The Importance of Being Myrtle

ULRIKA JONSSON

PENGUIN BOOKS

PENGUIN BOOKS

Published by the Penguin Group
Penguin Books Ltd, 80 Strand, London WC2R ORL, England
Penguin Group (USA) Inc., 375 Hudson Street, New York, New York 10014, USA
Penguin Group (Canada), 90 Eglinton Avenue East, Suite 700, Toronto, Ontario, Canada M4P 2Y3
(a division of Pearson Penguin Canada Inc.)
Penguin Ireland, 25 St Stephen's Green, Dublin 2, Ireland (a division of Penguin Books Ltd)
Penguin Group (Australia), 250 Camberwell Road,
Camberwell, Victoria 3124, Australia (a division of Pearson Australia Group Pty Ltd)
Penguin Books India Pvt Ltd, 11 Community Centre,
Panchsheel Park, New Delhi – 110 017, India
Penguin Group (NZ), 67 Apollo Drive, Rosedale, Auckland 0632, New Zealand
(a division of Pearson New Zealand Ltd)
Penguin Books (South Africa) (Pty) Ltd, 24 Sturdee Avenue,
Rosebank, Johannesburg 2196, South Africa

Penguin Books Ltd, Registered Offices: 80 Strand, London WC2R ORL, England

www.penguin.com

First published 2011

1

Typeset by Penguin Books Ltd
Printed in Great Britain by Clays Ltd, St Ives plc

A CIP catalogue record for this book is available from the British Library

ISBN: 978–0–141–04320–3

www.greenpenguin.co.uk

MIX
Paper from
responsible sources
FSC
www.fsc.org
FSC™ C018179

Penguin Books is committed to a sustainable
future for our business, our readers and our
planet. This book is made from paper certified
by the Forest Stewardship Council.

For my father, the late, great Bo Jonsson.
Jag saknar dig.

Yours by nature and by nurture.

The Going

Why did you give no hint that night
That quickly after the morrow's dawn,
And calmly, as if indifferent, quite,
You would close your term here, up and be gone
Where I could not follow
With wing of swallow
To gain one glimpse of you ever anon!

Never to bid good-bye,
Or lip me the softest call,
Or utter a wish for a word, while I
Saw morning harden upon the wall,
Unmoved, unknowing
That your great going
Had place that moment, and altered all.

Thomas Hardy

Chapter One

(2006)

It was the inescapable moisture in the cold, and the way it insisted on invading his bones for so many months of the year, that he really struggled with, and this Thursday was no exception. Despite this, Gianni D'Amico reminded himself that he had made a vow of friendship with the land of the Poms, to which he was determined to stick. This alone was normally enough to humble his aches and pains.

Today, however, the cold was dark, cumbersome and heavy to bear, and he found it harder to pacify his ailing joints. It was on days like these that he was eternally grateful for the salsa classes on Wednesdays and the occasional Friday evening – they kept him nimble, if not so quick. *Still*, thought Gianni defiantly, *there's life in the old bastard yet.*

True, he did miss the arid heat, the mildness of the winters and the domineering Aussie sun, which had gilded his skin so persistently throughout his childhood and beyond. He often longed for the large, cyclonic skies and the vast, magnificent plains of the Northern Territory he had encountered as a considerably younger man some forty years ago. He yearned for the grand open spaces, which, contrary to popular belief, did *not* induce a feeling of loneliness but instead awoke in him the very strongest sense of inclusion and belonging. Gianni was always at pains to point out, to anyone willing to listen to his ramblings, that he had never had such an overwhelming sense of belonging as he had experienced in the Outback. It was a native feeling somehow, inherent to this Italian immigrant boy, who perhaps should not have been in Australia in the first place.

On reflection, it had been the best decision he had ever made, he always thought, leaving his loving parents behind in an urban, densely populated Victoria, where they had established new roots. From there, he had ventured north to the great big Never Never – the nothingness that was the Outback – to engage his gritty determination and to liberate his curiosity. It had been the renunciation of the little Italian boy and the making of the adult Aussie.

He would never have imagined that his trip up north would eventually take him so much further north in the world than he had ever been – to England, a country of limited tolerance, whingeing and notoriously bad weather. He thought he'd seen it all until he'd discovered that in the UK it was, in fact, possible to experience all four seasons in just one day.

During irregular and unpredictable lulls in his daily life, Gianni's mind would wander and he would sometimes contemplate a return Down Under. But aside from the obvious climatic advantages, neither his roots nor his bones could face the upheaval once more, and with no family to speak of beckoning him back, he felt he lacked any real reason or, indeed, obligation to go. He had, by now, established a good but not extensive circle of friends and learned to live with the occasional snobbery of strangers – and the truly unreliable weather. Besides, on a more practical level, the flight alone was more than his small salary would facilitate.

The driver greeted Gianni as he boarded the relatively busy bus with a nod and a smile – a smile that was as baffled, amused and full of wonderment as it always was at the sight of bare legs sprouting from shorts in mid-November. He might not have known the passenger's name but it was clear he wasn't British.

You don't keep a tan like that in this country, he thought. *At least he's wearing socks and a good pair of walking boots!*

Gianni spent many of his bus journeys to work indulging in the warm, strong memories he harboured of the D'Amico family. Seating himself each time in the very front row, diagonally behind the driver, he had effectively secured himself exclusive access to the large front windscreen – a window on the world – as the bus drove along. The passing images became a source of entertainment but, equally, they served as indistinguishable background for his distracted, wandering thoughts.

As the bus approached the next stop, Gianni saw the outline of a lone figure, who stood out, upright and seemingly unmoved by the rain falling all around him, waiting patiently, enveloped and distinctly defined by a smart overcoat. The man's frame appeared solemn, yet distinguished, from what Gianni could make out from his prime observation point. The figure was topped with what looked like a trilby hat but . . . *That's a fedora for sure – it's what Papa used to wear.* He smiled in recognition.

It did not go unnoticed by Gianni that the man took a great deal of pride in his attire. So much, thought Gianni, that there was even an air of superiority about him. *Good on ya*, he thought admiringly. *You found yourself a style years ago and you've stuck with it. Just like me and me shorts.* He chuckled.

As the bus was brought to a somewhat faltering stop, the morning's rain, which had collected and failed to hurry down the drain, made a perfectly arched spray over the kerb where the man was standing. He glared down at the water as if it was poisonous. Gianni felt drawn to him and continued to stare, fascinated – almost in some kind of anticipation.

The man hardly lifted his head towards the driver and instead waved his bus pass in short, sharp moves just out of his pocket, slightly above his waist. It was a strange motion, agitated almost, and it had not gone unnoticed by the driver, who frowned with a mixture of surprise and annoyance.

4

As if further to draw attention to himself, the passenger who had just boarded the bus then grappled with his coat as he tried to return pass to pocket. For a brief moment, his head rose slightly but then, with an air of heaviness and an audible sigh of annoyance, lowered again, as if it had increased in weight. The man was about to be defeated by the bus pass and his machine-stitched pocket when he turned right towards the no man's land of the aisle.

Gianni's compulsion to stare did not relent.

Suddenly, in one very fast, sharp movement, the man clasped his head with a flailing hand and let out a loud cry of agony. The bus pass fell to the ground, followed very swiftly by the man himself.

There was a thud – the sound of solid life against wet linoleum – and this was quickly followed by a series of smaller scrapes as the man's overcoat and shoes settled uncomfortably on the floor.

Gianni took a sharp breath. Briefly he almost forgot himself – it was as if he had witnessed the man falling in slow motion, time and time again in a moment that seemed to last minutes.

But it wasn't minutes, it was seconds and, before he knew it, Gianni shouted, 'Get up, mate! What you doing down there? You haven't been on the sauce, have you?' in a manner that was as empathetic as it was accusatory.

But as the words left his mouth, he knew he wasn't truly directing them at the man on the floor – the words merely bridged the gap between him sitting in his seat and standing up to move closer to the still pile.

The man lay face down, the fedora to his side, near to Gianni, empty and purposeless alongside the smart overcoat, which only partially covered the wearer. There had not been time for him to secure a protected landing – his hands remained by his sides – and it appeared that the left side of his head had borne the brunt of the impact.

'Crikey!' Gianni bent down to the man.

A heavy, dark dribble of blood had formed a small pool by his left cheek. His eyes were not fully shut and as Gianni bent lower, his face close to the stranger's, he could hear soporific groaning with every shallow breath. It was the sound of regret, weariness and remorse rolled into one – all this from such tiny whispers of inevitability. Gianni wasn't sure if it was the sheer weight of the man's body that pinned him to the floor or whether he might soon end life's great journey face down on the No. 53 bus. Whichever, he was overwhelmed by a sense of urgency and a greater sense of responsibility.

He knelt next to the man who, it was clear, was in a bad way and shouted passionately, 'Someone call a bloody ambulance! Call an ambulance, for Pete's sake! We've got a fella here about to die!' With that, he closed in further on the man on the floor and decided his instinct was right: these were precious moments for both of them – yet Gianni had no idea why this was so. It was just a feeling.

The minutes that followed seemed endless and Gianni prayed that help was on the way. The driver communicated something to him but Gianni didn't hear, focusing instead on some instinctive responsibility and automatic sense of fate.

With every murmur from the man, who slipped in and out of consciousness, the urgency within Gianni crescendoed. He felt as if his chest was about to burst wide open with anxiety. But he remained calm – not out of diligence or lack of empathy but from necessity. You don't battle your way through Australia's Golden Outback fossicking for gold without learning a thing or two about human life, humankind and, more appropriately in the circumstances, about your own tenacity. And Gianni had not been found lacking.

Despite the distractions around him on the bus – other passengers whispering, gasping but mostly pointing – he kept his eyes on the man, but he felt a growing distance between them. The man had not moved since his fall and his position seemed most uncomfortable, but instinctively Gianni did not want to move him. He offered the man reassurance by stroking and patting him gently on the back, soothing him with words of comfort – 'Don't worry, mate. You'll be all right before you know it.'

By the time the ambulance finally arrived, the fallen

man was completely silent. There was no moaning or murmuring and his eyes were decidedly shut.

As a man in a heavy green uniform approached the disaster, he asked Gianni to step to the side.

'Has he died?' blurted Gianni, considerably more direct than he had intended to be.

'Let's just take a look here first, shall we? He a mate of yours?' asked the paramedic.

Gianni hesitated: he had temporarily felt close to the man. Then he confessed, 'Nah, nah, he just boarded the bus and then keeled right over. Easy as that!'

The man was heaved on to a stretcher by two men who, despite the weight, showed no awkwardness in their approach and execution.

As no one volunteered a name for the fallen man, and with no obvious sign of identification, the paramedics loaded him into the ambulance with the efficiency born of regularity.

As the rain continued to fall hard outside, Gianni found himself standing by the vehicle with a sudden and very deep sense of incompletion. Something compelled him to pursue his participation. 'The hospital is how many clicks away?' he asked nonchalantly, in the way a lone boy might ask a group of older boys where they were heading.

'Clicks?' frowned one of the medics irritatingly. 'It's three miles, if that's what you're asking. Are you coming?'

As he sat in the ambulance, Gianni remained silent

for the journey to the hospital – he wasn't sure if this was out of respect for the fallen man or if he was lost for words. It wasn't often that that happened.

After the ambulance had pulled up outside the hospital's Accident & Emergency Department things moved very quickly. Before he knew it, Gianni was without his new acquaintance, who had been swept away from him by staff with such urgency that he could barely trace their steps.

The hospital, Gianni noted, was a place of speed and panic, tragedy and trepidation, but most of all, it looked as if it was a place of waiting.

In a vague attempt physically to order those whose anxiety and restlessness kept them pacing or yo-yoing on and off their seats, four long rows of chairs had been formed. They might well have been straight before the night shift but by the time Gianni arrived the waiting room was chaotic. *What a terrible place*, he thought.

Much time passed and Gianni spent most of it looking out of one of the rain-spattered windows at the persistently wet grey day. He wasn't sure where he preferred to be: inside this hospital with its pungent smell of astringent substances or outside living through another cold and rainy day. But then he realized that, of course, he would have given anything to be out in the cold.

If he'd had one of those mobile phone things, he thought, he would have called work to *throw a sickie*.

His job was hardly of an urgent nature – it wasn't as if he saved lives. His lateness would have been noted but not remarked upon. He would make his way there as soon as he knew the fella was all right, and simply explain to them what had happened so peculiarly this morning.

Eventually a woman, dressed head to toe in garments designed to protect her from blood, tapped Gianni hard on the shoulder with an air of importance and impatience. 'Did you come in with the man on the bus?' she asked abruptly.

'Er, yeah . . . yes, that's me,' faltered Gianni. 'How's he doin'?'

'I'm afraid your friend didn't make it. We did everything we could but early signs are that he probably had a subarachnoid haemorrhage. We won't know for sure until an autopsy has been carried out . . .

'I'm very sorry,' she added.

'A sub-what?' Gianni was still two sentences behind.

'A b-r-a-i-n h-a-e-m-o-r-r-h-a-g-e,' she mouthed, in a slow, loud and deliberate manner, as if she was talking to the hard-of-hearing – and, as if to alienate Gianni further in this place of now most-definite tragedy, she began to walk away.

'Wait! What was his name? Where did he live?' questioned Gianni, keenly.

'Oh, I'm sorry. I thought you said you were friends. Well, I'm not at liberty to divulge that information – patient confidentiality . . .'

'Patient confidentiality? What's that when it's at home?' mumbled Gianni. 'Look, lady, I'm not some psycho from the back of beyond. He may not have been a mate of mine but I want to pay my respects to his family – I mean, it's the right thing to do. How does that fit in with your patient whatsit?' Gianni raised his voice as if to exert power that clearly wasn't his. He couldn't let this woman's rigidity and impatience go just like that. Today had been a strange day. It's not every day someone dies in front of you when you're on your way to work. Gianni was keen to see the day's unusual deviation through to its dignified end.

The doctor was clearly busy and she wanted Gianni to know it. She was consumed by her own sense of purpose and she oozed intolerance from every pore. 'Look, I can't tell you anything,' she threw at Gianni, in reckless abandonment of all empathy. 'It's up to you, Sherlock,' she taunted him. 'Now, *if* you'll excuse me . . .' With that she turned, smug and defiant, on her hygienic white clogs and joined the mêlée beyond the swinging doors.

Gianni was taken aback.

So that was that.

There he stood, a slightly dishevelled second-generation Italian from Australia who had failed to save the life of a fellow passenger on the bus that morning.

He felt bewildered, probably for the very first time in his life. But uncertainty and an instant and painful sadness partnered his consternation. Very briefly he allowed his mind to wander to the ripples of grief that this morning's drama would doubtless cause anonymous relatives and faceless friends.

He felt hot – and glad of his shorts. The heat was brought about by a sudden recognition of his deep unease. The memory of his father's death flashed before him and the terrible sadness Gianni had felt. The man on the bus, though – the fallen man – had been around Gianni's age and had clearly taken his last breath well before what should have been his expiry date.

With a heavy heart, Gianni brought his left hand up towards his face and, with the back, wiped moisture from the corner of both eyes. As he did so, his head bowed and his eyes creased shut.

When they opened he was shocked to find, secured between the thumb and index finger of his right hand, the dark grey fedora. The soft felt, which was creased, so definitely, lengthways down the crown and pinched in the front on both sides, had almost been dented by the pressure of Gianni's hand.

He let out a soft but audible whoop of near delight. The hat passed between his hands and, not unlike a potential purchaser, he balanced it and turned it to and fro with his short, firm fingers as if to display and view it in the very best light.

He turned the fedora over and looked inside, along the rim of its crown. There, in neat, handwritten capital letters, he read: 'PROPERTY OF AUSTIN LEWIS'.

'*Holy shit!*' exclaimed Gianni, in wonder and complete disbelief. 'What a nutter I've been!' All the while the man's identity had been balancing in his hands . . .

With a spring in his step, and in defiance of the pouring rain, he marched out of the hospital.

To work! thought Gianni, holding the fedora protectively against his chest out of the rain.

Chapter Two

As she sat on the pink chintz sofa in her bedroom, her legs about to be sensuously enveloped in the sheen of ten denier, Dorothy glanced up and caught the man across the room watching her intently. She recognized his look of desire and admiration because it was one she was very much used to. It was not a look she had ever grown tired of. She had always seen it as a pre-requisite whenever she engaged with a man. That look was as tempting to her as it was satisfying.

She glanced briefly at the man's bare chest, densely populated by a mass of greying and whitened hair, knowing his eyes were following her. She could feel them on her and it gave her a sense of importance and affirmation. He seemed content, and she thought she could even detect the hint of a wry smile. She avoided his eyes and returned her attention to her legs.

The room was still, quiet, almost peaceful, in direct contrast to the previous night's drama, which had unfolded out of raw passion in the kitchen, then moved with atrocious abandon into the bedroom, leaving behind it a footprint akin to that of a callous break-in. After reaching their summit, they had eventually settled down on the bed, exhaling mutual sighs of exhaustion and, ultimately, satisfied relief.

The urge and intensity, the haste and furious need of fulfilment and completion had hurried their heartbeats and rushed frantic thoughts of desperation through their minds. It had been a potent, heady cocktail, far outstripping the effects of any opiate, in Dorothy's opinion, and certainly worthy of a very real addiction. It was a feeling as irreplaceable as it was irrepressible. And it was the relentless quest for something so intangible that made it intoxicating.

That morning, it had seemed a shame to wash away the night's glow but she had felt the need for a soak, if only to allow her body to be immersed in the musky scent of sex. As she lay in the bath, she examined her slender frame, which bore none of the hallmarks of childbearing or premature ageing. Apart from the odd blemish and even a few wrinkles from too much sun, her skin was in good condition. Her length, she always thought, was all in her legs, and although they had been strangers to exercise classes, they had gained strength from dancing, walking and other more sensual physical activities.

She had noticed that the breasts of women over fifty tended to become either oversized or atrophic. They were often made ugly by childbearing and breast-feeding, but hers remained wholesome and full, if not a little more malleable than they had once been.

Physiologically, things were genetic, she understood

that, so she could take no credit for narrow hips, a neat, contained bottom and sculpted, shapely shoulders. Her mother hadn't been particularly tall so she guessed her legs had been a contribution from her father. Beyond that, it was unlikely he had given her very much more – an indictment of his idea of paternity.

The night before had been very good, even by her standards, she reflected, and her measure was the lateness and laziness of the morning. There had been no hurry and no need for punctuality. Time had been allowed to unfold at its own pace and without compromise.

After she had teased the stockings up her legs, she stood and allowed her skirt to hug her straight thighs. She turned around.

'Coffee?' the man suggested, with a confidence bestowed by the night before.

She raised her eyes to the mirror in front of her and, without looking at him, she replied, 'I only have one coffee a day – and I like to take it alone.'

Visibly disappointed, knowing he could no longer rely on his confidence, he got out of bed and dressed with purpose. With his blighted hopes hanging over him, but refusing to let go of his pride, he made his way positively towards the front door, where Dorothy stood ready to effect his quick dispatch.

As he brushed past her, he pinched her pleasing behind and, leaning his head towards hers, allowed his lips to make contact with her ear. She paused momentarily, then opened the door and closed it behind him without a promise or even so much as a remote sign of interest.

She made her way back into the kitchen and let out a loud sigh. The small but ancient radio, balanced precariously on a mound of magazines, was playing Elvis and, without delay, Dorothy responded.

As she jigged, her hips swayed from side to side and her nimble feet took little steps to encourage a dance. She had always thought she would have met her match in Elvis. *Together we would have set the world on fire* . . . But for now, all she needed to accompany her was some strong coffee and a thin slice of toast – on the hop, as it were.

It might not have been much of a meal – even a woman with her divine figure liked to keep tabs on her intake – but a slice of toast partnered with black coffee was hardly a crime punishable by cellulite.

It was a grey and increasingly wet day outside, not conducive to a good mood or a late-morning dance but, then, Dorothy did not tend towards conformity or – dare she say it? – normal behaviour.

Life had generally been good to her – she had always believed she had been born lucky. It had dealt her an upbringing that many people might have considered a little unusual but had allowed her to excel in an area where most women showed embarrassing weakness and an ongoing lack of understanding: men.

As a teenager, armed with the confidence of a

mature adult, Dorothy had braved the male-dominated world and discovered a nifty ability to coerce men, with speed and relative ease, into an arena where her rules applied. It had helped that she had been born a Leo, of course, inheriting such traits as independence, confidence and enthusiasm. But even on the darker side, her dominance and often snobbish superiority had not stopped her exhibiting her unlimited sexual lust and emotional indulgence.

However, Leos did not like the rain – they craved sunshine for the purposes of both heat and glory – so while she brushed her shoulder-length blonde mane in preparation for work, she was fully aware that her curls would take on a different shape in the weather awaiting her outside.

As she left the house and walked the few steps down her front drive, she saw the outline of her neighbour standing by the window in the front room. Dorothy shot her a bright glance and waved her hand high in the air with energy and gusto. 'Loitering with intent again, Myrtle?' she said, under her breath, while smiling broadly in her neighbour's direction. *If she would only stop looking so darn dull and depressed*, she thought. *And if she really isn't dull, depressed and miserable, she might consider telling her face so.*

Why that woman continued to give her the once-over, she didn't know. It was as if Dorothy represented some kind of physical threat. She thought it was quite clear there was no chance on earth she could ever be even *mildly* interested in the grey, matt, retentive husband, Austin. Him and his monstrous caravan parked so infuriatingly in the drive.

Dorothy thought it quite obvious that an extrovert such as herself would never in a million years consider Myrtle's conservative husband intriguing – not in the slightest.

The rain had already covered the roads and pavements with an inch or so of water, which made it rather tricky to negotiate in high-heeled leather shoes. Even so, she continued with all possible speed and purpose through the blustery wet.

About two hundred yards down the road, she saw the No. 53 bus – stationary, doors wide open. There were no passengers on board and the driver was moving around restlessly outside, smoking a cigarette to its bitter end, talking and gesticulating on his mobile phone.

Dorothy guessed there must have been another breakdown and wondered how anything ever got done in this inefficient country, where buses and trains were regularly held hostage to seasonal wind and rain.

Madison Universal World of Envelopes was, despite its pedestrian name, a reasonably decent, pleasurable place to work. The concrete seventies monstrosity of a building sat, a little like an abandoned family member, uncomfortably on the outskirts of town. Its exterior was unwelcoming, thanks to the tired concrete, which had fallen victim in large areas to graffiti. It stuck out like a sore thumb since the area surrounding it lay fallow and bare, awaiting overdue and much-needed regeneration. Of course, had the building been an older, historic one, at least it would have offered some endearing sign of heritage. Instead there was no reason to defend it against demolition.

Dorothy was a loyal and dedicated personal assistant to a sweet, greying man, who considered himself above and beyond the position of managing director but was equally aware that, at his age, he was considerably more the beggar than the chooser.

One of the major perks of his job, apart from the joy of overseeing the manufacture and shipment of envelopes nationally and internationally, was having a tall blonde for a PA.

Dorothy enjoyed the luxury of late starts and somewhat flexible working arrangements. Not that she necessarily needed flexi-time but it was, she thought, a sign of Mr Madison's faith in her and her abilities.

As she walked into the office she placed her handbag on her desk, close to a struggling gardenia. She eyed it with a mixture of regret and pity. No amount of watering or repositioning seemed to help the few sad dark green leaves that remained. She'd lost count of the number of times she'd threatened it with the bin, only to give it yet another chance to redeem itself. As if by divine intervention, it had always shown flashes of willing, as it clung to survival, sprouting a desperate new bit of greenery as if it was deliberately choosing to face death head on with new buds. But it had never bloomed.

As her boss had not yet arrived, Dorothy took the opportunity to attend to his office. While she was well aware that it wasn't strictly part of her duties to clean his desk she liked to keep an eye on what was going on in the business. These were vulnerable financial times – and while people would always need envelopes, the product's inevitable decline, thanks to electronic mail, had meant the company's future continued to be rather precarious. Dorothy took it upon herself to make sure she was as aware, protected and well defended as she could possibly be. She did not want a repeat performance of her previous employment.

She had been made redundant by a busy firm of solicitors in the centre of town: her boss had cited 'cut-backs', which Dorothy had taken as age discrimination. She had soon been proven right: she had been replaced by a considerably younger model. Not one to take injustices lightly, Dorothy had put up an uncompromising fight and won herself a handsome payout, not to mention hefty doses of dignity and self-righteousness.

Things had actually worked out better than she could have imagined. Mr Madison had made her feel valued and completely indispensable at the grand age of fifty-eight. She might be only two years away from statutory retirement but that was not a reality on which she liked to dwell.

She had never understood why a limit had to be imposed on so many things; why people had to be held back, hindered and restrained by something as innocuous as a number. She, at least, felt as young today as she had twenty years ago.

'Did you have a pleasant evening, Miss Dorothy? Do anything special? Anything you wouldn't want your mother to know about?' joked Mr Madison who, contrary to his suggestive questioning, was a rather short, stout man with a comb-over.

Dorothy leaned her head towards him and squinted. 'It was debauchery, Mr Madison,' she whispered teasingly. 'It was a bit of TV, a light supper and then a hot bath. Nothing short of fully fledged debauchery, I'm ashamed to say. I shall never be pure again!' She feigned a swoon, as she had so often while play-acting during their exchanges.

'Well, Miss Perkins,' he said, in a mock-authoritarian voice, 'as I always say, if you can't be good, then it's imperative you be careful!'

They both smiled.

The irony of the little sparring that had just played out was that Mr Madison assumed Miss Perkins had been joking and Miss Perkins knew that Mr Madison was blissfully naïve. For Dorothy the night before had been utterly indulgent and wanton – something her colourless boss might only dream of.

Dorothy embraced her professional role, which, she

felt, was based on equal partnership and mutual respect. Mr Madison paid her to work but he was not her master. Dorothy did not feel uncomfortable in the slightest at having a male boss – her feminism did not stretch that far. She loved animals but that didn't make her a vegetarian. On the contrary, she enjoyed the company of men tremendously – both in business and socially.

Unexpectedly, but as if on cue, four beeps came from her handbag. It was her mobile phone – a large, unfashionable, easy-to-use model, which had been partly responsible for changing her life. She rummaged around for it in her bag, feeling slightly compromised by the intrusion of a text message into her working day. It had caught her slightly off guard and she frowned as she accessed the message from the unknown number. The screen read: 'Delight me once more, Tiger.' It was signed off: 'Handsome1'.

Dorothy's frown was replaced with a smile and a sudden feeling of deep physical desire. Her heart started to race. She cleared her throat in a businesslike way, as if to remove herself from her current state of mind, then replaced the phone in her bag.

She looked up and around her. She straightened her skirt and blouse and headed for the kettle.

Anyone who referred to themselves as a Handsome1 was a cause for concern, she thought. Nonetheless, she had to admit she was sorely tempted. Not unlike Oscar Wilde, she knew she could resist anything but temptation.

Chapter Three

Myrtle looked down at her spreading wet feet as she stood in the shower and wondered if there had been any way of knowing that when Austin had left that morning he would not return. That when she had reluctantly leaned forward to accept his kiss on her right cheek, it was to be their final farewell.

The hospital had called some time after eleven. Austin, she knew, would have preferred her to be more precise about the time but she was not a person who had lived easily within the confines of precision. What she did know was that immediately after she had left a message for Gillian she had proceeded to the bathroom and taken a shower. It was all she could think of to do.

'Sandwich cut in triangles – brown bread, cheese and piccalilli, crusts off – six grapes, a yoghurt, small spoon, napkin folded in a triangle, carton of juice,' Austin had said, as he checked the contents of his Tupperware box meticulously before closing it and smoothing the sides anti-clockwise with his right hand.

Austin had left for work that morning, as he always did, at ten minutes past seven – smart, exact and distinguished in appearance. As he turned and crossed the threshold, leaving his wife behind, he had winked at her in the self-assured way only he knew, patted the stylish, structured hat that covered his head, then proceeded to close the door firmly behind him. His routine was as reassuring as it was unnerving, Myrtle had always felt. It created a kind of rhythm, and the silence between each slow beat of a single drum brought as much unease as anticipation.

Austin had been a man of extreme habit, there was no denying it. Myrtle had known that before she married him. This had brought a predictable tempo to their life – a continuum of events that meant Myrtle had always known exactly how things stood.

There had been times, though, when she had worried something might have been omitted from his regularity and it had caused her to fret momentarily – times when she had wondered whether he would forget to close the curtains in the orderly and symmetrical fashion he always did before they left the house, whether he would fail to press down the door handle systematically three times to ensure the door was truly locked, or whether he would inadvertently put the cheese on the wrong shelf in the fridge. But Austin's entire circle of life was so committed to the religion of routine that she need not have feared it would ever be broken.

So there Myrtle stood, that rainy Thursday morning, in their shower, which was tiled in dusty pink, with water flowing comfortingly over her rotund body, in a state of numbness and momentary calm.

'You don't want to swim in your own dirt,' had been Austin's constant mantra to anyone intent on defying his imposed rule on showers. Baths, he claimed, took up considerably more water and they certainly did not leave you as clean. And on both accounts he was, doubtless, right.

For an organized man, whose life was run like a regiment, it was not surprising. His need for rules was, Myrtle suspected, a direct result of growing up alone with a mother whose disasters and disorientations had given him a mission in life.

Myrtle, on the other hand, had been scatty from birth, according to her frustrated mother. Her deviation from rules and a distinct lack of self-discipline had created a messy bedroom, and that, claimed her mother, was the boldest indication of a messy mind. What Myrtle pleaded was merely forgetfulness became, in her mother's eyes, deliberate detachment and disregard.

She was a dreamer, a light, floaty person, incapable of being weighed down by the shackles of life. 'Her head's in the clouds,' was how her mother had constantly described her, and then she had gone on to forecast a life of doom for someone so naïve and unwilling to wake up to the harsh realities of life. She had been right, of course, Myrtle reflected. And Myrtle had paid a high price.

The nurse who had called from the hospital that morning had reassuringly pointed out that Austin had probably not suffered any pain, that he was fully intact

and that she, Myrtle Lewis, might like to bring someone with her when she came to identify him.

Identify, thought Myrtle. It was a strange word to use
in the circumstances. It did not sit easy in her mind.
She had seen him only a few hours ago, and after
nearly forty-one years of marriage, she would now be
forced to identify the man she had tried to identify *with*
for all these years. What if she didn't recognize him
when she saw him? What if they had the wrong Mr
Lewis and she was the wrong Mrs Lewis for the wrong
Mr Lewis? Her thoughts were random and removed
and she made no attempt to order them.

After she had hung up, the short walk from the telephone to the bathroom seemed to take for ever. So
many thoughts rushed to fill her mind and yet none
was of any substance or gave any relief. The closest
she came to comfort was when she looked down at
the pale green carpet lining the bathroom floor: it was
still moist from the shower Austin had taken early that
morning. *This water-soaked carpet is still Austin*, she
thought, just like the bathroom was still Austin, for
the pink and pale green décor had been yet another of
his impositions. As another random thought invaded
her mind, she remembered that, by unnerving coincidence, she and her husband had both been delivered
at birth by the same calm, reassuring hands – those of
her father – albeit four years apart. Perhaps it had been
inevitable then, all those years ago, that they would be
connected somehow for ever.

Their two families might only have been linked initially through general practice and Myrtle's parents' proximity to Austin's family home, but it had been a sign, Myrtle had always thought, that no matter how much her heart had wanted otherwise, Destiny had wanted something quite, quite different for her. From the outset, Myrtle and Austin's union had not been brought about by willingness or – least of all – love. It had been forced by mistake and circumstance. Now she had had no control over Austin's sudden departure from her.

In Myrtle's mind there appeared to be no middle ground between being a wife and becoming a widow. That morning, she had woken up a wife. Now she was a wet widow with feet that had given her no warning that her status was about to change.

The effects of her long shower had enveloped the bathroom mirror in a thick white veil of steam. The dusty pink wall tiles were weeping tears of condensation, which collected in small pools on the floor.

Myrtle couldn't quite make things out. The steam had created a swirling, milky atmosphere through which it was difficult to see clearly – everything seemed blurred. As she exited the shower and grabbed a pastel pink towel, the moist, dank air closed in on her and, for a brief moment, filled her mouth. She struggled to catch her breath.

She leaned forward clumsily, grasping for the handle, and managed to open the bathroom door enough for the fog to dissipate. Then, she turned to the mirror and rubbed it with all the force of her little, round hand. As she wiped frantically, the steam chased her little round hand, covering the mirror once again. In a flap, bewildered, Myrtle rubbed harder.

Suddenly she stopped.

For there, in the awkward, undefined clearing of the glass, she saw the vague, indiscernible outline of a flushed and reddened round face. Her brownish-grey hair, which normally bounced contentedly in curls, now hung lank around her face, lacking both will and co-operation, soaking two soft pale fleshy shoulders. All she could decipher of her face was two flushed rosy cheeks and a pair of small eyes framed by drenched lashes, like tiny starfish.

Who are you? Myrtle wondered. *I don't like the look of you one bit.*

The phone rang.

She gave a little jump. Immediately she turned away from the mirror and towards the door. She breathed in sharply, which seemed to indicate a small and sudden panic inside her. She felt light-headed but rooted to the spot. Glancing back up at the mirror she saw that the colour had drained from her face. She let out a melancholy sigh. The ring of the phone would never sound the same again, she realized. From here on in, it would always signal to her bad news from a hospital and, doubtless, death.

There was too much water for her towel to absorb

so its sole purpose was to hold her together as she padded across the landing, a little unsteady on her feet, to reach the cordless phone.

'Yes,' she confirmed, as if showing willingness to accept further bad news.

'Mother, are you all right? Good grief! I've just got your message. What on earth happened? Talk to me!' ordered Gillian's breathless, insistent voice. 'Are you all right?' she said again. 'I've been calling. Where have you been? I'm worried about you.' She moved seamlessly from one sentence into another, giving no pause for response.

Oh, yes – the children, thought Myrtle. *The poor children!* What on earth had she been thinking, taking a lengthy shower and completely forgetting that her daughters might need her? Then, out of nowhere, Myrtle realized that life without Austin could, in fact, involve long, spontaneous showers or even endless staring at her feet. *I might shower several times a day*, thought Myrtle, sheepishly.

As her mind strayed, her eyes wandered over the carpet, up the walls and all along the landing.

As if to wake herself up, she shook her head. It was a sharp appointment with reality – much needed with Gillian on the phone, she knew that. 'I'm sorry, dear. Yes, I'm fine,' she replied, reining herself into the here and now. 'I'm not quite sure of the details,' she faltered, almost as if she was responding to an enquiry about a drinks party.

'Oh, Mummy – all this now ... and so close to Daddy's birthday,' Gillian continued, as if to mark the inconvenience of her father's death. 'Right!' she went on sharply. 'I'm coming over. You're not to be left on your own.'

In one brief sentence, Myrtle's daughter had demoted her from adult widow to unsupervised toddler. And with that threat, Gillian ended yet another of her un-compromising and brusque conversations.

With trepidation and regret, Myrtle put down the receiver. How disappointing not to have been able to take control of the conversation. Her elder daughter always managed to railroad her. Myrtle shuffled across the landing with the towel, which was now doing a pretty good job of swallowing her from the ground up but had missed her shoulders, leaving them cold and exposed. She paddled forward and, as she did so, her right foot caught the hem of the towel, which, as it strained and tautened, forced her to trip and fall.

Myrtle wasn't entirely sure whether she was physically hurt or just embarrassed but she scrambled to an upright position and hoped that nobody in the empty house had seen her. 'Walls have ears,' her mother had proclaimed. *Oh, crumbs, let's hope that's all they have*, thought Myrtle, blushing, weighed down by her own awkwardness.

She felt protected by the towel: it acted as a kind of buffer between her sensitive skin and the stark, uncom-promising reality of her morning. She held on to it, summoning the resolve to enter the bedroom she and

Austin had shared. Her heart clenched at the thought of its emptiness. Would Austin's scent and presence somehow still linger? How would the solid reality of the room affect this most unreal of mornings? She stood still.

The house in which they had lived for thirty years – 'Not thirty, Myrtle,' Austin would have interjected, with great accuracy and assertion, '*thirty-one!*' – had offered husband, wife and their two young girls a great sense of comfort, another bedroom and a small, manageable garden.

The latter had given Myrtle unexpected satisfaction and the space to lose herself in thought at regular intervals during her week. To Austin's unease, she had become quite a skilful gardener. The planting, growing and dividing had fulfilled her overwhelming need to nurture. She wondered how many hours she had clocked up over the years, working to achieve her now fastidiously laid-out plot.

The lawn was skirted by jaunty perennials and shrubs. Spring was always marked by a palette of pink, white and purple, although with Austin forever guarding her, Myrtle had been forced to learn the merits of restraint even in her planting. Nonetheless, regardless of his uncharitable spirit, he had not succeeded in subjugating the pleasure it had continued to bring her.

The garden was square, and the shrubs had overgrown their boundaries with the lawn, reminding her of her own expanding waistline.

As she walked into the bedroom she looked around, as if for the last time. And yet, of course, it was for the first time in a life without Austin. The oak bed stood neat and made, lifeless and unwelcoming. The chest of drawers and the large oak wardrobe remained solid and unmoved by the dark news of death.

She walked over to the bed and sat down on Austin's side. Her body made a heavy impression in the mattress, and as it did so, she exhaled and her neck sank into her shoulders.

Myrtle dressed slowly and laboriously, every item of clothing heavy, like a piece of armour. As she carefully made her way downstairs, past the site of her earlier clumsiness, she wondered about Beth.

Beth would be greatly saddened, if not devastated, by her father's death – more so, perhaps, because their relationship had so unravelled with every year that Austin had refused to acknowledge that Beth's round character didn't fit into his square one. She would be cast adrift by her father's death, in some mistaken state of regret or self-doubt. All that Myrtle had wanted for them was that they might connect – as father and daughter should.

Has Gillian told her, she wondered, *or should I call?*

Her thoughts took her to little Molly. *Poor little girl.* Gillian's only daughter was a wholesome, inquisitive delight at barely five. Myrtle imagined her face dropping with the news that Grampy had gone.

'To where?' Molly would wonder.

'To heaven, of course, dear,' Myrtle would explain. It was unlikely that Molly would be confused by Austin's death. *That little girl always sees things so very clearly.*

Molly had enjoyed playing with her grandfather, and the discipline he had meted out had never been harsh – simply firm and correct – and it had proved a real winner with his only grandchild.

To Myrtle, Molly meant everything. It was with some degree of shame, although she had never fully articulated it even to herself, that Myrtle felt a greater love for Molly than she had, at times, felt for her own two daughters.

At the bottom of the stairs, she saw the second telephone, but although she was instinctively drawn to it on account of her concern for both Beth and little Molly, she walked past it at speed, pretending to herself and her conscience that it hadn't seen her, or she it. She hurried into the still and lifeless drawing room where the ticking of the grandfather clock seemed to call her back into greater consciousness.

She stopped abruptly.

Good God, Myrtle Lewis, your husband has just died, said a voice in her head. *Do something!* But the undeniable truth was that she didn't know what to do. She rubbed her hands back and forth, up and down, to and fro, as if to rid herself of the nasty residue of unease. Her hands were small and agile, with fingers a little too short to be dainty. The palms became moist and quite uncomfortable. Her heart was beating faster than she liked, and for the first time that morning she embraced the fear inside and the huge void awaiting her. She was overcome by a sense of weightlessness and helplessness – her head felt light again and, while she knew very well where she was, she looked around her in confusion. The truth was, she didn't know how to spend the next minute – let alone the rest of her life.

Since he had taken her in all those years ago, with her broken wings and ailing soul, Austin had been the captain of their ship. He had guided and steered her in a decidedly uncompromising way. It had been a huge relief for Myrtle: life had been beyond her control for as long as she could remember. Now, suddenly and without warning, she was at sea again, like a huge clipper with neither mast nor rudder. What frightened Myrtle most was that she could not go back but she truly did not know her way forward.

She paced the room erratically and with increasing speed, still rubbing her hands. She hesitated by the bay window and would, under normal circumstances, have tended the cacti on the sill, but instead she stopped to stare aimlessly out at the front garden.

When they had first viewed the house there had been only great swathes of willowherb, thistles and unkempt wild grass. Suddenly Myrtle felt deeply criticized by the order and organization she had created outside, when right now she wasn't even able to catch her breath or stop her heart slamming.

Out of the corner of her eye, she saw Dorothy,

from next door, like a blazing bougainvillaea, leaving her house. This was a daily occurrence, but as Myrtle followed the riot of colour that was Dorothy's clothing, she felt something strange stir deep inside her.

Dorothy hooked Myrtle with a solid and direct stare; she tossed her hair and shot her a knowing smile as she raised her left hand in a regal wave. All Myrtle could do was reciprocate unwillingly. She'd been found out. At that precise moment she felt her face had been the window to her soul and had given her away. She worried that Dorothy could see that among the darkest depths of Myrtle's loss there was an even more intense feeling: envy.

Envy is a ghastly word, Myrtle acknowledged. It sat uncomfortably on her tongue before it travelled down into her heart, where it paused and temporarily halted the thudding.

Myrtle blushed. She felt selfish that she was even contemplating her own feelings of jaundiced resentment when her husband had so unexpectedly passed away. She looked away from the window in shame.

Next to her armchair, nudging her left thigh, lay yesterday's unfinished crossword. She caught two across: 'Grudging praise (4) . . .'

Chapter Four

There was jam everywhere. A glutinous mass of cooked sweetened damsons had taken full advantage of the unfastened lid of the food processor and made a speedy bid for freedom. It had escaped with such velocity that it had succeeded in randomly spluttering the hot, sticky mess throughout the kitchen. Infuriatingly, rather than leaving just a finite area of gloop in a confined space, which would have been considerably easier to clear up, it had spewed out over everything within reach and beyond. Spots of the sugary viscous substance had landed on walls and surfaces alike.

'Good Lord! I have never made such a dreadful mess in all my life!' Gillian shouted, in sheer desperation. Her frustration was coupled with stinging pain from the hot jam, which had landed on her hands and arms too, but as she had long ago made a vow never to lose her temper, she was determined not to now, despite the pain and pure anger. Gillian had always maintained that nothing was ever gained from a loss of control – except perhaps indignity, which was something she had always managed to exclude from her life. However, it was immediately evident from the kitchen disaster that there was more to making damson jam than she had anticipated.

Today was supposed to have been a productive day — one of sorting, organizing, cleaning. She had taken on the jam-making project as an opportunity to reinforce her strengths, not only as a good mother but also as an excellent wife. Taking one day off work every couple of months enabled her to fulfil her role as both. She was well aware that this subtracted six whole days from her annual leave but it was a sacrifice she was more than prepared to make because it was, for her, as satisfying as it was rewarding. Besides, above all else it gave her a sense of achievement and pride. But while her alibi for this absence from work was her aspiration to reach the highest echelons of mother- and wife-hood, the truth was much plainer: she had an over-whelming need for order and control.

Gillian glared at the food processor with fury in her eyes: fury at the machine, which had failed her so readily, and fury at herself for not securing the lid properly. This, she knew, was a moment in which to show absolute self-restraint. In the thick of domestic disaster, she would have to concentrate on correcting the mistake, rather than the indulging the innate desire to scream and shake uncontrollably, like other mere mortals would. She would win this battle between heart and mind in the determined way she had always won in the conflict between emotion and appropriate behaviour.

Her apron was covered. In one hand she held a spatula coated with jam, and the other was a clenched fist, which refused to open. Gillian looked up at the ceiling, rolled her eyes and took a very deep breath.

'Give me strength,' she growled, through tightly clenched teeth, and proceeded to count to ten. For a woman so intent on organization, order and tidiness, this was as beastly as things could get.

By her own admission, the day hadn't started well. A pounding headache, which she knew only too well had the potential to develop into a ghastly migraine, had disrupted her concentration: first thing in the morning she had inadvertently used Geoff's haemorrhoid cream to clean her teeth. She was as disgusted by the taste in her mouth as she was by his affliction – the mere thought of it made her wince and retch. She couldn't bear to think of nether-region problems any more than she could bear to remember the torture of childbirth.

While she was fascinated by all things medical, she believed that if it hadn't been for her revulsion in the face of other people's illness, she might, in another life, have made an excellent doctor. Geoff had often joked, peering into their well-stocked medicine cabinet, that Gillian alone kept the pharmaceutical companies in business.

But the dawning of a day like this had, without doubt, contributed to a tense atmosphere in the house and she had immediately gone on the attack.

'I don't understand why you simply can't fold your dirty laundry instead of throwing it in a pile, which

39

takes up much more space than a little bit of order. Show some consideration for once!'

Geoff felt watched, scrutinized and dissected. 'Because, Gillian, it's dirty and it doesn't really matter – it's going to be washed anyway. Why do you have to pick up on every little detail? I don't do it on purpose, love,' came his reply. And there it was – Geoff's use of the word 'love' to soften the blow and attempt to keep things in perspective.

'I'm trying to run this house and it really doesn't help when you leave the bathroom looking like a public convenience, or when you don't push the chair in after you've finished at the table. *Or* that I find myself tripping over dirty socks on your side of the bed. I'm merely asking for a bit of common sense and reason. That's all.'

'Good Lord, Gill, you're starting to make me feel paranoid – everything I do seems to be an unhealthy option between completely wrong and not quite right. You don't half have the ability to make someone feel unworthy, love. And that's on the days when you don't make me feel utterly discreditable.' With that, he had patted little Molly's head reassuringly as he had turned to leave the room.

The very thinnest veil of shame had enveloped Gillian but she rejected it immediately. 'Nonsense. What kind of talk is that? I would suggest it has more to do with your own self-esteem than it does with my judgement.' Her voice was raised as she placed the blame back in his lap.

'You're right, Gill, but then it's hardly surprising, bearing in mind you've even taken to correcting the way I speak.' He paused. 'You know, it's really getting to me. It would be nice if I could just "be" and be myself . . .' He left the room.

There was another pause – not a comfortable one.

'Mummy, when you shouted with your voice it hurted my heart,' articulated Molly.

Gillian softened. 'Hurt, darling. It "hurt" your heart – not "hurted". There, there. Sometimes daddies just need telling how things should be done. Just like Mummy has to tell you how to do things. Now, you need to get your book bag and put your shoes on so we're not late for school . . .'

Gillian hadn't realized that telling her husband and daughter what to do had become mutually indistinguishable. Over the years they had, in her implacable eyes, become one and the same person, requiring one and the same treatment. Geoff's behaviour had become less responsible, increasingly negligent and considerably less acceptable. Like a child refusing to listen and make eye contact, so Geoff's behaviour had regressed. And it was this, above all else, that compelled Gillian to try to bring him back into line.

She had waved them both goodbye earlier since Geoff had offered to take Molly to school. She had kissed Molly with an air of impatience, then had proffered Geoff a cheek. She didn't make physical contact with him, instead shutting her eyes and tightening her lips. Her pursed mouth, she knew, made what Geoff referred to as a 'cat's bum'.

And yet it was in such sharp contrast to how they had kissed when they had first met and started dating: she had been open-mouthed, generous and insatiable. It had been a relationship based as much on passion as it had been on intellect and suitability. Even by Gillian's own admission, Geoff had actually seemed infallible at the start. He had provided her with more reasons to marry him than she could ever have hoped for. He had, for instance, given her no hint that there was anyone of significance in his past; he was incredibly intelligent, regularly showing flashes of brilliance that left her impressed, if not awestruck, and he possessed a cracking sense of humour, which had been integral to his romancing of her. To top it all, Geoff had secured the approval of his future father-in-law – and that had been the absolute subjugation of Gillian. She had been in his thrall and had bestowed on him her adoration – something normally only reserved for her father. And, indeed, once her relationship with Geoff had been secured and had settled down, Gillian had made sure there was room for both men in her life.

Thinking that she had once been so desperate to make Geoff her husband, and that over the last few years had hardly been able to touch him, was not so much a cause of consternation, it was simply the way things were. She would frequently muse that it would be healthier if everyone acknowledged that wanton love and distraction inevitably made way for practicality and pursed lips. It was simply the price you paid for a long-term marriage and small children – nothing more, nothing less.

And small children did take their toll. Gillian had struggled with her daughter's inability to conform. She had not expected her life to be turned upside-down by the presence of such a little person. She had certainly not anticipated the turbulence Molly would cause even before her arrival: Gillian had sent herself into a spin of unadulterated hysteria about her own health and that of her unborn child. She had studied every book available on the subject in great detail. As bad luck would have it, she seemed to suffer every ailment associated with pregnancy and didn't enjoy the luxury of relaxing, like every other mother-to-be around her. While Geoff would pat and stroke her stomach, Gillian just rued the way her body's shape was changing and moved his hand away.

When her mobile had rung, so very inconveniently in the aftermath of her contretemps with the food processor, Gillian had wiped her forehead with the back of her hand, transferring jam to her face and into her hair. Then, as she had moved quickly towards her phone, she had managed to knock a picture frame off the dresser in the hallway and realized too late that her hands were spreading freshly made damson jam wherever she went.

And then, of course, the day had gone from bad to worse: from beastly to breathtakingly shocking. It was her voicemail, with a call from her incoherent, dithery mother who, between sighs and hesitations, managed somehow to impart the dreadful news of her father's death.

Why her mother couldn't be sharp and to the point at such a pivotal time as this was not only irritating to Gillian but verging on insulting. She paused. Perhaps it had been a bit harsh to criticize her mother – she had been caught on the hop – but it was still frustrating.

'Oh, poor Daddy! Poor, poor Daddy!' she exclaimed, and just as the tears were about to gather in her eyes, she knew she needed to focus: she must think logically, efficiently and responsibly.

She had wasted no time in phoning to check on her mother, smearing the telephone with more jam as she did so. For some moments, Gillian allowed herself to forget about the kitchen and thought of her family, in a deliberate act of distancing herself from the tragedy of her father's death.

She bent down next to the dresser to pick up the picture frame – once more forgetting her sticky fingers. The glass had smashed into dozens of pieces, large and small. The glorious picture of her and Geoff on their wedding day was now sliced, carved and divided. The photograph lay face down – and when she lifted it, it was clear to see it had been permanently damaged.

For Gillian this was not only an inconvenience but also yet another cause of frustration. Her mind went back to their wedding day, eleven years earlier, which she had organized with military precision. She had translated her dreams into a wedding-day reality but her overwhelming control of the whole operation had been the one thing to make her heart swell with pride and confidence. Everything in life deserved a system in which things could be structured and compartmentalized – that way there was no room for clutter and disarray or, God forbid, havoc and turmoil. Gillian had learned very early on that a tidy life invariably meant a tidy mind – she felt convinced she had inherited this wisdom directly from her father.

What had happened this morning, however, remained unclassified within the system and would stay in a pending folder somewhere in the far reaches of her mind.

Prioritize, prioritize! rang a voice alarmingly in her head. She scrambled the shards of glass into a small pile with her tacky fingers as tiny splinters tried to penetrate her skin. Gillian winced, but continued with determination until the majority of the glass formed a small mound by the leg of the dresser.

Then, with rejuvenated focus and purpose, she headed back into the kitchen. She held her hands under the tap, which took for ever to run warm, rinsing off a mixture of gooey jam and glass splinters. Then she delved into her handbag on the countertop with damp hands, searching for her car keys with a deep, underlying anxiety. She scrabbled inside the bag, turning the search into a lucky dip.

But this wasn't a lucky dip. Gillian's life was *not supposed* to be a lucky dip. Gillian's life was predetermined, planned and intended. It was about structure and foresight – not much was left to chance. If she had wanted odds on her life she would have played the lottery, like all the other idiots who believed in taking chances, sacrificing reason and sensibility.

But without car keys she was without mobility – she would be housebound and unable to get to her parents' house at such a crucial time, as she had promised. Her mother ought not to be left alone at a time like this. Internally, at least, Gillian was despairing, and it seemed the more desperate her need, the less likely the keys were to make themselves available.

She spent the next few minutes hunting for them – she looked everywhere, increasingly shocked that something belonging to her had actually gone missing. This was out of character and could not have come at a more difficult time.

Gillian was at a loss. She had tried every drawer, every cupboard, every surface – but she drew the line at looking behind the sofas: she would not have been daft enough to lose them there.

She went back into the hallway and decided that Geoff's coat pocket might be the wild card. She found nothing but a couple of pieces of paper – a restaurant receipt and another receipt. Gillian held on to them unconsciously, crumpling them in her hand and treating them like worry beads, passing them between her fingers in agitation and distraction, trying to draw from them some comfort.

Oh, the shame and irony of having an impeccable house in which something so vital had gone missing!

'Your house is more like a museum than a home,' one of her friends had commented. 'There's nothing out of place and I, for one, am too scared to sit anywhere.' She had laughed nervously.

Gillian had taken the remark as a compliment when, in fact, it had been intended to jolt her into seeing her ordered house as the cold, remote exhibit it really was.

She needed one of her tablets – the migraine was now firmly established, throbbing and stabbing above her right eye – but she hoped she could still catch it before it had her in a darkened room, vomiting into a bucket. The tablets were on repeat prescription: she had never believed in all that hocus-pocus nonsense about natural healing. If you had a pain, an illness, a condition, it was surely preferable to swallow a pill than crush a plant leaf or rub yourself with some fragrant oil. This was as much down to Gillian's sense of urgency as it was efficiency: time was never on her side. Besides, she felt very strongly that it was much less of a gamble. As a result, she was no stranger at the doctor's surgery – they knew Mrs Lloyd very well because she would go there with a shopping list of just-in-case medicines, such as antibiotics, steroid creams or pain relievers. She would use medical terms for problems, refer to medicines by the generic name, not a brand, and she would discuss doses with the GP as if she were a colleague rather than a patient.

On her way to the bathroom she peered into the living room where there was very little, if anything, to indicate a lively family life. The sofas – all three – stood perfectly puffed; the coffee-table was polished and unused, as if awaiting the arrival of magazines or some literary stimulus, and the dresser had been evenly adorned with frames, ornaments and reference books, all placed according to size and colour. Gillian had banished Molly's toys to cupboards and had, at times, even insisted on tidying up while Molly was playing, much to the frustration of the nearly five-year-old who had not yet fully grasped the virtues of neatness and order.

'Mummy, I don't *want* to tidy up,' Molly had said, resisting. Hardly unexpected from a child but it was as if she was forcefully rejecting her mother's influence. Gillian had tried not to take it personally, explaining to her daughter the importance of 'need' rather than 'want', and that if everything had a place and it was put there, nothing would ever go missing.

How she was eating those words now! Her father would have been disappointed in her – she was disappointed in herself.

And then, as she looked into the living room, she saw her father standing by the French windows, looking out on to the garden, clutching a cup of tea, as he passed a critical eye over the flowerbeds.

Gillian stood fixed to the spot. 'D-a-d-d-y,' she uttered hesitantly but no sooner had the word been spoken than the apparition disappeared.

Gillian fell to her knees, then sat back on her haunches. She took a sharp breath. 'Oh, Daddy!' she exclaimed. Her eyes welled and her lip quivered. 'Oh, Daddy! What happened to you?'

And what has happened to me? she thought. *I've lost control* . . . A pristine house soiled with spewing jam, lost car keys and a head darkened by pain and exhaustion. This was not how her father would have liked to see her. They had shared a passion for order, discipline – temperance, even. Where were the skills her father had taught her now? He had instilled in her the integrity of everything from dressing well, which showed discipline and care, good behaviour, which showed respect for those around you, and finally he had impressed on her the need to control one's temper, which, more than anything, showed a healthy amount of emotional intelligence. She was her father's daughter, there was no doubting that.

She felt ashamed. She needed to get to her mother and was unable to because she couldn't find her car keys – in her own house.

Tears were still threatening but she refused to release them. Instead she wiped her eyes with the back of her clenched hand.

She sighed with the slightest hint of self-pity. Looking down into her hand, where she clutched the receipts from Geoff's coat-pocket, she saw that one was a dinner bill from last Thursday night and the other – she held it out in front of her – was a receipt for two cinema tickets, which triggered no memory in her whatsoever.

Today's hideous events had left her with an immense dark shadow hanging over her. And so Gillian's exemplary, superior intact life took a challenging new turn. Picking up the phone, she dialled her younger sister's mobile.

Chapter Five

The coffee shop in which Beth found herself had made every effort to entice customers in, and more recently it had tried even harder to make them stay by placing chunky, homely sofas and armchairs randomly on its premises. The idea that coffee might be taken in anything other than a rush was in direct contradiction to the way it had originally been promoted in this little corner franchise. When it had first opened the café, along with most other modern coffee shops, had relied on speed and efficiency – the quick, easy and no-nonsense dispensing of hot drinks for the ever-so-busy preoccupied inhabitants of the fast world.

Gradually, however, the world, and indeed the coffee shop, had experienced a rather gentle revolution: the arrival of families to occupy the softer seats in the café replacing the men in suits who rushed in and out without so much as a thank-you. Mothers with young babies and children would seek an hour's refuge from the inclement British weather; teenagers met up there because there was nowhere else to go and it seemed so adult and outrageously trendy to drink coffee in a place so central and permissible. Slowly but surely the pace of the café had eased to match the requirements of its customers.

Out had gone the hard wooden chairs and the tiny round uninviting tables to be replaced by sofas with scatter cushions and large, solid, rectangular tables. The shift had not only been born out of pace and speed but ergonomics – the proprietors wanted to make sure that staff and customers alike were well seated and comfortable within their environment. A little notice board had suddenly appeared at the far end: now local groups and charities could easily access the community, and display their pleas for help or advertise their services. Soft easy-listening music was piped through the speakers, replacing the pop music and untimely chat of national radio stations. All this made for a calm, relaxed atmosphere. There was also much mention of 'organic' in the coffee shop's signs and literature. All of these factors had gradually engendered feelings of spiritual goodness, generosity and environmental awareness in the customers.

For Beth the change had been very positive – not least because she wasn't a hurried, rushed kind of person. She was laid-back and, in her father's words, 'lacked the urgency gene', which she had at first taken as a compliment but had later understood had not been meant as such.

However, she had decided that she needed to be 'relaxed' because she believed the virtues of patience and understanding had been bestowed upon her to guide her through life and help her navigate her unnervingly imbalanced family.

Having often felt at odds with her parents and elder sister, Beth had done what was necessary for her sanity, and withdrawn her involvement.

'Darling Beth,' her mother would whisper, in a last-ditch attempt at persuading her younger daughter to attend a family lunch or dinner, 'Gillian and Geoff are coming. Please don't make such a fuss – it's so upsetting.'

'And you don't think it upsets me? I wouldn't want to embarrass Dad by forcing him to be seen out with his loser of a daughter. What was it he said? "Hopeless, deluded, ineffective and without serious qualifications"? Well, that's nice, isn't it? Just because he doesn't understand art or value it, I'm considered without aptitude. Why don't you say something to him *if it means so much to you, Mum?' had been Beth's angry response.*

'Oh, Beth, please let's not make a fuss,' was all her mother had been able to offer, and Beth had, once again, ended up not joining in.

As a result, she had often felt like an only child but she couldn't recall ever being uncomfortable in her own company. In fact, she would go so far as to say that she found the greatest peace in solitude. Perhaps that was why she so often enjoyed the inspiration that came to her at the café – placing herself on its periphery, studying the people in it and using the atmosphere to feed her imagination. She would then create images and scenes in her mind and sometimes there was enough colour in them for her to transfer what she had observed and experienced to large canvases in her tiny flat.

She enjoyed the verbal entertainment, too – listening to people sharing gossip, sometimes laughter and the occasional gasped 'I *cannot* believe she said that', before she respected the privacy of their conversation and lives.

She loved studying people's moods, movements and behaviour – it was all a great luxury to her and in some respects even a source of comfort. She had a genuine and passionate interest in people, which had created in her an enduring ability to empathize, pity and, most importantly, to respond.

She often wondered if this was what had originally compelled her to become an artist or whether it had just been lack of interest in other subjects at school, and a feeling that whatever she did in them, she never did quite well enough. Art had been different. It had offered Beth a creative outlet, which she had enjoyed beyond compare, and to top it all, it was a subject in which she had excelled from early on.

No matter how excited she had been, at the age of fifteen, to have found her 'calling', it was always going to be squashed by her disapproving father's blatant rejection of art as not being, in his view, 'a real subject' and certainly not one that counted as education in any way, shape or form.

And yet it had been art, and nothing much else, that had opened and broadened Beth's mind. It was art that had kept her constant and stable during those times when she had thought she might lose the plot entirely.

This morning, courtesy of the rain, the café was particularly busy. It was one of those wet days that brought about a shortage of seats and consequently created a fraught and fragile atmosphere, but as Beth had already been there for nearly an hour and a half, she had secured a great position by the window, away from fractious adults and unwilling children.

She sat with her sketchbook on her lap and a large jug of coffee, which she had bought with the intention of it lasting her a very long time – and it had. Despite it having gone cold some time ago, she couldn't help but wallow in the warm, sombre aroma of exotic black steamy coffee and the enticing scent of melted-cheese-and-ham toasted sandwiches.

Neena was already more than a little late, but Beth had come to accept that as part of her charm – and she *had* accepted it, truly. It was not a cause for anger or irritation – it was just who she was: Beth understood and liked that.

The café door opened. 'Sorry, honey, I just couldn't get away!' Neena shouted for all to hear, as she approached Beth, briefcase and newspapers tucked in her hand. She was wearing her work 'uniform' – navy skirt and tights, white blouse and jacket. But the lapel of her blouse was sticking up above her jacket on one side, so she didn't look as smart as she'd intended.

'Sorry, sorry, sorry, sorry – a million times sorry! Please forgive me. It was totally unintended and it's completely reprehensible – I'll fully understand if you refuse to treat me to a muffin now – but it was mad getting into work and it was equally mad trying to get away . . .' Neena was almost breathless.

Beth liked that. She liked her breathlessness, her disorganization, her apologies and her neediness. She liked her neediness above anything else. She liked that it mattered to Neena that she was late. It was impossibly endearing.

Neena kissed Beth hurriedly on the cheek, and all the while Beth just smiled – she smiled with contentment, familiarity and a great sense of belonging. 'You crazy woman,' she said calmly. 'Of course I forgive you but I'll have to think about the muffin . . . I'm not sure a woman who looks so dishevelled is quite worthy of a fruity muffin – not to mention the sin of failing to turn up on time. When will you ever learn, Neena Gupta?'

This was met with a broad and grateful smile from Neena as she fumbled to tuck her runaway blouse lapel under her jacket collar. They held each other's stare, smiling like two naughty schoolchildren, ignoring the hustle and bustle around them.

Neena let go of her belongings in one fell swoop and undid her coat, which she draped carelessly on the back of the chair Beth had reserved for her. Her thick black hair hung in luscious swathes around her shoulders. It was the colour of liquorice. Her skin, Beth had always thought, resembled unbaked gingerbread. It was flawless and had remained so in spite of the onslaught of the morning's wind and rain. Every time Beth saw it, she wanted to touch it – it seemed so soothing.

'Right, then, sweetie,' Neena started. 'I'll wait till the queue's died down before I get my own hit of caffeine but I haven't actually got *that* long – despite this being a so-called "meeting". What's on your mind? What couldn't wait until tomorrow?'

Beth felt slightly compromised by the idea of rushing this. While a huge part of her wanted to throw the suggestion into the air, as you might the idea of catching a movie and a bite to eat, the other part of her wanted it to be given the credence and consideration it truly deserved, not dismissed lightly. This was important.

'Well, I've just been thinking . . . and . . .' She hesitated. She wanted Neena to be properly seated when she said it. She wanted her anchored so there was less chance she would be distracted or, worse still, rush away and disappear into the mass of people.

'What?' asked Neena, sounding impatient. 'What is it?'

Beth didn't like her urgency: she didn't want to feel compromised by Neena's anxiety to get away – that sense of being under the pressure of time, which Beth had never actually known. *Perhaps*, she thought, *this is a terrible idea. A heaving café on one of its busiest days is hardly a place conducive to serious conversation.* She began to change her mind – but thoughts about bringing up the subject had been running through her mind for some weeks now . . . months, if she was honest. Well, if she was going to be *brutally* honest, they were thoughts she'd had from the moment she had first met Neena.

Now, as she was on the threshold of broaching the subject, she was transported back to her childhood when, time after time, she would ask for permission to meet up with friends at the weekend only to have her request flatly rejected by a father intent on absolute control. She remembered very clearly that turbulent feeling in her stomach and the week-long build-up before she had been able to pluck up the courage to approach him.

The very first time, she had suggested it to her mother, who had reciprocated with an encouraging, resounding 'Yes.' The following day, before she had had a chance to approach her father, she had over-heard him talking to her mother in the sitting room . . .

'How dare you go behind my back and undermine me in this way?' His voice was agitated and raised.

'I'm so sorry, Austin, I thought it would be harmless – she merely wanted to meet friends at the cinema,' her mother had responded quietly.

'Harmless? How can it be harmless when she's in such dire need of qualifications? She's not likely to get them at the cinema, is she? Not only will it cost her money, but it will also cost her a decent future. I cannot believe you even contemplated giving her permission without first consulting me. Unadulterated liberties,

nothing less,' he had said forcefully, harshly and loudly. Her
mother had not replied.

Beth hadn't liked the way her father had spoken to her mother – it had come like a sharp stab in the stomach – and it proved not to be an isolated incident. The feeling it left her with endured: there had never appeared to be any form of reconciliation between her parents, which might have taken away Beth's own sense of pain and guilt. There was not the smallest gesture – a pat on the shoulder, a brief holding of hands – or warm word to heal the rift between her mother and father.

Beth had found herself grounded – and concluded painfully that her poor mother would be a useless ally in her battle for social freedom.

That feeling she'd had, aged fourteen, was now sitting like a stone in her belly and wouldn't shift. Beth didn't know whether to seem casual or profound in her approach – she didn't want it to sound as if this was the kind of suggestion she made every day of the week. Equally, she didn't want to scare Neena off. It was a tough call to strike just the right balance.

While awaiting a response from Beth, which did not appear to be forthcoming, Neena started to sort her belongings. She was grappling with the contents of her handbag, then decided to empty them out on the table in front of her. A mobile phone with a shattered screen was first to fall out, followed by three lipsticks, several hairbands and a biro, which had leaked on to a wad of tissues.

Beth was anxious that she might have paused a moment too long and lost Neena to organization. 'Er, well . . .' she cleared her throat '. . . I was just thinking that it would make sense for us to merge our resources. You know, the two of us. It would be far more practical in the long run – both financially and from an efficiency point of view. And, actually, you could say that by reducing the amount we travel, we're limiting our carbon footprint and so, in turn, we would be doing something positive ecologically, too . . .' The words came out of her mouth before she'd had a chance to edit or review them, so Neena's reaction was no surprise.

'I'm sorry, Beth, but what the hell are you talking about?'

'I want you to move in with me,' she blurted out.

There! She'd said it. And it hovered, for a moment, like a huge red hot-air balloon right above their coffee-table. It was inescapable, and Beth knew that until Neena opened her mouth again, the agony would not be over and the balloon would not budge.

There was a prolonged pause. Beth's eyes did not shift from Neena, and the hot-air balloon hung, still and permanent.

'Oh, Christ, Beth,' Neena finally uttered. 'Are you seriously telling me that you want us to save the world by moving in together?'

She was right to be appalled – the suggestion was as absurd as its presentation had been. After all these months of deliberating and pontificating with herself, Beth had managed to reduce her deepest desire to an environmental project. *So much for planning.* She winced.

'If it's a greener environment you're after, or even a recycling buddy, why don't you just advertise on the board in the corner?' Neena signalled over her shoulder towards the notice board, without turning her head.

Beth thought she looked a little cross. It wasn't surprising. Her proposal had sounded practical, if not just a little clinical. It was the first time the atmosphere between them had been hard for Beth to gauge: normally their friendship and, indeed, the basis of their entire relationship was one of ease with a distinct lack of complication. But for the first time Beth felt both uneasy and insecure.

'Honey,' Neena leaned in towards her, '*I* would want us to live together because that's what you and I both want – not because we're signing up to the Green Party and want to show willing!' was her frank response. 'I love you and I couldn't imagine anything nicer than waking up next to you every morning. But I won't live with you under the pretence of an environmental commitment – and certainly not if that's what you're intending to tell your parents!'

Beth smiled – she grinned. She felt embarrassed and relieved all at once. She leaned forward to give Neena a kiss – but Neena turned away.

'I mean it, Beth. It's time you came clean with your parents. It's not fair on them or on us. We should be able to live our lives the way we want to, without having to skulk in corners and initiate covert missions during national holidays. If this is important to you, you're going to have to face them. Head on.'

She was right, of course. Beth's parents hadn't been told of the true and very real nature of her relationship with Neena. Two years ago she had introduced Neena as a friend, which, of course, came naturally as she was indeed very much Beth's friend – there was no lie in it.

But when love had so unexpectedly unfolded between them it had become increasingly difficult for Beth to explain things to her parents. Her mother, bless her, was most unlikely, Beth thought, even to be familiar with the word 'gay' – especially not with its more modern interpretation – let alone understand its meaning and intention. And her father, well, he, she knew, would be nothing short of appalled, disgusted, disapproving, if not in a state of absolute disbelief and denial. It would be a minor miracle if he were to believe her in the first place, and not think she was saying it to provoke and annoy him – further widening the unbridgeable gap between them.

So, with such mountains to climb, it was easy to understand why Beth had chosen to keep her personal life to herself. Although this was not something she was proud of: she had always congratulated herself on her openness with other people, her honesty and integrity. But she didn't see her parents as 'other people':

they were so much more than that – and, in many ways, so much less.

Families bring an inherent need for communication and association – but, as Beth understood from the magazines and books that had enlightened her, many people struggled to form a natural relationship with their parents. So she was not alone. And she was not alone in loving them while not necessarily liking them. Her mother was harmless enough – she wouldn't say boo to a goose – but with her father, things were different and therein lay the sticking point. She had to concede there was something about him that she feared. She would, at times, be forced to admit to herself that, in fact, she hated him. She hated him because – unreasonably or otherwise – she just didn't understand him. The differences between them made her feel as though she was no more the product of him than she was of the stranger serving behind the counter in the café.

'I know,' Beth said reluctantly, looking down. She couldn't escape the sense of shame she felt. Neena had outwitted her by miles, and it was testament to how well she knew Beth that she had gone straight for the jugular. 'I know I must talk to them about it. And I think that if I make this announcement, it will force them to understand that I'm very serious about you – about us. There will be no escaping the issue.' And it would be an issue, there was no denying that.

Strange how love worked. Suddenly Beth rather

relished the prospect of telling her parents. She felt strong – and determined to fulfil her promise to Neena.

Her mobile rang. While she was inclined to revel in this moment of unity, clarity and proposed cohabitation, she knew she would have to answer it, just in case it offered the possibility of work.

She picked her phone up from the table, and as she put it to her ear she mouthed to Neena, 'It's *Gillian*,' rolling her eyes and sticking out her tongue in a playful show of contempt. '*Yes!* Gillian, what can I do for you on this shitty morning?'

'There's no need for that kind of language, Beth, regardless of the weather,' came her sister's speedy and breathless response.

Beth gave her head a brisk shake.

'Are you sitting down, Beth? Are you on your own? Have you got someone with you?' The onslaught of questions was not unexpected from Gillian, although its nature was.

'What? No, I'm not on my own.' She paused briefly, knowing that the mention of Neena would force a frown on to her sister's face. A wince and a frown were the only indications Beth had ever had that her sister understood her relationship with her lover. Gillian had refused to acknowledge it in words. 'I'm with Neena and the coffee shop is pretty full so speak up. What do you want? Signatures on one of your petitions or what?' Beth had no hesitations about taunting Gillian. She was Teflon-coated – nothing ever seemed to stick to her.

'Beth. This is serious. I don't know how to tell you . . . It's . . . er . . . well, I can't . . . Daddy has died. It's so entirely awful. He collapsed on the way to work and then he apparently died in hospital or on the way there. I'm not sure which. It's just so awful. It's ghastly. Beth, can you hear me?' Again Gillian didn't pause for so much as a breath.

Beth felt her jaw drop and, with it, heard her own sharp intake of breath. She stared at Neena. *No! No! No!* was ringing in her head and flashing before her eyes, but she couldn't be sure she had said it.

Neena was gazing at her with concern.

And then it came.

'NO! NO! NO! It's not true! It's not true!' she shouted, rocking violently from side to side in the chair. Strangers' faces turned towards her and, had she been more aware, she would have noticed that, at that precise moment, life in the café stopped. Abruptly. Momentarily.

Neena was mouthing, 'What?' at her, respecting the fact that she was still on the phone but keen for a response.

'Oh, my God . . .' was all Beth could say. She wasn't thinking – she was just reacting. 'Mum . . . What about Mum?' she yelled.

'I've just spoken to her. She doesn't sound good. She's on her own. I'm hoping to go over – she really shouldn't be alone at a time like this. And can you imagine? So close to Daddy's birthday, too.' Beth noted inconvenience rather than grief in Gillian's words but she could hear, too, that her sister was fighting for breath.

'OK, OK, OK . . .' Beth's thoughts were falling like hail in her mind, icy stones of agony and panic. 'Cool, cool . . . I'll head over, too,' she said distractedly.

'It's not *cool*, Beth!' scolded Gillian. 'It's all deeply upsetting.' She hung up without so much as 'goodbye'.

Beth dropped her phone into her lap and stared straight ahead.

'Oh, honey, what is it?' asked Neena, for the second time that morning.

'My dad's died.' The words tripped from her mouth with ease and simplicity, as if it was something she had said many, many times before.

And that was that.

From where Beth was sitting it seemed nothing had changed. Nothing had changed since the news of her father's death – life had carried on with neither acknowledgement nor sympathy. She could see people continuing their conversations, drinking their coffee and eating their food. She felt sickened by their consumption and their ability to remain untouched by the brief but clandestine visit of the Grim Reaper – taking a life, as he had, without warning or announcement. She felt angered by his taciturn malevolence. She was shocked by his ability to cause such turmoil in her life with one big, silent sweep of his scythe. And yet things around her remained unchanged. People walked about freely, unmoved by Beth's tragedy.

She could feel Neena embracing her and kissing her cheeks, yet all she could do was sit there, arms by her sides. Her phone slipped out of her lap and fell to the floor but she did not stir.

Then, galvanized, she stood up. 'I've got to go,' she said, with sudden urgency – as if she'd just awoken from a trance. She put on her jacket and placed her mobile in her jeans pocket. She was moving automatically – robotically almost – and her eyes were focused as if she was already in a different place, somewhere dark, far removed, somewhere Neena wasn't. She put her cycling helmet under her arm and turned to walk out.

Neena abandoned her belongings and followed her. 'I'll come with you!' she urged, reluctant to let her go.

But Beth wasn't listening. She turned at the door. She looked sad and confused. 'He'll never know now,' she mumbled. 'He'll never know who I am. And I will never know who he was.'

Neena stood helplessly at the door, which had shut confidently behind Beth. Her head lowered, her body rigid, she remained there for some time as it opened and closed for people forcing themselves out into the driving rain.

She took a deep breath, lifted her head and walked back to where they had been sitting.

The moment that had changed everything replayed in her mind. How she had bent down to pick up Beth's phone and seen one of her own tears drop on to the dirty tiled floor, leaving a dark, round patch by Beth's shoe. How she had looked up, seen tears running down Beth's cheeks, forming solid streams to her jaw where their lament had finally delivered them to her chest. She recalled Beth biting her downturned lower lip and squinting in a vain attempt to stem the flow, but she was ultimately defeated by her own lack of control. Beth's tears had rolled without the slightest constraint: the tributary had overflowed with nowhere else to go.

Neena's instinct had been to cup Beth's face in her hands. At that precise moment, she had thought, Beth had looked like a little girl – like a vulnerable child, lost in life and confused by the advent of death. That must have been what she had looked like as a child, she had thought, and that warmed Neena. She had felt such a surge of amazing love for her. An unconditional need to protect Beth had shot right through her.

With tears still filling her eyes, all she could think now was that she wanted to shield her darling from all the pain that inevitably lay before her, but as she slumped into the chair Beth had just left, she felt helpless.

Chapter Six

(Gloucestershire, March 1965)

As they stood in young Myrtle's tiny bedroom – walls dressed haphazardly with prints of her heroes and heroines – the air between them was unusually heavy with anticipation and agitation.

Austin had come to the house under the pretence of passing by, but Myrtle had felt he was checking on her. She felt mildly irritated by his duplicity but not enough to point it out, perhaps because there remained some truths that had not passed between them. Some, perhaps, never would. But she couldn't help feeling he was making sure she wasn't somewhere else, doing something else. What was to him protectiveness and care, she interpreted as suffocating possessiveness. Yet, as good friends, she knew there was nothing wrong with one person looking out for the other.

Austin stood, head bowed, as far from Myrtle as he could place himself – by the window overlooking the Hale family's small apple orchard. He had a distinct way of looking away when he was talking to her, as if deliberately without acknowledgement and showing undue interest in anything else. It was, she felt, as if he was addressing the room. Many times in the past she had found this rather endearing – charming almost – but lately she couldn't stop feeling irritated by him.

'It's not that odd, really, when you think about it,' Austin said, with a flippancy that filled Myrtle with unease, picking away as he spoke at some chipped paint on the sill. It was a kind of subliminal reference to Myrtle's doubt and her undeniable misgivings but it was not acceptance. 'We've known each other all our lives,' he continued, 'for longer than either of us can remember, and there's a lot to be said for friendship nowadays.'

She knew that. She had felt generous amounts of sympathy for him when she had first got to know him. There was a sadness in his eyes that at first she had found hard to see because he insisted on looking away when she talked to him. It had become an enjoyable challenge for her to force his eyes to meet hers, whether it was across the keys of her father's piano when she had tried so hard to teach him to play or when he suffered her pitiful attempts at mathematics homework. His avoidance and nervousness had always served to make *her* feel more in control. What he lacked in social and communication skills, she more than made up for in enthusiasm and a sense of fun.

Today, however, the physical and emotional distance between them was so noticeable that Myrtle felt afraid to move. She didn't want him to come closer and her body refused to move nearer to him because she was scared he might read that as encouragement – and that was the last thing she wanted. She was adamant he must not think there was any more substance to their emotional equation than friendship. Even though he was a friend, she resented his appearance today – he looked too proper and orderly, standing there by the window, dressed in a shirt and tie, sweater and plain, well-ironed trousers. His attire showed such utter disregard for fashion. His thick dark hair, which she normally admired if only for its sheer perfection, was now annoyingly shiny and had been so meticulously slicked back into place with a fine-tooth comb that it nauseated her. He was neat and organized – he looked so safe. Inside, Myrtle felt chaotic. She had an almost irrepressible urge to make a startling noise – like she had felt inclined to do at exam time in school when the hall was deafened by the strictest of silences. Then Myrtle couldn't trust herself not to stand up and scream at the top of her voice. Now she wanted to unsettle Austin and provoke in him a spontaneous, uncalculated reaction – she wanted something unexpected.

Instead she, too, chose to look away, in clear and plain avoidance of the atmosphere between them – and, undeniably, in pain.

'I know . . .' She looked down at her short but slender fingers, which had gathered around her somewhat turgid stomach. 'I just don't feel . . . I just don't feel . . . er . . .' The words were like spoonfuls of sand parked on her tongue. 'I'm not sure . . . about love, so to speak.'

'Myrtle.' Austin cleared his throat and his tone became considerably more serious. 'Marriage is the summation of companionship and trust. I would estimate the ratio to be positively divided – say, fifty:fifty. Out of those two parts will come love, continuity and a sense of belonging.'

There was an awkward silence. She couldn't stand the awkwardness and formality of his words.

'Oh, but you know I'm painfully bad at maths, and there you are, confusing me with numbers, equations and solutions. I speak in words or music, Austin,' she braved, 'not in figures – I'm not clever like you.' She looked up briefly in hope, but found him frowning.

'You like reading books, don't you, Myrtle?'

'I do. I do. But books about people and circumstance, about sadness and happiness, about love and colour.'

'See?' He was desperate to encourage her. 'You're already touching on the metaphysics of life.' He moved closer and Myrtle flinched.

'You see, I'm sure you will learn to love me. In fact, I know you will. I'm a reliable, dependable man – I can offer you security.' At which point he directed his stare right into her eyes. 'Myrtle, there are some real snakes in the grass out there – as I'm sure you know.' He waved his finger, then glanced down her body, eventually stopping at her feet. 'I will look after you, Myrtle,' he said, confident of his solution. 'I will. I swear it.' That was his solemn promise. 'I will not let you down. I work hard. I will soon inherit the house. We have a friendship that has stood the test of time and I think you will not find me wanting.' He aimed that sentence at her eyes and, she imagined, at her soul. It would have been difficult to contradict it. On this occasion he wasn't lacking in direction – that much was true.

Myrtle closed her eyes. She could deny it no longer: she wished he was someone else. But when she opened them, it was Austin standing before her. And she knew that that would not change, no matter how much she wished for it.

She was dumbfounded, silenced by her own sadness. He had stolen her words and used them to his own advantage. 'I just feel so young and foolish.' She had meant it in every sense – they both knew that.

'We might be young but we're both old enough,' was all he was prepared to concede.

Myrtle's eagerness to please others – her naïvety – had not been at the expense of complete stupidity or common sense. Her kindness and generosity of spirit had not entirely been blotted by ignorance. She understood, very well, that the offer Austin had made was exceptionally kind, not to mention generous, in the circumstances, no matter how much she hadn't wanted to consider it.

Austin had immediately put an end to her self-deprecation – he would hear none of it – refusing Myrtle's attempts to try to change his mind or turn him against her. Presumably he didn't want to hear them, she thought, because he didn't wish to be reminded of the disaster she had become.

The only thing she could comfort herself with, at that precise moment – tears were once again on the precipice of her cheeks – was the fact that he hadn't asked her outright to marry him. There had been no actual proposal. He hadn't chosen to use those precise words or actually make her commit to them. Love itself was a commitment, and it wasn't one that she could presently spare him. She had already pledged herself. Her heart was somewhere else. And this fact had invaded her body and consumed her soul.

'You see, Myrtle, all is not lost. We have plenty in common. So, it's decided, then? There is a solution, after all.'

And with that he left, closing the door behind him. She wanted it to remain open to allow her deception and insincerity to flood out of the room. Instead she was sealed inside with her poisonous, ungrateful pretence to suffocate her. She sat down on her bed and wept silently into her hands until her eyes ran dry and her head ached.

Love was involuntary, Myrtle had always felt, spontaneous and intuitive enough to render man or woman helpless and at its mercy. Romance was pure indulgence. Marriage, on the other hand, was an intention, a decision made consciously and very deliberately.

*

Austin walked back to the house he shared with his mother. It would have been a waste, an extravagance, to use his late father's car to drive just a few miles. He couldn't help feeling that the meeting – the discussion, the suggestion – had been a success. Doubt was not a characteristic that sat easily with him, and to that end he had chosen to ignore Myrtle's hesitation. His friend needed guidance at a time like this, if not a little control – something he had been forced to take from a very young age.

At twenty-one, it was Austin Lewis's intention to marry Myrtle Hale and, after very short deliberation, it had become clear that it was the right answer for them both. He hadn't anticipated objection and he had not been disappointed. There were very few things in life of which he was uncertain and this was not one of them.

Before he even knew it, Austin had subconsciously laid claim to Myrtle – the smiling, happy girl with the sparkling, starfish eyes. It was the twinkle and the light in them, the like of which he had never before encountered, that he had been unable to shake from his mind. He liked this calm, kind-natured girl: her sense of fun and happiness was a clear sign to him that she would not present him with any of the malignancy and disorder with which he had hitherto had to cope. *She will be manageable*, he reasoned.

The road ahead was black and icy. The only sound was the confident beat of his shoes making forthright contact with the lane he had so often walked. His mind wandered. It was obvious that marriage had become a necessity and suddenly urgent for both of them. It made complete sense. He liked her. It would be an opportunity to broaden himself and give his life another meaning. As he saw it, with this union he would create a family of his own, a much-needed distraction from what was left of his own family. It was about time his world became more about living and less about surviving.

His foot slipped on the frozen lane and he swiftly steadied himself. His mother entered his head. His body stiffened, his pace quickened and his jaw tensed.

He stopped at the end of the drive, looked up at the house and inhaled sharply.

'Gerald, is that you, dear?' came a woman's slurred, feeble voice, the moment he closed the door behind him. It was swiftly followed by the all-too-familiar and inevitable stumbles and knocks against the atoll of furniture as she doddered her way from the sitting room to the hall. A tumbler with only the dregs of a pale golden liquid hung limply out of her sinewy hand.

'Oh, it's you, Austin . . .' Mrs Lewis was incapable of hiding her disappointment. 'Is Father working late again? He mentioned nothing to me about being late back tonight . . . I don't recall.' She grasped her forehead, frowning. The glass crashed on the stone floor.

'Mother!' Austin lunged forward to catch her before she missed the door frame. 'I told you, Father is not working late.' He took hold of her, smarting at her breath and turning his head away. 'Where on earth did you get that – that drink from? I disposed of all the bottles.' He was in no mood for his mother's behaviour – especially not tonight. For too many evenings he had been forced to endure this welcome.

'Ah, you silly boy! You hadn't counted on the cooking sherry in the larder, had you? Cheap and nasty, dear, but a remedy all the same. You should smile more. Smile, dear boy, smile.' She pinched one of his cheeks hard. 'I may be in the winter of my days but I can still dance,' she taunted, with a laugh that cut right through him.

As she tried out some dancing steps, he grabbed her firmly and guided her upstairs to her bed, as he had done so often, aware that once tonight had worn off there would be little he could do to stop her recreating the scene all over again. He did what he could to control her. In the past he had tried to give her a stern talking-to because pleading had got him nowhere. He had created a routine for her, pinning notes and lists to walls telling her what to do and where to put things after the drink had begun to steal her memory. Then he had locked the door behind him on the way to work.

At the heart of his mother's misery was the unexpected death of her husband eight years ago and that was the one thing he could not change or control.

When he had imagined the evening during which he had hoped to persuade Myrtle to marry him, the last thing he had wanted was to undress his mother for bed and wash the smell of her poison off his hands and face. He left her, mumbling in her sleep, flat out on a bed that had been made for two.

Little surprise, he reflected, that hitherto he had had neither the time nor the inclination to develop a colourful personality or life for himself, being forced instead to concentrate on the huge task so close at hand.

It was pertinent, then, that tonight, like so many other nights, only served to reinforce his loneliness. He had become withdrawn especially from his mother, whose turbulence unsettled and alarmed him. It was little wonder that he had sought solace at Dr Hale's house and all that came with it. Alcohol had become his enemy just as much as it had become his mother's – and he had never touched a drop.

Austin sat down on the edge of his bed, bent forward and clasped his head in his hands. 'Damn woman! Damn drink!' he whispered, through clenched teeth. 'Damn, damn loneliness! Oh, Myrtle . . .' He looked up to the ceiling, flung his head backwards and his slick, greased hair tousled in a dozen strands about his face.

He lay down on the bed fully clothed, face up. His right hand reached out to the empty side of the bed and rested there momentarily. Then he clasped his hands together, in prayer, and closed his eyes. 'Dear Lord, bring me companionship and love, and forgive my impatience with my mother . . .'

*

'Austin, you've not had an easy life,' Myrtle's father had confirmed, as the two men had sat in the sitting room one Sunday afternoon. Austin was a competent cook through force of circumstance but Dr Hale had taken pleasure in inviting him over regularly. While he was medically responsible for Austin's sick mother, the gesture he had extended to her son was an act of pure kindness and compassion towards a young man who had been expected always to fend for himself. 'You've endured the kind of childhood no young person should ever have to. Your patience and perseverance is much admired by all of us here. I have witnessed at first hand your mother's sickness and how it has compromised her as well as you. You have a great sense of duty, Austin, something many young people today appear to have abandoned in favour of freedom and frivolity – although quite what freedom they are seeking is beyond me . . . But no matter. The kindness and friend- ship you have shown to our Myrtle has been second to none, and I want you to know that you are always welcome here, always welcome.' He had patted Austin gently on the shoulder.

A subliminal agreement, of sorts, had passed between Myrtle's father and the man who had become her friend. It was nothing short of a nod and a wink – a suggestion of destiny – between two men who, for entirely differ- ent reasons, had the very best of intentions.

The words had been kind and generous, and Austin had felt a flush of pride when Dr Hale had spoken them. It was not only recognition: it was, he had felt, an invitation to extend his presence in their lives and he wasn't going to decline.

Myrtle had always been a distracted soul. What she lacked in concentration and focus, she had always made up for with an abundance of enthusiasm for a notional life brought to her by characters in books she read and by her own creative imagination. While she lived happily in the real world, she had felt more at home in the hypothetical one where she knew her fertile, resourceful mind was rooted. Her mother continually referred to her as 'fanciful, fantastical and conceited', words that Myrtle understood to be directed at her pretension, but in her own defence she believed she was simply a helpless dreamer.

Nevertheless, throughout her teenage years, aided by her vivid inner life, Myrtle surrounded herself with literary tales of romance. The authors had spent much time, thought and energy in contemplating how, exactly, to go about catching and securing a man. Myrtle had been intimidated by the sheer number of options. She had understood this much: it was important to remain realistic in the pursuit; it was fundamental not to set one's expectations either too high or too low. Her thoughts were following the path of possibility far more than that of expectation.

'I believe I'm going to be a translator,' piped Libby, looking up from the book in her lap. 'I'm excellent at languages. I love French and Latin and Mother says I've got an ear for them.'

She swung her long, slender legs off the end of Myrtle's bed and lifted the book closer to her face. She had the kind of legs Myrtle dreamed of, and the greatest waste of all was that Libby didn't even know it. She walked around oblivious to the fact that her legs were the envy of other girls – girls like Myrtle, whose own legs had been made for playing hockey.

'*I* can't imagine going out to work,' Nibs confessed, leaning back against the wardrobe door, curling her legs under her skirt. 'I don't really see the point. When school's over, that's it for me. No more being told what to do, no more homework and no more ghastly uniform!'

'Nicola Brown!' frowned Libby, keen as mustard to take the moral high ground. 'You need to work, you know.' She lowered the frame of her glasses to the very tip of her nose and shot Nibs an irritated look. 'How on earth will you live? What will you do for money? You'll have to work. Everyone has to work!'

'That's what men do,' Nibs hissed, pointing her nose up to the ceiling and rolling her eyes. 'Men work. I'm going to enjoy myself – I want to have fun. Life will run its course and I with it.' Intent on provocation, she added, 'Who knows? I might not even marry . . .'

Myrtle gasped in horror. 'Surely you want to marry, Nibs? Everyone wants to marry. Why would you say that? Everyone wants to have that special somebody.'

'I didn't say I wouldn't have a "special somebody". In fact, I may have more than one "special somebody". We're young, Myrtle, it may take time to find someone who'll be good enough. I don't want to settle for just anybody.'

Libby looked up, interested and slightly shocked by the turn in the conversation. 'You girls need to think about more than just marriage and men. There's more to life than finding a husband, you know. You could work, travel . . .'

Nibs shot Myrtle a look. 'I bet you've already chosen yours, Myrtle,' she teased. She grabbed a copy of *Honey* magazine from underneath Myrtle's bed.

Myrtle smiled and closed her eyes. 'Well, naturally, he'll be unfathomably handsome. He'll have darkness and mystery about him,' she said, as she stared contemplatively out of the window.

'Mysterious, hey?' queried Nibs, leafing through the magazine slowly, pausing briefly to look up. 'I can't imagine bothering with mystery. It'll be enough to deal with life itself, without worrying about a complicated husband. I couldn't be doing with that.'

'But I should imagine he might be a writer,' continued Myrtle, dreamily, 'or perhaps an artist – prone to mood swings and definitely with a strong, difficult temperament. I will be the only one to unlock his creativity. He will need me – and I him. We will be tormented by each other's desire and our passion will be irresistible and inexplicable. He will catch sight of me from quite some distance – and *bang*!' She clapped her hands together. 'His eagerness will rush through his veins, compelling him towards me. His love will be as infectious as it will be frightening, but I shall be fearless,' she said. 'We might spend the best part of a lifetime in pursuit of a love undiluted by the interference of others, infrangible and undiminished by time. But, most of all, it will be a love victorious.' She was breathless and smiling.

'Good Lord, Myrtle!' gasped Nibs. 'You've been reading too many romantic novels! A love victorious, indeed! You should read factual books and less of this rubbish.' She waved the magazine around.

'Quite!' interjected Libby. 'Next you'll be telling us he wears a uniform and rides a horse . . .'

But with her boundless imagination, Myrtle had no trouble in committing herself to the prospect of romance. Her heart was a rainbow of emotions that was keenly awaiting the advent of flirtation, passion and infatuation. She was the perfect candidate for speculation on love: her mind was uncomplicated by the cynicism that consumed others. It was free and virtuous. She was young at heart; she was submissive and passive with a generous, unquestioning trust in everyone. In truth, she was naïve.

When Fate finally dealt Myrtle a hand in the romance stakes, she was, cruelly, left without choice. When the decision was made, she had grown anxious about marriage to Austin for many reasons – not least because her heart did not jump when she saw him. But she was also increasingly aware of his close attachment to her family, especially to her father. And as marriage was, to her, an unknown quantity, she was hesitant about severing those family ties.

Myrtle had lost count of the number of times her father had made attempts to tenderize her defiance to marry Austin, but it didn't seem fair that she would be made to marry someone about whom she was so ambivalent.

'Dear Lord! Myrtle, you cannot call this a dressed table!' her mother called from the dining room, one Sunday, when Austin had arrived for lunch. 'I asked you to lay it, and Austin has no knife, your father has no glass and the serviettes have been placed so haphazardly it looks as if you threw them on with total disregard! And for goodness' sake be careful with that bowl –'

Before she could finish the sentence her daughter had missed the small step down into the dining room and tripped. The fine ceramic dish she was carrying crashed to the floor and splintered into hundreds of pieces.

Myrtle got up and stared down at the mess of blue and white china scattered among perfectly round new potatoes and cauliflower florets. She turned her head to one side and then the other, her eyes fixed to the floor.

'Look! It's made a pattern – a beautiful pattern. The cauliflower looks like mounds of snow on thawed ground and the splinters are sharp peaks of ice.' She gazed, transfixed, at the result of her clumsiness.

Her mother's face wore an expression of sheer disbelief mixed with pure anger. 'Myrtle Hale! You silly, silly girl! I've never known such ham-handedness!'

Austin watched, frowning. He made no attempt to assist Myrtle, instead retreating to his seat at the table and looking away.

Mrs Hale pulled her daughter into the kitchen by her arm, faced her straight on and hissed in her ear, 'Have you taken complete leave of your senses, girl? Look at yourself – dreamy and thoughtless, careless and useless! A speedy appointment with reality is what you need. You're no good to man or beast in your whimsical state. Austin Lewis is a fine man and you would do well to realize that before it's too late. He's made you a fine offer – one which, I might add, you do not deserve. Not in your state. The very least you could do is to show him and the rest of us a little respect!'

Myrtle hung her head and whispered a compliant 'I'm sorry, Mother.' She walked away, ashamed and embarrassed.

She battled with the hopelessness of a future founded on practicality, and she couldn't reconcile her heart's true desire with the fundamental sense that wrong had been inflicted on her. It was as if she was being asked for her head to do away with her heart – to shut it up and leave it be. She was being asked to forgo her natural instincts and passionate impulses in favour of a prefabricated tailor-made proposal that was sorely lacking in colour and depth. She would be forced to do penance by accepting it and look ahead to a life in black and white – a monochrome life – in which everything would be sharply defined and outlined by Myrtle's own wrongdoings. It would be an emotional chastisement – to live without light and shade would be to live with a silent heart – suffocated by expectation and encumbered by a misplaced sense of duty. And she, for one, didn't dare to contemplate what she should do with her relentless supply of hopes and dreams. The prospect was unthinkable.

After lunch, when the men had retreated to the drawing room for tea, Myrtle helped her mother clear the table. Her sister, Wren, had been excused this chore and had promptly placed herself with delight in front of the small wooden-framed television.

Mrs Hale, intent on getting her message across, continued, 'You'd do well, Myrtle Hale, to remember that you're a very lucky girl indeed. Through no design of your own, you've managed to capture the heart of a very good man and you should place a great deal of value on that – you ought to be grateful.'

Myrtle bowed her head and nervously, with her hands, ironed the wrinkles on her skirt as she did habitually. 'It's not that I'm not grateful. Really . . . It's just . . .'

'It's just what, girl? There's always something. What is it? Spit it out or for ever hold your peace!'

'Well, it's just that I see Austin very much as a friend

and not as a husband. I rather imagined I might marry someone towards whom I was romantically inclined. You know, the kind of man who makes your heart skip and your cheeks blush at the very thought of him. The kind of love that makes you forsake all others – someone you would die for, like Romeo and Juliet, someone you can't live without . . .'

'Myrtle Hale,' said her mother, grasping her shoulders, 'the day you get your nose out of those darn novels and take a look at yourself will be the day the rest of us no longer have to run behind you, mending all the gaping holes you leave in your wake. Instead, you're going to have to make the best of a very bad job.' She lowered her eyes to Myrtle's feet.

'But perhaps there's no need,' said Myrtle, fuelled by possibility and the opportunity perhaps to sway her mother in her favour. 'Perhaps it doesn't have to be this way. Perhaps I don't need Austin. I could manage . . .' Her voice petered out.

'Manage? You? Dear girl, you weren't even able to get yourself through school without getting yourself into trouble with the police – and you think I could trust you with your own life? Less procrastination and considerably more appreciation.' She turned away.

Myrtle bowed her head again and whispered ever so faintly under her breath, 'I don't want to.'

Her mother swung around, put her face up close to Myrtle's, raised her hand and clipped her across the top of her head.

Myrtle turned away. She felt her cheeks flush as tears welled in her eyes.

'You bring shame on this family with your selfish ways and ingratitude. Shame on you, Myrtle Hale.' Mrs Hale stared her right in the eyes. It was an unfailing, penetrating, steady scowl, the kind that was always preceded by the use of Myrtle's surname. At best she could hope to be referred to as 'Little Miss' but with profundity at its peak, her mother went on the attack.

It wasn't her mother's hand that had hurt her, Myrtle quickly saw. It was the shame that had pierced her so enormously. It was the shame she couldn't expel. It burned her heart and had been growing like a cancer deep inside her for the past few months.

'I'm sorry, Mother. I'm truly sorry,' she pleaded softly.

'Oh, you'll be sorry, all right, sorry for all the disappointment and pain you've caused.' Mrs Hale raised her eyes to the heavens. '"For all seek their own, not the things which are Jesus Christ's". And you will pay your dues – the Lord will see to that. Or woe betide you!'

Myrtle never quite knew what it was about profound situations – conversations, even – that made her mother draw on God for support. She was not always so God-fearing.

And deep down Myrtle knew she was without choice. None was offered to sinners and deceivers. Her only hope would be her father. She was depending on him to show pity – to throw her a lifeline. She would do whatever it took to make him understand that life with Austin was beyond her. She was relying on his loyalty to her, his imagination and, most of all, his instinct. But she had left her father with no choice either.

'Myrtle, Austin is a good man and he will care for you and look after you. You will have a nice life together, I'm sure of that. Besides, you two have been very good friends for a long time – as long as either of you can remember. What could be a better start? You could do considerably worse.' Her father winked at her reassuringly and he smiled as he ruffled her hair lightly.

She grabbed his hand, which had just touched her head and held it to her heart. 'I don't want to lose you, Daddy! I don't know what I'd do without you. Things will never be the same, I know it. Oh, Daddy, I'm so scared. I'm just so scared – scared I won't love him and that he'll be cross with me for not being able to love him. Then he'll be cross that you agreed to it and you'll be cross with me for making such a terrible mistake. And I can't, Daddy, I just can't. I know he's a good man – but he's not "him".' She mouthed the word as if making her father privy to a secret code.

There were tears streaming down her cheeks and her father lifted her chin with his solid, reassuring hand, convinced that his daughter's passionate speech would eventually turn itself into love for a good man. 'Now, now, Myrtle. No need for drama and tears.'

*

It was appropriate that, in keeping with Austin's staid proposal-of-sorts, their wedding was of a subdued and muted nature.

It was a Wednesday afternoon in May 1965. There was to be no pomp and virtually no ceremony. All things traditionally indulged in by a bride for her wedding had been denied Myrtle, as if the futility of her dreams was to be reinforced on such a day in all its incredible starkness.

The rain beat hard against the window.

Myrtle's head was deep in the toilet bowl.

There was a knock on the bathroom door. She raised her heavy head slowly.

'You'd better hurry up, Myrtle. Mother's furious. She says we're going to be late.' It was Wren.

Myrtle retched once more, wiped sick from the corners of her mouth and swept loose hair away from her face.

'I know. I'm coming,' she managed. 'Please, just give me a moment.'

She stood up and looked at herself in the mirror above the wash-basin – there were tears in her eyes.

'You're in a lot of trouble,' hissed Wren, and ran off.

Don't I know it, thought Myrtle, as she dabbed the tissue on her mouth, scrunched it in her hand and flushed it down the toilet.

She went into the bedroom and found her mother holding out a mass of pale blue polyester. It looked stiff and uninviting.

'Get yourself into this dress, Myrtle Hale,' she ordered. 'There's no time for dilly-dallying. It's already eleven o'clock and at this rate we shall be late – thanks to you, Little Miss.'

Myrtle stepped inside the dress, struggling to keep her balance. She made a concerted effort to pull it past her hips and smooth it over her thighs. Her mother stood behind her, working it over Myrtle's shoulders. She turned her attention to the zip.

'For goodness' sake, breathe in, girl! You stand like a sack of potatoes. Hold yourself properly and smile. Lord, give me strength.'

Myrtle bowed her head. 'This material itches. The dress is cold and hard. I'm breathing in as much as I possibly can, Mother. I can only think that satin might have been more obliging.'

Without hesitation her mother lifted her hand and gave her a tap on her behind. 'You ungrateful little madam! Ideas above your station – as always. Satin, indeed. You're lucky to have the good fortune to be wearing a wedding dress at all in your state. I ask you! Satin, indeed.'

Myrtle bowed her head deeper into her chest. The relentless tears were in her eyes once more, as she worked to contain her nerves and nausea.

'It's raining,' piped Wren, enthusiastically.

'Of course it is, dear. What else could we expect? I can't imagine the sun wanting to shine on a day like today. Your sister, no doubt, envisaged sunshine and a horse and carriage in her fanciful way,' replied her mother, flapping around her elder daughter and fussing with the ill-fitting dress.

Wren raised her eyebrows and smirked. 'Did you, Myrtle? Did you? Is that what you were dreaming of? A horse-drawn carriage and a prince?' She giggled.

Myrtle clapped a hand over her mouth and ran past her mother straight into the bathroom where she made it just in time to the toilet bowl.

'Sensitive as the day is long, your sister is,' huffed her mother.

Despite Mrs Hale's earlier anxieties, they left the house on time. Myrtle's shoulders were covered with a small, powder blue cardigan. One hand tightly clutched a few dozen bluebells while the other clung to a sodden tissue. Both hands were trembling.

The dress made Myrtle perspire while she tried desperately to contain herself, breathing deeply into the tissue. Her father drove to the register office, looking back at Myrtle regularly, winking and smiling. Her mother's mouth was decidedly downturned and her eyes refused even once to make contact with her daughter's.

'Nervous?' whispered Wren, pertly, leaning across to her sister on the back seat.

'Well, yes. I don't feel well at all,' came the hesitant reply.

'I should think not!' pronounced Mrs Hale, whose trained ear was capable of hearing the merest undertone.

*

The registrar's office was concrete and impersonal, and in the greyness of the day's persistent rain, it was hard to distinguish the building from its neighbours.

The bride's legs were shaking and she felt sick – she was trembling not only with anticipation but also because of the physical demands of the day and its looming, ultimate pronouncement.

They came into a room that was memorable only for its insignificance and coldness. Her father squeezed her hand a couple of times as they walked the short distance to the front of a large, heavy oak desk.

There stood Austin, immaculate and polished in a navy suit and a dark tie, an upright dichotomy of anxiety and certainty. Myrtle glanced at him briefly, purely for identification purposes.

'Myrtle. You look . . .' he whispered, as if grappling to find the word 'different' but he left the sentence unfinished. He cleared his throat.

Myrtle blushed and looked away – elsewhere, any-where – inadvertently catching Wren's eye. Her sister was a reluctant bridesmaid, gazing at her with disdain, in disbelief and with inescapable pity.

The proceedings blurred. Myrtle faded in and out of the ceremony lifelessly and unwillingly.

'I do solemnly declare . . .' Austin repeated after the registrar.

Myrtle swayed from side to side. Austin nudged her. 'It's your turn,' he said.

She took a deep breath, as if she was about to jump

into deep water. 'I'm sorry. What do I say?' she faltered.

'Speak up, girl,' she heard her mother call from behind her, adding insult to matrimony.

'Are you, Myrtle Mary Hale, free lawfully to marry Austin Gerald Lewis?' repeated the officiating registrar.

She lowered her head, looked down at her white shoes and inaudibly uttered, 'I am.' She spoke the rest of her words vaguely and slowly, in a hushed tone, as if she was hoping vainly that an unexpected interruption might save her.

The ceremony was over and Austin leaned forward to kiss his bride, but as he did so, Myrtle turned her head to escape his lips and they collided. Awkwardness and embarrassment enveloped her once more.

Wren rushed forward. 'You're Mrs Lewis now! How does *that* feel?' she yelled, putting her face right up to Myrtle's.

'Oh, well . . . nice, I guess,' Myrtle lied.

'Well done, my girl,' said her father, turning to her after he had congratulated the groom. He gave her shoulders a gentle rub and kissed her forehead.

'Congratulations, Austin. Myrtle is a very lucky girl,' her mother said, facing Austin. She turned and gave Myrtle a look of utter disinterest. 'Now, let's go back to the house for some tea and wedding cake. I baked it myself – I hope you'll be impressed, Austin.' She smiled.

And so the wedding party of five returned to the Hale household with the newly inaugurated Mr and Mrs Lewis.

Despite nausea, nerves and a growing self-hatred, Myrtle smiled as much as she could bear to. She made every attempt to look happy but was sure that the closest she got to exuding joy was an expression of agonized gratitude.

'My dearest Austin and Myrtle – congratulations!' said her father, raising his teacup in the direction of the newly married couple. 'I'll keep this short and sweet – not unlike the ceremony itself. As the father of the bride, I feel it is wholly appropriate to share some thoughts with you on this poignant day. This is, indeed, the beginning of your new life together and you have my unconditional blessing.

'Myrtle, from an early age, literature and music facilitated your escape into an imaginary world. When you were a child, I noticed more and more how you were liberated by books and prose, how you came alive with music and how you resonated with the imaginative and – at times – the improbable. So much so that I think you've struggled in the past to extricate yourself from it.' He gave a light chuckle, which was met with silence.

'Your creativity has enabled you to absorb the world in your very own joyful way, which, as your father, has given me great pleasure to see. In many ways this has enabled you to skirt the parameters of life's realities but never to be drawn in. To your detriment you have, at times, battled to . . . how shall I put it? . . . remove yourself from the imaginary – often allowing the facts of real life and fantasy to merge.

'Today, however, my darling Myrtle, is the first day of the rest of your real life. You stand together with Austin on the threshold of fact – not fiction. Today, the two of you together are making your own history and, indeed, your own future, and it's a joy and comfort to witness it.

'Myrtle,' he said, raising his cup and saucer in her direction, 'I hope you continue to light up our lives with all the colour of your imagination, with all your kindness and generosity of spirit, with all your empathy and humility.

'Austin,' he turned to Myrtle's husband of an hour and a half, 'you are charged with guiding our dearest Myrtle when she strays from the sensible and necessary. Your responsibility is to love this dear thing like no other. If you achieve that, I know you will both be very happy – very happy indeed. Here's to Austin and Myrtle and the future Lewis family!'

As he raised his cup one final time, he took a swig of lukewarm, sweetened tea, then wiped the corner of his right eye and smiled gently at Myrtle.

Mrs Hale did not smile. She cocked her head in the direction of her husband. 'That was much too much – quite unnecessary. You spoil that girl. Had you been a bit harder on her she wouldn't be in the state she's in now – just look at her!' Scowling, she turned her stare to the young bride and narrowed her eyes.

Myrtle had wept silently throughout her father's speech and was trying hard to compose herself. She attempted to smile to hide her relentless nausea.

That was where the little tradition their wedding had been built on ended. There was no honeymoon or even a night away; there was no passion or dream fulfilled; there was no dowry.

Chapter Seven

Myrtle paced anxiously by the window in the front room, her eyes flitting nervously between the front garden and the grandfather clock in the corner. *Austin was a good man and I was fortunate to have him in my life – very fortunate indeed,* she thought.

Briefly, this calmed her pounding heart and gave her sanctuary. She exhaled.

Outside, the weather was grim. It was sad and grey as if it, too, had been told of Austin's passing. There was a distinct murkiness about the sky, Myrtle thought, almost as if someone had forgotten to turn on the lights.

Out of the grey, wet air, Myrtle could vaguely see someone walking up the drive. A big shapeless mass of black with a heavy, laboured walk left her in no doubt that it was Beth. Her head was bowed and she was carrying her cycling helmet.

Myrtle's heart skipped, lifted a little, and she felt a rush of blood to her cheeks as relief spread across her face.

As soon as she opened the door Beth – without hesitation – threw her satchel and helmet on the floor and thrust her wet, strong body in the direction of her mother. Myrtle flung her arms as wide as she could, then closed them securely around her daughter. Briefly, sorrow ran hot and heavy through her veins. Mother and daughter held each other tightly and Myrtle could feel Beth sobbing into her shoulder.

'My dear girl.' Myrtle stroked her damp hair. 'My dear, dear girl.' She couldn't bear the sound or sight of Beth's sadness but at that precise moment it was overwhelmingly good to feel like a mother again – the way she had when Beth had been small. It was an undeniable pleasure – a rare wonder – regardless of the tragedy, to feel so needed. 'There, there, my love. Please don't cry. Please don't upset yourself. I can't bear to see you cry.'

Beth curled herself into her mother's bosom, like a little girl. She held on to her and refused to let her go. 'Mum, I just can't believe it,' she sobbed. 'What happened? I mean, what was it? How did he die? And why so suddenly?'

'There, there. Let's get you dried off. My darling Beth, thank you for coming,' said Myrtle, as she guided her daughter inside.

She made them strong cups of tea and they sat down in the living room.

'I think I need something stronger than tea, Mum.'

'Well, you know your father won't have any alcohol in the house. He'll be mortified if he realizes his death has driven you to drink,' replied Myrtle, unaware that she was still referring to her husband in the present tense.

'I'm not being *driven to drink*, Mum! I'm just saying that my nerves – my head and my heart – could do with a tipple to soften this bloody blow.'

There was irritation in Beth's voice and Myrtle was keen to dispel it. She understood what Beth was suggesting. There had been plenty of times when she, too, had wished for the soothing effects of alcohol during the past forty-odd years – times when she had struggled tirelessly to suppress her emotions, and others when she had fought to set them free. But the thought of conspiring with alcohol against her husband would, she knew, be a step too far. There was nothing he loathed more in the world than spirits – apart from dishonesty, of course . . .

'I believe we've only had wine in the house once.' Myrtle tried to distract Beth. 'On our tenth wedding anniversary, your father brought home a bottle of . . . Oh, what was it now? . . . I think it was called Soave. He chilled it a little before dinner and let me have a taste.'

'He let you have a taste?' Beth frowned in disbelief.

'Well, yes. You know your father doesn't drink, so on that one occasion he let me have two glasses and then he poured the remainder down the sink.'

'What a waste! Not like Dad to waste things . . .' A small smile crept across her lips and she looked at her mother with raised eyebrows.

Myrtle smiled back, and relief appeared to lighten the air. She looked at her daughter and thought how like her father she was. They were of the same build – neither especially tall and comfortably stout. Beth's face was also slightly rounded – doubtless accentuated by her short, abrupt haircut. She could have made more of her hair, Myrtle had always thought – it was thick and dark, like the very deepest mahogany – but Beth had always vehemently rejected the idea that she should be defined or judged by a hairstyle: she had chosen to dismiss her long, voluptuous tresses at the unhesitating age of thirteen, chopping them off herself, to her mother's utter consternation, with blunt scissors. And that, more or less, was how she had kept it ever since.

But it was the nose, above all else, that Beth had directly inherited from her father – if inheritance was anything to go by. They each had short noses, with a neat roundness to the tip. It was actually more forgiving on Beth than it had ever been on Austin. On him, it had always looked less confident, less forthright and distinctly lacking in conviction, Myrtle had always secretly thought.

'Well, these things do happen,' Myrtle said, desperate to cling to the temporary lightness, fearing her daughter's inevitable sorrow, just as she feared her own. She decided to take full advantage of the trivia this opportunity presented. 'And nine months later you were born, my love. My darling, darling Beth.'

'Oh, that's charming, that is! I'm the direct result of your only drunken night . . .' Beth wasn't sure whether to laugh or cry.

They both let out a brief snigger.

'I was hardly drunk, Beth,' Myrtle smiled, 'and you were very much wanted – very, very much.'

It was true that Beth had been wanted. She might not have been planned but she had been cherished and welcomed.

As a result of the traumatic memories of her first pregnancy, Myrtle had recoiled over the years and turned her back on all things intimate. On the few occasions when she had forced herself to endure it, it was as if she had very deliberately and negatively closed her body and mind to the idea of impregnation.

Austin and Myrtle's contraception had been an unnerving mixture of the primitive and unnecessary. But it was impossible for her to forget how the wine had made her feel that night, all those years ago. She had been relaxed, warm, agile and content.

On reflection, she felt sure that the soothing effects of the white wine Austin had poured for her on the night of their tenth wedding anniversary had helped her drop her guard so that her reproductive defences had dramatically diminished. She had let him in, closing her eyes and wishing he was someone else.

Less than a year later, their darling daughter Beth had given her mother a considerably easier labour than her elder sister had. And Myrtle had loved her, as she did now, wholly and unconditionally. Just the way she was.

Beth was wiping tears from her eyes and clutching a damp tissue. 'I can't get my head around it, Mum. He's gone. He's really gone. I'm not going to see him again and he's not ever going to speak to me again . . .' Beth's voice was faltering under a swell of emotion. 'So, not much change there, then.' She succumbed to a little smile. 'But he's never going to understand . . .'

'Understand what, my love?'

'Me. Know me. Understand me. He never did understand me. Why was that, Mum? What was it about me that riled him so?'

'What is there to understand, Beth? You're a lovely girl and a wonderful daughter, and you're here with me now – that's all there is to it.' Brushing awkward questions under a heavy carpet was familiar territory.

'But, Mum, what about *you*? How are you? What are you going to do?'

Myrtle looked down at her hands writhing in her lap. She had put such pressure on her thumb that her finger had left a mark. Her heart began pounding again. For reassurance she looked out to the back garden searchingly, pleading for some space in which to lose herself. 'Oh, me? I don't know, Beth. I have no idea. He does everything, your father. I'm sure it will all work itself out.' Her breath shortened.

Beth was alarmed by the tone of her mother's voice – she seemed distracted and removed from the situation, yet at the same time there was a hint of something more profound, which Beth had never heard before. Her mother's eyes glazed and, Beth noticed, she was rubbing her hands perpetually.

Beth pushed aside the small vase of blue freesias on the coffee-table and reached forward to still the anxious hands. She held them firmly and laid her cheek against her mother's flushed one. As she did so she felt the heat of Myrtle's anxiety. 'Mummy, we'll get through this together,' she vowed. 'But I think we must go and see Dad. We must. We must see him.'

Together they sat holding hands, consumed by the reality that had so suddenly invaded their lives, looking out through the wide French windows, excluded from the rest of the world by death and the unexpected. Each clutched the other in the hope that they would, at some point, comprehend this most abstract day.

'Mum, you must tell me what happened. Was Dad unwell this morning?' enquired Beth, intently.

'No, my love. I don't think so. You know your father. He was never poorly – he had the constitution of an ox.'

'But there must have been some sign. Are you sure he wasn't ill last night? How did he look when he left for work? Did he say anything to you?'

Myrtle sighed. 'No, no, he didn't say anything. He didn't look any different from any other day. He certainly made no mention of anything . . .' At which point, she felt just a minuscule shred of doubt, questioning her memory and, indeed, her standard of care.

'But perhaps he acted oddly . . . Last night, how was he? Did he complain about anything? Mum, please try to remember.' Beth was insistent.

Myrtle blushed, staring back at her daughter. 'No, I don't recall . . . He watched the evening news.' Myrtle moved her eyes to the armchair. 'He folded the paper neatly – as he always did – closed down the house . . .' She looked at Beth pleadingly. 'You know your father, switching off lights, turning off sockets, checking the doors,' she gave way to a little smile, 'and he took himself up to bed. Regular as clockwork, your father.

'I'm so sorry, my darling Beth, that's all I know. It's not much use, is it? I'm so sorry for not being able to offer you more at this terrible time.'

'It's OK, Mum. Just tell me again – just tell me one more time. What was it the nurse said? Exactly?' Beth pleaded.

And Myrtle retold the conversation, then she looked her daughter straight in the eyes.

'My beautiful, beautiful Beth. I can't tell you how proud I am of you. I'm so grateful you're here. Thank you for coming. I'm only sorry that I can't seem to furnish you with any details. But I love you so very, very much. You know that, don't you?'

'I know, Mum. I know.' She took her mother's hand and kissed it. Tears filled her eyes once more.

As the two of them sat there together, Myrtle reflected with gratitude on the strong and secure bond with her daughter. Beth had always felt like *hers*. She belonged to Myrtle. And with this child she had not been exposed to derogatory remarks or condescending rumours.

Nor had Beth been deemed a misdemeanour or a mistake. Beth had been wholly permissible – utterly justifiable – and Myrtle had taken great joy in that fact alone. And her maternal instincts had not faltered once – not even the very first time she had set eyes on her baby daughter. She had fully expected her to be recognizable, immediately familiar, but instead she had encountered a little individual who at birth looked like neither her father nor her mother. Myrtle had embraced this wholeheartedly and thrived on the strangeness of her little creation – and a good job, too, because an individual she had certainly turned out to be.

She appeared, to Myrtle at least, to fear nothing and no one. It was as if, over the years, Myrtle had personally encouraged Beth's independence and individualism. In so doing, she had channelled through her daughter her own tempered imagination and restrained freedom, dreams and desires. It had been wonderful to watch Beth blossom and acquire such an unexpected palette of colours as she matured. She was painted with undeniably vibrant tones of pride and uncompromisingly intense shades of empathy, tolerance and openness. It was something Myrtle had never seen before.

Sadly, this vivid personality had unsettled her father greatly.

Austin had felt deeply uncomfortable in Beth's world of positives and endless possibilities. Her way of life was sorely lacking in moderation, he observed, and in his more outrageous moments, when Myrtle would bow her head in shame, he would even go so far as to say she was 'a considerable distance from sanity'.

Myrtle would often offer up a silent prayer that father and daughter might one day find a way towards each other. Then she, and indeed Beth, would feel complete. But her wish was never granted. Beth did not have a father who embraced her unconditionally, and Austin never had a daughter, of his own, shaped to his specifications.

The doorbell rang.

Myrtle and Beth looked at each other. Neither moved, and Myrtle's heart persisted in beating hard inside her chest. She inhaled a short, sharp breath.

'Who's that? Surely you're not expecting visitors,' Beth asked.

Myrtle stared back blankly.

Their hesitation was long enough to warrant another interruption by the doorbell.

'Let's go together, Mum.'

It was a short, tentative walk, Myrtle wringing her hands and Beth drying her eyes. As they reached the front door, Myrtle straightened her skirt, placing her hands by her sides. She glanced at Beth for reassurance. Beth nodded encouragingly and Myrtle opened the door.

Before her on the doorstep, stood a short, solid man, in the pouring rain, wearing a mac and, rather disconcertingly, shorts. His face was rugged – tanned, lined and framed with light grey hair. He was holding a bright yellow potted primula, Myrtle noticed.

The man cleared his throat. 'Pardon my intruding like this . . . out of the blue – I wonder if I might come in?' he asked cautiously.

Beth and Myrtle looked at each other. As if their day hadn't been disjointed enough in all its resplendent turmoil and confusion! Now this.

'I beg your pardon. Crikey, this ain't easy. Right, I've come to offer my condolences. I was with Mr Austin Lewis when he passed out on the bus this morning . . . I've come to say how sorry I am for your loss and to return this,' said the man, stretching out a hat he had been holding behind his back.

As his last words left his mouth, Beth let out a loud gasp and automatically covered her mouth with her hand. Then she reached forward tentatively and took the hat as if she was afraid the man might not let it go.

The man, relieved that it had been accepted, still remained unaware of the commotion his arrival was causing. He looked down into his hands and falteringly held out the primula in the direction of Myrtle, as if to suggest she would be the rightful recipient.

There was a long silence.

The man cleared his throat again. 'Can I come in?' he repeated.

It was Beth who finally welcomed him in – treating him with all the relief and gratitude she might have bestowed upon the missing piece of an unsolved jigsaw puzzle – while holding the fedora tightly. 'Oh, please do! Come in and sit down,' she begged, completely ignoring the fact that her father would have insisted the stranger take off his shoes first.

The man bowed his head, walked through the hallway, with Myrtle following, and slowly sat on the far edge of the living room's floral sofa. Once again he cleared his throat. 'I hope you don't think I'm being a bit previous. I guess I should have introduced myself. My name is Gianni – Gianni D'Amico. I take the number fifty-three most mornings to work. That's why I was on the bus, you see . . .' His voice was marked by reluctance.

Oh, goodness, thought Myrtle. *He's wearing great big chunky walking boots. It's raining outside . . . the carpet. Austin will be furious.*

She remained in the doorway, clutching the primula and staring at the stranger on her sofa with his illicit footwear. She felt as if she was standing on the sidelines, watching a significant story unfold before her eyes – a story in which she played no part but with which she had some tangible connection. She felt as if she was bearing witness to something fundamental, but couldn't shake the feeling that she was on the outside looking in. All the while she didn't take her eyes off the stranger's boots.

Beth, on the other hand, was fuelled and energized by the man she considered must have been the last living person to have shared a space with or, indeed, touched her father. Consequently she clung to the stranger as a survivor might to a piece of shipwreck. 'Oh, thank you so much for coming over. I can't quite believe you're here. What happened?' Beth was virtually breathless with excitement.

Gianni looked across the room at Myrtle, still standing in the doorway. He tried to catch her eye but her gaze was fixed to the floor by his feet. He turned his attention to Beth, who had placed herself close enough to him for their legs to touch. 'Right, well, you'll have to forgive me if I miss anything out but it was all a bit of a surprise – not the kind of thing you expect on your way to work.' He exposed a brief smile but immediately reined himself in and straightened his face. 'I saw Mr Lewis – your pa, I'll guess?' He nodded at Beth.

'Yes, he's my dad.'

'Well, I saw him standing at the bus stop in his overcoat and his hat. That's a fedora, I thought. My own father used to wear one. I thought he looked proper smart.' He straightened out the word so much there was virtually no trace of his Aussie drawl.

'Well, he got on the bus and his head – well, it was kinda hung low, like this.' He lowered his own in slow, graduating movements, as if he was nodding off to sleep. 'He didn't seem to be bothered by the rain, but I thought he was a bit off when he didn't even look up at the driver.' He threw a glance in Myrtle's direction.

Beth sat still and her eyes remained firmly on the

story-teller, who held the key to her father's final moments.

'I mean, I thought he had the wobbly boot on. Suddenly – BANG! – he fell . . . straight on to the floor of the bus. It made a ruddy great thud, I can tell ya. And that was it . . . really.'

'What do you mean? Did he die on the bus?' Beth's eyes welled.

'Ah, nah, I don't think so, love. Someone called an ambo and I thought I should go with him – I don't know why. It was just one of those feelings you have. I was with him all the way to the hospital.'

Tears stained Beth's cheeks. Gianni put his hand on her knee briefly.

'What did he say? Did he say anything? Was he in pain?'

'I don't think so, love. I don't know. He didn't say anything – he just kinda murmured all the way. I couldn't make out what he was saying.' There was a long pause. 'I waited quite a fair while at the hospital until someone came out. They said something about a sub-something haemorrhage . . . Yeah, I think that was it but the doctor wouldn't tell me any more.'

Gianni looked at Myrtle again, but her eyes still refused to shift in his direction. She said nothing.

Myrtle's hearing was muffled – by anxiety and the unreality of the situation. She could barely hear the voices, let alone make out what they were saying.

'I'm sure he was a bonzer bloke, your pa,' Gianni

said to Beth. She started sobbing and, instinctively, he put his arm over her shoulders in a gesture of pure reassurance.

She asked him to repeat the story, which he dutifully did. It was a narration spiked with darkness and the unforeseen, burdened with tragedy and death, and distinct only by its lack of dénouement.

'Well, I think it's time I bade you two ladies g'day,' he eventually said, when he felt he could impart no more. He drew a huge breath and sighed heavily. 'I mustn't take up any more of your time – you probably think I'm a right drongo turning up like this but I just wanted to hand back the hat and let you know that he wasn't alone . . .' He paused. 'I'd best go.'

Despite Beth's reluctance to let him, he got up to leave.

As he passed Myrtle in the doorway he raised his eyebrows and said to her sympathetically, 'I'm so sorry for your loss, Mrs Lewis. I'm sure you must be in a fair bit of shock right now.' He reached out his hand. Myrtle continued to stare at his feet so he was forced to retract the hand.

'But how can we get hold of you?' Beth called in desperation. 'Can I have your number in case I need to call you?'

Gianni turned around. 'If it's any use, I can leave you my home number. I don't live far away.'

Beth scrambled around for a pen, pulling out drawers in the hallway dresser and hurriedly tearing a piece of paper from the pad next to the telephone. Myrtle watched him scribble something down, then shaking Beth's hand as he said farewell.

He crossed the threshold. At the last moment he turned around, looked straight at Myrtle and said, 'Oh, and the primula – bet you know it hates the winter damp.' Then he was out of the door, disappearing into the wet remainder of a bleak day, which now had the semblance of night.

Beth closed the door behind him and leaned against it. Her eyes looked up to the heavens and she smiled. 'What a lovely thing to do, don't you think, Mum? To take the trouble to come around like that to tell us about Dad ... What a kind gesture!' Her mood had changed: her sadness and mourning had been replaced by relief and calm – temporarily, at least. 'And to bring you a flower, too. How lovely was that?' As she walked past her mother, she took the potted plant out of her hands and placed it on the dresser next to the telephone, then disappeared into the kitchen.

All Myrtle could think of was the dirty footprints on the carpet.

Not long after, the phone rang.

'Mummy, goodness, this is most frustrating. Apart from anything, it's annoying, if not painfully embarrassing, but I'm afraid I'm not going to be able to come over.'

Myrtle had almost forgotten about Gillian.

'I've lost my car keys. I've looked high and low and

can't for the life of me imagine where they are. I know, I can't believe it myself.' Her voice faltered. 'You know only too well I'm a stickler for tidiness – I take a very dim view of clutter and mess – but what with the food processor taking on a life of its own and nigh on exploding, and your call telling me about poor Daddy, I simply can't find them! I'm furious, Mother – the house looks like a gypsy camp! I swear, if I find that this is Geoffrey's idea of a practical joke – To top it all he's gone to Birmingham for the day and isn't back until tomorrow! – I shall have his flaming guts for garters.'

Myrtle had wanted to interrupt – to sympathize, console and reassure – but there had been no pause for breath in her daughter's monologue, no time for Gillian to ask how Mother was.

As Gillian talked, Myrtle stared at the carpet and saw another speck of dirt left behind by the unexpected visitor, which she tried to bring closer with the tip of her shoe in order to pick it up but it proved unwilling.

It was, clearly, a fate worse than death for Gillian, Myrtle quickly grasped – an untidy house and a missing piece in her perfect puzzle. No apology, no remorse and very little in the form of comfort was forthcoming on her elder daughter's part.

'Not to worry, dear,' Myrtle forced through Gillian's congested plethora of words and complaint. 'It's fine. Beth is here.' She managed to nudge the speck of dirt close enough to pick it up. She heard a vague pause at the other end of the line.

'She is?' came the waspish retort. Clearly, the elder sister felt outdone by the younger. 'Oh, I see . . . Well, I shall be around first thing in the morning. I simply can't make it before . . .'

Myrtle wondered if Gillian felt snubbed by Beth's ability to come to her at such a critical time. What made things worse was that Myrtle was so keen to placate her but she didn't know how. As if to inflame the situation, she realized that this was the second unsatisfactory conversation she'd had with Gillian in one day.

Now it was twenty to five and darkness had enveloped the garden. Normally it wouldn't be long before Austin's footsteps would be coming up their short gravel drive and he'd report on the events of his day at the office without a hint of a question about Myrtle's doings.

She exhaled. She didn't want to go to the hospital as Beth had suggested earlier. She wanted to stay at home and hear about Austin's day. 'I'm not ready to go to the hospital, Beth. Not even if Gillian was here now. I can't face it,' she said.

'Well, there's no need, Mummy. You've no need to face anything alone just yet. Tell you what, I'll stay over, OK? How does that sound?' was Beth's immediate response.

It sounded like a huge relief, thought Myrtle.

Beth had made the proposition for her own peace of mind: her mother appeared to be drifting into uncertain waters and needed safe harbour. It was a little unprecedented, to say the least: Beth hadn't stayed over since she had so defiantly and noisily moved out at the age of eighteen.

Much later, when Beth had had a bite to eat while Myrtle merely looked on, they had gone upstairs and Beth had insisted on bedding down on her father's side in the bedroom – fully clothed. Myrtle draped a blanket around her in the way she used to tuck her in at night when Beth was as small and vulnerable as she appeared tonight.

Then she sat on the bed for a while, looking at her daughter, curled up like the child she still was, sobbing into disintegrated bits of tissue, littering the area around her on the bed and refusing to let her mother turn out the light. Beth mumbled to herself and occasionally out loud, groping her way forward in her own darkness with words, memories and questions. She required so much that night – but most of all she needed something Myrtle couldn't give her: her father.

As soon as she thought Beth had settled into a deeper sleep, she had no idea why but she went straight to the cupboard under the stairs, took out the vacuum cleaner and proceeded to vacuum the length of the hallway and into the sitting room, tracking the footprints of the stranger's cumbersome boots. Then she turned and repeated the chore with overbearing vigilance.

Myrtle did not want to go to bed for fear of a visit from the old intruder: insomnia. Little pieces of the day flashed before her, at times making her feel light-headed, but most of all she was concerned about the stranger's boots marking the carpet. *It just won't do.* She could hear Austin's voice. He would be most distressed to know she had not been capable of imposing the rule of no shoes in the house – especially on a complete stranger.

The house felt cold. There was an incessant silence and a punishing sense of anticipation, which manifested itself in Myrtle's constant pacing. From time to time her heart would rush and pound, accompanied by shortness of breath.

As she walked past the telephone, she looked at the dresser and saw the sunny yellow primula given to her by the stranger, whose name she couldn't recall . . .

What a lovely colour, she thought.

Chapter Eight

Myrtle was running as fast as her little legs could carry her. She was struggling to catch her breath, her mouth dry as sand, her cheeks burning. She ran between the pavement and the hard asphalt road, desperate to silence her panting, fearing she would be heard and stopped. Sweat on her neck ran down her back. Her head was pounding as if it might explode.

People with blank faces lined the streets, standing by as Myrtle tore past them. Here and there, they would stretch their necks out into the road, gnashing long, spiky, yellowing teeth at her, close enough for her to feel their breath on her skin. The noise was loud, irregular and distorted – she couldn't make out what they wanted.

Someone was coming up behind her. She shot a glance over her shoulder. It was a man. He was tall, large-limbed, wearing a uniform with bright buttons and a dark, heavy jacket. Myrtle nearly lost her balance. She hadn't seen his face. Her legs began to burn in agony and the pain in her chest was suffocating. Terror engulfed her. The man wasn't running: he was walking, eating up the road with huge steps, gaining ground.

Suddenly and abruptly she stopped. The road had come to an end. In front of her stood a house with a red front door. Fuelled by fear of the man behind her, she banged on it and kicked it. 'Let me in! Let me in!' she screamed, but no sound came out.

Panic set in. Her heart was going to force its way out of her throat. She banged harder. Her hands hurt. She couldn't breathe. She pushed against the door and fell into a tiny, unlit vestibule. She scrabbled around, then stood up and pressed her back against the door.

It was impossible to see – the darkness was all-encompassing. She used her hands to try to orientate herself.

She heard rustling by her feet and knelt down. She could just make out a holdall with large handles flopped to either side. As Myrtle leaned over, in the vaguest, dappled light, she saw the little face of a baby lying in the bag, its fair skin lighting up the cramped, dismal place. Myrtle gasped. Gently she levered out the little being and cradled it in her arms. As its hands reached out for her she started to sob. She pulled her face back and saw the child looking straight at her – as if it knew her; as if it had been waiting for her. She pulled it closer, holding it tightly and caressing it, whispering softly, 'It's all right, little one. I'm here now. I'm here.'

Suddenly there was a loud bang on the door and the whole building shook. Then came another and another and finally the sound of wood against glass as the door crashed wide open.

Myrtle sat bolt upright on the sofa in her living room, flushed and trembling, dazed and confused.

'Mummy, it's me! Where *are* you?' came a voice.

It was Gillian's. It reverberated from the hall and was moving closer. She was spitting fire.

Myrtle felt hazy and blurred by the recurring nightmare. She rubbed her eyes and opened them ever so slightly. The light was invasive and she was forced to shut them again. Words were flying around – angry words. Myrtle tried to piece them together to form a sentence, catching snatches here and there. They sounded like accusations – directed, from what she could make out, at a husband who was not present to defend himself. There was urgency about the situation – that much was clear. In trying to stand up, Myrtle got her leg stuck between the sofa and the vacuum cleaner. She fell forwards, bumped her head on the coffee-table and found herself on all fours, straddling the badly positioned appliance, just in time for her daughter to march into the room.

'There you are, Mummy!' she said. 'I've been looking for you. What on earth are you doing down *there*?'

Myrtle looked up through a little mop of hair bouncing playfully in front of her eyes, which made it hard to see Gillian clearly. She tried to stand up as her elder daughter turned away and continued to rage. From what Myrtle gathered, it had something to do with lost car keys and a jewellery box in Molly's room.

Eventually Myrtle found her feet. She smoothed

her hair, which had taken on a life of its own, and straightened her skirt. As she opened her mouth to speak, Gillian turned on her heel and headed out of the room, blazing a trail through the rest of the house, calling to her mother as she went. Myrtle set off in pursuit, finding it hard to keep up with her daughter. It was like trying to catch a fly, Myrtle thought. She had – very deliberately – not been granted the time to interrupt Gillian's fury. Nor did she, if she was perfectly honest, have the strength or inclination to try.

'Where is Beth, then?' shouted Gillian, stopping suddenly. 'Mummy, I thought you said Beth was here. I wouldn't put it beyond her to be having a lie-in – and on a day like today, too. I don't suppose she's likely to grace us with her presence much before noon. Honestly, Mother!' Gillian's frown returned – not that it was ever far away – creating a well-established, deep crease between her eyebrows, the one Myrtle always wanted to smooth out with the back of her thumb.

As if on cue, Beth appeared at the bottom of the stairs, eyes puffy from tears and restless sleep. 'You shouldn't be so judgemental, Gill.' She yawned. 'I've *actually* been awake for ages. In fact, if it makes you feel better, I hardly slept at all. So, no lie-in for "lazy Beth".'

Myrtle sensed the tension and moved closer to her daughters.

Beth took a deep breath, walked straight up to her sister and stretched out her arms to embrace her. The hug was big enough to envelop Gillian in a mixture of sadness and goodwill. Beth held her sister firmly and just long enough for her to rest her chin on Gillian's shoulder. 'Hi, sis. I can't believe he's gone,' she whispered. 'I miss him already, the old fart.'

Gillian stood there in the hallway, both hands rigidly at her sides, unmoved by Beth's gesture. Uncomfortably she lifted her right hand to her sister's back in a short, sharp, impatient tap, as if she were patting a dog in acknowledgement of good behaviour.

'Right. Let's not fuss,' she said, re-establishing her superiority. She released herself from her sister's hold and marched into the kitchen. 'We really must get going to the hospital before Daddy utterly decomposes. Goodness knows what state he'll be in when we get to see him.'

Beth looked at her mother with raised eyebrows and a mouth that showed an equal measure of disappointment and offence. Myrtle smiled back. 'But, Gillian, dear,' she started, looking in disbelief at the clock in the hallway, 'it's barely eight. It's still early morning. Don't you think we ought to phone beforehand and check whether it's a suitable time for us to pop in?' Myrtle wanted to swallow her words. She felt ashamed to have used an expression such as 'pop in' with reference to a trip to identify her dead husband. It seemed not only wholly inappropriate but also ill-timed – especially as the day before had seemed so wholly inappropriate and disjointed.

'Yeah, nice to see you too, Beth! Your sorrow's overwhelming, Gill. Oh, and I'm fine, thanks for asking.' Beth raised her voice sarcastically. 'Could we maybe just take a moment to talk things through rather than approaching this trip to the hospital like a school visit to the zoo? This is not *all* about rounding up the troops – I mean, these are pretty exceptional circumstances. I don't know if you're aware, Gill, but our father has just died,' she spat, with what she felt was justified derision.

'Right,' said Gillian, ignoring her sister and turning very deliberately to her mother. 'Mother, might you be ready to go sooner rather than later?'

'I rest my case.' Beth slapped her hand hard on the sideboard.

'Oh, goodness . . .' There was trepidation in Myrtle's voice. 'Girls, please don't fight. Let's try to be civilized, shall we? Your father wouldn't want to see you argue.'

'I wouldn't be too sure of that. I think he rather enjoyed us fighting. It fuelled his belief that one of us was inferior to the other,' Beth snarled.

Myrtle cleared her throat. 'Why don't we have a nice cup of tea and a little sit-down? Give everyone a chance to . . . to just settle a little. I'm sure we're all very upset. Beth, please let's have some tea.'

Myrtle and Beth sat down at the kitchen table while Gillian made a pot of tea in deafening silence. Beth put her hand under the table to touch her mother's. She looked at her with a smile and a gentle wink. Myrtle smiled back.

'When we get to the hospital, I think it's best I deal with things, Mother. You're in no state to be talking to people, especially anyone wearing a name badge and in a position of authority – you know you're easily confused. I'll go in first and have a look at Daddy, but you ought to think twice about seeing him – both of you. You never know how this might affect you,' declared Gillian, not anticipating a challenge.

'What?' spluttered Beth. 'What the hell are you talking about, Gill? We *all* want to go and see him. Who are you to decide for Mum what she does? Or for me? I *need* to see him. Besides, I haven't seen him for weeks.'

'I think you'll find he's changed quite a bit,' Gillian cut in.

'Stop being so damn pernicious, Gill. What's wrong with you?'

Gillian wouldn't be drawn. Instead, she rolled her eyes and hurried out of the kitchen. Beth retreated upstairs, leaving Myrtle alone at the kitchen table, disappointed, confused and with a rapidly developing case of indigestion.

Gillian was not prepared to allocate enough time for Myrtle to change out of the previous day's clothes, let alone have a shower. The best Myrtle could do was to attempt to iron out the creases in her skirt with anxious hands.

With every tick of the clock, Myrtle continued her aimless pacing of the previous night, longing for Beth to make her way downstairs in order that the tension might ease – or at least be shared.

Finally, Gillian hustled her mother and sister out of the front door, turning to look Beth up and down. 'Are you going in *that*?'

Beth was dressed in a tired black bobbled sweater, which danced loosely above black leather trousers. Her biker boots were scuffed and greying at the toe. 'I wasn't aware there was a dress code for viewing the dead,' she snapped.

'Well, sackcloth and leathers is hardly what you might call respectful . . .' hissed Gillian.

Myrtle opened her mouth. At first nothing came out. 'Girls, please, I beg of you . . .' she stuttered. 'Today of all days, I don't . . . I don't have the strength . . .' She trailed off.

A minute later she found herself sitting in the back of Gillian's robust and practical car with her head slightly bowed. Beth had first gone to the passenger seat in the front, then taken one look at her mother cutting a lonely figure in the back and jumped into the seat next to her.

The silence in the car was thick, solid and hung heavy. Myrtle was on the verge of starting up a conversation – a passing comment about the bumpy roads, the changing colour of the leaves, the state of the hedges along the lanes – but she was terrified Gillian would cut her off or, worse still, blatantly ignore her.

The air outside was damp and milky. Inside the car,

it was frozen – crippled by anticipation, fear and two daughters whose personalities curdled at every turn. Myrtle looked down at her lap where her hands were once more writhing uncomfortably. Beth reached across to still them.

Gillian's untimely attack on Beth had made Myrtle feel deeply conscious of what she was wearing. As she stared aimlessly out of the car window she reflected that it had been many years since she had worn trousers. If she wasn't mistaken, there had been a time when she would only have worn a skirt on special occasions. But she had gradually come to understand that she looked more dignified in a skirt and therefore worried less about her spreading body. Skirts seemed to contain her better, and the emergence of some extra weight on her legs had not discouraged that belief. As Austin had always said, 'You're solid and reliable, Myrtle, and you stand, not unlike a traditional oak table, with a leg at each corner.' When he had said it he had looked at her very seriously. Myrtle hadn't known if he had meant it light-heartedly. At any rate, she might have preferred to be as reliable as a nightingale singing in spring, rather than a piece of furniture. Doubtless, Austin had been right – she was rather solid.

And a skirt seemed very fitting for a widow. Trousers might have appeared disrespectful – perhaps Gillian was right. And she was grateful that, although her mind wasn't all it should have been that morning, her clothes would give out the required air of reverence.

'Thank God for that!' said Beth, as the car finally came to a standstill in the hospital car park. 'You're the worst driver, Gill. I've never known so many stops and starts. What's with the hesitations and emergency brakes? It's enough to give you whiplash . . . Perhaps that's what you were hoping,' she added slyly, as she climbed out.

Gillian ignored her sister and headed for the ticket machine with typical speed and efficiency. Beth and Myrtle watched as she fumbled in her handbag, shaking her head as she did so. They waited patiently. Eventually Gillian returned to the car, head held high. 'Not a word, Beth! Don't say a word,' she hissed, through clenched teeth. 'I'm simply not having a good day. It looks like I've left my purse at home.' She held her hand out, palm up, and clicked her fingers several times. 'I need some change,' she said, avoiding eye contact, jiggling her hand impatiently under Beth's nose.

'"Please",' insisted Beth.

After she'd deposited the ticket in the car, Gillian hared off, leaving the other two floundering in her wake. At the hospital entrance she stood waiting for them to catch up, tapping her foot irascibly and looking at her watch. As they all reached the reception desk, a sizeable woman gazed up with a look of extreme boredom and disinterest, almost designed to niggle Gillian. 'Can I help you?' asked the receptionist, sounding even more bored than her appearance suggested she was. When Gillian asked for directions to the mortuary, the woman's demeanour changed minutely, her head tilting to one side with just a hint of pity. 'Ah, poor thing. I tell you,' she said, leaning forward, 'my Phil's going to end up in there one of these days, if he doesn't give his liver a break.' She let out a quick and inappropriate guffaw. 'It's in the next building to your left,' she continued, no longer bothering to look up. 'Take the lift up to the first floor, and it's right there in front of you. You won't miss it.

'Good luck, love,' she whispered, a little contritely.

Gillian turned and muttered under her breath, 'What a foul woman! Hardly suitable material for a hospital reception desk.'

Beth took her mother's hand in the lift. She was desperate to stop it twitching but it appeared to have a mind of its own.

Silence, once again, enveloped the reluctant trio. It felt, Myrtle thought, as if a giant bear was asleep in the corner of the lift and she was terrified of breathing for fear of waking it.

The doors opened, and the three mourners found a grand reception area with glossily polished white flooring. Bright, fluorescent light was beaming down from a high ceiling on to gleaming, spotless, incandescent walls unmarked by frames, signs or human hands. Myrtle squinted. She saw staff moving about smoothly and silently, as if on castors, rolling and floating before a lifeless untarnished background of cleanliness and purity. In one corner there were two sets of tables and chairs, neutrally upholstered in cream and off-white, and there was a large plant in a light pot – a monstera, if Myrtle wasn't mistaken. She couldn't quite make out whether it was plastic or the real thing. Instinctively she wanted to move forward to rub the leaves between her fingers but she knew her place was behind Gillian.

'We've come to see my father, Austin Lewis. He died yesterday and is resting here, I believe,' said Gillian, at the desk.

The receptionist's face wasted no time conveying empathy and understanding.

As Myrtle sat in one of the high-backed chairs she felt deeply ill at ease in the salubrious atmosphere of the waiting room. There was an undeniable cleanliness about the place – to be expected in a hospital, she thought – but she couldn't bring herself to feel grateful for its newness and brilliance. Instead the smell of disinfectant made her feel queasy. It reminded her of the time when they – she and Austin – had been forced to rush Beth to hospital after she had fallen out of the large tree at the bottom of the garden and landed on her head.

'What the bloody hell was she doing climbing a chestnut tree?' Austin had demanded furiously, time and time again, as he paced the hospital's Accident & Emergency Department.

'I'm so sorry, Austin. I'm so sorry ... It's all my fault, not Beth's. Please, forgive me ...'

Meanwhile Beth, who had seemed so small in

Myrtle's arms, had faded in and out of consciousness and Myrtle had thought her heart might burst with terror. She hadn't wanted to cry, she hadn't meant to cry, and she had definitely not wanted Austin to see her cry. But all the while her mind punished her with the thought that this hospital was where her first child had been born . . . and where her second would die. Austin had simply continued pacing the same few square feet of the hospital, cursing his curious daughter for being so utterly foolish, and Myrtle had never forgiven herself for allowing Beth to fall out of the tree.

Now, in the mortuary waiting room, Myrtle looked at Beth and felt proud of her daughter. Beth squeezed her mother's hand and gave her a reassuring smile. But Myrtle could see the tears building in her eyes. Meanwhile, Gillian was striding the length of the building. She reminded Myrtle of Austin.

Eventually a nurse appeared from nowhere, glancing at her watch as she approached the visitors.

'I'm looking for a Mrs Lewis? Is Mrs Lewis with you?' she asked.

Gillian nodded in the direction of her mother.

'Now, Mrs Lewis,' the nurse said, in a hushed tone, 'I feel I should take this opportunity to inform you that your husband did have a serious fall and sustain some injury to the left side of his head, just above his left eye. The fall appeared to have been so sudden that he had no time to put his hands out to protect himself. Having said that, the damage is not too severe – but I felt it was right you should know,' she finished, smiling hesitantly.

A quick and uncomfortable sequence of images flashed before Myrtle: Austin slipping on the bus; crashing down; the thud; blood; a dent in his head. What if his eye had fallen out? Myrtle didn't dare to ask. Instead, she gazed at Beth, who had tears streaming down her face, and Gillian, who stared at the nurse expectantly, as if waiting for a finale.

The nurse hooked Myrtle with a serious look. 'Ready?'

Myrtle lowered her head, burying her chin deep in her chest. Beth took her hand, but not before Gillian had squeezed in ahead of them.

The doors led to another set. These had flaps at the bottom and made a whooshing sound when they opened. Myrtle saw a glass corridor to her left framed by stainless-steel shelving that ran the entire length of the room. It was bright, with fluorescent light shining blindingly and coldly on to steel benches under which bright blue hoses were tucked neatly around reels. To the right there were a dozen large, heavy white doors with oversized handles and small notices on the front with writing Myrtle couldn't possibly read.

As she looked from left to right, frantically searching for something and nothing, Gillian stopped in her tracks. 'Oh, Daddy!' she cried. Then she lunged forward at a mass of white sheeting on a bench directly ahead of them.

'*No!*' shouted Beth, as she rushed up behind her sister.

Myrtle could see the top of a head at the far end of the bench, uncovered by the mass of whiteness below it.

And there lay Austin Lewis, calm, still and very, very dead.

That was when Myrtle collapsed.

Chapter Nine

Gianni lay on his bed as stiff as a board, flat on his back, with only his head exposed to the outside world. He opened one eye slowly but the light was blinding. He forced it shut, creasing it into a tiny pinprick in his lined, weathered face. Instinctively he covered both eyes with the back of his arm.

A single white sheet draped his solid body in sharp peaks and troughs, then gradually flattened out in unison with the rest of the mattress in smaller folds and creases. Gianni grasped his head. 'Damn the Scots!' he mumbled. 'Damn the Scots for making bonzer whisky . . .' he cursed.

His mouth was dry – *as dry as a dead dingo's donger.* 'Yuk!' He yawned, attempting to mobilize his unyielding jaw up and down, forcing his dry tongue to make contact with the roof of his mouth in a laboured attempt to generate moisture but to little avail.

As he lay there, eyes closed, face up to the ceiling, it was difficult not to dwell on the fact that his body was increasingly sore at the start of every day. There had been a time, he was quick to remind himself, when his *little fella* had been rigid first thing every day, but even he had succumbed to the fossilization of old age. The

hint of a smile ambled across Gianni's well-worn face –
those were the days. Still, not bad for a sixty-year-old . . .
Slowly and gingerly he rolled over to one side and let a
foot escape the cotton sheet to test the rawness of the
bedroom air. It might have been October, and the
house was definitely nippy and draughty, but Gianni
was still wallowing in the heat of the wee drams he
had consumed so copiously the night before.

He lay there for a while, eyes shut, foot bouncing
playfully between the mattress and the cold floor until
he felt obliged to get up.

'Come on, you old bogan!' he egged himself on, as
he swung his legs around and lifted himself up in one
fell swoop – made all the harder by the fact that he
insisted on not owning a bed. As he stood up he
glanced briefly out of the bedroom's sash window
before scratching across his shoulders, then one side
of his back and his bare behind in a lame effort to
rejuvenate himself.

The mattress lay bare, white and suddenly redundant
on the floor of a bedroom devoid of any luxuries – in
fact, it was sorely lacking in any fixtures and fittings at
all. But Gianni liked it that way. The estate agent had
proudly walked him through the house, boasting
about the stone porch, the glazed panel above the
door, the traditional coving and cornicing and, finally,
the master bedroom, which she had haughtily described
as 'impressively spacious and with a sublime double
aspect'.

As he had walked out of the bedroom – the first and only time he'd viewed the house – the chubby little woman, manhandling a huge cluster of keys, had tugged determinedly at his jumper and whispered proudly that the bespoke damask pencil-pleat curtains with Regency valances and tie-backs were included in the price. Then she had winked and squeezed herself past him.

If she had hoped this would persuade him, she couldn't have been more wrong. Gianni D'Amico was not a fan of frills and sashes, of piping, pelmets, voiles or valances, so he had torn down the window dressings on the very day he got the keys, and had proceeded to use them as dust sheets while he redecorated.

The stripped floorboards were bitterly cold that morning and in his mind he bemoaned the fact that he had forgotten to set the timer on the heating the night before.

In the kitchen the gas range purred and hissed reliably with heat. On inclement mornings like this it was a great source of comfort.

He adored the heat of Australia – of course he did – but he hadn't been drawn to England by the weather. There had been other factors, which he wasn't willing to dwell on that morning, although yet again he silently reaffirmed his love of the country.

Gianni liked England's large-hearted people, their generosity and especially their kindness. He liked the fact that he could strike up a conversation with a complete stranger at the bus stop or in a supermarket queue.

He filled his father's old steel coffee pot, placed it on the scorching stove and breathed a sigh of relief.

He needed something for his head. He put a couple of Nurofen in his mouth but no sooner had he swallowed them than he gagged and was forced to spit them into the sink.

'Aaaah, you old geezer! You can't take the juice, hey?' He smiled at himself. 'Look at you, chundering like a drunk teenager.'

He rested over the sink for a moment.

The night before was gradually coming back to him, recovered by some far-reaching, still-working parts of his brain: the bereft young woman in the sitting room and her widowed mother; the tears and the sadness of a daughter who'd lost her father – but the mother had seemed so vacant, so lost, so desolate. There was something still and mysterious about her.

Death does that to you, he thought. Death does all sorts of things to you. It can poison the mind, destroy the body and unsettle the heart to the point of no return.

Gianni felt dark and sombre as he sat down on one of the pine chairs, put his elbows on the kitchen table and stared morbidly out of the window. *Death is a terrible, terrible thing*, he reminded himself. *It comes in all shapes and sizes – sometimes completely unannounced.*

Involuntarily, Gianni recalled his mother's small,

exhausted frame bent over, her hand clutching her belly, sobbing loudly in her sparse kitchen in Victoria, lamenting, '*Il mio bambino, il mio bambino.*'

Gianni hadn't dared to touch her.

At only seven he had been too young to understand what was causing his mother's pain and worried that it was a progressive illness, which had made him fear for her life. After each and every premature loss of a baby eroded his mother in some way, Gianni noted that part of her recovery was to envelop him in adoring caresses and swathe him in bandages of tenderness as if to atone for what had amounted to a temporary rejection of him. He was left in no doubt that he was adored – worshipped, even. His mother never recovered from the loss of her babies, which left its mark on Gianni. His early encounter with death had eclipsed his naïve belief that it only visited the old.

Death was a dreadful thing, but he had learned on his extensive travels, and during his time with the Abos in the Outback, to accept it and move on.

The coffee pot let out a guttural sigh to signal that its work was done. Gianni shot out of his chair and rushed towards the stove. Leaning forward in a hurry to move the pot from the hotplate he forgot that he was naked.

'Damn it!' he said, dispatching both hands to his manhood. As he turned around his backside made contact with the range and he jumped away.

He had to laugh. His naked exploits on such a cold

and misty morning would have been enough to make modest Mrs Daly next door turn crimson. He poured his coffee, closed his eyes, inhaled and took a sip.

Cup in hand, he switched on his battery-operated wireless in time to hear Melvyn Bragg pause amid a verbal essay on the history of ideas to announce that the time was nine eighteen. Gianni slammed his cup on the table and made a bid for the bathroom. He was going to be late at the garden centre for the second day running.

Chapter Ten

'What news, D?' asked Marjorie, who desired something to colour her hitherto dull day. Her chores were done: the house was not only tidy but it had been cleaned thoroughly and she was rather thrilled with the new lemon verbena fragrance she had applied to the toilet bowls. Things were just so and she felt decidedly sanctimonious.

'Oh, Marj,' sighed Dorothy, heavily, 'nothing of particular interest, really. Oh, except – I almost forgot! – the outrageously dull little man next door keeled over and popped his clogs the day before yesterday. Just like that! Collapsed on the bus, from what I understand.'

'Oh, that sounds dreadful, D,' said Marjorie, with a fittingly sharp intake of breath. 'Was he old?' she enquired, considering for a brief moment the vulnerability of her own years.

'Well, no. I mean, he looked old and he behaved old but I don't think he was much over sixty – so in man-years he was still officially in his prime, I guess,' she replied, marginally slighted by Marjorie's interest – this was not really what she had wanted to talk about.

'How awful,' Marjorie persisted. 'How awful for that poor wife of his. He was married, wasn't he, to that little woman?'

'Oh, yes, he was very married. Although I suspect she was considerably more married than he was. She clung to him like a limpet. I don't think there was much to her life but pacing around the house, doing the garden and glaring defensively at me whenever I passed. She seems desperately dull.'

'Poor woman,' sighed Marjorie.

'Still – every cloud has a silver lining. Perhaps she'll get rid of that monstrosity of a caravan parked in the drive now that he's gone. It's an eyesore, if ever I saw one. I don't think she drives. Besides, what on earth would she want with a caravan? To be frank, I don't think she's capable of very much at all.' Dorothy swapped the telephone to her left ear and rested it on her shoulder so that she could examine her nails. They were still perfectly manicured in red.

'Now, D, don't get your claws out. The poor woman's just lost her husband. I trust you'll do the sisterly thing. If not, at least the neighbourly thing,' pleaded Marjorie, who suddenly wished she lived nearby so that she could have brought the newly widowed dear a nice lamb stew straight from her slow-cooker.

'What? Tow the caravan away myself?' joked Dorothy.

'Don't be wicked, D. Charity starts at home, and all that . . .' said Marjorie, her mind wandering to a coffee and walnut cake, which would be more suitable for someone with whom you have but a nodding acquaintance.

'I'm only pulling your leg. Of course I'll pop my head around the door – I just don't want to frighten the dear old girl.' Dorothy paused. 'And just when I needed to ask them about trimming their flaming leylandii, which left me in the shade for most of the summer.'

Marjorie wanted a change of subject – all this talk of death was morbid. She might be in the autumn of her life but there was no reason to start fretting about winter just yet. 'And how about you – how are you, my love?'

'Oh, you know – it would be ungrateful of me to complain. Work is fine. The house is fine. And there's just the hint of intrigue wafting around the place.'

'Oooh! Do tell. Someone new?' Marjorie perked up.

'It's been half a dozen occasions and I know you'll not want to hear this but the sex is heart-stonkingly good.' She ran her hand through her hair and looked at herself in the mirror that hung above the chest of drawers.

'Dorothy! I've told you, I don't want that kind of detail! Is he charming? Age? Baggage?' fired Marjorie.

'Yes, well – all that. He's of a certain age, he's quite, quite charming, and I suspect he needs both hands for his baggage. But, rather unnervingly, he does make me laugh. And he leaves me wanting more. Which can never be a good thing.' Dorothy leaned into the mirror, inspecting a slight protuberance on her otherwise smooth chin.

'Well, that sounds marvellous, D! It's been quite some time since I've heard you speak so highly of any man.' Sparring was a given in this relationship.

'Hmm . . . Yes, quite agree. But it doesn't take away from the fact that I couldn't bear for things to get . . . you know, messy.' A frown settled on her doubting face.

'By "messy", I presume you mean "involved",' suggested Marjorie, who knew her friend only too well. Without allowing Dorothy the time to respond, she continued, 'Well, perhaps you need to go with the flow a little more. Stop trying to anticipate. You have a tendency to be a little overbearing sometimes – you know you do. You have a penchant for control, D, and – let's face it – we can't always control everything. There are some things in life we aren't *supposed* to control. Like Trevor's desire to keep working, in stark contrast to his boss's insistence that he retire. That's out of his control. But I'm not ready to have him at home yet. God works in mysterious ways, D. Perhaps you just have to trust him, hey?'

'Trust who? *Him* or God?' She smiled wryly.

'You're playing with me now, D – you know what I'm saying.'

'Of course I do.' Dorothy turned to another view – it was late afternoon, dark and, annoyingly, the bulb in her outside light had gone, she noticed. 'Sometimes it's hard being quite as autonomous and unfettered as I am. I only have myself to rely on.'

'Darling girl, you have all that freedom and yet you restrict yourself with rules and game plans. Perhaps your approach should be a little more *laissez-faire*. Relax and enjoy it for what it is. And don't be scared – what have you got to lose, my love?'

Dorothy didn't like Marjorie's encouraging, carefree tone, sitting, as she did, on the moral high ground of an infuriatingly long-lasting functional marriage. She appreciated Marjorie's friendship, she even respected her opinions, but she did feel, from time to time, that there were areas of life in which Marjorie was considerably less experienced than herself. To that end, she could only treat her views as well intended but ultimately – when it came down to it – Dorothy would have to walk away from her advice and sort the wheat from the chaff by herself.

'There's always something to lose, Marjorie. We both know that. And you know me, I like things as they are. I'm not keen on change,' came Dorothy's reply.

'You're not keen on not being in control, dear. That's what you're not keen on! The only constant in life is change – it's inevitable. Don't fear it, D – try to relax a bit more. Now, look at the time! I must get Trevor's sandwiches made – he's off to the allotment first thing in the morning.'

'Oh, Marj – the day of your emancipation is long

overdue! I should have thought Trevor was quite old enough to make his own sandwiches!' teased Dorothy.

'I know, I know, and he is, but he prefers it when I make them – says I get the pickle just right.'

'Of course he prefers it! He's got a woman-who-does – what more could a man want?'

'Ham and Branston is what he wants, that's what. Now, I must dash. Let me know how you get on and I promise to come over soon,' finished Marjorie.

'You'll come when Trevor's on the golf course, that's when!'

They said their goodbyes, and as Dorothy put the phone down, she picked up her mobile and looked at it for the hundredth time that day. Fancy a neck tonight? I'll cook. Handsome1 read the text in her box of saved messages.

The riddle had occupied her mind for much of the day at work. Between phone calls and filing, she had found herself returning to the text to check whether she had read it right.

Was this what he wanted? Was it part of his plan to gain her undivided attention – to confuse her so that he would linger in her thoughts for the entire day?

She couldn't help but feel uneasy, if not increasingly infuriated. She had to confess to finding Handsome1's approach a little unsettling. She was interested – she certainly was – but she didn't like the idea or, indeed, the reality of his persistence.

Relax, Marjorie had said. But for Dorothy things

were best on her terms and she didn't have full control of the reins with this one. Relaxing was not an option.

She felt as if he was making little inroads into her unwillingness – his powers of perception and persuasion appeared to be a good match for hers. Perhaps he didn't even know it. Perhaps he wasn't being manipulative but was simply behaving instinctively and impulsively. There was the possibility that he wasn't playing games but was actually being transparent and honest.

Accepting a change like this would be a considerable challenge for Dorothy. It would be an invitation to erase or rewrite the rules by which she had lived over the past twenty or thirty years. It would be tantamount to an internal revolution, and she wasn't convinced she was ready for that. She needed to regain control of her intrigue and not succumb in a way that might be potentially damaging in the longer term.

She *did* have a lot to lose. She had lost so much before – once before – when she *had* accepted change and altered the way she behaved, when she had reciprocated and been persuaded, had allowed herself to become undefended and vulnerable. She had engaged in forlorn hope by sailing too near the wind and, as a result, courted disaster. She had been left hanging by a thread.

Her loss then had been two-fold. It had been so great that it had taken her some time to get back on her feet. She had learned, among other things, that loss could quite literally take your breath away. In life you might be forced to endure the loss of something other than in death. And often that loss was just as enduring as bereavement. Lost love was one thing but the loss of an unborn child was another. For Dorothy it had been the two together that had left her so utterly exposed. So, while she respected Marjorie's encouragement – indeed, welcomed it in many ways because it meant Marjorie believed good could come out of something so 'trivial' – she found it hard to banish the need only ever to trust herself.

She looked down at the mobile phone in her hand, played with it a little, gazed up to the sky and sighed heavily. *He'll cook, he says*, she thought. *Cook . . . a meal! Yes, that's it! A meal . . . He must have been using predictive texting and not checked it before he sent it.*

She tried it on her own phone: *m-e-a-l* came out as *n-e-c-k*.

What a relief. He wasn't trying to confuse and baffle her: all he wanted was a meal – that was it.

While Dorothy acknowledged that it was a lovely suggestion, she felt – strictly according to her own rules – that seeing him twice in one week was a bit much. She would defer it to next week, thereby making up for some of the consternation she had been forced to endure today. It was important she continued to show restraint and temperance. She would return to her former stoicism and quite simply abstain. Handsome1 could wait. He would have to.

Dorothy had a widow to visit and, from what she could remember, all she had in the fridge was the remnants of Wednesday night's cheeseboard. It would just have to do.

Chapter Eleven

Geoffrey wanted to treat Gillian with care and sensitivity. Most of the time it was like handling a fireball, but on this occasion he was hoping she would be less resistant to his calming, sensible, well-meaning hands and allow him to take care of her – as he'd always intended.

On her return from the hospital, Gillian had turned her nose up at the supper Geoff had so caringly prepared and gone on to take pot-shots at his inability to rinse the shampoo out of Molly's hair. Then she had completely demoralized him by pointing out how inept he was at dressing their little girl: Molly was in mismatched pyjamas.

Geoffrey had bitten his tongue for Molly's sake.

If he hadn't been the kind of upright, logical chap that he was, his relationship with his wife might, some years ago, have taken quite a different course.

To most of his colleagues, Geoffrey was simply too nice at times. He had a marvellous sense of humour, *joie de vivre*, and was always willing and helpful. Some had wondered whether he was really cut out to be an estate agent. After all, the one who takes pity on a purchaser and pleads with the vendor to sell for less is probably not the hungry, cut-throat character you want at the helm. And yet Geoffrey's approach had always won the day. He was extremely popular, as much with the sharks who infested the waters where he worked as with those who flocked to his office in search of their dream home on an often limited budget.

Geoffrey never blew his own trumpet – he was far too self-deprecating for that – but he did acknowledge that the difference between him and his peers was that he never treated people or houses as mere figures, percentages or targets. He genuinely saw them as entities, each requiring care, attention and, above all, patience. Patience was the key to calming the nervous, twitchy purchaser and unnerving the arrogant vendor.

Tonight Geoffrey needed to draw abundantly on his pool of patience. In many respects, of course, his father-in-law's death had been ill-timed. Not that there ever was a good time to die. But the death of Austin Lewis had come at a shamefully tricky time for Geoffrey. His marriage was hanging rather precariously in the balance – as it had done over the past few years. There was an overdue need for honesty and it was eating away at him. Geoffrey had harboured to himself things he needed to get into the open. There were changes he wanted to make and changes his marriage desperately needed.

Austin's death was not the change he'd been hoping

for, though. He'd been thinking more of bringing back some romance into it or, failing that, affection.

'Daddy, I don't like buttons. I have to wear these pyjamas the other way around. Buttons are lumpy. I like smooth, like my blankey,' pleaded Molly, as she snuggled up on her father's lap.

'Doesn't sound as if Mummy likes the pyjama combination I chose either, Molly Moo,' he whispered into her ear, which was hidden by shoulder-length light-brown curls. He kissed her on the temple.

'Will we have a story tonight, Daddy? I read one page and you read the other,' she suggested, abandoning her phobia of buttons. She leaned in towards him and whispered, 'Mummy looks very cross again. Do you think she has the devil in her?'

Geoffrey was startled. 'What on earth made you say that, Molly Moo?'

'Well, you always say you're going to squeeze the devil out of me when I'm having a tantrum ... Maybe we could squeeze the devil out of Mummy?' she whispered. She looked at him with her innocent eyes, and with all the courage and conviction of someone who had very easily come up with the quantum theory.

He ruffled her hair and lifted her off his lap. 'Perhaps we could, poppet. In the meantime, it's bed for you or you'll be grumpy in the morning.' He patted her on the bum – he couldn't bear two grumpy ladies at breakfast, regardless of age.

As Molly skipped up the stairs, Gillian was relentless in her pursuit of sorting, clearing and generally making a nuisance of any object standing in her way.

'Goodnight, Molly,' she called out absent-mindedly.

'Love,' said Geoffrey, placing a hand on each of Gillian's shoulders. 'How was it at the hospital?'

She shrugged him off and paced up and down the kitchen. 'Oh, well, you know . . .'

'No, I don't know. How was it? How was your poor mother?'

'Well, she decided to collapse. No sooner had she set foot in the mortuary than she dropped to the floor. I don't know if she fainted or just overheated. Frankly, it really was quite embarrassing, Geoff.' Her voice had softened slightly, but empathy was lacking.

'Oh, poor Myrtle!' exclaimed Geoffrey. 'What on earth did you do?' He frowned, leaning towards the hurtling missile, attempting to get a bit closer in the hope that she might calm down.

'I had to give her a slap,' replied Gillian, full of self-righteousness. 'What else was I supposed to do? It was that or mouth-to-mouth – and that would hardly have been appropriate in the circumstances . . .'

Geoffrey didn't know if she was being serious or whether his wife had seriously lost her marbles. As he listened to his heartbeat in the long silence that followed, it became clear that he was too scared to contemplate either. 'Dear, oh dear,' was all he could think of to say. 'I'll go and check on Molly and then perhaps we can have something to eat and a . . . talk.'

Gillian remained in the kitchen, thinking of how much she hated the way he'd used 'talk' as a noun – it sounded ominous yet specific. If he'd used it as a verb it would have been a general chat with no specific subject but tonight she was in no mood for talking – he must, surely, have realized that. If anything, he should have read her body language – it was loud and clear.

The last couple of days had been exhausting and Gillian still had to make plans, funeral arrangements, *and* she had to remember she also had a job where she was very much needed. It really was a strain to be so much in demand and to be pulled in every direction – but life *was* demanding, there were no two ways about it. There was no point in sitting around – you just had to get on with it. Efficiently.

Gillian bent down and looked into the oven. Fish pie – what on earth had possessed him to make a fish pie? She had never been keen on it – and he *knew* she didn't mix carbohydrates with proteins. Now she'd be forced to sit and pick mashed potato off the top of a lumpy mess of fish and cream. The idea was not appealing at all. Her top lip drew into a snarl.

Sitting on her haunches by the oven, she spotted a dried-up gloop of damson jam on the skirting-board.

When Geoffrey walked into the kitchen he found his wife on her hands and knees scrubbing the stubborn mess so hard her entire body was shaking. 'What are you doing, love? Molly wants you to kiss her goodnight,' he said.

'Well, she'll just have to wait. Besides, I said goodnight to her before she went upstairs.'

'Gillian,' he bent down and, with gentle strength, lifted her upright by her shoulders, 'I think you should go and see her. She can sense the tension. She knows something's wrong. Forget this, I'll clear it up. Your daughter needs you.'

The words stung Gillian's heart. *Don't you dare question my maternal abilities*, she thought. *I'm a very efficient mother.* And with that she put down the cloth and made her way upstairs.

Molly still had the light on in her room and she'd propped herself up with a second pillow, reading a book about a little pig with a temper. She looked up as her mother walked in. 'Are you *very* cross, Mummy?'

'Darling, I'm not cross at all. Mummy's just very busy at the moment.' She pondered whether to share the news of Grampy's death but didn't want Molly to go to sleep feeling sad.

'Today we had to change places in the classroom. At first I sat next to Annoying Elliott and then Mr Dawson moved me to sit next to Enemy Hannah.'

'It's *Mrs* Dáwson, Molly. Your teacher is a lady. Oh dear, Enemy Hannah doesn't sound very nice. But perhaps we could talk about it in the morning. We'll have more time then.'

'All riiiiiight . . .' sighed Molly, from the comfort of

a bed laden with cuddly toys – the disorder irritated Gillian.

Dinner was played out in virtual silence with Geoffrey topping up his wine as soon as his glass was empty, Gillian not touching a drop of hers.

'So,' he cleared his throat nervously, 'what did they say at the hospital?'

'Subarachnoid haemorrhage, they reckoned.'

'Wow – what the hell is that?' he blurted out.

'A brain haemorrhage,' Gillian answered firmly, looking at her husband with widening eyes. She might have used the same tone to point out he had got his twice-times table wrong.

'Oh, I see, and how does that work, then?' he asked, nerves making him sound stupid.

'Work? What do you mean "work"? It can happen to anyone. It's a haemorrhage – the rupture of a blood vessel in the brain. He made it to the hospital – just about. Oh, poor Daddy.' She put her hand to her mouth. 'The thing is, Geoff, what I don't understand is that he wasn't even poorly . . . It's just a bit odd that there weren't any signs . . .'

'Well, maybe there aren't,' he said. 'I mean, you know about these things, love . . .' He smiled gently.

'I thought I did. I simply couldn't help feeling there might have been a warning sign. After Mum dropped to the floor, I took her straight to the doctor, for all the use he is . . .'

'Oh, that sounds like a good idea. Can't be easy for her.'

'After causing an almighty fuss, I got to see Dr Neil and I told him – in no uncertain terms – that she clearly needed some two-milligram diazepam tablets – at the very least – to tide her over.'

'Wow, Gill. Can you do that?' Geoffrey didn't attempt to hide his surprise.

'Well, I did.' She looked directly at him. 'I also came back with some of Daddy's belongings they handed to us at the hospital. Mother was in no state to look after anything. I've got his briefcase, his wallet and his clothes here.' She got to her feet, glad to be deserting the fish, which was no longer a pie.

While Gillian had a quick look through the briefcase and turned her attention to the wallet, Geoffrey finished what was on his plate and sheepishly ate Gillian's leftovers. He needed comfort, and if he couldn't get it from his wife, he'd get it from food.

Damn! He hadn't wanted her to get up and become distracted by other things. He wanted her full attention. He wanted to know how she was coping and then perhaps extend their chat . . .

'You have some mash on your chin.' Gillian had rematerialized at the table holding a wallet. 'You might like to wipe it off,' she said, with disdain.

Geoffrey blushed and used his napkin hastily.

Gillian was slipping her fingers through sections of the wallet, feeling for paper, cards and coins. He took a sip of wine and started to fill the silence again: 'Well, things are quiet at work at the moment – it's that ghastly pre-Christmas lull, nobody wanting to commit and everyone wanting to make sure they have a last Christmas in their home before they sell – so I'm sure I'll be able to help out a little more with . . .' He wasn't sure what Gillian would want him to help with. 'With Molly, or your mother or . . . arrangements.'

'Hmmm,' was the only reply he received, as Gillian remained fixated by the object in her hands.

Geoff opted for a change of subject. 'Poor Simon. He's having a terrible time of it at the moment. Says Paula's really putting him through the mill. Not only is he forced to do nights with the youngest, but now that she's expecting again, he says she's turned into a monster – it's like living with Stalin, he says, though I'm not sure she has a moustache.' He continued, 'From the sound of things, she's become quite unreasonable – she's making all kinds of peculiar demands on the poor sod and he can't do right for doing wrong. Poor bugger!' He hoped Gillian might cut in and either jump to her friend's defence or see the blatant comparison with herself.

If not, he had hoped she might reassure him and express relief that *they*, at least, weren't in that boat. He had wanted Gillian to nod and agree – he'd even hoped for a little laugh or at least a smile, but he was disappointed and dismayed. Her head was bent firmly over the wallet and he wasn't sure she had even heard what he was saying.

'Gill?' He prodded her with his finger. 'Did you hear me? Did you hear what I was saying about Si and Paula and Stalin?'

'Hmm – what?' She leaned back in her chair. 'No, sorry. I don't understand it. I don't understand . . .' Her voice faded.

'Well, I guess it's just the hormones. Must be dreadful for you gals, having all that stuff to deal with.' He put his arms behind his neck. 'Just you wait, I told him. Just you wait till you've got three little blighters – then you'll be outnumbered. Then you'll be screwed!' He laughed loudly.

'Something funny?'

'No, no, nothing funny. Just reflecting, you know. I was thinking, Gill, about how things have been. It's been a bit tough between us of late and now, what with Austin passing away, you're going to be under a lot of pressure. I want you to know that I'll do what I can but I need to hear from you –'

'Hear what from me?' replied Gillian, curtly, head buried in the papers from her father's wallet.

'You know . . .' he fumbled '. . . hear that everything's OK, you know, with us – that we're OK.'

'What are you *talking* about, Geoff?' she shouted. 'My father has died. My mother has lost the plot. My sister is beyond aggravating. I have a daughter and a job to attend to – not to mention the house. The house, Geoffrey – I have the house to look after. And now this!' She threw the wallet across the table at him and got up, waving a card. Her face was uncompromisingly mean: she was flustered and red with fury – and her use of his full Christian name was never a good sign.

The dissected wallet knocked the salt cellar over. He picked it up and gave it the once-over, wondering what the fuss was about.

'I had no idea Daddy was a blood donor. I would never have guessed. Not Daddy. So unlikely,' she said.

'Wow,' said Geoffrey, hesitantly. 'But that's a good thing, right?' he faltered.

Immediately he felt Gillian's face close to his and her breath on his face. 'Apparently not! Read that!' she snapped, holding the donor card right in front of his nose.

Chapter Twelve

Myrtle couldn't remember much from the hospital. She guessed, under the circumstances – of her husband dying so very suddenly and unforeseeably – that memory loss wasn't entirely unexpected. But she couldn't fathom why she could recall some things but not others.

She could not, for example, recall walking into the mortuary but she knew she must have done because that was where she had collapsed. She could remember hearing a loud smacking sound and then feeling a hot, burning sensation on her left cheek. That was when she had come to and she very definitely remembered seeing Gillian slap Beth and Beth retaliate with a slap of her own.

She had remembered Gillian more or less pulling her by her arm into the surgery and how painfully embarrassed she had felt when her calm and sympathetic doctor had explained that he wanted to hear from *her*, Myrtle, how she was feeling and not from her daughter.

Myrtle had blushed. And she had blushed even more when she noticed the awkwardness between Gillian and Dr Neil. Myrtle didn't want to be there. And she certainly didn't want anything to do with tablets.

Fainting had seemed most undignified. She remembered the indignity of lying on the floor and a distinct sense of shame.

She had called out but didn't remember what she had said, and then it had all become a bit vague and blurred again.

Now, lying in her room, she looked up at the ceiling, unable to remember coming to bed. She was still fully clothed, and as she touched her left cheek, she was sure it still stung. It certainly felt sore. And her head ached. Her body felt solid and heavy and she wasn't sure she wanted to move just yet. The house was silent, and as she turned her head slowly to the left, there was no sign of Austin next to her.

Suddenly she felt a stabbing pain in her chest and her breathing became shallow. Her hand was shaking as she guided it towards Austin's side of the bed and touched the cover. *He'd be so ashamed*, thought Myrtle, *me falling over like that – making a spectacle of myself*. She turned back and looked at the small carton of tablets Gillian had insisted on at the doctor's, lying untouched on her bedside table. Instead of a pill, she settled for a deep breath.

Eventually Myrtle got up and made her way downstairs but she couldn't stop her hands shaking. As she went into the kitchen she saw a little piece of torn paper supported by the kitchen-roll holder on the table. Myrtle picked it up, her shaking hand making it hard to read:

Mum,

Thought I'd leave you sleeping – you looked exhausted! Have had to dash to the studio – I've got a commission. I'll bring you supper tonight. Call me at any time, if you need me. You will NOT be disturbing me – that's what my mobile is for!

   Love you tons! Everything will be all right – promise. We'll get through this!

   B

Lovely, thoughtful Beth – whose handwriting hadn't much improved since she was twelve, scribbly and scrawly, long giraffe-neck and crow's-feet letters, which Myrtle had always attributed to her artistic side.

She didn't want to let go of the note – it made her feel she wasn't alone. She clung to it, like she had clung to Beth the previous day, for support, for steadiness.

It was awfully quiet, and as she moved towards the radio, the front-door bell rang. Myrtle gave a little jump and froze mid-step. *Crumbs,* she thought, *will I be like this every time the phone rings or the doorbell goes?* Just for a moment she thought she might be able to pretend she hadn't heard it.

The bell rang again – this time more persistently.

She peered into the hallway. Through the frosted-glass panels of the front door she could see something brightly coloured – the vague outline of a woman. She was moving around, and from the little she could make out the figure had blonde hair.

I don't want to see anyone, thought Myrtle. *I can't.*

Without a second's hesitation, she got down on all fours. She didn't know what possessed her but in some peculiar part of her mind she had a compulsion to make herself smaller – ultimately she wanted to be invisible. The bell went again, this time its impatience coupled with a voice: 'Myrtle! Mrs Lewis! It's Dorothy from next door. Are you in?'

Myrtle – still on all fours – bowed her head. She couldn't breathe for fear of making a noise. She closed her eyes and prayed her neighbour would give up and go away.

To her shock and utter horror, the letterbox flap opened.

'Myrtle! What on earth are you doing on the floor? Have you fallen over? It's Dorothy from next door – I've come to check you're all right . . .'

Myrtle had no choice but to reply. 'Oh, yes, thank you,' she called. 'I appear to have lost . . . er . . . something.' Crimson with embarrassment, she could barely make herself stand up, but as she walked towards the door she could see that Dorothy had retreated from her position.

Myrtle opened the door and there stood her neighbour, looking the other way, running her hands through her immaculately coiffured blonde hair. This was the woman who, without knowing it, had spent so much time in Myrtle's head, and without Myrtle knowing why:

Dorothy intrigued her to the point of fascination, awe and even, she thought, fear.

'You poor thing,' started Dorothy, tilting her head to one side. 'I'm so sorry to hear about Austin. Must have been a dreadful shock. So unexpected. I brought you this – just a little something, a token gesture. It's the thought that counts and all that . . . Now, I know how you like your garden and your plants and things. I'm afraid I'm the kiss of death in the horticultural department – one look at me and most plants lose the will to live and make a bid for the bin. Apparently this is some plant or other – can't remember its name – but, quite frankly, you're its only hope. It's been living on borrowed time on my desk at work and I thought your green fingers might bring it back to life . . .' Dorothy handed over a pot. The plant and her neighbour might be a match made in heaven.

'It's a gardenia,' said Myrtle, gazing at the sad, dry, lifeless twig Dorothy had thrust into her hand.

'It is? Well, I hope you have more success with it than I did.' Dorothy felt pleased that she was giving the dull little woman a project to engage herself in. 'And you know I'm only next door if you ever need anything. Just pop over. In fact,' she glanced up to the sky, 'you must come and have a drink sometime soon – it's always half past *wine* time in my house! Anyway, I don't mean to be rude but I really must get to work.' She went on her way, waving her hand high over her shoulder.

As she passed the caravan, she waved a final time to Myrtle and disappeared into the lane.

And there stood Myrtle on her doorstep, having spoken a few words to the woman who lived next door and with whom she had never properly conversed. Yes, there had been the odd 'hello' across the drive but that was the extent of their neighbourly relationship. Now Austin had died and suddenly there was Dorothy, in front of her, right on her doorstep.

Myrtle closed out the cold, feeling a fool for initially having tried to avoid her neighbour, who was merely and quite innocently expressing her condolences by donating a dying plant. She placed the gardenia next to the primula on the dresser in the hallway. She knew exactly what to do: with a bit of love and care she'd have it back on its feet in no time.

Myrtle was still in yesterday's clothes. In fact she was in the day-before-yesterday's clothes. It occurred to her that she hadn't showered for two days. With no packed lunch to prepare for Austin, she was at a loss.

Meanwhile, ten miles away, Geoffrey was dreading getting up. In the more puerile part of his male mind, he was rather hoping that if he lay in bed long enough he might be forgotten about. He was also hoping, as he closed his eyes briefly, that he wouldn't have to face the inevitability of yet another joyless morning with his wife.

If she was still in the house.

He'd been deeply unsettled by Gillian's behaviour

last night, and some of the things she had said had sent a chill down his spine. What she had intimated had been pretty shocking. In all honesty – and this situation lent itself to some personal honesty – he wasn't sure he was fully able to agree with her accusations. Neither was he ready to. Perhaps accusations were not there to be agreed with – especially when they concerned other people – but he feared she was running away with wild assumptions, jumping to the wrong conclusions and, frankly, she was putting the fear of God into him.

He needed to tread carefully, very carefully indeed, from now on. It was going to be yet another eggshell morning, and that was quite a challenge for a man with such big feet.

He frowned his way into the bathroom. Head hanging low, he lathered up in the shower. Baths had become a thing of the past since Gillian insisted showers were more economical – but sometimes, just sometimes, when she was out at her French class on Wednesday night, he would run himself a big bath, pour a big beer and put Van Halen on the portable cassette recorder. He would then tell Molly – who by that time was normally tucked up in bed – that Daddy was doing some serious reading and he needed the music on to help him relax. She, of course, being of a considerably more generous spirit than her mother, had accepted that this was not only an essential part of Daddy's routine but also that it was very serious. Geoffrey had been careful not to swear her to secrecy. The idea of forcing his daughter to withhold something from her mother – no matter how minor – would, he had always felt, be entirely wrong. He didn't like secrets. But just as he understood it was wrong to swear, he also accepted that there were circumstances when you couldn't avoid it – and the same was true of secrets.

By the time Geoffrey placed his foot tentatively on the bottom stair, he was enveloped by equal measures of disquiet and dejection. He took a deep breath. Just as he was about to turn the corner into the kitchen, Gillian came rushing past, like a hedgehog with its prickles standing on end. With all the poison and hatred of a woman possessed, she hissed, 'Don't you even dare speak to me, Geoffrey. I've just remembered today is the class photograph at school and I've been forced to spend the best part of this morning plaiting Molly's hair while you've had your lie-in! We're going to be late now and Molly is most likely going to miss Assembly – but as long as you've had your sleep, Geoffrey, as long as you've had your sleep.'

'But you should have –'

Gillian raised her hand towards him in an aggressive jerk and disappeared into the ether that was *her* utility room.

Geoffrey sighed, then popped his head into the kitchen where Molly stood to attention. 'Hey, poppet – look at your fancy hair. You look lovely, my darling girl,' he enthused.

Molly shrugged her shoulders. 'Can you marry an apple, Daddy?'

Before he could answer, in rushed a frantic Gillian, grabbing her car keys, her handbag and reaching out for the hospital note she had pored over with such intensity last night. She waved it in the air and gave Geoffrey a glare.

They were out of the door before he'd had a chance to give either his daughter or his wife a goodbye kiss.

This morning's school run was never going to be pleasant. For one, Gillian was stressed at being late but, more significantly, she felt severely compromised by the events of the night before.

The fuse had been lit by the news she had stumbled upon – information her family should have told her, sensitively and long ago. But the facts had revealed themselves accidentally, and she had wondered all night if she oughtn't to have worked it out for herself earlier. Why, oh, why, if she was so good at mathematics, had she not put two and two together before?

There were no two ways about it: Gillian Lloyd had been made a fool of. She had been shocked by the stampeding anger that had hijacked her. Her mind was ablaze with such fury she found it impossible to control herself. The indignation and confusion alone put her in a flat spin – she was overtaken by panic and fury the like of which she had never previously experienced.

When Geoffrey had grabbed her fists as she attempted

to beat them against his chest in the throes of her bilious screaming fit, she had been forced to a standstill – dazed and overcome by exhaustion. It had been an immediate detachment – a detachment of hypnotic proportion. The trembling, quaking rage had been replaced by a kind of stony consternation and emotional lethargy. Through her trance she could vaguely hear her husband trying to reason it out, but the words rang hollow and did nothing to reassure her.

In the car, as soon as Molly started singing, Gillian slammed her hand down on the passenger seat, turned and shouted at the top of her voice, 'Stop it, Molly! Stop singing! Stop it, for goodness' sake – I can't think when you're making that noise!'

Molly's response was a shamed silence, eyes welling with silent tears and her little fingers rubbing her new school satchel. She looked out of the window and wondered at the huge task ahead, how hard she would need to pray to God for him to take the devil out of her mummy and, while she had his attention, she wouldn't mind a pair of those nice pink satin ballet shoes Amelia had worn yesterday. She wanted the exact same pair.

By the time they pulled into the school car park, which was always over-subscribed with cars double- and triple-parked by wives whose husbands had bought them expensive unmanageable models, Gillian wasn't even relieved to find empty spaces. It meant only one thing: they were extremely late.

She swerved her cumbersome Volvo and parked it in an unruly fashion across the lines of two bays and threw herself out. She tapped her feet as she shouted at Molly to get out and they ran across the forecourt to the main reception, Molly falling behind, laden with games and swimming kit, and a bulging reading satchel.

On entering Matron's office, Gillian was briefly overcome by the musty old smell of a room that was home to files and folders, replacement uniform and missing games kit. 'I need to sign Molly in – I'm afraid we're very late,' she said hastily, to the stony-faced, disapproving woman.

As Gillian bent to open the register she dropped the pen. She wanted to swear but managed to restrain herself. 'For goodness' sake, Molly, stand still,' she exclaimed, blaming Molly for her irritation. But she knew she was clutching at straws – if not clutching at life – her nails digging perilously into the thin, bare edge of the living world, hanging on to reality by a thread. She felt she might spontaneously combust at any moment.

Under Reason for Lateness, she finally put pen to paper, took a deep breath and exhaled. What she wanted to write was 'paternity problems' but decided, on very hasty reflection, to withhold her anger and retain her dignity for Molly's sake.

She wrote 'traffic', turned around, patted Molly on the head and ran out towards her car. She got in, pulled the belt across her chest and put the keys into the ignition. Then she leaned forward and rested her head on the steering-wheel, eyes closed.

She had to see her mother. She needed to let her know in no uncertain terms how she felt about a stranger possibly intruding into her life.

Whether she liked to admit it or not, for the very first time in her life Gillian needed her mother.

Chapter Thirteen

Gillian pulled into her parents' drive with considerably more speed than normal – so fast, in fact, that the front of her car hit the towball on the caravan and her head ricocheted off the headrest. She paused briefly before getting out and slamming the car door as hard as she could. She stormed up to the front door, flung it open and deliberately disregarded the shoes-off rule. She had no intention of removing her footwear today.

She marched in, determined to catch her mother unawares. This – this meeting should be as much of a surprise and shock to her as the news had been for Gillian the night before.

She thrust her head into the dining room. No sign of her. Like a sniper intent on his target, Gillian was on a mission. She pounced into the sitting room without so much as a pause for breath.

And there Myrtle was – plumped in front of the television, propped up by puffed cushions, relaxed, ripe and ready for the picking – a sitting target, in other words.

'Mother! There you are!' said Gillian. She might as well have screamed, 'Ha! Found you!'

Myrtle almost leaped out of her skin and looked at her in horror.

'Mother! A word. Now. Turn that bloody thing off.' She snatched the remote from her mother's lap so brusquely that Myrtle let out a yelp. Gillian switched the television off and threw the remote on to the coffee-table with a bang. 'Is there anything you wish to say to me?' she shouted, despite the fact that there was barely a foot between them.

'Er . . . say?' replied Myrtle, clearly astonished.

'Yes! Do you have anything to say to me, Mother?' Gillian continued, in an even more severe voice.

'Oh, well, I'm terribly sorry about yesterday . . . about passing out like that. I don't know what came over me. I'm so sorry, Gillian, that I embarrassed you.' Myrtle bowed her head.

'Embarrassed me? You don't know the meaning of the word. Embarrass, indeed! I'm afraid that's just not good enough, Mother – forget your embarrassment. How about *shame*? Do you feel ashamed, Mother?'

By now Gillian had moved even closer, leaning over Myrtle, who was forced to push the back of her head deep into the back of the floral sofa.

Myrtle realized suddenly that she was frightened – she hadn't seen that look in her daughter's eyes before. She felt hot and flustered and could feel her cheeks burning. 'Gillian, dear, whatever is the matter? Whatever has happened?' she stuttered, pressing the words out of her mouth with all the strength she could muster.

'I don't know, Mother. Why don't *you* tell *me*? I mean, there I was' – she pulled away from Myrtle and began pacing the room – 'carrying on with my life, going about my business, carving out an enviable career, choosing a suitable husband and even starting my own family . . .' She stopped and turned to Myrtle. 'Would you know anything about that, Mother? Creating a family, a family of your own – a nice, happy family all of your own. Would you?'

'Well . . .' said Myrtle, without the slightest idea where Gillian was heading. She tried to show willing. 'I suppose I –'

'You suppose what, Mother? What do you suppose? What do you suppose in your ignorant, heavily insulated little mind – what have you ever supposed? That everyone would live happily ever after? Is that it? That if you put a brave face on it, things would just be fine and dandy?'

'Gillian, why don't you sit down, dear? I don't know what's got into you, my love,' tried Myrtle, effectively pleading for mercy.

'Got into *me*? Yes, indeed, that's a very good question.' She looked up to the ceiling. 'What *has* got into me? Or, more to the point, what got into *you*? I have here . . .' She started to root through her handbag.

Myrtle noticed she was shaking so much her entire body was moving.

'I have here . . .' she began again, extracting her father's wallet from her handbag with such force she nearly lost her balance. She waved it high in the air. 'In here, among a bank card, receipts, bits of cash . . . is a blood donor card. Yes?'

Myrtle wasn't sure whether she was supposed to agree or to challenge her daughter – but there was a distinct air of accusation in Gillian's questioning. She felt deeply unnerved – terrified even. Gillian had never behaved like this before. 'Yes, Gillian,' was all she could muster.

'It tells me . . .' she drew a deep breath, then stared straight at the card, reading aloud '. . . that Mr Austin Gerald Lewis is blood group O . . .'

There was a silence that was hard, cold and very, very solid.

It was a silence Myrtle did not wish to encroach upon. She didn't know what had possessed her daughter and she couldn't think beyond Gillian's malevolence.

'Well, *Mother* – you *are* my mother, I presume? Are you? Because if I'm blood group A, and you and Daddy are blood group O, then Austin Gerald Lewis sure as hell was not my *father*!' She threw the card at Myrtle.

But not all the bombshells dropped, or all the curve-balls thrown, or all the missiles of war fired, hit their intended target. Nonetheless, like the card Gillian had thrown, they often land close by, exploding as they do so, sending shockwaves and wreaking destruction. This particular plastic bombshell twisted, sliced through the air in a slant and eventually found its resting place near Myrtle's lap.

Myrtle watched it fly, as if in slow motion, Gillian's words echoing in her head. It was like watching a car crash. Myrtle could have looked at Gillian. She could have spoken. She could have got up to wipe the whole conversation away – remove it, rub it all out. But instead she looked down.

'Well?' Gillian asked. 'Well, Mother, did you know two Os can't have an A?'

She threw herself across the coffee-table, grabbing her mother's arms, shaking her. 'Say something, for God's sake! *What have you got to say?*' she screamed, so loudly it deafened Myrtle. Gillian's eyes had never looked wider and had certainly not been in such close proximity to her mother's since she had been a young child.

Myrtle's mouth opened.

Gillian shook her by the shoulders. 'Tell me I'm wrong – tell me all my years of studying biology have stood me in terrible stead and I'm wrong about this, Mother. Tell me this is some terrible nightmare – one *hell* of a bloody mistake. *Tell me!*' she shrieked.

Then, just as quickly as she had grabbed hold of her mother, she let her go, pulling herself back to the other side of the coffee-table – ensuring there was a physical and very real distance and divide between them. 'You appal me,' she whispered. 'You disgust me.' The words dripped with such disdain that Myrtle felt nauseous. 'I don't know who you are. But I do know that I don't like you. How could you do this to me? Did Daddy even know?' She stared at her mother, eyes narrowing. 'You are a wicked, wicked woman.' And with that, Gillian picked up her bag and walked slowly and very precisely out of the living room and, seemingly, out of Myrtle's life.

Chapter Fourteen

(Gloucestershire, 1964)

Myrtle was sixteen when he first came into her life.

PC Julian Horton strode into their kitchen as if he belonged there, Myrtle thought. He placed his helmet on the table and sat down on the kitchen chair directly across from where she stood. His fair hair was immaculately greased back, the tousled quiff shining at the front in the dappled sunlight leaking through the window from the orchard. His sharp shoulders were accentuated by his smart uniform; his slightly coarse face was clearly defined by a sharp and uncompromising jaw, interrupted only by a deep, rugged dimple sitting defiantly at the centre of his chin. Dark, dark lashes and plentiful eyebrows framed his blue eyes, indicating to Myrtle both authority and kindness in one fell swoop.

'How are the preparations going for the village fête, Mrs Hale?' he asked, turning with disinterest to look out of the window.

'Oh, you know – rushed off my feet as usual, PC Horton, rounding up the troops again. Clearly, it's one thing asking people to do something and quite another to get them to oblige. At the moment I'm still awaiting confirmation that someone can organize the cake stall. I've been sorely let down by Mrs Wetheridge – at very short notice, I might add – but it's hard to show frustration with a woman who has just one kidney. I'm hoping Mrs Craig will take her place – though I'm fiercely dubious about her motives. The past two years she's walked away with the top prize for that *delightful* lemon drizzle cake,' she continued, with contempt, but hadn't finished yet.

'Quite why the committee place such high regard on what is nothing more than a lemon sponge I will never know. It has always been a Victoria sponge that has done the trick in years gone by. Still, the times they are a-changing, PC Horton, they are indeed,' she said, as she wiped her perspiring forehead with the back of her arm.

Just then PC Horton looked up at Myrtle, attentively somehow. He parted his lips in a smile – exposing vaguely asymmetrical teeth, chipped and defaced in the corners by passionate games of rugby – and winked shamelessly.

And it was at that very moment – so utterly out of the blue – that Myrtle felt as if his entire being had jumped across the room and right into her chest, invading her heart without warning and sending a rush of blood to her soft, pale cheeks. That small gesture – a look from him to her – had lasted just a moment too long. It had rendered her immediately and unexpectedly intoxicated by this man of honour, whom she had known for so many years but who had suddenly, that day, become someone else.

In that very second her entire body had virtually convulsed with the excitement of his presence. At that moment and from that day forth, a dangerous and inexplicable tension and effervescence manifested itself in her head and heart. Whether this was destiny was largely irrelevant, but it was an encounter that made Myrtle's life urgent and imminent for the first time.

The intensity of this instant and prodigious emotion forced her to steady herself on the steel bar soldered to the Aga while she tried to listen as PC Horton spoke to her mother.

'They are, indeed, Mrs Hale,' he said, his voice fading as he continued to look Myrtle up and down.

Myrtle was unable to register anything else he said: she listened and gazed but couldn't hear. She watched his lips move confidently and invitingly around the shapes of the words but the phrases were empty and meaningless.

Myrtle had had every intention of leaving the kitchen but found she was physically unable to move. She was grounded to the floor and spellbound by the sorcery that had passed between her and the smart, handsome gentleman. She felt heady and light – consumed by emotions that had never previously visited her.

'I'm still several prizes short of a decent raffle,' continued Mrs Hale, 'and I'm quite behind on my jam-making – and if I hear one more objection from Mrs Barnaby about the ferret racing so close to her land, I fear I may not be responsible for my actions!' she said, in a raised voice, looking over her shoulder while straining steaming vegetables through the colander into the sink and disappearing beneath a veil of steam.

PC Horton nodded in agreement, raised his eyebrows and smiled again at Myrtle, conspiratorially this time.

Mrs Hale was unaware of what was passing behind her back while she clattered and clanged with saucepans and lids in a kitchen that was never at rest. She was glad that PC Horton popped over for a cup of tea once in a while – it was the clearest indication of all to her that she was, indeed, at the very centre of the community. Her involvement with the WI and her relentless desire for responsibility had seen her elevated to the higher echelons of regard in the area. She understood very well that, while her husband was expected to provide medical expertise to the villagers and beyond, she played an equally important role in upholding the duties of the doctor's wife and sustaining many of the activities and events that contributed to their strong, wholesome community. In her more private moments, she had admitted to herself with some regret that, in marrying a doctor, she had forfeited her shot at being a vicar's wife, which she had set her heart on when she was very young.

PC Horton didn't stay long and whatever had been exchanged between him and Myrtle had lasted only moments – but he had cast a spell over her. Myrtle felt as if he had physically cupped her face with his gaze and then, as he stood up to leave, he winked again as if to acknowledge this mutual understanding.

And with the come-hither look safely deposited in her heart, he politely and charmingly made his exit from the kitchen and from her day.

Myrtle remained where she was, fixated and fidgeting by the hot stove until her mother pushed her out of the way.

'In the name of all that is holy, will you mind your back, Myrtle Hale? You're in my way – you're in everybody's way. Stop dawdling and loitering, right now!' Mrs Hale said, at the top of a voice that embraced reprimands.

Myrtle heard the words – not for the first time – but while before they had injured her and pricked her feelings, now she had become immune to them. It was as if she was standing in a large bubble, impenetrable by anyone – except perhaps the honourable man who had just left.

She moved herself deliberately slowly, then proceeded to skip down the hallway to her room. She closed the door and backed against it, holding the handle for support, shutting out the rest of the world. She wanted to be alone to revel in the warmth and glow with which his presence had infected her.

Myrtle Hale had never known such distraction. A gentle, subdued, restrained teenager had, in an instant, become a highly flammable creature of some unpredictability. Her body pulsated and her heart felt as if it might combust.

She sighed loudly and heavily, rolled her eyes searchingly and gratefully up towards the heavens of the new world in which she now found herself. She let go of the door and sauntered gracefully, hands flowing either side of her, towards her record player. She crossed a floor dotted with soft toys, walls shelved with passionate literary inspirations and a desk cluttered with sketches and a private diary.

There in the corner of her room, resting against the flowery wallpaper, waited her loyal LP of the Searchers, whose songs of love and lament she regularly played but whose lyrics had remained a coded message until this very day.

She slid the vinyl out of its cover, got down on her knees and placed the record carefully on the turntable. She guided the arm to track number four. As the guitar strummed the opening bars, she danced with her arms behind her back and without much rhythm to the sounds of 'When You Walk In The Room'.

She closed her eyes and surrendered to the vocals of Mike Pender and John McNally and suddenly she knew that their words were meant for her. Indeed, she *'could feel a new expression on her face taking place every time he walked in the room'*. The song carried on and it was as if the words had been deliberately penned for this particular day of her life – that if '*she closed her eyes for a second she could pretend it was her that he wants . . .*'

Myrtle didn't quite know what this was, but she felt it was an epiphany of some sort. Dared she imagine it was love? That the burning sensation in her heart, which was holding her hostage to all things normal, was what made the world go around? Was this what all the world was talking about?

She spun herself in circles in her bedroom, lifting her arms to the sides in a wayward, floating, angelic shape. She felt exhilarated and feverish with dangerous love.

Her new sensation drowned all other sounds. She was blissfully unaware of her mother calling from the kitchen for her to come and help.

Eventually Mrs Hale came thundering down the hallway, spatula high in the air, and forced her way into Myrtle's room. 'Young lady! I've been calling you for quite some time. I suggest you get yourself into the kitchen, stop with all this fancy music nonsense and join the rest of us in the real world.'

Myrtle smiled in her delirium, even in her mother's presence.

'And wipe that irreverent grin off your face.' She raised the spatula threateningly high in the air, turned on her heels and marched back to the kitchen. Spiking through the music, Myrtle could hear her mother cursing piously as her heavy feet carried her down the hallway.

Myrtle walked over to the record player and took the needle off the worn vinyl.

In the kitchen, her sister Wren was already at the table and looked up with scorn from her plate of supper, shaking her head and tutting as Myrtle walked in. Myrtle, who had always had an undiscriminating appetite, pushed her food around the plate, occasionally lowering her hand under the table and stroking the pine chair next to her where PC Horton had sat earlier.

She knew her mother wouldn't accept her rejection of food but equally she knew she wouldn't understand what had possessed Myrtle. Besides, Myrtle was in no position to explain. Instead, she forced a little down her throat and then piped, 'Mother, I'm really not feeling well . . .'

'Idle, more like!' shouted her mother, from the stove. Myrtle was made to sit at the kitchen table until every last piece on her plate had been consumed, while Wren looked on in triumph. Myrtle's only comfort was stroking the chair beside her and the thought of the music waiting for her in her room as soon as she was done.

That meal rather compounded the situation Myrtle faced at home. Life was a tricky combination of unconditional love from her beloved father and a suppressed but at times very real rejection by her mother. Many times she had borne witness to her mother's favourable treatment of Wren. Myrtle had seen bonds and connections between mothers and daughters among her friends but had failed to grasp why this was not forthcoming for her at home.

'Look at your sister,' Mrs Hale said. 'She's finished every little bit on her plate. That is all it takes – a few minutes and a grateful mouth. Wren doesn't while away her days titillated by trivialities – she works hard and concentrates. You'd do well to take a leaf out of her book, Myrtle Hale.' It was her mother's usual mantra.

Wren smiled wryly at her sister and nodded in agreement.

Despite a persistent sense of inadequacy, Myrtle now held on to something much stronger, which left her feeling untouchable – invincible even. She clung to this for distraction and dear life in order to blot out daily life. Her imagination was in full bloom.

It could not have been further from coincidence that PC Horton was present at the dance that was held at the village hall the following Saturday. This, she knew without question, was quite within his remit as the local bobby but his presence made her tingle with excitement.

'That's a very pretty dress you're wearing, Myrtle Hale,' said PC Horton, as he stood on the steps, smoking a cigarette as she walked past.

Her heart jumped and she felt as if her whole body had been struck by an electrical current. She blushed. It was a plain dress – one she'd worn a hundred times – and was not only distinctly ill-fitting but had been ill-chosen. It had not been Myrtle's choice – her mother's dress-making abilities had made for a very safe and dull dress code. A poor dress, however, was not going to get in the way of politeness and a chance to answer the man directly.

'Oh, thank you. That's very kind.' She smiled to hide her nerves.

'I've just been checking around the hall as there was a bit of trouble out the front last week – some scoundrel trying to make his way in with half an eye on the toaster and some chairs, I should think.' Now he smiled, exposing his damaged but tantalizing teeth again. Teeth that said, *I'm not afraid to get stuck in. I'm just not afraid.* And Myrtle could feel her knees weaken as her eyes stayed on his mouth.

'I shall have to hang around for the duration, is my reckoning. If you need a lift home, I'm sure your pa would appreciate me getting you back safely.' He blew the final puff of smoke from his mouth.

All this and now. At that moment she couldn't escape the feeling that this was a very deliberate attempt on his behalf to share space with her again, but she didn't dare count on it.

Her mind wandered to the chance of sitting next to him in his Ford Zephyr even for just a very short time. And she would be doing nothing wrong. On the contrary, she would be pleasing her father by making a safe journey home. It would not only be rude to turn down such a kind and well-intentioned offer, it would be foolish – her heart knew that. Moreover, she felt sure that her mother would approve.

'Oh, yes.' She hesitated without meaning to. 'That would be . . . very kind.' Myrtle smiled shyly and proceeded into the hall, which was still flooded with summer daylight and lined with teenagers sitting on benches and chairs along the walls or standing in small clusters near the far end.

True to his word, he was waiting in his car outside the hall at the end of the dance. Myrtle had thought of nothing else all evening.

As she climbed in, she was grateful that her dress, though contrary to the current fashion, was long enough to cover her chubby knees and pale legs. Once again she longed for Libby's – long and slender, with their olive tone. What she wouldn't give for those legs right now. If she'd had Libby's legs she would skip through the village barefoot every day.

But she had neither slender legs nor a short skirt. Myrtle Hale had shoulder-length wavy brown hair and might best have been described as compact. 'All the best things come in small packages, my love,' her father would say encouragingly, which, rather than making her feel better, served as a constant reminder that she had inherited her mother's build.

The car journey was short, prolonged only by PC Horton's insistence on going the long way around so that he could 'keep an eye on parts of the village', which Myrtle thought admirable.

With the exception of this excuse, and the music

filtering quietly from a radio in the car, there was silence between them. Myrtle found the lack of conversation unnerving and she struggled to rid herself of the extraneous energy that was suddenly occupying her – her hands were writhing in her lap. She stared intently out of the side window, trying hard to find something other than fields and houses of any significance.

As he pulled up outside her home he justified not driving up to the front door by claiming it might wake Dr and Mrs Hale. *He's a true gentleman*, thought Myrtle.

As she prepared to get out of the car, he placed his left hand on her knee and looked straight at her. 'You've got wonderful eyes, Myrtle. They're like starfish, framed with those long lashes.' He smiled.

Myrtle could feel the heat of the flush rushing to her cheeks but words failed her. She got out and walked towards the house without daring to look back – she feared it had all been a dream, a fantasy, and the car an apparition.

Myrtle Hale did not sleep that night. She felt dizzy with possibility – consumed by it. She was falling, from the very greatest height, into the heavenly hiatus that was love.

What ensued was nothing short of an illicit affair: PC Julian Horton was married with two daughters. What had started off as a number of subtle rendezvous in and around the village, and had skirted the parameters of wrongful behaviour, had unravelled and become a distinctly irresistible connection between two people who claimed helplessness in the face of powerful infatuation.

Julian Horton had been persistent in his pursuit of Myrtle, turning up unexpectedly outside school and in her mother's kitchen. His intention showed itself with such humility that Myrtle felt utterly defenceless. He had disarmed her with flattering words of tormented affection, which he laced with pleas of weakness and imperfection. He was flawed, he claimed, which made him vulnerable to Myrtle, and it was this, she always knew, that had driven her into his arms – the compelling self-abnegation he had exposed.

Sitting in PC Horton's car overlooking Summer's Hill – a view that on any other day would have inspired and moved Myrtle but on that day went unnoticed – he had turned her face towards him with one hand and kissed her directly on the mouth.

Myrtle hadn't known what to do so she parted her lips tentatively and allowed him to explore her mouth gently and probingly. Her naïve emotions were hard to define but she couldn't help sensing a strong connection with this man – an affinity. Equally, she felt imprisoned and couldn't escape the feeling that her heart had left her without a choice.

After the kiss she had pulled away, covering her mouth with her hand and searching for something to say – but all that came out was 'Oh, you shouldn't. Mother says I'm most likely coming down with a cold.'

Then she had cringed at her feebleness, immaturity and lack of sophistication.

Covert missions brought them together regularly and irregularly, whenever an opportunity presented itself – and sometimes even when it didn't Myrtle's imagination won the day. Everything about her daily life had become forbidden, unspoken and uncertain and, most frighteningly, something to which she felt remarkably suited.

Whenever he dropped in to her mother's kitchen, he sat down at the table, hooked Myrtle with long glances and nudged her feet with his own under the table. Myrtle justified this sinful behaviour to herself as a keen, hopeless, urgent and, above all, devoted love. She was defenceless. And it was his urgency that confirmed he was dedicated to her.

She could not reject the very strong feeling that their union was intended by a greater power than the two of them put together.

She began to fall behind with her schoolwork. She lost her appetite – much to the fury of her mother, whose main role in life was to feed her family – and all ability to reason with herself and those around her. She became more and more reclusive, consigning herself to her room and her record player, immersing herself in the words of love sung by the Searchers, and frequently lying on her bed wallowing in her helplessness.

He had avoided all talk of love. Myrtle thought

about it constantly and knew, unquestionably, that it was love which had undone her. Despite his reluctance to say the words, she felt that his actions spoke them instead – and the fact that he had presented her with a delicate silver charm bracelet just moments before he had taken her virginity had made her heart positively burst.

From that moment of abandon, their connection was not only reinforced but fuelled by furious desire that entirely changed Myrtle. She felt she owned something no one else knew about, and she was sure people looked at her differently. Her life became a precarious balance of shielding her new-found maturity from her parents and exposing it to its full potential with her lover.

The change in her did not go unnoticed by her father. 'Myrtle, my love, you look exhausted and you're not eating properly. I'm worried about you. Is school getting the better of you? I know it's important you work hard but not to the detriment of your health. Our health is all we have. I know your mother is very concerned but . . .' he winked at her and touched her shoulder '. . . you know she's too proud to show it. You're not worried about anything, are you, my lovely?'

Desperate to stop her father's probing, she shrugged off his concern but conceded that she was, indeed, struggling to keep up with her schoolwork.

'Well, you must just concentrate on being a young lady. You're growing up faster than I would like. Seems only last week I could hold you in one hand.' He had kissed her forehead – as he always did – and returned to his newspaper.

Myrtle's remedy was PC Horton – and he was all she ever thought of. Her obsession alienated her from her friends and she was unable to focus on anything but that irresistible man.

'I can't stop thinking about you, Myrtle Hale. All the time I'm away from you, all I see is your little face. What I wouldn't do to have you fixed into the back of my car every day!' he said on one occasion as he slid his hand under her skirt and along the inside of her thigh.

She had no way of stopping the words that had been so desperate to escape for so long. 'I do love you, Julian,' she said, looking directly at him.

His hand remained where it was and he closed his eyes. 'Me, too,' he replied, clearing his throat and pursuing his desires.

Myrtle trembled uncontrollably and reached forward to meet his mouth. There was something distinctly Romeo and Juliet about the wrongfulness of their relationship – although she doubted Juliet had been a contortionist forced to double up in the back of a Ford Zephyr parked in remote parts of the village.

She continued to dream of a time in the future when they could be together in full view of the world and could display their reciprocal love.

PC Horton continued with his double life, which enabled him to have the best of at least one world. He had no intention of leaving his unsuspecting wife or jeopardizing a life with his children. Myrtle Hale's keenness, availability and innocence made things very easy for him. He issued no promises above and beyond their next encounter and he was rather proud of his honesty to that extent.

But as Myrtle's waist narrowed due to her inability to look at food in quite the same way as she had done previously, her father became concerned that she might be suffering from a thyroid problem or possibly even anaemia.

He ordered a blood test, and two weeks later, as he stood reading the results in his surgery, he fell back, shocked, into his large leather chair. His glasses dropped to the floor.

Still in shock, against his better judgement and for the first time in his life, Dr Hale forced himself to challenge the indisputable scientific truth of medicine. He resolved to approach his daughter directly in the absence of his wife. There was no need to upset Mrs Hale – at least, not yet. He hoped against hope that perhaps, by divine intervention, there was some other logical explanation for the evidence before his eyes.

He called Myrtle into his study, a dark and sombre room with shelf upon shelf of leather-bound books stacked ceiling-high with good intention but in no particular order, much to the frustration of Mrs Hale. It was furnished with a large oak desk, inherited from his own physician father, which was strewn with papers, pens, notes and a glass vat of black ink. Dr Hale thrived on the seriousness of the room, not least because it gave him sanctuary from the world outside and was capable of inspiring in him the greatest state of concentration.

The sobriety of the study had never bothered Myrtle – it was a room in which she'd shared many fascinating and profound conversations with her father: talks about life – past, present and future – that had been creative, insightful and always inspirational.

She stood now to the right of the desk, opposite her father, and began to handle the silver-plated letter-opener her mother had bought him many Christmases ago.

'My darling Myrtle,' he started, in a gentle but nonetheless unfamiliar voice. Usually it was laced with enthusiasm but on this occasion it faltered somewhat. Myrtle couldn't help but identify an underlying tone of dejection. Her father sounded tired and flat. 'I'm worried about you,' he went on.

Myrtle expected yet another mild lecture about her deteriorating achievement at school and resigned herself to the loss of some of her vinyl records and possibly even a couple of magazines as punishment.

'I have had the results of your blood test. They're a cause of grave concern to me. I wonder if you've had any symptoms of any kind, Myrtle dear – have you been feeling yourself?'

Myrtle's mind had already left the room and was

somewhere else. She tried hard to contain the relentless energy she was harbouring inside. She was twitching and drawing the knife up and down the side of the desk. 'No, Daddy, I'm absolutely fine – you've no need to worry about me in the slightest. I'm very, very well. In fact,' she said, looking him straight in the eye in the hope this would bring their conversation to a close, 'I've never felt finer.'

'You know you can always talk to me, my love. We're always straight with one another, aren't we?'

'We are, Daddy,' Myrtle responded.

'This is a tricky time and you're under a lot of pressure at school. But you know I'm proud of you . . .' he hesitated '. . . and so is your mother. She doesn't always show it but she is. You know that, don't you, Myrtle?'

'Yes, Daddy,' she lied, in an attempt to placate him.

'Now, I've chosen to speak to you alone because I don't want to make your mother any more anxious than she already is. Therefore it's important you're honest with me, Myrtle. It appears that you are pregnant.'

Myrtle wasn't listening. She was waiting for her father to finish his sentence so that she could simply reassure him that everything was fine, then skip back to her records and a Hardy poem she was keen to finish reading. But his abrupt ending forced her to replay the words in her mind a couple of times before she understood what he meant.

'Pardon, Daddy?' She breathed in sharply and the knife dropped out of her hand.

'It's true, Myrtle. You're pregnant. Now, before this conversation goes any further, I want to hear from you what and, more to the point, *who* has brought about this unfortunate circumstance. Remember, honesty, Myrtle – honesty is integral to our communication.'

She was overcome by dizziness and was forced to steady herself against her father's desk. She didn't know what to say. She couldn't possibly tell her father about PC Horton. She would have to invent something and lie – for her own and everybody else's sake. But what could she say?

'Oh,' she blushed, 'I don't know. I don't really understand. I don't know,' she repeated. It was a ridiculous answer and she felt almost more ashamed of her reply than of the subject of their conversation.

'Myrtle! Look at me!' There was anger in his voice, which she had never heard before. He had always been her refuge, her protector in stormy times. Now, for the first time, she had compromised herself – but, more importantly, she had compromised their bond.

'Myrtle Hale, if I didn't know you better I would think you were ignorant and rude. Don't take me for a fool – don't ever take me for a fool. You tell me now who has got you in this condition. Were you goaded? Set upon? Good Lord, you weren't attacked, were you?' His eyes were as big as saucers.

Myrtle wanted to look away but her eyes were stinging with tears. His anger scared her. 'Oh, Daddy, no, it wasn't anyone,' she tried again, her words muffled by sobs and fear. 'It's love. I've fallen in love, Daddy, and I knew you'd be disappointed because it has distracted me somewhat, but I'm helpless, Daddy, I'm so in love. And he loves me, too,' she added, hoping her last words would make everything all right.

'Who loves you, Myrtle? Who?' he shouted, forcing his face into hers.

There was no point in evading it any longer. Her time had come. 'Mr Horton,' she whispered. 'PC Horton – Julian.' She gave her voice strength: 'He loves me. I know he does.' She moved closer to her father, in the hope that he would understand and the anger in his voice would dissipate. She threw her arms around him and rested her left cheek against his broad chest, sobbing uncontrollably.

Dr Hale stood there, arms steadfastly at his sides. He was sure he had heard his heart fall to the bottom of a very dark and empty pit. He opened his mouth and said automatically, 'I shall have to speak to your mother, Myrtle.' He raised one arm to his brow. 'You cannot expect me to shield you from her. You have confessed, and I credit you with that, but you have been a foolish girl – a very foolish girl. I shall have to deal with *Mr* Horton separately.'

'Oh, Daddy, please don't tell Mother! Please, Daddy, I implore you. I beg of you, Daddy, don't be cross with Julian. His only weakness is to love me . . .' She grabbed her father's arms and stood on her tippy-toes, eager to stop him leaving the room.

Dr Hale extricated himself from his daughter and walked out of the study. His love for her had been contaminated with the most terrible disappointment and anger. A trace of jealousy brushed his heart. Her love for such a weak, selfish, unscrupulous man flew in the face of everything he had ever tried to instil in her.

Myrtle heard her father's footsteps diminish. She heard his muffled voice, a pause – and then she heard her mother scream as if she had been stabbed. She heard Mrs Hale's heavy feet make their way towards the study. The door was flung open and rocked the shelves. Her mother marched up to her, raised her hand and brought it down with great force on Myrtle's cheek. 'You vile, vile girl. You wicked sinner.' She raised her eyes to the heavens. '"Let sinners be consumed out of the earth and let the wicked be no more!"'

And with that she left the room.

Myrtle looked up briefly and saw her father standing in the doorway, his head hanging low.

Those were the last words her mother spoke to her in more than a week.

Back in her bedroom, Myrtle put a hand on her belly and stroked it gently. She leaned her head back and looked up to the ceiling in gratitude. While her body remained still, her head was whirring in disbelief and wonder. She was carrying a child – a being that had been created with her lover and she could not believe her good fortune. Calm and serenity flowed over her and a big smile crept across her pale, round face.

But when she remembered the night's confrontations, pain and panic set in, accompanied by the ever-present nausea, which pricked her conscience, as it had not at any other time in the past months. Clasping her mouth with her hand, she rushed over to the wash-basin in the corner of her room and threw up.

When she looked into the mirror, she saw a new and different Myrtle Hale. She turned her face from side to side and wondered whether others would see the change in her: her preparedness, her womanhood, her completion.

She knew now what it was to be a woman of conviction, a woman with a purpose. But there came also a nagging fear.

She had ruptured the bond with her father and now she felt lost, but she knew that she wanted the baby more than anything.

Chapter Fifteen

The atmosphere in the house over the coming days was not lost on Wren. She had missed out on the main action, but she was neither too young nor too stupid to fail to notice the icy atmosphere. She, too, found herself thrust into the mêlée of anger, frustrated expectation, dissatisfaction and, most of all, unbearable silence.

Passing a boiled sweet from side to side in her mouth, Wren sidled up to her sister on the walk home from school one day and tried to persuade her to share the events that had so changed life at home. 'You really must – *must* – tell me, Myrtle. Have you done something wicked? Something truly wicked?' She smirked.

But Myrtle would not be moved. Before too long, her sister and everyone else around her would surely be aware of her condition. 'There's nothing to tell, Wren. Really there isn't,' she lied.

'How can you say that when Mother can't bear to look at you and even Father is keeping away from you? You think I'm too young to know, Myrtle, but I swear I'm not.' She paused, swallowed the sweet and looked at her sister. 'You can trust me,' she lied back.

And those were the two words that hung heavy in Myrtle's mind: swear and trust. She had sworn to her father she would not speak of the situation to anyone. And she knew she could trust no one.

Some days later, as Myrtle stood in her bedroom, she saw his car come up the drive slowly and tentatively.

She watched him walk up to the front door and, from the confinement of her bedroom, she heard him enter her father's study.

'Mr Horton – Julian – do you have any idea why I've asked you here today?' asked Dr Hale.

'No, Dr Hale – has anything happened? Have you had a break-in? I know there's someone going about it in the village. They're only breaking into sheds and the like, mind, but it's theft nonetheless,' he replied conscientiously.

'It appears there is more than one thief on the loose, then. It seems there is more than one criminal in the village . . .' Dr Hale moved towards his study window and looked out.

'Has there been a crime? Blimey, we don't see much action around these parts but we're always willing and ready. How can I help?' he continued, none the wiser.

Dr Hale turned away from the window and stared straight into PC Horton's eyes. 'Oh, you've been very willing, I know that.' He paused momentarily. 'You really have no idea, do you, why I've called you here? This means either my daughter's imagination has run away with her or you are not being honest with me.

Which is it, Mr Horton?' His stare did not budge.

'I'm sure I have no idea what you're talking about –'

'Stop right there! Choose your words very carefully, Mr Horton. We're more than likely to fall out over what the ensuing exchange will result in, but let's not fall out before we've even started!' He spoke forcefully.

PC Horton passed the circumference of his helmet between his fingers quickly and nervously.

'It's regarding Myrtle. Did you not think I would be alerted to the situation – eventually, at least?' Dr Hale moved closer to his target.

'Oh, er, I see . . .' he stuttered, stunned but resigned in equal measure.

'You, Mr Horton, may I remind you, are a married man. Why, you're a father! Not to mention a supposedly honourable, upright man of integrity and honesty. Your role in this community is one of responsibility and trust – you are supposed to be incorruptible!' Dr Hale's voice was raised but tempered with a need for reason and superiority.

'Look, it got out of hand – she's a pretty girl. She charmed me. What can I say?' PC Horton replied, facing his opponent straight on.

But he had misjudged Dr Hale if he had thought the affair could be dismissed out of hand. The tall fifty-three-year-old doctor might have been no physical match for the younger man across the room but that did not deter him. Lunging forward, he grabbed PC Horton by his tie. 'She's pregnant, for goodness' sake, man! Did you know that? And you stand there talking about her as if she was nothing more than a fleeting mistake – none of which was your fault! How dare you? You are not beyond reproach . . .' He let go of the policeman and shook his head.

'Well!' PC Horton smiled – as much with embarrassment as with a sense of achievement. 'Well, now, that is something . . . I'm shocked,' he said, offering his own surprise as a kind of remorse.

'As well you might be – but not as shocked as Myrtle was. She is my daughter – nothing but a girl. How could you? How could you find it in you to shatter her like this, paralyse her life before it has even begun?' He stood close enough for PC Horton to feel his breath on his skin.

Suddenly the policeman seemed to grasp the magnitude of the situation. 'I can't be expected to marry her. I hope that's not what you're suggesting. I couldn't . . . I mean, that wouldn't be right!'

'There is more than that which is not right, I can tell you. Of course you're not going to marry her, but if you want to stay married to your good wife, then I suggest you speed a transfer to another part of the country before I get a chance to put pen to paper to your superiors. Have I made myself clear?'

Never in his life could Dr Hale recall ever having felt so incensed by a situation that he had allowed his emotions to project in such a threatening way.

'Well,' started PC Horton, bringing his sanity up to

speed with the reality of what his actions had resulted in, 'I – I will do, indeed,' he mumbled.

'Never darken our doorstep again. Ever.' Both men knew he meant it.

Myrtle's ear was glued to her door for the long, painful duration. She held on to the handle for support, desperate for a glimmer of hope, a sign of any news or, at the very least, the sound of his voice. Eventually she heard his footsteps quicken to the front door.

She ran to her window and watched him walk down the drive hastily, his head bowed.

She knocked on the window frantically, needing him to prove to her that he, too, was thrilled by the confirmation of their relationship. But very little acknowledgement was forthcoming. He looked over his shoulder and immediately turned his eyes straight back to the ground. Myrtle knocked again and waved furiously – she called his name, gently at first but then she was bawling it. Her hand fell from the glass.

'No!' she whimpered, as tears cooled her burning cheeks. She fell to the floor.

But it was not the last time she saw him.

Some days later, in the village, she ran up to him – something she had never had the courage to do before. She yanked at the sleeve of his uniform. 'Julian, it's me! Please don't ignore me. I haven't seen you for ages. Father told you my news, then?'

He refused to make eye contact with her, instead

reaching inside his breast pocket for a cigarette. 'What news? That you've got yourself in the club? Well, you should have taken more care. How do I even know it's mine?'

Disbelief overwhelmed her. 'How can you say such a thing? It's you I love and you know it . . . Now we can finally be together – we're going to have a child! We don't have to bear our secret any longer – we have been set free!' she enthused.

'Free? *Free?* You don't know the meaning of the word! This isn't freedom, you fool. Look,' he said, turning to face her but looking over her shoulder into the distance as he spoke, 'what we had was a bit of fun, all right? It was nothing more than that. I'm a married man with two kids already. I don't want any more. And now you've spoilt it all by getting yourself into trouble. You know what this means, don't you?' He didn't pause for a reply. 'It means I have to leave. I can't run the risk of her-indoors finding out. You stupid girl.' He took one last drag of his cigarette and threw the butt at her feet.

Myrtle was dumbfounded. She couldn't move, she couldn't breathe, as she watched him climb into his car – their car – the car in which they had shared their unspoken passion so many times while overlooking Summer's Hill.

And there she stood, satchel at her feet, alone and yet multiplied inside.

*

On her return from school she was called into her father's study, where she wept, exhausted by the turmoil and confusion. She sat in the chair opposite him, sobbing.

'Your mother cannot bring herself to discuss your situation with me – she's been rendered speechless by recent events, as you might imagine. To that end, I feel it is for the best that, as soon as you start showing – God willing, it will not be any week soon – you will leave school. What will happen thereafter, I am still not sure.

'I intend to try to talk about it with your mother but you must understand this is very hard for her and has come as a dreadful shock. I understand arrangements have been made for Mr Horton – and his family – to move away to another post, somewhere up north. I do not think the village need know our business and it seems highly unfair to make your mother suffer any more than she already is.

'This way, you will no longer have to be reminded of your . . . your error of judgement, at least not on a daily basis and in the form of such an unscrupulous man. What will come after remains to be seen. Either you will remain here and have the baby – though, Lord knows, that would be testing for your mother – or there may be an opportunity for you to go away and have it and return once the waters have calmed . . .'

His words were soporific. She was drained. She didn't understand why he spoke of this as an 'opportunity' when PC Horton had been forced away, but she felt too heavy to question him. All she could muster was 'No, Daddy,' in a faint, listless voice.

He looked at her with eyes that knew better but he knew better than to say so. 'Myrtle, this whole affair . . . this whole business is a damn disaster.' He brought his hand down hard on his desk. He looked away, composed himself, then turned back to his daughter. 'You, young lady, have disgraced yourself, your family and beyond. You have shown utter neglect and disregard for other people's feelings and have put on the most vulgar display of selfishness. This will be a lesson to you, Myrtle Hale, a very big lesson indeed.'

Then he asked her to leave his study.

In his heart he had wanted to walk around to the other side of his desk, pull her into his arms and hold her – just hold her – but that would have been dangerous. Instead, he had chosen to warn her off, to frighten her into realizing the disastrous choice she had made.

His daughter had changed: she was no longer the girl he had once known, and while he understood he could not save her heart – it was too late for that – he was determined to make every attempt to save her mind.

Her mother – his good and faithful wife – was quite a different matter. Dr Hale sincerely doubted he had any chance of stopping Mrs Hale condemning their daughter to eternal damnation. Myrtle had blotted her copy-book with her mother for ever. The damage, he had deduced, was irreparable, which troubled him greatly for Myrtle's sake.

Instinctively he wanted to handle his daughter with kid gloves and kill her with kindness but he knew that, from this point forward, he had to be cruel to be kind. Myrtle needed to learn the hard way – much as it pained him to stand by and watch it unfold.

Chapter Sixteen

Beth wondered if she should have done it. In her heart of hearts she felt it hadn't been the best idea but on the other hand she figured – in her willing, well-meaning mind – that by bringing it up with her mother now, the blow might be softened or even obscured by her father's death. After all, as she had learned over the past ten years or so, there was never going to be a 'right' time for anything.

To that end, Beth decided it was best to arrive at her mother's with ammunition. The mixed-bean casserole would not only be gratefully received but would, she believed, serve as a distraction. The presence of Neena would put a real focus on the subject and Beth would be unable to wriggle out of it as she had done so many times in the past.

She knew her mother liked Neena. She could tell by the way she looked at her and smiled in a truly warm and welcoming way, which was more than she could ever have said for her father's approach. Beth only hoped her mother would look at Neena in the same way once the cat was out of the bag. But she couldn't be sure of it.

*

When Beth and Neena arrived Neena expressed her condolences, taking Myrtle's hands in hers and reaching forward to touch her cheek. Her eyes welled, and Myrtle felt embarrassed by this show of emotion but relieved that Beth had such a good friend by her side.

Still numbed by Gillian's visit, she didn't quite know how to respond to Neena's softly spoken words and generous gestures. All she could do was thank her and bow her head.

Beth sensed the tension and her mother's incoherence and quickly replaced it with sanguine, counteractive banter between herself and Neena. They bustled around the kitchen, heating the food, and Neena took it upon herself to lay the table. Myrtle stood by helplessly, watching them go about their business, thinking nothing and everything.

Over the meal, which Myrtle noticed was distinctly lacking in meat, Beth talked excitedly about her day and her latest commission. Myrtle's appetite was non-existent, and after the first bite she found herself pushing the food around her plate, putting very little into her mouth. Her unease was not lost on Neena, who insisted she tried one of her home-made samosas. Both girls watched intently as Myrtle took a bite.

With flakes of pastry falling from her mouth and the spice burning her virginal palate, she managed to say, 'That's nice.'

The girls turned to each other and smiled.

Beth cleared her throat. 'Mum, I know you must be feeling so shocked at the moment – we all are – but you really must eat. I know none of us have much of an appetite but it's important we keep ourselves going.'

But Myrtle didn't want to keep going. She wanted to lie in a darkened room and be left alone.

'Now, Mum,' continued Beth, munching her third samosa, 'you know Neena quite well, don't you?'

Myrtle was brought back into the room by Beth's question. She didn't know what Beth was implying. Her face was serious, still and focused. Myrtle hoped she wasn't leading up to anything 'Gillian'. She would hold on to the belief that Beth knew nothing – until it was proved otherwise.

'Yes, dear.' Myrtle nodded and smiled. 'I do.'

'Good. She's my very best friend. I don't know what I would have done without her over the past few years – not to mention since Daddy passed away. So,' she said, turning to Neena and taking her hand at the table, 'we're thinking of moving in together properly.'

'That's nice, dear,' responded Myrtle, relieved. She looked at the pair in front of her and then at her plate.

'We want to live together. Like a couple – a proper couple.' Beth smiled at her mother, euphoric that the burden was now very nearly off her shoulders.

'We love each other, Mrs Lewis,' Neena interjected reassuringly.

'It's really cool, Mum. We're so connected we even

know what the other is thinking – we can anticipate what the other is going to do and say. Even our cycles run concurrently! It's weird but they say that happens, don't they?' said Beth, gazing at Neena.

'Yes, they do. It is strange but it does happen,' Neena confirmed.

Myrtle looked at them sitting across the table from her, like two young schoolgirls thrilled that their collusion for a midnight feast and sleepover was about to be approved.

'Do you have a bicycle, too, Neena?' Myrtle asked meaningfully.

Both girls let out irrepressible giggles, then straightened their faces as it dawned on them that their news had been neither absorbed, nor accepted, nor understood.

'*No*, Mum,' Beth said. 'I meant our menstrual cycles – you know, our periods.'

Myrtle blushed. She felt a fool. She had not only misunderstood the words but she was ignorant enough not to know that such a thing might be possible. She looked down at her plate again. 'That's nice, dear.'

'So, are you OK with that, Mum? Us being a couple? It's just that I've been wanting to say something but Daddy always made it so incredibly hard for me to talk to him or even have a proper conversation with you. And I know now is a stupid time but, as Neena quite rightly pointed out, there's never going to be a good time.'

Myrtle wondered what had happened to that nice boy David, who had been such a good friend to Beth since they were at middle school. She wondered why she hadn't seen much of him lately and why Beth never talked about him any more. 'What about that lovely David? He was a very nice young man. Well-mannered, your father always said.'

'Mum, Dave is just a mate. He was never my boyfriend. I haven't had a boyfriend. If it wasn't going to work with Dave, it wasn't going to work with anyone. I'm a lesbian, Mum. I'm gay . . .' she said, raising her voice slightly, undeterred by her previous anxieties.

Myrtle was trapped. She couldn't look away. Beth had commanded her attention and was telling her something important, but she felt stifled by it. She didn't understand – she didn't know how she was supposed to respond. Beth's sentence was incomprehensible – impenetrable. 'Well, that's nice, dear,' she said again. 'Shall we all have a cup of tea?'

Beth and Neena looked at each other. Neena frowned, elbowed Beth and nodded in Myrtle's direction.

'Mum, I'm not sure you understand what I'm saying. I'm telling you I'm in love with Neena and we're in a relationship. What do you think about that? How does it make you feel?'

Myrtle got up from the table and headed towards the kettle in a trance-like state. She shook her head. 'I'm wondering when this rain's going to let up. It feels like it's been pouring for months. It can't, surely, go on for ever. Your father would hate it. He won't like the idea of being buried in the rain. Not one bit.' She switched on the kettle and reached for three cups and saucers in the cupboard above.

Beth and Neena looked at each other with equal measures of relief and dismay.

'Mum, did you hear me? Did you understand what I said?' persisted Beth.

'Yes, dear. Neena and you are going to live together.' Myrtle didn't turn to look at the happy couple behind her.

Beth couldn't help feeling there was something distinctly automatic about her mother's reaction and, while she had finally made the announcement, something niggled at her. 'Mum, why don't I run you a bath and you have a long soak? I bet you haven't had a bath in ages . . .'

'Oh, no, your father would hate . . .' Her words came to an abrupt halt. Myrtle's mind disappeared into the pot of tea she was tending by the kettle. She peered up at the ceiling to stem some tears.

'I could give you a massage, Mrs Lewis. It might help you relax a bit. I do reiki healing, too. It's very effective,' Neena suggested.

But Myrtle did not reply. It didn't sound relaxing, what they were suggesting. Besides, she didn't deserve anything relaxing in her state of mind. 'Milk and sugar?' was her reply.

And there the three of them sat. At a kitchen table

which, over the years, had been host to so many family meals, always held in austere silence as Austin had been a firm believer that food should be eaten and respected solemnly.

Later, Beth washed up and Neena dried – their relationship had always been based on an unspoken equality. Beth's strengths lay in the artistic and spontaneous, Neena's in being articulate and detailed. It had been that way since they had first met and was what had made things feel so right. They had understood and supported each other in a way that had not initially needed pronouncing. There had been declarations of love, but as theirs was an all-encompassing love, it had never required dissecting, labelling or compartmentalizing. It was an unconditional statement of affection Beth had not encountered before.

She had dreamed of it in her first relationship, but Yvonne had wanted to play games with Beth's mind, challenging her to struggles of power and control. She had laid down conditions that had sent Beth to hell and back. After such a destructive relationship, Beth had gradually realized that she would rather be on her own than tortured by someone living rent-free in her head.

Her relationship with Neena had not only come as a breath of fresh air but had helped her understand that life need not be made more complicated than it already was.

It was with Neena's support that she had finally found the courage to face up to who and what she was. She had come to accept that she was still a whole person *without* her partner but that her life was greatly enhanced by Neena's presence, and Beth felt all the better for knowing it.

However, Beth's awkward relationship with her father and her inability to confide in her mother had rattled her confidence in exposing who she was. The death of her father, she felt, had given her the opportunity to pave the way for a clearer, more lucid relationship with her mother, although it was hard to accept that the situation with her father would remain for ever unresolved.

'I don't think she quite gets it,' Neena whispered, nudging Beth by the sink.

'I know. She just needs time to digest the news. Perhaps it will be a welcome break from mourning – a distraction even. At least we know we've told her and we know she knows – even if she doesn't understand. We just have to keep reminding her of us at every opportunity. That way it will become inescapable,' reasoned Beth.

Myrtle was gazing out at the sodden garden, its sad plants pleading for the rain to stop. She couldn't stop thinking about Gillian, her strong words, her terrifyingly erratic behaviour. She was still shaken by their encounter and felt paralysed with fear at the prospect of seeing her again, let alone hearing from her.

And then there was Beth: she felt sure she hadn't been told but Myrtle needed to know for certain.

As the girls put on their coats to leave, Beth begged her mother to have a long bath to help her relax. She reached into her coat pocket and handed Myrtle a small bottle, which she told her was Rescue Remedy and that she was to put a couple of drops on her tongue before she went to bed: it would help her to sleep. *Rescue*, thought Myrtle. *I need rescuing*.

Neena reiterated her offer of reiki healing, but Myrtle thanked her and said that although the samosas were lovely she was too full for any more Indian food.

As Beth and Neena were about to walk out of the door Myrtle plucked up the courage to ask, 'Beth, dear, have you heard from Gillian?'

'No, I haven't, actually. She's not answering her mobile. I thought she might have lost it. I'll try her again.'

'Oh, no need,' said Myrtle. 'I'm sure she'll be in touch. You know Gillian — it's all rush, rush, rush.' With that, she kissed her daughter goodbye and accepted a hug from Beth's best friend.

'That went all right,' said Neena, as they walked down the drive.

'Did it? I'm not so sure. She definitely didn't take it in. She seemed so — I don't know — distracted. Her mind was elsewhere,' replied Beth.

'Oh, love, it's a tricky time for you all. But surely

this is a weight off your shoulders. Things can only get better, can't they?' Neena put her arm around Beth and gave her an encouraging squeeze.

'Can they? I don't know about that.'

Chapter Seventeen

Myrtle needn't have worried about Austin being buried in the rain. The funeral had taken place on a cold, dry, cloudy day and he had been cremated.

The arrangements had been made without Myrtle's knowledge. Geoffrey had phoned her on the same day as the funeral director, who had been appointed by Austin. Both calls were simply to inform Myrtle of arrangements that had been made by Mrs Gillian Lloyd. The funeral director needed Myrtle, as next of kin, to confirm and approve that the preparations were acceptable.

Myrtle had understood that she was powerless to approve anything. She felt unworthy, if not incapable, of organizing or sanctioning something as profound as the funeral of a man of such relevance and stature.

Beth, on the other hand, was furious with her sister for marshalling such a significant event, *their* father's funeral, without consulting her or allowing her any input whatsoever. She was seething – and confused by her sister's lack of communication. She had no other choice but to take it personally. She would have gone on the offensive if only Gillian had made herself available – but she had not. Instead, she had effectively gone underground in some covert operation, which had infuriated Beth.

Four days had passed since Myrtle had spoken to her elder daughter – five, including today, the day of the funeral.

Geoffrey came to pick her and Beth up. Gillian sat in the front refusing even to look at her mother.

Beth could not find it in herself to put aside the immeasurable anger she felt towards her sister – even for this day, although she was civil to her brother-in-law.

'All right, Geoff?' Beth leaned forward to kiss him as he opened the car door for her. Out of earshot of the others, she said, 'Listen, thanks so much for picking us up. Good to know that *someone* in the family understands the meaning of inclusion . . .'

'Oh, I'm glad to be of some help. You know how it is . . .' He grinned, then whispered, 'It's like walking a tightrope at home. And you know my sense of balance . . .'

'Hmm, I guess Gillian wins first prize for suffering the most,' she replied.

It was a small, insignificant gathering at the crematorium – Myrtle, her daughters, their partners, a couple of former colleagues of Austin – Myrtle was unsure if she remembered them – Austin's bank manager and his wife, who had become acquaintances of sorts. Myrtle's sister, Wren, had expressed her sincere condolences over the telephone and sent a wreath from

West Africa, where she was tirelessly spreading the word of Jesus.

Mr Lovell, of Austin's old firm, had taken it upon himself to say a few words about his former boss, describing him as 'measured, hard-working, profound and disciplined' in a somewhat emotionless voice. As he returned to his seat, music started up: '*I will not cease from mental fight, Nor shall my sword sleep in my hand . . .*' crackled through tinny speakers in the small chapel and Myrtle thought how appropriate 'Jerusalem' was for Austin, who had remained so loyal to England's green and pleasant land to the very end. The words made her heart swell and her eyes burn but she shed no tears – not even when the coffin was wheeled across rollers through the heavily woven brown curtains into its pit of fire. She could not think of anything other than her daughters.

She comforted Beth, who steadfastly refused to let go of her mother's hand throughout the service – indeed, throughout the day – but she constantly found herself one person away from Gillian, who repudiated her with something more than disdain. Myrtle wondered how Gillian managed, in such a confined space, with such a small number of people present, on such a significant day, to avoid her so successfully. But shame, embarrassment and fear stopped Myrtle making the first move.

After the short service, Beth had been determined to stay with her mother but Myrtle insisted she was fine to be on her own. In fact, she wanted to be alone – after all, she might as well get used to it. Beth reluctantly left her – after venting a tirade of anger about her sister. 'What *is* it about her and always having to be in control, take control or assume a God-given right to do everything *her* way? I know she's older and I know she was the real daddy's girl – I know all that. Christ! But why does she have to remind me – today of all days – by blanking me like that? It was like she couldn't even bear to speak to me!' she shouted, pacing the living room, arms gesticulating.

When she eventually ran out of steam, her anger was replaced with several open-ended questions about her father, punctuated by the occasional long, steady silence.

Chapter Eighteen

Despair. Everything seemed hopeless.

When she had first opened her eyes that morning, for the very briefest moment everything had felt as it should. Then, like a giant truck smashing into her, it had all come back to her with shocking speed.

Austin had been burned to ashes. There was still no word from Gillian – and Beth regretted her relationship with her father almost as much as Myrtle did.

She closed her eyes and surrendered to the bleakness of it all.

Alone again.

Myrtle wondered how many times over the past few days she had picked up the telephone, dialled Gillian's number and put the receiver down before it even rang out . . . Half a dozen, perhaps?

The loneliness that had been her enemy for so many years but which she had gradually learned to befriend was now on the offensive again. When Gillian had arrived, wailing, and inflicted on her mother immeasurable pain, Myrtle had felt as if she had reached her nadir.

The loneliness had started all those years ago when she had paced the floors of Austin's mother's house, agitated and unnerved by her confinement, waiting, at only seventeen, for the arrival of a child – a child that would only ever be hers.

Her inability even to cook her husband's supper had added to her sense of uselessness. As time had passed, her diminishing self-confidence had left her speechless. With only the company of an obtuse, disorientated mother-in-law, and unvisited by her own family, who felt she was best left to get on with things, Myrtle had become desolate and depressed.

Then, being alone with a baby had exacerbated her despair. Unable to communicate it, she had piled her black moods on to wretchedness and despondency until she had gone to bed in the hope that there would be no morning. In the park, where Myrtle would push the pram aimlessly, she had met another woman pushing a pram with equal detachment. She had dark skin, brown eyes and black hair – Myrtle presumed she came from India. She was dressed in swathes of material and much of her face was also covered. Reluctant smiles and nods had, over time, given way to an exchange of simple words, which indicated to Myrtle that the stranger felt equally lost in her surroundings and just as alienated by motherhood.

It had become clear that the woman spoke little English but her presence affirmed that Myrtle was not alone in her situation. Despite the limited communication between them, Myrtle became reliant on her new, reserved, voiceless friend.

She wondered about the woman's life – had she too

been subjected to a marriage arranged by others, a convenient solution to unwanted emotions, a union that smoothed over uncomfortable cracks? Was she, too, trapped in a soulless relationship, forced to play the role of loving wife to a man she neither knew nor liked and had grown quietly to despise? She wondered if loving her child had come naturally to her and whether it was more responsive than Myrtle's.

She had never mentioned anything about her acquaintance in the park. First, when Austin came home he never asked about her day: instead he merely enquired how 'the baby' was – as if he couldn't even bring himself to mention Gillian's name. Second, she knew he disapproved of people with dark skin. He was a stifled racist. 'Fancy sending an Indian around to mend the television!' he exclaimed, under his breath, to Myrtle when the Asian man had turned up with a smiling face and broken English. 'What do *they* know about televisions?' Myrtle hadn't known how to answer him. She didn't understand his objection, especially in light of the fact that the 'darkie' had so speedily succeeded in mending the fault.

In many respects this had fuelled Myrtle's friendship with the woman in the park. It was a very little something she had away and apart from Austin – something clandestine – and that alone gave her some small satisfaction.

But Myrtle's days continued to be filled with the silent maintenance of a screaming newborn baby who lost weight with every day she continued to refuse her mother's breast. Myrtle couldn't help but take the rejection personally. She felt to blame, but her over-bearing feeling was of guilt – guilt that she was not even capable of nourishing her child, which appeared to come so naturally to other mothers. Austin, too, had shown dismay at Myrtle's failure.

'For goodness' sake, what's with all the moping around? Pull yourself together, woman. You're making such a meal out of the whole affair. Why can't you just get on with it?'

All this compounded Myrtle's conviction that not only was she a useless mother but, more importantly, she must try much, much harder to succeed.

She had wept silently with relief and gratitude when a locum midwife had patted her shoulder and recommended she fed the baby with bottles. From that day forth, baby Gillian had thrived and within three weeks was as fat as a cherub.

'Myrtle, it's Geoff,' he said, even before the receiver had reached Myrtle's ear.

'Geoffrey!' Myrtle's heart raced and she grasped the telephone with both hands.

'How are you, Myrtle? I've been meaning to call,' he asked, in his honest, languid tone.

'How's Gillian?' came Myrtle's immediate response.

'Well, she's not in a good place right now. I guess you two have some things to – to talk about.' He had been on the verge of saying that Myrtle had some 'explaining to do' but felt it would have been a bit harsh and a tad unfair, bearing in mind his wife's fly-off-the-handle reaction to so many things and that he himself was still pretty much in the dark about the exact circumstances. 'Look, I'm just calling because I wanted to check how you were and also to ask if you still wanted to have Molly on Saturday – like you nor-mally do. I mean, there's no need for her to get caught up in all this, is there?'

'Oh, Geoffrey, that would be lovely. I've been trying to get hold of Gillian but I can't seem to get through,' she lied.

'Things are a bit tricky at the moment. I think there has been rather a lot to take in – what with Austin's funeral and now *this* . . .'

Who would have thought such a small word could cover so much? thought Myrtle.

'If you need any help at all – you know with any-thing practical – just you give me a call. You have my number, right?'

Myrtle looked down at the sideboard where Austin's meticulously filled-out address book remained and nodded. She thanked Geoffrey for taking the trouble to call and hoped, to herself, that by the time Saturday came, there might have been a change in Gillian or that at the very least Myrtle might be spared a few moments to explain herself.

*

There was a knock at the front door.

Myrtle hesitated. She wanted to be left alone.

Unwillingly she made her way to the hall and looked through the uPVC glass panel but couldn't see anyone.

Reluctantly she opened it.

There was no one there.

Cautiously she put her head outside. Nothing. Embarrassed, she was about to shut the door when she looked down and saw a potted plant on the doorstep. On top of it lay a card. Myrtle looked around, bent down and picked up the plant. Inside the house, she opened the card:

> *Thought you might like this auricula: small but impressive and quite underrated, if you ask me. Lovely flowers March time. Hope you're feeling better. From one plant lover to another, Gianni*

Gianni?

The man in shorts and big boots.

Myrtle examined the terracotta pot and went through to the kitchen where she put it down. She rested the card against it, wandered into the sitting room, turned on the TV and positioned herself comfortably on the sofa.

Two men were driving cars, dressed in what Austin would have referred to as 'scruffy get-up'; they were laughing and joking, the wind blowing their messy hair. They whooped with the thrill of jumping up and down along bumpy roads.

Myrtle switched over.

A woman was weeping about her waistline and sobbing over pictures of her former self.

'It's all right, darling, let it all out, my love. Age changes things . . . But, you know, I'm just going to measure your hips and then Genevieve will take you off and give you a little make-over, darling. Does that sound OK? Who knows? Maybe you'll come back blonde and then you really *will* have more fun!' said the slim blonde woman, as she passed the plump, crying one to someone else.

Myrtle eventually settled for the man with the weathered face, who was bent over a herbaceous border, talking about the virtues of early planting and the need for aerating the lawn in spring if it hadn't already been done.

Saturday came and Geoffrey turned up with a bright and beautiful Molly accompanied by her cuddly bear, Lucky, clasped firmly in her hand. There was no sign of Gillian.

'I'll pick her up at four,' said Geoffrey, and leaned forward to give Myrtle a kiss on the cheek.

Molly wasted no time. She walked inside and dropped Lucky on the floor. 'Daddy says Grampy's gone to heaven.' She sighed and stared her grandmother in the eye.

Myrtle was caught on the hop. She looked at Molly's sad face and felt compromised: she didn't know what Gillian had told her exactly. 'Yes, that's right, dear,' she replied, wondering what was coming next.

'But why did he? He didn't even tell me he was going and now we won't be able to read the story about the very angry crocodile together. How long will he be, Granny?' she enquired, with an innocence that Myrtle was loath to dispel.

'Oh dear. My darling Molly, I don't think he's coming back . . .' She knelt down.

'But *why* did he go? He didn't even tell anyone he was going. Mummy says I mustn't go anywhere without telling her. I think it was very naughty and when he comes back, Granny, you must be sure to give him a "consequence",' she said, bringing a lump to her grandmother's throat. Then she ran into the sitting room where the small box of toys and the books were stacked neatly for her visits.

Consequences, thought Myrtle. *There's no shortage of those at the moment.*

Over a fish fingers and peas lunch, Molly took it upon herself to run through the advantages and disadvantages of eating vegetables, and Myrtle was sure she could hear Gillian's voice coming through loud and clear.

'Hannah at school says that if you eat too many carrots it will turn your hair ginger. But Mummy says that carrots make you see in the dark because they're full of vitamin see. I like carrots. Do you, Granny?'

'I do, Molly. But I've always been rather more keen on spinach.'

'Like Popeye, Granny? My, oh, my, you must be very, very strong, Granny. I bet you could lift two watermelons with your bare hands . . .' she said, her eyes as big as saucers.

'Oh, golly, I don't know about that.'

Molly took great pride in showing off her reading, completed a floor jigsaw of the human body, and turned to play with a couple of dolls she took out of her toy box.

She looked at one of the dolls, with long blonde hair, slender legs and a short floral skirt, and turned to her grandmother. 'Granny, you're not much of a party girl, are you?'

'I'm not?'

'Well, you never wear pretty dresses, do you?'

Myrtle thought for a moment. Molly was right on both counts, of course. Myrtle had been afforded neither the time to be a party girl nor the luxury of pretty dresses. 'Well, why don't we see if we can do something about that right now?' She led the way upstairs into her bedroom and opened her wardrobe.

Molly and Myrtle were met with a drab display of largely dark colours with a rare and occasional break of beige. Underneath the cheerless, dejected and dreary garments a sober, ordered row of black and navy shoes stood to attention.

'Oh, Granny!' exclaimed Molly. 'There's no hope! You haven't even got a pink top!'

Myrtle gave way to a smile. There was, indeed, little hope in her wardrobe – or anywhere else for that matter.

'Well, Molly, right at the back here I've got a very special little box which I've never shown you but I think it's just perfect for today,' she said, as she reached into the very depths of the doomed, dismal wardrobe and brought out a large, navy velvet box.

'Gosh, Granny, what have you got in there?' Molly was fascinated.

'This, Molly, is my box in which I have kept some things from a very long time ago – before you were even born – and I think you might like them,' said Myrtle, opening it slowly. 'Shall we have a look?'

'Oh, Granny, I never knew you had a secret box. What's this?' she said, digging her fingers right to the bottom to pull out a book covered with decoupage.

Myrtle took a sharp breath. 'That's Granny's diary. Well, it was Granny's diary when she was a young girl.'

'A diary?' shrieked Molly, with delight, immediately opening it. 'What lovely writing you have, Grandma!' She didn't hesitate to leaf through it. 'Oh, Granny, is it all about your friends – the friends you had?'

Myrtle stroked her hair and nodded. 'I've also got one or two necklaces in here you might like.' She was trying to distract the little girl.

Molly held on to the diary as Myrtle unpicked chains, a couple of bracelets and some earrings.

'This necklace here, Molly, was given to me by your great-grandpa – my father – shortly after I married Grampy and I would like very much for you to have it,' she said, handing over a thin gold chain with a little heart dangling from it. 'It's very special to me and *you* are very special to me, too.' She hung it mid-air for inspection and admiration, in the hope that Molly might loosen her grip on the diary.

'That *is* beautiful, Granny. Thank you!' She threw her arms around her grandmother and the diary fell to the floor. 'I'm going to save it for special occasions. I really love it!' she piped.

Then, with an air of seriousness, she asked, 'May I try on some of your shoes, too, Granny? The ones with the little tiny heels and the buckle on the front?'

Myrtle wondered why she hadn't thought of showing her granddaughter the wardrobe on previous occasions, but she hadn't wanted to bring out the box before.

Right at that moment Myrtle longed to be five again so that she might not make quite such a mess of her life. How would Molly's unfold? She could only hope she wouldn't end up as reluctant a participant in life as her granny had.

Geoffrey picked Molly up as arranged at four o'clock, and Molly held the precious necklace tightly in her left hand. She sprinkled fairy dust over her grandmother with the right, in the hope that it might help her sleep better or turn her into more of a party girl. And then she was gone.

Chapter Nineteen

Dorothy felt obliged. At the same time, she had to admit to herself that she wanted to show off a little, too. But most of all she wanted to send a rocket up that dreary woman's behind to ensure she snapped out of her dull comfort zone and spiced up her life. You could tell a mile off, thought Dorothy, that she had led a miserable life – her face said as much. She'd been disabled by restrictions and a highly unappealing lack of confidence. She needed liberating – urgently.

Dorothy wasn't up to dealing with this in a one-to-one and decided, therefore, to kill two birds with one stone and lose the sad, pathetic little widow in her mêlée of friends, thereby giving her a perfectly rude awakening *and* doing the neighbourly thing.

Warning her neighbour would only scare her off and give her time to think up excuses so Dorothy made sure she had as little notice as possible: she telephoned her only half an hour beforehand to invite her around that same Saturday night. In the end, as she had expected, she had been forced to go next door and march Myrtle to her house. It was an event her friends referred to as the Cheese and Whine Party and it never failed to disappoint.

As they passed the caravan parked in the drive, Dorothy said, 'So, you won't really have much need for this *thing* any more, will you? I'm sure you'll get a good price for it. I can help you sell it, if you like.' She linked arms with Myrtle in a conciliatory fashion, to reassure her that she was doing the right thing by her.

Before they reached Dorothy's front door, Myrtle could hear women's voices and a constant hum, spiked with the occasional guttural laughter swiftly followed by a raised voice here and there. She was sure she could smell smoke. Her stomach turned. She wanted to go straight back home. She wasn't ready for this. She wasn't ready for new faces and new people; she wasn't ready for people who were so firmly someone else's friends.

But Dorothy's vice-like grip was not about to ease and she guided Myrtle inside with a gentle shove.

'What on earth are you doing?' Dorothy exclaimed, as Myrtle bent over in the hallway. 'Good God, woman! You don't need to take your shoes off in this house!' She leaned towards Myrtle. 'You need all the height you can get, my love. Keep them on so we don't lose you in the crowd.'

Myrtle felt embarrassed and promptly did as she was told. Dorothy disappeared into a room to the left where she was greeted by the women.

Myrtle stood rooted to the spot.

'Come on! Come on!' Dorothy called, gesturing force-fully with her hand. 'Ladies, I've brought you a gift,'

Myrtle heard her announce. It was met with a whoop of delight, a few seconds of chat and then a silence.

Myrtle was incapable of moving. Dorothy came out of the room. 'For goodness' sake, woman. Now's not the time to be backward in coming forward.' She waved frantically. 'What are you doing standing there?' She grabbed Myrtle by the shoulders from behind and pushed her towards the voices and the smoke. 'There's nothing to be afraid of. They don't bite. Well, Vivienne might – but it'll only be a nibble . . .' She nudged her into the room. 'Ladies, ladies! We have a new friend – a new member of our sisterhood, a surprise contribution to our little *soirée*. This plain, faded, lank little creature is Myrtle Lewis from next door. She's in dire need of attention. She's recently been widowed so go gently on her, girls. Please!'

Myrtle saw three women sharing the sofa facing her. Out of the corner of her eye to the right, she saw another sitting on a *chaise longue*. Her eyes ran quickly from side to side across a group of women planted irregularly in the sitting room.

Dorothy turned to her. 'Now, Myrtle,' she said loudly, 'these are my very good friends – and if you're lucky, they'll be yours, too. Now, what's your poison?'

Myrtle just stood staring.

'What's your tipple?' Dorothy urged, poking her with her elbow.

'Er,' said Myrtle. 'I'll just have some tea, if it's not too much trouble.'

'Nonsense! It's wine or a cocktail – I'll compromise at sherry, though in the circumstances it seems pretty desperate. Sherry is, after all, for grey ladies who get the same sensation from a rocking chair as they used to from a rollercoaster. So, I'll accept nothing less,' Dorothy announced forcefully, as she exited the room.

Myrtle – rigid, speechless – stood rooted to the spot.

'My dear, sit down,' said the woman on the *chaise longue*, patting the seat next to her gently. Her hair, Myrtle noticed, was well styled – cropped short at the nape of her neck, with soft, blonde-grey waves on top. She had large, pleasant, welcoming blue eyes and a friendly mouth framing yellowing teeth.

'Oh, but I shan't be staying, I must get back to –'

'Back to what, dear?' the woman interrupted, continuing to pat the seat. 'Seems to me you've suffered a great loss and could well do with some company and support. Sit down next to me. We can get to know each other. Take no notice of Dorothy – she doesn't mean any harm.' She smiled. Myrtle smiled back, defeated.

Dorothy marched in with a small glass in her hand. 'Nothing is more telling of age than a grey raincoat, dull shoes or a glass of sherry. You really should try something . . . younger.' She placed the drink on the table directly in front of Myrtle. 'Now, then, no need for formal introductions but over there is Margaret,' she said, pointing at a dark-haired woman perched on the edge of the sofa, wearing a bright pink twin-set, pearls and a navy skirt. Margaret exposed a short, sharp smile after which she turned away and looked with greater interest out of the window.

Dorothy nodded in Margaret's direction. 'We call her "Mad Margaret" because she quite, quite lost the plot when she discovered – *in flagrante delicto*, I might add – that her beloved Arthur had, with unbearable predictability, exchanged her for a younger model. So, in return, she thought it only fair to cut a small hole in all his suits, scatter prawn shells under the driver's seat of his car and give his credit card a good airing before packing his bags and chucking him out. She's not bitter,' Dorothy winked, 'just a bit slow on the uptake. She'll get there in the end, with the help of a nice settlement and a few decent bottles of wine along the way. Don't get even, hey, Margaret? Get everything!' She giggled.

Mad Margaret rolled her eyes to the ceiling.

'Next to her is our dearest Vivienne. She is one of a kind – one of the original libbers and a great believer in comfortable shoes, as you can see. If ever there was a feminist among us, it's our Viv. She may have turned her back on fitted clothes but she does run a tight ship in extremism, liberalism and speaking as she finds.'

Vivienne sat in the centre of the sofa smoking a thin cigar attached to the end of a long stick. Her hands were congested with large silver rings. She had long, straight jet-black hair that spiked on either side of her chest. She was draped in black clothes and her eyes were blackened with makeup. Her large, ornate earrings had, over time, elongated her lobes. She gazed back at Myrtle and, like Dorothy, winked.

'So you're finally free, then?' Vivienne observed. 'Released from the shackles of marriage, liberated by death and ready to join the rest of us in the twenty-first century . . .' She raised her eyebrows as if to provoke a response.

'Viv, please!' exclaimed the woman next to Myrtle. 'The poor girl has just been widowed – her husband has just died. Don't talk like that! It's disrespectful and inappropriate. Give her a chance.'

Myrtle blushed.

The woman at her side patted her hand reassuringly and smiled as if to apologize. Myrtle reciprocated. She couldn't deny this was rather exciting.

Dorothy carried on: 'Next to Viv is Daft Deirdre.' She lowered her voice. 'Bless her. She's one token short of a pop-up toaster – she's only sixty-three but already she's trapped in the viper's nest of dementia. God bless her.'

The woman with grey hair cut into a smart bob had slanted, withering eyes and a bright shade of pink on her lips. 'The secret to happiness is a bad memory, I've been told.' She smiled.

'I see you've met Marjorie.' Dorothy waved towards the woman beside Myrtle. 'She's one of my nearest and dearest friends. She, like you, chose a life restricted by immanence. She has been doomed by the confirmation of her existence through marriage for some forty years now. Isn't that right, Marj? Though, if you ask her, she'll tell you she has the love of a good man and will insist, outwardly at least, on sitting contentedly within the confines of her suburban house and middle-class friends – but really, I believe, she's sexually frustrated and partially, at least, regretful.'

'Oh, stop it, Dorothy! Don't take any notice, Myrtle. She always sets out to shock. Take it as a compliment – it means she likes you.' Marjorie touched Myrtle's hand. She chuckled quietly to herself.

Vivienne, whose cigar smoke was clouding the room, turned her attention to Myrtle again but without looking at her this time. 'You're a blank canvas. No sign of war-paint on your face. Good for you. It's a slippery slope, you know, avoidance of the gratification of time, and before you know it you'll be injecting yourself with poison in some sad, degrading and dangerous attempt at staying young. It's a sign of desperation – the downfall of the modern woman. It only serves to prolong your dying youth. Look at me, and take delight in the fact that you'll know you're getting older when fortune-tellers offer to read your face . . .' She winked again.

Myrtle wasn't sure where to look.

'Ahem!' Dorothy cleared her throat. 'There's nothing wrong with a bit of colour on your cheeks. You could do with some brightening up, Myrtle. Have you considered blusher – accentuating your cheekbones, for example? Even a bit of mascara on those enviable lashes of yours would work a treat.' Then she whispered behind a hand, 'Vivienne may profess to come from the de Beauvoir school of thought and have you believe we're all morbidly trapped in some cycle of self-mutilation but even her eyes are darkened with kohl.'

'I heard that!' sniped Vivienne. 'Besides, it's not the school of de Beauvoir, more the *church* . . . Feminism, sister, is my religion. You religious, Myrtle?' She took a slow, seductive drag of her thin cigar.

Myrtle looked around the room unsure where to direct her attention. She wanted to reply but she didn't know what to say.

'Well, yes – I mean, we do go to church occasionally . . .' Awkwardness enveloped her, like the leaves of a giant triffid, and she wanted to disappear into the floor. She was not well rehearsed in social situations and certainly not without Austin by her side. Should she have stayed quiet and maintained a shred of dignity?

Deirdre shot up from her seat, clasping her hips. 'Oh, this arthritis is killing me! Give me strength. I don't care what Dr Flaming-Feelgood says, those glucosamine-whatsit supplements are doing nothing for my hips. At this rate I'll be going up to bed in one of those geriatric stair-lifts. It doesn't bear thinking about.'

'You really ought to give HRT a go, dear. It's worked wonders with me,' suggested Mad Margaret.

'Not a chance!' interrupted Vivienne, perching on the edge of her seat. 'HRT is nothing more than the pharmaceutical manipulation of women and you should just accept that arthritis is the price you pay for having children. You only have yourself to blame for insisting on perpetuating the species and exploiting your fecundity to the extreme.'

'Ladies, please.' Marjorie clapped her hands. 'I have to say, I've never quite been the same since my hysterectomy . . .' Myrtle blushed ' . . . and I was left with very little choice. I don't feel my joints or my energy levels have ever recovered, and to be quite frank,' she lowered her voice, 'without my womb, I feel half the woman I used to be.'

Myrtle thought she might burst with discomfort.

'Well, all the more fool you for allowing the medical profession loose on you! Nature should be allowed to take its course. I, for one, do not believe in the mutilation of women as standard practice,' interjected Vivienne, loudly.

'Oh, nonsense!' Dorothy got up and did a little jig in the middle of the floor with an imaginary partner. 'A few salsa classes of an evening is what *you* really need, Deirdre. That'll do the trick . . . They'll loosen you up a bit! But you'd do well to remember that the dance floor can be a very dangerous place.' She arched her eyebrows provocatively and danced off into the kitchen.

Marjorie turned to Myrtle. 'Personally, I don't necessarily think Deirdre's looking for male company and,' she shot a glance at Vivienne, 'at least *I* go to bed at night with the man I love.'

'Poppycock,' said Dorothy, dancing back into the room with a glass in her hand. 'There's no such thing. In my experience men cannot resist temptation and to that end it's best to be shrewd with your investments. Remember, mirror, signal and manoeuvre. Look in the mirror, send out your signal across the dance floor and then make your manoeuvre!'

Mad Margaret nodded, in partial agreement. 'I have to confess I don't want to be alone for the rest of my life and maybe life with a wayward Arthur is, after all, better than a life alone with my electric blanket and a copy of the *TV Times*.'

Myrtle thought of her bed, how empty it now was, and she admitted, to herself at least, that Margaret was a woman after her own heart.

'You really need to broaden your mind *and* your sexual fantasies,' Vivienne complained. 'Try Nancy Friday. It will certainly change the way you look at Arthur. And it might even change the way he views you!' She laughed.

'Oh, not another conversation about that blasted G-spot!' exclaimed Margaret, rolling her eyes. 'I can't bear the humiliation of trying to look for it any longer – I'm too old and it hurts my neck in the bath when I try to look further south than my belly button.'

'I can't believe that at your age you haven't got to know your body better. Fundamentally you do *not* need a man to reach an orgasm,' shouted Vivienne. 'I certainly never have. It's time you took control and set yourself free, Margaret.'

Myrtle had never blushed so much in her life. She didn't know where to look but settled for the window. She smiled to herself – there was an air of excitement about it all. She had never before been part of a conversation like this one, and there was something complicit about being there . . .

Marjorie nudged her gently, interrupting her thoughts, to ask if she had any children.

'Two daughters,' Myrtle said.

'How wonderful,' rejoined Marjorie. 'They must be a great comfort to you at a time like this. There's something very special about a mother–daughter relationship.'

Myrtle was doubtful but she nodded because she liked Marjorie. She had warmth about her, which, during such a lively, exciting conversation, Myrtle found soothing. She was grateful that the woman had taken her away from the other subjects.

Myrtle stayed a little while. She couldn't deny she wanted to stay longer but these weren't her friends and she felt obliged to go home. She mumbled some excuse about a casserole when she knew there was no such thing – she didn't even have an appetite, let alone anyone to cook for.

Dorothy protested, claiming there was still so much to talk about. But Marjorie asked Dorothy to let Myrtle be and escorted her to the front door, leaning forward to kiss her cheek.

'You girls really have no shame,' Marjorie said sternly to her group of friends. 'That poor, poor woman – you were like vultures on a bare carcass! There was nothing there to feed on. She's only just a widow, for goodness' sake.'

Dorothy sidled up to her, glass in hand, bent over and whispered, 'She's not a widow, darling, she's a project!' then danced back into the kitchen.

Myrtle was grateful for the time she had spent at her neighbour's – it had killed a few hours and had actually been, rather unexpectedly, a daring delight. She smiled as she put the key in the front door, took off her shoes and walked into a cold and murky hall, neither lights nor heating making the house a home. Silence. All she could hear in her head were the voices from her visit next door. She felt a headache coming on and she could still smell smoke on her clothes. The thought of opening the door to the bare fridge was not something she relished.

She passed the potted auricula, which stood neatly and sweetly next to the potted primula on the sideboard. It needed to be planted out, but she would postpone that until she was ready to face her garden again.

In the bedroom, she saw Austin's reading glasses on the bedside table, untouched and unworn since the night before his death. His book – science-fiction, she deduced from the cover – lay closed and undisturbed.

Myrtle didn't undress. Austin would have been in utter disbelief – the idea of not changing from day into night clothes and back again would have horrified him. Instead, she just lay down on her side of the bed with snippets of the women's conversation whizzing through her head, like a swarm of mosquitoes. Myrtle closed her eyes.

On reflection, the evening had been as much a disappointment as it had been enjoyable. She wished she hadn't been so ill-equipped to join in the conversation and contribute – she smarted at her lack of courage. She was left feeling vulnerable, exposed and a tad inadequate. But, above all, she had felt lonely. All the while she had sat in Dorothy's front room she had been a spectator, on the periphery of a warm, close social gathering; she had had nothing much to share with anyone or anything. She had so desperately wanted to join in, to have an opinion – not be so vague, so hazy and bewildered. It was hard to fight off retrospective humiliation. She wondered what they had made of her . . .

Her heart raced and her breath shortened. She reached her left hand across her body between the bed and the bedside table and flicked the switch on the electric blanket.

'Now, you must use this prudently. It's not for everyday use but only for the very coldest of nights,' Austin had said, as she unravelled the blanket and its cord from the wrapping at Christmas fourteen years ago. Myrtle felt cold and shivery and she consoled herself with the thought that Austin would have been proud that, after all these years, it still did its job.

Chapter Twenty

Modern architecture should have suited Gillian. Characterized by its simplicity of form, its unfussy, minimalist approach, it was nothing if not straight to the point: all function and no frills. Gillian always approved of a no-nonsense approach and transparency. Now, sitting in her office, which was marked out by the sharp horizontal and vertical lines of glass encased in steel, she began to detest everyone's ability to look in on her through the windows. She fiddled distractedly with the paper clip in her right hand, passing it through her fingers over and over again. She had tried to read the document on the desk in front of her in at least half a dozen positions and with searching enthusiasm every time but the information had failed to sink in.

What was usually a buzzing office with plenty of unwanted activity and noise had, over the past two weeks, become a muted, restrained place, silenced by what Gillian considered to be over-indulgent, misplaced sympathy on the part of her colleagues.

Added to the hush of sympathy enveloping the office was a feeling that she was separated from the rest by a physical exclusion zone. Everyone, including her boss, appeared to tiptoe around her, as if fearing to say the wrong thing at such a sensitive time. The quiet was unnerving – it was as annoying and frustrating as it was bloody ill-timed. What she really wanted was noise and normality so that she could go on with life as usual. Why couldn't people just get on with things – like she did?

When she had lost her car keys, on the day she had lost her father, the ensuing hunt had led her to a cinema receipt for two in Geoffrey's coat pocket. Apart from the fact that it was for a ridiculously soppy comedy that she would *never* have gone to see, the point remained that he had taken someone else. And as the dust was beginning to settle around her again, the memory of those tickets was growing sharper.

There wasn't a huge cloud of doubt hanging over her in any way, shape or form – that was not why she found it so hard to concentrate on work. In fact, there was absolutely no doubt about it: he had been to an early-evening performance, mid-week, to see a film with someone who wasn't his wife. A woman, she had been sure.

When she had confronted him with the crumpled receipt, he had had the audacity to say that she wasn't thinking straight and that she was being 'highly emotional'. His insistence on trying to talk to her rationally had only served to fuel her rage.

'I can't believe the cheek of it – let alone the duplicity. How dare you hide behind the excuse that I'm in mourning and in shock and am therefore behaving *irrationally*?' she had shouted at the top of her voice. 'I am a woman! I am perfectly capable of dealing with more than one issue at a time, Geoff. Not only have you insulted my intelligence by your inappropriate – not to mention ungrateful – high jinks with some bloody woman but don't you think it's a bit of a coincidence that I should find you out at such a time, huh?'

She gave him no space to reply, and as her voice had nowhere else to go but down, she hissed at him, 'You're deliberately trying to topple me, to bring me down and show me up to prove that I'm not capable – that I can't have everything, a child *and* a career. It's nothing short of a conspiracy,' she had directed in his ear as she stalked out of the kitchen.

'There's no conspiracy, Gill – for goodness' sake! This has nothing to do with your ability to cope with work and Molly. Let's keep Molly out of this. In fact, let's keep work out of this, too.' Geoffrey couldn't resist raising his voice any longer.

'Well, you would say that, wouldn't you? Cover your tracks, lie, distract and cheat,' Gillian spat.

'I have not been unfaithful to you, Gill. And, in particular, I didn't cheat on you to prove you can't manage a healthy work–life balance – as the Tory press would put it.'

'Oh, so you do admit you cheated, then? It just happened to be for another reason! Well, I hope she was worth it – I hope *she* can give you everything you need.'

'I'm going to say this for the last time – I did not cheat. If you want to know the truth, I'll tell you.'

Gillian looked out of the window and was met by pitch black. All she saw was her own reflection.

'I went to the cinema with Francesca from work. It was nothing more, nothing less. I didn't meet up with the rugby lads for a drink after work. Instead I went to see a film. It was a comedy. I had popcorn and she had a 7-Up. That's all it was.'

Gillian turned her head. 'That was *all* it was? You laughed with another woman – and you say, "*That's all it was*," as if you bumped into each other at the corner shop? You chose to spend time with another woman and you say, "That's all it was." Have you taken leave of your senses?'

Geoffrey knew it was a question that required no answer but he wanted to answer her – he needed to.

'Yes, perhaps I have, Gill.' He turned away from her and walked up to the fireplace. 'Perhaps I needed some light relief.'

'*Light relief?* Lord, give me strength! From what? Is your life *that* hard? Is your life *that* unbearable that you see fit to engage in a leisure activity with another woman who, I might add, is not only younger than you and barely of childbearing age, but is doubtless impressionable and suggestible *and – and – and*, above all else, knows you're married? You think that's acceptable behaviour, Geoff?'

'Look, love, I didn't cheat. Nothing went on. I just

wanted to do something that didn't require handling with diplomacy and special tactics of manipulation or walking on eggshells or even having to think –'

'Well, you certainly didn't do that, did you?' interrupted Gillian.

'It's just that you and me – us – we don't seem to have much fun any more. In fact, we don't have *any* fun. Our life is a never-ending timetable and list of things to do, no mindless, hedonistic, senseless fun. We never relax together. Your life is weighed down by an overwhelming, overbearing sense of duty and you put that over on me, too. The times we *do* sit down together in the evening – which you know full well are as rare as rocking-horse shit –'

'Don't swear, Geoff!'

'– we end up watching some depressing programme about sick or dying children or some painfully dull documentary about scientific advances. Those are *your* choices, Gillian. Not mine! Whatever happened to the colourful, affectionate, happy, smiling, carefree Gillian Lewis I met, hey? I can count on one hand the number of times you've come up to give me a hug in the last couple of years. That's no way to live, Gill, that's just . . . existing.'

'Ah, so she gives you hugs, does she? Is that it?'

'No! You're not listening to what I'm saying. I don't know what happened to me – to us. I try to show you how much I love you but you reciprocate with a glance at your watch or a complete change of subject. I don't want to live like this any more. I can't. I'd always hoped Molly would bring us closer together. Instead, having a child has done nothing but drive a wedge between us and change beyond all recognition the people we once were.' He sighed in defeat.

'Don't you dare bring Molly into this!' Gillian shouted, reminding him of his earlier plea. 'Don't you dare hold her responsible for your illicit behaviour.'

'Look, what happened . . . it just happened . . .'

'Chicken pox happens, Geoff. Infidelity is considerably more Machiavellian!'

'I keep telling you – I wasn't unfaithful!'

'You were! Maybe not with the flesh but with the heart and mind – and that's far, far worse!' She glared at him.

'I give up, Gill. Once again, you're not listening to me. I don't know why I bother. You've turned yourself into an island – untouchable and unreachable.'

And with that last and most painful recrimination, he had walked out of the kitchen and left her with the person she understood the very least: herself.

With the paper clip still passing between her fingers, she convinced herself it was no coincidence that the object she was manipulating was supposed to hold things together. The sharp end of the clip pricked her finger. She winced and let it go. As it dropped on to her desk it looked disfigured and beyond recognition but, more poignantly, no longer capable of holding anything together.

Chapter Twenty-one

Myrtle had lost track of the days. One seemed awkwardly and painfully to succeed the next with neither focus nor direction. Before Austin's passing, the days had segued neatly and completely into each other. Now they blurred a pattern of miserable solitude, relentless pacing, nervousness and an anxiety she had not experienced for many, many years. Austin's birthday had even been forgotten – it had come and gone before she knew it.

She couldn't help but liken life as it now was to an unsettled and untreated case of dreadful indigestion – the kind that sits tense and hard in the solar plexus and makes you prone to light-headedness, shallow breathing and momentary confusion. She wasn't sure if it had been two or three weeks since Austin had died and the subsequent unexpected encounter with Gillian. In her head she had been able to count it only in days – not weeks.

This particular morning, she had been startled by sirens blaring. She had hurried out of bed and stumbled in a dazed state to the front of the house in time to hear the noise dissipate into the passing traffic. Looking out of Gillian's old room on to the gabled roof that hung over the sitting room she could still see the imprints on the black tiles of Austin's big, outdoor boots, which had so impressively and precariously walked across them as he had endeavoured to clear the guttering not long ago. When Myrtle had pleaded that she feared for him so high up – balancing on ladders and the roof – Austin had quite plainly rebuked her: 'Myrtle, for the umpteenth time, if a job's worth doing, it's worth doing properly. Furthermore, I'm doing this because no one else could possibly do it the way I want it done.' And with that she had been forced to let the matter lie.

A small panic enveloped Myrtle. What would she do if the roof leaked now? What if the plumbing stopped working? She didn't even know how to change a light-bulb. She had been restrained from doing so by a husband who always told her not to bother her 'little head with all things physical and practical'.

Myrtle pulled away from the window, slid down with her back against the radiator and, as the tears started, she put her head in her hands. She felt so utterly helpless – helpless and hopeless. She sobbed, gasping for breath until her jaw stiffened. Although her hands pressed hard on her eyes, the tears refused to stop. The increasing pain in her chest was making her head throb relentlessly.

The sound of footsteps approaching the front door drew her back to the window and she thought she could see the rough outline of someone passing beneath the porch. She rubbed her eyes, trying to eliminate any signs of pain and self-pity. Her nose was streaming. Whoever it was knocked. Myrtle wiped her nose on her sleeve and went to the door.

She kept the chain on as she slowly opened it, peering through the gap with one eye and her nose poking out into the chilly winter air.

'That's a cute little nose,' said an enthusiastic voice. 'I just thought I'd pop by to see how you were doin'. I work over at the garden centre and we've just had a delivery of these gorgeous big heathers and I wondered if a certain lady, who clearly loves her garden as much as I do, wouldn't like to have one.'

It was the man in shorts again.

She looked him up and down with considerable confusion.

'I know a green-fingered lady when I see one,' he continued. 'There's no flies on me, love. Just a glance at this front garden tells me you must be down on all fours every day or so . . .'

Myrtle continued to stare.

'I'm sorry,' said the man, pulling himself back a bit so Myrtle could see a large purple heather in his hand. 'I've surprised you too much. I shouldn't have come. It's not like you're short of surprises right now, is it?' He smiled in a conciliatory fashion. 'Look – no dramas, forget the whole thing. I'll take the heather back with me, and when you're feeling better, you can come and get one, choose your own colour. Blimey – I don't even know if you like purple . . .'

Myrtle felt embarrassed. It was, she had to admit, a lovely big heather but she was not in a fit state to be choosing colours, plants or greeting strangers. 'Thank you,' she uttered. 'Very thoughtful. Lovely plant.' What should follow? Was it customary to invite strangers in for a cup of tea? Should you keep them on the doorstep? Would it be too rude to ask them to leave? One thing was for sure, in her nightgown she was not really in a position to play host to this man.

'You're thinking, Shall I invite the mad bugger in for a cup of tea? Honestly, don't worry – I don't drink the stuff anyway. I just wanted an excuse to come by and see that you were all right. You looked like you were in a fair amount of shock when I saw you last. How's your daughter doing? All right?' he asked.

Myrtle's mind blurred.

'Don't you worry. I'm going to leave the heather right here,' he said, bending down and placing it on the step, 'and you just plant it out when you're ready. Unless, of course, you want me to do it? No.' He paused. 'Course you don't. The last thing you want is someone fussing up your front patch. It's the Aussie in me – I talk too much. Just tell me to shut up and go away!'

But at that moment, despite her early-morning shock, despite her nightgown and her tousled hair, she realized that there was something about the man she liked, and she didn't want him to go away. His kindness and generosity had been so unexpected – much as his visits were – and there was warmth in his face. He smiled, he joked, and she had given him nothing in return. He had spoken but she had not said much back. And the fact that he had complimented her garden had stirred something inside her.

'I'm sorry,' Myrtle forced out. 'I would invite you in but I'm not dressed yet. Thank you so much for your thoughtfulness. It's a lovely heather. I shall be sure to plant it near my ornamental cabbages . . . And thank you so much again.'

'That's all right! You get stuck into your garden. I'll pop by again in a couple of days and see how you're getting on. You must think I'm an annoying old fart. Anyway, you take care and give my best to your daughter, won't you?' He winked and was on his way, leaving Myrtle's nose poking out between the door and the chain.

Gianni had seen tears in her eyes. She had been crying. He didn't like to leave her like that.

Myrtle closed the door and pressed her back to it. She smiled to herself. No sooner had she regained her composure than the phone rang. Like a cat on a hot tin roof, she jumped.

She picked it up.

'Hello, Mrs Lewis,' said the voice. 'It's Mr Pegg from the bank. Is this a good time?'

*

259

Beth sat with her back firmly against the arm of the sofa, one leg bent and the other crossed over it. She was chewing gum – which she rarely did, perhaps only when she was really restless. She wound a piece of the gum around her finger and stretched it as far away from her mouth as she could before it broke off and fell limply in slow motion on to the inside of her forearm.

She had hoped that telling her mum about the plans she had with Neena would take a weight off her shoulders, that she would feel lighter in herself, freer, and that life would be more lucid, more defined. She had to acknowledge that, in the circumstances, this had perhaps been more than a tad optimistic. She had to confess to a little something inside her that was still eating away at her – the burning sensation. It reminded her that she had failed to make the statement while her father was still alive. The embers of the fire of failure and inadequacy, not to mention cowardice, were still burning somewhere in her heart. Now she felt that the path should have been clear for her to make a life for herself and Neena that was no longer conscience-stricken or besieged by her inner voice recalling the unresolved issues with her father. But it wasn't. She had tried so hard to feel buoyed by the prospect of living with Neena but even the commission of a new work for a private client had done nothing to lift her spirits or fill her with confidence.

Perhaps it didn't help that the weather was so damn bleak and that the heavens appeared to be mourning the death of her father even more than she was. The fact that it had now rained pretty much non-stop for at least three and a half weeks put more than a dampener on her potential new-found happiness.

It had been a struggle to display enthusiasm and excitement in the presence of Neena and this worried her because it was with Neena that she had always felt most natural. 'Could you, *please*, not put that huge box there?' Beth had sighed exaggeratedly. 'My God, you have so much *stuff* . . . So many little ornaments and things without, well, function,' she had found herself saying, without pausing to edit her irritability.

'OK, hon. I was just putting it down there because there didn't seem to be anywhere else,' Neena had replied, smiling and moving towards Beth to express her contentment and understanding in the form of a stroke of the cheek.

Beth had ducked and walked past her. 'Exactly. There isn't much space, so it would be great if we could just be smart about what we have and where we have it,' she had growled. She couldn't quite believe what she was saying, especially as normally she thrived on relaxed, unordered surroundings. She had felt increasingly aggravated by her own irritation.

Neena, of course, had shown nothing but understanding. Beth had just lost her father and she needed time to mourn. She reassured her constantly with smiles, kisses planted softly on her temple. She had even gone as far as scrambling together a thick, hearty *rasam* soup mid-week when she was usually home late. She had left work at a reasonable time and stopped off to get what she needed at the shops, then set about cooking when, Beth knew, she had better things to do. The warm, fragrant smell had almost seduced her – had she not remembered what a mess Neena had left in the kitchen.

On the four occasions Beth had called Gillian, her attempts had been met by a highly irritated voice: 'It's Gillian . . . obviously . . . Well, I guess you should leave a message . . . if you must.'

It was so definitely Gillian – so very her – and it had initially been a relief that Beth had been redirected to a voicemail without having to speak to someone so irascible. However, by the fifth time she had tried, she had been close to throwing her phone against the wall. Part of her – the part that knew her sister so well – had reminded her that Gillian had never been very emotionally accessible and that perhaps this was just her way of dealing with things. But most of her felt that it was not only rude of Gillian to ignore her but downright selfish. This was a time when sisters should be able to reach out to each other. But since the funeral, Beth had been met by this persistent wall of silence and she was left feeling as if Gillian had taken all the grief and mourning and ring-fenced it for herself. It was as if she was assuming a greater right to their father.

It wasn't because she wanted to be more like Gillian

or fit in with her dad that Beth envied her sister's relationship with him but because she didn't understand why she had never had the credentials to join their exclusive members-only club. She felt it wasn't natural to be so disconnected from her father, and wondered whether she would have segued more easily into a functional relationship with him if her mother hadn't waited so long to have her. There had been times in the past when her days had been dark and gloomy and she had wished for a happier accord with her father. She had sometimes wondered if she had been a complete mistake altogether. Perhaps her parents had planned to have only one child – the perfect, bright, beautiful daughter, without complications and awkwardness – until, unexpectedly, another had come along all those years later and spoilt the whole picture.

Beth had tried to banish these thoughts because they were pure speculation on her part, although at times it had seemed like a very probable scenario. She hadn't bothered asking her mother about it, first because she couldn't imagine *any* mother in the world giving her daughter a straight answer to such a question, but most of all because she would never want to upset her. It was hard enough to get angry with her for not standing up to Beth's father, let alone try to shatter the frail core of a woman who had been such a loyal wife, obliging mother and didn't have a bad bone in her body.

But, of course, her mother had got caught up in the crossfire between her and her father. It had been unavoidable. And it had been such a struggle for Beth to try to hurt and provoke her father – to get his attention – without upsetting her mother, who stood on the sidelines pleading with them to keep their voices down.

Beth understood her mother's need to keep the peace but there had been moments when she had lost respect for her completely and perhaps, on reflection, irrationally. When Beth had failed so miserably at maths and declared to her father that she wanted to go to art college, he had looked at her with the most uncompromising disappointment – the kind that had told her that with every fibre of her being she had failed him, that he had hoped for better.

'You cannot be serious. Art college? What kind of fancy idea is that? That's what people who want to *play* at life do – not those who take life seriously. How on earth do you think you'll ever make a living by doodling and scrawling with crayons on a piece of paper? You need proper qualifications, young lady, ones that mean something to employers – something meaningful . . .' His voice had trailed off, as if he were giving up.

His expectations had not only been dashed but his face had spelled out his sheer hopelessness. His 'something meaningful' was so clearly the very opposite of all she represented to him. It was this comment that had stabbed her heart and had continued to do so for years. She had not let him forget it. Every time there was a clash between them she would bring it up, not unlike a hammer out of a tool-belt hanging heavy around her waist.

'I'm just working on another "meaningless" piece for my art degree. You know, the kind that won't get me a job and will see me destitute and reviled by society for the rest of my days. But don't worry, *Daddy*, I'm not expecting anything from you. Nothing. Nothing meaningful, at least.'

It was from the very first mention of 'meaningful' that Beth had known she would never, ever be able to agree with her father, and she had turned to her mother for support – or recognition or rationale. At the time, her mother's face had shown pain and torn loyalties but the following day her actions had betrayed nothing. It was as if the argument had never happened. It had been swept safely and swiftly under the carpet and would remain there until the next time Beth decided to challenge her father's opinions.

Right now Beth was unsure as to what to do. She certainly didn't want to burden her mother with her sense of displacement and awkwardness – the situation must be intolerable for her already: she had lost her husband so unexpectedly. And Beth had no desire or intention to turn up without warning at Gillian's because she couldn't bear the potential – perhaps inevitable – rejection and disappointment with which she would be left subsequently. Gillian did not like the unexpected.

It was no coincidence then, she thought, that she

had kept on her at all times the piece of paper with the phone number, like an unstable person might have the number of their therapist in a pocket, or a seasoned offender might always carry the number of their solicitor. Never had a piece of paper given rise to so much comfort. Despite its lack of monetary worth, never had anything else seemed so valuable and tangible. Beth had taken it out of her purse regularly, played with it, then folded it diligently along the creases and placed it back in the zipped pocket.

So, when Neena was working late on one of her cases – which she had tried recently because she felt that Beth shouldn't be alone too much – Beth knew the timing was right. She had taken a few sips of the screw-top wine they had opened the night before; in the background the radio was subtly reminding her that Christmas was around the corner and she figured it was neither too late in the evening to phone nor likely that she would catch her contact mid-supper.

She picked up her mobile and pressed in the numbers firmly, mouthing them to herself as she did so for fear of getting them wrong. Then she took another large glug of wine, closed her eyes and waited for the tone.

It had been Beth who had suggested the coffee shop because she wanted to have the comfort and luxury of being in truly familiar surroundings. When meeting someone you didn't really know, she reasoned – in fact someone you didn't know at all but whose world had collided with yours – the very least you could do for yourself was to be in a place you knew well.

She had been relieved by his response when she had called. He had, he confessed, been surprised by her call but not because it had 'freaked him out', as he put it. No, it was more that calls to his home were rare. He didn't have a mobile, he had explained, because he didn't quite see the point, and that was why he was so delighted that Beth had suggested they could meet face to face. It was the best way to talk to people, he said, looking them in the eye, like people used to do in the old days.

Beth had smiled with relief – she couldn't help taking to him even if it was just over the phone. When she had ended the call and they had made their arrangements, she had wondered – she had kicked herself, really – why she hadn't had the courage to make the call before.

She didn't tell Neena about the meeting, not out of the slightest bad intention or any desire to keep a secret from her but because it made perfect sense for her to test the waters first. If the whole idea turned out to have been badly conceived, she wouldn't have to say a word or feel a fool or even justify acting on a whimsical notion. But if the experience turned out to be good, meaningful and positive, as she hoped it would, she could share it with Neena and together they would take things from there.

She was, of course, hoping for the latter as she perched on one of the armchairs in the café, sipping a large mug of coffee. She had made sure she was early – she needed her caffeine kick, and in this foul weather there was something comforting about a warm mug in your hands, something to anchor you.

It was a particularly noisy morning, with prams, pushchairs and mothers, some cradling newborns close to their chests, having been blown indoors by the relentless harsh wind and driving rain. And yet, despite knowing she was frightfully early, she couldn't resist looking up each and every time the door opened. It felt ironic as well as foolish that when he actually walked in, Beth's eyes were fixed on the rim of her coffee mug. And when she eventually looked up, Gianni was waving from the doorway and she smiled, giving an enthusiastic wave in return. As he walked towards her, he turned on his heel. Beth's heart sank almost as quickly as it had lifted. He turned to hold the door open for a woman battling a double-buggy: she was weighed down by shopping and being outwitted by a toddler who stubbornly resisted her will to leave. The man lowered himself and looked the small boy in his eyes, said something, winked, and the child hurried outside to join his mother.

Beth smiled to herself.

As he approached she hesitated, unsure whether to shake his hand or embrace him, but her insecurities vanished when he greeted her with a huge smile and his big hand on her shoulder, as if to ward off any physical awkwardness that might have arisen between them.

'What can I get you? Coffee, tea, herbal?' she offered enthusiastically.

'Ah, no, don't you worry yourself. You've already got something. I'll get it. I'm not having you stand in the queue for me – it's no skin off my nose. I'm old but not that old yet. Besides it does my knees good to keep upright. Can I get you a top-up?'

She watched him as he stood in the queue with the regular patrons, in his shorts, bare legs and walking boots. He glanced briefly at the overhead menu and waited patiently. Beth liked his calm. At the till he reached far into the pockets of his shorts and brought out a cupped handful of coins from which he plucked six or seven and extracted a smile from the normally miserable cashier.

'So, how're you doing, then?' he asked, as he sat down opposite Beth.

'Oh, you know ... It's not been easy – on many fronts. Mainly, I guess, because there was no warning – it was all so sudden ...'

'Well, death is always a hell of a shock,' said Gianni, and had a sip of his simple black coffee. 'That's the point, isn't it, I guess? Even if you've had time to prepare, like I did when my dad finally carked it – crikey, that's a few years ago now – it's still a shock. Maybe that's the idea – to shock us, give us a bit of a jolt.'

'Hmm, yes. Well, it's certainly done that. I'm really

grateful you agreed to come. It must have seemed a bit random, me calling you up like that, but I just needed to know about the morning on the bus. Do you mind?' she asked.

And Gianni generously obliged, reciting to her, once again, the exact movements and nuances of that Thursday morning when her father had collapsed and died.

Unlike the first time they had met, Beth did not shed any tears. There was nothing new in the story, nothing that enlightened her as to what had happened or why. There was certainly nothing that made her feel any better about her father dying so suddenly.

'How's your ma doing, by the way? I passed by there yesterday to drop off a plant for her. She likes her garden, doesn't she?'

'Now that's the understatement of the century . . . Sometimes I wonder if she didn't actually love it more than she loved Dad.' She smiled at the absurdity of her suggestion. But as she continued, the smile faded: 'It's just that she always seemed to come alive in the garden. She had this amazing energy when she was in it, but when she came indoors it was as if she went on automatic pilot somehow. It was as if she did what she had to do for us and Dad, but it wasn't until she was out in the garden that she really seemed happy.'

'Well, speaking as a gardener, I have to tell you that gardening can do that to even the most red-blooded of blokes . . . You ever been interested? If not, I bet there's still time for you to be converted,' he said.

They laughed, and Beth went on to tell him where she really came alive: in the studio, in front of her canvases. He knew a surprising amount about art, thought Beth, more than she would have expected of a man in shorts and walking boots. He seemed genuinely interested in her work, and when they joked about some of the modern art installations, she let out an internal sigh of relief that this man – this stranger – was so easy to talk to.

'To be honest, Dad never understood art. He was never interested in it and he couldn't comprehend why I would want to spend my life on a career that was so chancy – so volatile and precarious. But we never did see eye to eye . . . about anything, really.'

Gianni smiled. 'I'm sure your dad was real proud of you and all the things you've done.'

'Nah,' said Beth, shaking her head. 'I can categorically say I was not a source of pride to him. More a thorn in his side, I think. It was my big sis he really admired.'

'Oh, you have a sister? Well, it must be good to have someone to share with,' he offered.

'If only. Anyway, that's a whole other story . . . I wouldn't mind so much but it's Mum I worry about. She needs all the support she can get at the moment.'

'Yeah, I bet. Look, it's not for me to say, but when I was there the other day, she'd been crying. She looked kinda frightened and . . . well, a bit alone,' said Gianni, putting his mug down on the table between them.

'I do worry about her,' Beth said, staring vacantly into space. 'She has so much to deal with. I mean, she's been with Dad all her life and I'm not sure she's coping very well. In fact, I don't think it's actually hit her yet that he's gone – or, at least, that's what it looks like. She seems to be behaving so *normally* – almost as if nothing's happened. That's quite odd in the circum-stances, don't you think?' Beth didn't pause to wonder at the wisdom of asking a complete stranger for advice about her mother.

'Well, people react in different ways. Some have breakdowns and others, well, they just get on with it. Maybe your mum just needs to get on with things – with life.'

'But she has no life. Not without Dad. And I haven't exactly made things easier for her.'

Beth waited for Gianni to ask why, but his question didn't come verbally: it came in his eyes and in the slight tilt of his head to one side.

'I think I've overwhelmed her. For years – ever since I can remember – I had a tricky relationship with my dad, to say the least.' Beth rolled her eyes. 'For the past couple of years I've been wanting – needing – to tell him how I feel, and how I've felt, and ask him to accept who I am. It's long overdue . . . Except he went before I got my act together. So, I should be relieved, right? Maybe that's what I'm feeling right now – relief. What a terrible thing to say . . . But to top it all, I decided that the best way to clear my conscience – to explain and declare myself – was to tell Mum. What kind of a daughter does that? Burdens her mum with so much at such a crap time . . .'

Gianni touched her shoulder again. 'A good, honest daughter, I think. Sometimes life throws you these curveballs and sometimes, as you English say, it never rains but it pours. Sometimes it all comes at once, doesn't it?

'Perhaps it's all a bit much for your mum at the moment,' he continued, 'but I bet her friends are rallying around, helping her through this. You mustn't feel so responsible,' he chided.

There was a pause.

'You know,' said Beth, sitting forward in her chair, 'it's funny you should say that . . . I've never really thought about it until now, but I don't think Mum has any friends. Not that I know of anyway – apart from a few of Dad's work colleagues. I mean, she does things with the WI once in a while – not cooking, of course, she's a useless cook – but I know she goes to meetings sometimes. But she's never talked about anyone – mentioned anyone's name . . .'

'I can't believe that! Surely she's got some friends – she's got such a kind face. Everyone has someone, don't they?'

'Weird, isn't it? I really don't think she has . . . Which makes the whole thing so much worse, so much more tragic,' she said, her gaze wandering off into the distance.

'Is there anything I can do?' Gianni asked, pulling her back into the conversation.

'I'm not sure there's anything anyone can do. I think it's up to me to get hold of my sister and give her a bloody good telling-off, and then I need to make sure Mum is really OK.'

'Well, I'd be happy to help. I could always give her a hand in the garden, if it's getting too much for her,' he offered.

'You are kind. I really appreciate that. And thank you so much for indulging me and taking time out to meet me. Perhaps we could stay in touch . . . if that's, you know, appropriate . . .' Beth said hopefully.

'Hey, that'd be great. I'd love to see some of your art, too, one day. I bet it's great.' He winked, smiled and gave her a nod.

Beth replied that she'd like that, and as she made her way home she felt rather pleased that the meeting had turned out so well, even though she'd opened up and said more than she'd intended. But death does that to people – it does strange things, she thought.

Odd, too, that she had liked the relative stranger who had come into her life only recently, and how she had spent her entire life struggling to like her father. But, then, just because you loved your parents, it didn't necessarily mean you liked them. And she liked Gianni. She definitely liked him . . .

Chapter Twenty-two

'Take a seat, Myrtle. It must have been a terrible shock for you, all this business. I mean, sixty-two? It's no age, is it? Not nowadays. Today there are more centenarians than ever, I believe . . . No, there's no doubt about it – going at that age is most unreasonable.'

Myrtle stared blankly at Mr Pegg and thought how out of place a man in his sixties wearing a tweed suit and tie looked in a modern office with clean, white walls, floor-to-ceiling window blinds, wood-veneered desks and ergonomic chrome armchairs. She remembered Mr Pegg's original office from the one and only time she had accompanied Austin to the bank to put in place the loan on the new house all those years ago. Myrtle recalled having felt intimidated by the solemnity and heaviness of the dark oak-panelled room, which not only lacked windows and natural light but was distinctly comfortless.

She hadn't understood at the time why she had been requested by Austin to attend: it wasn't her money they were using, after all. Now, as she sat on the other side of Mr Pegg's desk in a padded navy office chair, she thought how clinical it all was, with bright fluorescent lighting bouncing on light, crisp, cold surfaces. A painting of a vase of flowers on the wall behind him had replaced the fake Constable that had hung so grandly in its gilt frame in his old office.

'You must have a lot to deal with at the moment, dear Myrtle. I think you did a splendid job with the service. Both Maureen and I thought it was a very touching tribute to such a commendable man – especially your choice of hymn. Austin would have been very proud . . . very proud indeed,' he said, as he tilted his head to one side.

Except, thought Myrtle, *it had absolutely nothing to do with me.*

'Now, Myrtle, we must deal with the most urgent matters at hand. As you know, Austin made me executor of his will, and while that is a separate matter from my agenda with you here today, I think it's worth noting that I had the greatest respect for your late husband and, clearly, I hope the feeling was mutual.

'Austin, you see, was not only a customer here at the bank for more than forty years but he became a good friend, a colleague of sorts . . .'

I didn't know he had named you executor. It hadn't crossed my mind. I know so very little.

'I feel it is my place and duty to stress to you the value and importance of loyal customers such as Austin in the transient, disposable world of today. Men like him are few and far between . . .'

They are indeed. He was loyal and he was extremely valuable, I'm sure.

'It's doubtful you need me to point out what a dignified, consummate professional he was. He was a shrewd man, your Austin. Not only was he clearly a brilliant accountant – as the success of his company will surely testify – but he was a man who might be considered a little ... What shall we say? ... old-fashioned by today's standards. That's no bad thing, I might add, Myrtle. Tradition and thoroughness are qualities rarely encountered in today's business where it appears everyone is out to make a "quick buck" in return for not very much at all. But, no, Austin worked very strictly within the law and he was as quick to dismiss the manipulation of accountancy rules as his counterparts were eager to break them.' He leaned forward across his desk and lowered his voice. 'That sort of practice is more common than you'd think, Myrtle. But while others were happy to cream off unjustifiable profit and cut corners, Austin was a man of the greatest integrity – a man who made sure his clients were safe and, more importantly, were able to sleep at night.'

Oh, yes, he liked to stick to the rules, Austin did. Myrtle knew that. *He was a stickler for rules, regulations and obligations.*

'So it falls on me, dear Myrtle – I am duty-bound,' he was peering over the top of his narrow glasses, 'to relay the details of the accounts you and Austin held here at the bank.'

I've never held an account in my life. What on earth is he talking about? I do wish he'd get to the point. She shook her head. Her hands were writhing in her lap.

'As if to vindicate his professionalism over the years, to prove the sheer brilliance and efficiency of his mathematical mind, you have no need to worry, Myrtle. The private accounts are in very good order. In fact, they're in excellent order. Seems he was quite the little squirrel, Austin was – quite the little squirrel.'

Myrtle hadn't known there might be anything she ought to be concerned about, so being told she had nothing to worry about indicated that she should have been very concerned all along. She frowned.

'As you are well aware, Austin made a full repayment of the loan on your house some years ago – in 1989, if memory serves me – so there is nothing left outstanding on the mortgage. A shrewd man, indeed – there aren't many people in his position, I can tell you. Most people walking through my door here at the bank are leveraged to the hilt. It makes for very uneasy living, I can tell you.'

He moved the papers on his desk, shuffled some around and raised one in his hand. 'Now, let's have a look . . . Your current account is certainly very healthy and will doubtless see you through the next months or so until you decide what you want to do with things. You must know that you need have no concern about using your cards or chequebook. There is a very accommodating overdraft facility, as you know, but not one I advocate using – not with today's rates anyway. Austin never dipped into it – not even by so much as a penny – in more than forty years. So, unless you're planning a major shopping spree – I know what you ladies can be like,' he grinned, 'because my Maureen is no stranger to the "plastic", as they say – I would suggest you'll be fine with the contents of your joint current account.'

Joint? What 'joint' account?

'Before I turn my attention to Austin's savings account, I should ask you if there is anything you don't understand or that gives you cause for concern, Myrtle?'

Myrtle was stunned, and while it went against her very nature to ask for anything, she knew that this matter was of some urgency and, without Austin, she simply didn't know a way forward.

'Well, there is something and . . .' she hesitated '. . . it feels very awkward to ask. I wouldn't normally, and it seems strange bringing something like this up, but I don't quite know what to do. As you rightly pointed out, Austin liked to stick rigidly to rules. He insisted on a household kitty to which he contributed a sensible weekly allowance. I'm afraid it's some weeks now since any money went into it. I was wondering whether it might be possible for me to have a little advance – only enough to see me through the week.' Myrtle's cheeks pinked.

'Why, I'm sure we can arrange that. How much are we talking about?'

'Er, well, normally Austin allocated me sixty-five pounds for the week's budget,' she confessed.

Mr Pegg picked up a piece of paper from his desk. 'I know it's customary nowadays to do all this on the computer but Austin was never keen on the whole concept of Internet banking and I have to confess to agreeing with him. I know everyone's keen to save on paper but I think you'll find there's no substitute for feeling a sheet between your fingers and seeing the figures in front of you in black and white. So, as he has not registered for our frankly superb Internet banking service, I just want to make sure you are aware of how things stand. It's not often – in fact it's very rare indeed – we ever see you in here, Myrtle. So, there you are. There in the bottom right-hand corner is the balance of the account,' said Mr Pegg, as he handed the paper over the desk to Myrtle, pointing with his pen at the figure. 'I will be in touch regarding his various investments and trust funds in due course.'

Myrtle looked at the piece of paper without touching it and her jaw dropped.

When things had been normal – as normal as Myrtle had always known them – in November, with Austin's birthday out of the way, her thoughts had always turned with enthusiasm to Christmas. When the girls were young she had spent time with them preparing and making decorations in early December. It was at such times that it had become obvious Beth was by far and away the more artistic and creatively talented of the two.

After the girls had left home, there had been a fallow period of many years when Myrtle's own creativity had been put to one side. Instead of making new decorations, symbols and festive trinkets, she had felt compelled to rely on the things the girls had made years ago, which were neatly packed away in the loft by Austin.

Then along came Molly – lively, eager, and with eyes on stalks. The past two years, in particular, had been such a treat for Myrtle and had given her an unforeseen boost of energy as she dedicated many hours to preparing for Christmas with her enviably uninhibited granddaughter. Much to Austin's dismay, the two of them would take over the kitchen, spreading sheets of paper, paints, beads and glitter on the table, and spend at least one Saturday ahead of Christmas making decorations. Even the temporary mess was difficult for him to witness and he would often head for the TV so that his irritation didn't give rise to comments in front of Molly.

Myrtle had wanted to extend her enthusiasm to cooking and baking, but Austin had always said, 'Know your limits, Myrtle. Know your limits.'

They both knew what he meant by that. It was important to remain realistic.

But this year the advent of Christmas felt not only awkward, sinister and inauspicious but wrong and, most of all, incredibly untimely.

The Saturday after Myrtle's meeting with Mr Pegg

at the bank, which had left her confused and uncertain, it was a joy to spend time with Molly again. Unfortunately, the little girl's visit was marked by the distinct absence of Gillian at the door. It was Geoffrey who dropped his daughter off and Myrtle had to admit that even he looked rather peaky and out of sorts. He was curt and seemed impatient – preoccupied, even.

For Molly, however, it was just another super Saturday with her granny and she arrived a ball of energy.

As they sat at the kitchen table, with Myrtle showing deliberate and determined intent to keep things as normal as possible, Molly was in full flow about the Christmas carol concert at school. 'Oh, Granny, Jesus was the newborn baby king, you know.' She stuck some felt covered with glitter to a piece of card.

'He was. That's quite right, you clever little thing,' her granny replied. 'And what did he look like, this newborn baby king?'

Molly rolled her eyes. 'I don't know, Granny. I wasn't born then. But he didn't have much luck because he got himself killed by King Somebody.'

'Oh, that's not very nice. I bet God had something to say about that.'

'Well . . .' she thought about it for a moment '. . . if you do something mean to someone he loves, God will make you get hurt or something. That's serving me right,' she said, with great conviction.

'Oh, I see.'

'But he does nice things as well,' she said reassuringly.

Myrtle smiled to herself and thought what a joy it was to have Molly with her. At a time when everything seemed so dark and gloomy, fearful and full of uncertainty, it was not only calming to be in the company of such an innocent but it was also a welcome distraction. Then she felt a pain in her heart. Part of Gillian was sitting at the table with her . . .

Myrtle could not have known the awkwardness that was about to follow.

The second she heard Dorothy shout, 'Coo-ee!' through the letterbox, she almost jumped from her seat. She felt niggled by the unexpected arrival of her neighbour – it was a blatant, unwelcome interruption of her precious time with Molly. And before she knew it, there, at waist height, stood Molly with her neck bent so far backwards Myrtle thought it might break in two, staring up at her grandmother with large, pleading eyes. It would have been very difficult, if not impossible, to disappoint her, although she felt sure her own face must show plain desperation at Dorothy's suggestion.

Myrtle's hand was, of course, eventually forced by the sheer delight of a five-year old: it would have been nothing less than cruel to turn down such an exciting invitation but it had not been without some resistance.

'Well, I'm not sure if I have any reason to go. I don't really think we need anything. No, we have everything. Besides, it does seem an awfully long way,' she tried.

'Sssh,' Dorothy cut in, with a firm, slender finger

across her lips. 'I can tell you right now, Myrtle, I'm not in the mood for excuses. I will *not* take no for an answer.'

'Well, I've never actually been . . .' Myrtle confessed.

'Oh, dear Lord, it's like pulling teeth . . .' Dorothy clasped her forehead dramatically, much to the delight of Molly. 'Just take a look at that adorable little face, would you? How could you deny that darling face a bit of fun? Besides – you need to face it, Myrtle Lewis – you're outnumbered!' She pinched Molly's cheek and turned back to her neighbour. 'And you know what they say, Myrtle? Once you've seen one shopping centre, you've seen the mall!' She laughed and bent down to share the joke with Molly.

It was the fact that Dorothy had somehow got Molly on side before Myrtle had had a proper chance to reject the proposition outright that made Myrtle feel such a stick-in-the-mud.

Molly was looking up at Dorothy in awe, especially when she went on to announce that she wanted to take Myrtle shopping because 'It's about time we got you out of that dull navy and grey!'

This, Myrtle knew, would guarantee Dorothy a place in the fashion-conscious mind of her adorable granddaughter. She felt shame and a momentary twinge of jealousy that a relative stranger had come along and suggested something so simple but so manifestly appealing. Dorothy might as well have been offering a sardine to a hungry kitten.

When Myrtle admitted that the car in the driveway was only used by Austin – that she couldn't drive – Dorothy tutted and suggested they catch the bus. The look on Myrtle's face put paid to that idea and Dorothy kicked herself.

To make up for her *faux-pas*, she ordered a taxi on her mobile. Molly could barely contain her excitement.

When they entered the shopping centre, Myrtle gripped her handbag tightly. The place was bustling, with people rushing from place to place, some smiling and laughing, others walking with force and determination to the sound of Christmas carols blaring from inconspicuous speakers. Myrtle's eyes were met with fluorescent and multicoloured fairy lights, vivid window displays, shiny gifts and garish decorations wherever she turned. The sense of occasion was undeniable.

Myrtle fell behind and watched Molly skipping and swinging Dorothy's hand to and fro, chatting non-stop as if this was the moment she had waited for all her life. Her eyes were sparkling. The pair danced from shop window to shop window, Molly rushing to point it all out and take it all in, her mouth gaping with anticipation and possibility.

Myrtle tried to speed up but she couldn't keep up with Dorothy's long legs and confident strides. She was pleased to see Molly so boundless and full of excitement and she smiled with satisfaction when she noted that Molly hadn't looked back at her grandma once.

'We've got to bring a bit of colour into your life,' Dorothy shouted at Myrtle, from where she had placed herself at the entrance of a large, vibrant and shiny store.

'Oh, Granny! Isn't this fun?' squeaked Molly.

'We're going to sort you out with something smart and bright, which will bring out those sparkly blue eyes you've been hiding since God knows when,' said Dorothy in a raised voice as Myrtle caught up, and then she prodded her into the shop. 'And who knows? We might even find a special little something for you too, sweetie-pie.' She smiled at Molly.

'Oh, yes, please!' Molly giggled. 'Yes, yes, yes!'

'Now then, Myrtle, let's get you something jolly and fun. It is the festive season, the season to be merry.' She marched on into the depths of the shop, clearly expecting Myrtle to follow. 'I think, considering your shape – a cross between a pear and a lampshade – it's safest we stay away from knits. They always look so . . . heavy and dowdy. If anything, they scream safe, dull, and might as well come with a free white flag with "defeat" written on it. And it was with good reason we threw out the vulgar knits of the eighties. For what it's worth, I think you need to stay away from anything fussy around your neck. Let's discount all bows and frills – they'll only draw attention to your cleavage, which, although quite, quite handsome and considered pert and petite by most standards, is not really worth exaggerating. You might, however,' she said, leaning in towards Myrtle and cupping her hands under her breasts, 'like to consider a better bra. Something that just gives you that extra little . . . hoick up.' She gave them a firm lift.

Myrtle gasped and stood frozen to the spot as Dorothy walked off, zigzagging through the assault course of stands, displays and endless rails of clothes.

'Colour-wise . . . now, I don't want to put the frighteners on you,' she said, as she came back, 'but it's about time you befriended something brighter – pink and possibly even a dash of red. Navy and grey tell me you can't be bothered to make an effort – you've surrendered, and have no intention of coming out of your comfort zone, Myrtle.' She stopped and looked straight at her. 'Just out of interest, for the record, so to speak, where do you *normally* shop?'

Myrtle's head was spinning. 'Er, Austin would normally take me to M and S but only when it was absolutely necessary.'

'My dear girl,' said Dorothy, 'this has nothing to do with "necessary". Shopping is not about "needing" and all about "wanting" – and one more thing,' she said, grabbing Myrtle by both her shoulders. 'You *never* shop *with* a man and you *never* dress *for* a man. You shop *with* yourself *for* yourself. Is that clear? No wonder he's dressed you in a camouflage of dulls and darks – he wanted you to go unnoticed. We clearly have a lot of ground to make up!'

Molly was grinning and nodding so fast her head was

in danger of falling off. Myrtle raised her eyebrows in disbelief.

'We need something to accentuate your waistline – it's somewhere under your heavy knit, I hope? – and then we need to try to give you that much-needed height. Don't panic. It doesn't have to mean heels – often it's just the length of a skirt,' she said, hoisting Myrtle up a little by her waistband, 'or the shape of a blouse.' She was off again, weaving through the myriad hangers and rails.

Myrtle was speechless. It was sensory overload – the soothing music oozing from speakers, the sparkle of colours, the clear bright lights and the well-intended advice. Never had Myrtle felt such concern or kindness from someone she barely knew – or anyone, for that matter. It was the kindness of a stranger and she felt reluctantly poised at centre-stage in a new and unfolding relationship she could never have anticipated.

Myrtle felt a tingle inside her – a heady mix of excitement with unexpected and undeniable indulgence, something she hadn't experienced since she was a teenager.

Before she knew it, Dorothy had returned with four or five different pieces, stating that there wasn't time to try them on. Instead she, with her vast experience and unchallenged opinion, could immediately tell if something had potential or was a non-starter.

Talking to herself, she held things up to Myrtle's

chest, turned her head from side to side, pushed Myrtle in front of a mirror, this way and that.

'I love it, I love it, I love it!' shrieked Molly. 'Granny, you look like a princess!'

This was pointless, she thought. She shouldn't spend money on things like this – when on earth would she ever have a reason or occasion to wear them? She bowed her head and closed her eyes. If ever there was an exercise in humiliation, this was surely it.

Dorothy took a couple of items up to the till, Myrtle mumbling that she couldn't possibly warrant the luxury of a pale pink satin blouse and a slender black skirt.

'Look,' said Dorothy, squaring up to Myrtle, 'I can't bake you a cake or make you a cottage pie. That's what people do to be neighbourly and helpful, isn't it? But I *can* contribute in a number of different ways, so instead, my dear, think of this as a treat – a gift from a friend indeed to a friend in need.' She turned to the cashier to pay. 'In fact,' she swung back to Myrtle, 'consider it an early Christmas present.'

Dorothy bent down to Molly and whispered, 'And now we've simply got to find something for you, angel face!'

'Aren't we lucky girls, Molly, being spoilt like this?' Myrtle joined in.

Molly jumped up and down on the spot. 'Now it's all about me! It's all about me!' she sang.

And it was. Molly picked out a chunky pink scarf

with pink and crimson flowers embroidered on it, and a diary covered with beautiful pink Chinese silk. She brushed it against her cheek and looked at her grand-mother. 'Now I can have a diary just like yours, Granny. I'm going to fill it with stories and secrets!'

Myrtle smiled back, clutching her handbag in one hand and the crisp new carrier bag with her premature Christmas present from the relative stranger in the other.

Dorothy wanted to stop for coffee but Myrtle politely suggested that they really ought to get back in time for Geoffrey. Molly looked disappointed but Dorothy reassured her there would be other times and that was enough to placate her. And Myrtle really hoped she meant it.

Myrtle had had no idea that shopping could be so exhausting. She barely had the energy to climb the stairs. She placed the carrier bag with the generous gift on the bed and lay down. She didn't need to wonder what Austin would have thought of her day – she knew. 'A lot of unnecessary shenanigans': those were the words he would have used, of that she was certain. And he wouldn't have stopped there. The whole point of the day would have been lost on him and would have been nothing less than an insult to common sense. 'If there's no purpose to it then I fail to see the point, Myrtle,' he'd said calmly, when Beth had asked her to go along to the shopping centre when it had first opened. 'It's an ineffective use of time, if nothing else. We have plenty of things to be getting on with. Shopping is for the leisured classes, the shirkers and slackers of this world. What on earth would *you* do there?' he had tutted.

And it had been the way he had stressed 'you' that had made her feel so ridiculous for having asked in the first place. The innocently posed question seemed only to serve as yet another reminder to Myrtle that she was, for any number of reasons, a source of annoyance and disappointment to him.

Myrtle had made up an excuse to Beth – so convincingly, in fact, that Beth hadn't asked her again.

It might have been Austin's objection to the free market and increasing commercialization of a world he enjoyed scrutinizing but it certainly wasn't Myrtle's. She had wanted to go – see what all the fuss was about – but, as with so many situations between them, she hadn't had the courage to face up to him.

Austin wanted to keep Myrtle on a tight rein – and he had succeeded. Feeling obliged, as she had since the day they had married, was a heavy burden. And one that, apparently, even kept you away from shops and dawdlers.

Myrtle looked at the shiny shopping bag she had dropped at the end of the bed and her eyes wandered across the room. The wardrobe door was still slightly ajar and she could see the old diary Molly had found lying among her shoes.

She sat bolt upright. The day after tomorrow she would have to put her fears aside and catch the bus. She simply had to go to the post office.

Chapter Twenty-three

The last will and testament of Austin Lewis was read at Reed & Ryder Solicitors in town. Beth had insisted on accompanying her mother and held her hand throughout the appointment. She wasn't much interested in what the will said. She wasn't even relieved when Mr Pegg from the bank assured her, as soon as they walked in, that she would doubtless be well looked after. Words of praise for her father followed – she had to hear that he had been a man of principle and dignity – but they were of no comfort to her and she steadfastly refused to look at Mr Pegg when he addressed them, choosing instead to focus on her mother.

Once again, there was no sign of Gillian. She had been requested to attend but Beth had still been unable to get hold of her. She had concluded that her sister must be well and truly messed up.

Not turning up for the reading of your own father's will brings a whole new meaning to the word 'selfish', thought Beth, whose face hid not an ounce of her anger. *There I am, thinking I'm the one with all the issues, but Gill is turning out to be a prize bloody idiot. I don't know who the hell she thinks she is. She must be up to her ears in self-pity. Well, I hope she bloody drowns in it! I can't forgive her for this – I really can't. Poor Mum.* She squeezed her mother's hand.

Both Beth and Myrtle smiled a little when Mr Ryder cleared his throat and threw his head back as he started reading the statement accompanying Austin's last will and testament.

"'To my dear daughters, Gillian and Bethany, I leave only my wisdom and experience. My unfaltering support for you both ended the day you graduated from university. I see it as a point of great principle that from then, in adulthood, you make your own way in life and relinquish any further financial dependency on your parents . . .'" read Mr Ryder, authoritatively, his face giving every indication he was basking in the supremacy of his speech.

Ha! Well, there's the second joke of the day! Beth rolled her eyes, crossed her legs and let go of her mother's hand. *Dear, precious Gillian was the only one to have benefited from a paid-for university education, you might remember, Daddy dearest. I seem to remember having paid my own way through art college by working part-time. Yes, that's right. I 'relinquished' all dependence on you at the earliest opportunity – I had no desire to be on your payroll for a second longer than absolutely necessary. It may have been something to do with the look of repulsion on your face when I told you I was pursuing my art degree that really sealed it for me. Still, perhaps I should be thanking you for the steely determination that makes my heart beat now, hey?* She looked away, incapable of hiding her anger and frustration.

294

And that was it. Everything Austin Lewis possessed was bequeathed to his beloved and loyal wife Myrtle.

Well, that's just fine with me, thought Beth, knowing she really meant it. *I hadn't come here expecting anything. I'm certainly not one of those people you read about in tacky magazines whose superficial veil of bereavement hides a blood-sucking, asset-stripping, distant relation. No, I'm not here in the expectant hope that my dad was going to soften the blow of his sudden death and our disastrous relationship by giving me thousands of pounds. I'm here to support Mum – and for that reason alone. No, the hardest and most painful lesson I've ever learned in life is that expectation – without a single exception in relation to Dad – leads to burning, irreconcilable disappointment. What I really want from him right now – the only thing I've ever wanted from him – is love and understanding.* Her eyes stung with tears.

Myrtle couldn't help but note that Austin had made a point of using the words 'beloved' and 'loyal' in reference to herself. The latter had made her wonder if it had been a deliberate expression of his true feelings or whether he wanted to have the last laugh about her pre-marital dalliance. It certainly felt like it.

Beth sat in silence and her thoughts turned to her mother, whose only sign of bereavement had been to carry on pretty much as normal, not break down in tears, wail uncontrollably or even show – perhaps – relief. Beth was increasingly worried about her, and while neither of them was particularly interested in what Mr Ryder had to say, she couldn't help but feel a gap between them. It was as if her mother had things to say and hadn't found the courage to voice them.

This isn't how you react when you lose the person with whom you've shared some forty-odd years of marriage. Beth had offered her mother plenty of opportunities to talk and share, but she had given Beth nothing to go on. It was as if her mother's emotions had been frozen. Most worrying of all was the garden: it had stood untouched since her father had died. Beth decided on a change of tack.

With all things official out of the way, Myrtle was left feeling empty and complete in one fell swoop. It seemed there was even less to deal with or think about. This meant less purpose to her days but potentially less fretting.

Old habits died hard, and with Wednesdays having always been set aside for the week's food shopping, Myrtle felt she needed to make a concerted effort to change her routine.

For weeks now she had continued to buy for two – always choosing the cheapest cuts as instructed by Austin: mutton, lamb shin, beef skirt and brisket. She had still found herself looking for items in the reduced-to-clear baskets with their sell-by-dates calling out to her in desperation.

Hitherto, any food she had bought had gone to

waste – and it was extraordinary, really, that even though she wasn't eating properly, Myrtle couldn't seem to conjure up even the slightest hunger. Instinctively, she had carried on picking out Austin's favourite foods automatically: roast for Sundays; cold meat on Mondays; Tuesdays had always been shepherd's pie; sausages on Wednesdays with somewhat lumpy mash, and so she had carried on.

In the past, she hadn't dared to try something new. The one time she had – many years ago – it had caused such a furore that she had been frightened into next week and resolved never to stray from Austin's weekly meal routine ever again.

'Myrtle, I don't know what you were thinking!' Austin had said, in hushed but firm tones across the table. 'I can't eat this steak and kidney pie. I can't and I won't. It's perfectly reasonable of me to expect some continuity in the kitchen. We are both acutely aware that your talents lie in the garden and that there is no evidence of them here in the kitchen. I don't believe it's too much for a man to *know* what he is coming home to after a day's work. And it isn't this sort of thing,' he said, as he flipped the end of his fork on the plate and watched it fall to the floor.

He had grasped his forehead and rested his elbow on the table. His frustration was clear for Myrtle to see, and she instinctively knew his outburst extended beyond the meal. Other times she had caught him looking at her in bafflement, staring blankly and sadly into open space – it was as if their entire situation was a cause of great despair to him. She noticed it because she couldn't help thinking that even he – the meticulous Austin Lewis with his great plan back in 1964 – had surely hoped for more than this.

'Are we agreed then, Myrtle?' he had asked, forcing her to look up at him.

She had had no choice but to whisper, 'Yes.'

In many ways it had been a relief to be forced to stay within the confines of regularity, predictability and routine. It meant she always knew where she stood. But since Austin's passing she appeared to have survived on cups of tea and Digestive biscuits – nothing more, nothing less – and it had grown tiresome. It was time for a change, in more ways than one.

Beth came around specifically to discuss the plans for Christmas because, as she pointed out, this year would be like no other and she didn't want bereavement to stand in the way of tradition. Besides, she was adamant about the inclusion of Neena as her rightful partner – until now she had kept her waiting in the wings.

Myrtle decided to agree with whatever Beth would suggest. But the conversation turned out to be about more than Christmas.

'I'm sorry to say this, Mum, but bloody Gillian – bloody, bloody Gillian! – I just don't get it. Where the hell is she? It's like she's vanished off the face of the earth. I've lost count of the times her mobile has gone to voicemail, and when I call the house Geoff fobs me off with some feeble excuse that she's not there, or they don't bother to answer the phone.' There was aggression in her voice.

'Try not to be so hard on your sister,' Myrtle responded, in the hope of calming her down.

'Hard? I'm trying to talk to her and mourn with her. Besides, why shouldn't I be hard on her? She's not the only one to have lost a father. Or is this more to do with the fact that they were close and that means she has more right to mourn him than I do? She'd do well to remember that he was my father, too, regardless of the shit relationship we had. If we're going to compete in the mourning stakes, I'd win hands down. This is bloody harder on me. I have to carry on in the full knowledge that our relationship remained unresolved, unreconciled. I have to live with the fact that he probably hated me, and that although I loved him I didn't much like him.' She got up from the table and slammed her plate on the counter.

'Oh, Beth, he didn't hate you, of course he didn't.'

'How do you know? How can you be so damn sure?' Beth's energy was unnerving. 'I'm sorry to say this, Mum, but I still can't work out why you never defended me. Why did you never stand up for me when he put me down, dismissed me or just plain ignored me, hey? You just stood there like some – like some unconcerned, uninvolved bystander. I know I rubbed him up the wrong way but I never knew why.

I didn't do things the way he wanted – but that's what kids are for, isn't it, to push the boundaries, strike out and be individuals? And all the while Gill got the praise, the smiles, the approval. I felt like a sodding outcast in my family. It's little wonder I couldn't wait to get away . . . and you, quite frankly, didn't even seem that bothered when I left. I mean, were you *that* scared to stand up for me – to rock the boat?'

Myrtle stood up and walked out of the kitchen.

'Where are you going?' shouted Beth. 'Don't walk away from me now! I have every right to say these things – you can't take *that* away from me and, more importantly, you need to hear them!'

'I'm not walking away. I just needed to get out – out of the kitchen. I'm sorry, Beth. It wasn't *you* . . .'

'What do you mean, it wasn't me? It clearly *was* me who riled him. It *was* me he couldn't bear to look at. I sometimes wonder if it was because I was gay that he couldn't stand the idea of me.'

Myrtle stood by the french windows, looking out on to the garden. 'Oh, Beth, I'm so sorry. It wasn't how I thought it would be,' she said, not turning around.

'What do you mean, it wasn't how you thought it would be? What wasn't?'

'If anything, I thought it would be Gillian he'd take against. All those years,' she sighed, 'all those years of hoping it would all work out – somehow – that we'd be a happy family . . .'

'What are you on about, Mum? How is this about Gillian?' Beth asked, her face bewildered.

'Beth,' said Myrtle, turning to face her daughter at the other end of the room, 'I'm afraid it's all a terrible mess. And it's neither your nor Gillian's fault. It's all my doing. I've made a dreadful mess of everything by agreeing to your father's demands – the secrecy of it all.'

'Mum, you're freaking me out! What are you talking about?' Beth moved towards her mother.

'Don't come any closer, Beth. I'm afraid you'll never think the same of me again after I tell you this. Don't be too quick to judge your father – he thought he was doing the right thing and, deep down, he was a good man. And don't be too hard on your sister. Please, Beth, I know I'm in no position to ask for anything, but I beg you, please go easy on Gillian.'

'You're not making any sense.'

Myrtle turned away from her daughter and faced the garden. 'I suspect the reason Gillian is not talking to us is because she's had some news – something I mistakenly and very wrongly kept from her under the assumption that I was doing the right thing. But it wasn't the right thing, Beth. Instinctively, I knew it was wrong but I was obliged by your father. And I'm afraid I made a terrible mistake. But it wasn't for the first time. And now poor Gillian is paying the price . . .'

'Mum, you're scaring me. I've never heard you talk like this before. What the hell is it?'

'I'm afraid to tell you – and this is neither the time nor the place, but waiting for the right time and place has turned out to be a luxury I've never been afforded ... In the turmoil and shock of your father's death ...' she paused to pluck up courage '... Gillian has discovered that Austin was not her father.'

Beth fell into the armchair behind her. 'Bloody hell, Mum! You are kidding me, right?'

Chapter Twenty-four

Gillian knew it was a coincidence that the day she had asked Geoffrey to move out for a while, to give her the space she longed for, was the day she'd received a small parcel from her mother. It might have been a coincidence but it was also wholly appropriate.

She had not needed to open it to know who the sender was – she'd have recognized her mother's beautiful handwriting anywhere. At first she hadn't been that fussed about it. Christmas was only weeks away and she'd convinced herself it was a present for Molly. But then, gradually, the doubts had started forming in the front of her mind where she couldn't avoid them. She began to wonder whether her mother would be stupid enough to think she could make it up to her with a little help from Royal Mail. If that was what she was thinking, she had another think coming. As things stood, Gillian couldn't foresee a time when she could even be in the same room as her mother.

Conversely, it seemed a relief and a peculiar comfort to leave work early and pick Molly up from school, knowing that when they came home, she would be able to size up the parcel again.

It felt odd with Geoffrey away from the house. But,

Gillian had reasoned, it was the lesser of two evils. Having him around only wound her up – just the sound of his voice either irritated or infuriated her. And it wasn't as if he was being particularly hard done by – she'd hardly sent him to Siberia. Coventry, yes, but that was where his parents lived and she knew his mother would take great delight in doting on her only son.

She had made a conscious decision not to pander to Molly. Instead, Gillian had explained that Geoffrey was away on business. Molly had accepted it, just as Gillian had anticipated.

'Has Daddy gone far, far away? Or did he just walk there?' asked Molly, in bed one evening.

'Darling, let's read your story now, ok? It's way past your bedtime. I'm sure Daddy took his car to the conference.'

'I miss him, though, Mummy, don't you?' She looked her mother straight in the eyes. 'I don't like it when Daddy isn't here.' She paused. 'Are you cross, Mummy?'

It was one thing not being able to control other people's emotions but quite another not being in charge of your own. 'Of course I'm not, darling. What makes you say that?'

'Because you always look angry when you look at Daddy, and when he hadn't taken the rubbish out the other night you made that tutting sound and rolled your eyes, like Mrs Roberts does when Callum needs the toilet during Assembly.'

'Does she? Well, that's not very nice, I'm sure. Now,

let's just read your book, sweetheart, or you'll be very tired in the morning.'

Molly started reading, stopping only to insist that her mother read the right-hand pages and she read everything on the left.

When they came to the end of the book, Gillian kissed Molly on the forehead and got up to walk out of the room.

'Mummy, can you do that sleep-dust thing when you sprinkle the dust on my eyes to make me sleep? Please, Mummy?'

'OK, but then it's straight to sleep.' She scattered the imaginary dust over Molly's eyes, which were concentrating hard on being shut.

Before Gillian had finished, Molly opened her left eye. 'I miss Daddy,' she whispered. 'I miss him like I miss Grampy. I bet he's lonely in heaven. Don't you miss Grampy, Mummy?'

Tears brimmed in Gillian's eyes before she could stop them. Overwhelmed, she rushed forward to bury her face between Molly's head and shoulder. She held her so tightly it even pinched her voice and she could barely get the words out. 'Oh, my darling girl, I do, I do, I do. And I love you very, very much. Always remember that.'

'And I love you, too, Mummy.' She smiled. 'And, Mummy . . . tomorrow night I think I'd like to read the dictionary,' she whispered.

*

Gillian went into the kitchen, opened a bottle of red wine, poured herself a large glass – by God, she needed it – and took the parcel into the living room. She made herself comfortable on the sofa, took a deep breath, exhaled loudly and had a mouthful of wine.

She ran her finger along the top of the bulging envelope, put her hand inside and pulled out the contents. She looked at the slightly battered corners of a book covered with decoupage. She opened it and a note fell on to her lap.

It read simply:

My dearest Gillian, This is for you, about you. You were a most wonderful thing to happen to me. All my love, M

Gillian hadn't expected to read the entire diary – certainly not in one fell swoop – but it proved irresistible on so many levels. Not only was she looking for clues and pieces to the giant cryptic puzzle that was her past but between every line she was frantically searching for redemption on her mother's behalf.

31 January 1965

I can't bear the thought of losing him. A life without him is stifling – I cannot breathe without him. They cannot take him from me. They cannot tear us apart. It would be the undoing of me. I won't live. I won't, I won't, I won't!

Who in their rightful mind would ever think Austin
could be a match for him? He doesn't move me – not in the
slightest. When he brushes past me, his presence burns me.
He is impassive where I am passionate; he is stuffy and staid
where I am vigorous and so very alive. He will silence me, I
know he will. I will be stunted and hushed. I cannot give to
Austin. It is barbaric of anyone to even contemplate that I
could one day love Austin the way I love him. It simply won't
happen. I am not armed with the power to make it . . .

At the outset, Gillian rejected calls from her heart to
cry, deciding instead to engage her mind's most profound concentration to maintain absolute emotional
control, but in the end she was rendered powerless by
the story and succumbed to tears. Her upright, hard,
cold front weakened and she found herself crumbling,
piece by piece, into smithereens, tiny insignificant
particles. To begin with, she had been quite capable of
stemming the flow of tears with the back of her hand,
but ultimately the dam burst and Gillian Lloyd – forever
contained and controlled – became unrecognizable
even to herself.

Her very identity was smashed to pieces; her reputa-
tion as an upholder of moderation and the sovereign of
restraint was blown apart by the discovery of a different
truth from the one she had always known and loved,
facts to which she had not been privy before. She cried
tears of sadness, injustice and self-pity but mostly she
lamented another person's life – a person she neither

knew nor recognized. Either, she told herself, this was the stuff of fiction derived from a dangerously vivid imagination or it was becoming increasingly clear that she didn't know her mother at all. Perhaps she never had – and now, rather terrifyingly, she wasn't sure she ever would.

I don't know what I'm supposed to feel. I'm angry and relieved all at once; I'm baffled and confused. Oh, God, I'm all over the place . . . What the hell am I supposed to do with this?

How could someone live with a secret like that? This is the stuff of movies – it isn't my life . . . This is too unreal. Why would someone hide something like this? How did they think they could get away with it? And whatever happened to 'him'?

15 May 1965

The only thing keeping me alive is the thought of this child growing inside me. If it is God's will for me to be with Austin, as Mother says it is, then why is it not his child I'm carrying? They would have to kill me before they take this child from me. If ever there was a sign that I was meant to be with Julian, it is this child. I have never loved anything as much as I love this little being – whatever it is, a boy or a girl. I do not mind. It will be mine and mine alone.

The contents of the parcel had not made everything clear for her. In fact, if anything, the ramblings of a passionate, confused seventeen-year-old had made a disaster area of Gillian's emotions and wreaked havoc with her mind.

If Mum thinks sending me this means everything will be all right – put to rest – she must be completely naïve. I, for one, am not ready to be understanding. Not yet, anyway.

Less than half an hour away Myrtle Lewis, too, was in pieces. Beth had departed fairly swiftly after her mother's confession, not because she was angry or because she wanted to make Myrtle feel any worse than she already did but because she, like Gillian, needed space to review and digest.

Beth had not pursued the intricate detail: she had told her mother that she needed to see how the single fact of Gillian's parentage would sit in her mind before she or anyone else went on to dress it with what might turn out to be bias or superfluous opinion.

She had given her mother a cursory peck on the cheek as she left, in sharp contrast to her usual enveloping hugs.

As soon as Beth had gone – the front door shutting with a loud bang behind her – Myrtle sought refuge on the sofa and dissolved into tears. She sobbed so loudly she no longer recognized the sound of her own voice. The wailing came from somewhere deep inside, somewhere she hadn't been for many years, and while it scared her, she just didn't care. She certainly didn't care about herself, and as things stood, it didn't seem she had anything she could care about either. It was all such a mess. Not caring about herself was one thing but tainting the lives of those she loved was beyond unforgivable. She had come undone for the second time in her life and this time seemed worse: so much more was at stake. This time was fraught with the dissolution of relationships, death and shameful lies. Her own dishonesty, wickedness and loose morals had led to this. She had only herself to blame. She was unworthy, depraved, and her unspeakable weakness had not only paved the way for her own downfall but her inability to be honest had deeply compromised Gillian. And her inability to face up to the truth had made her fearful of defending or supporting her younger daughter.

There was no release from this interminable guilt and no accommodation for forgiveness. But no matter how much she wanted to un-be, she could not deny the feeling of relief.

She exhaled. Her shoulders dropped. She raised her hands to her face and wiped away some of the tears.

Enough now, she heard a voice say in her head. *You can only go in one of two ways, Myrtle Lewis, and down is not the answer.*

She pushed back her shoulders and straightened her spine.

Gianni was a patient man. A few unanswered knocks on a door were neither here nor there to him. But as well as being patient he was also persistent. When the knocks went unanswered, he walked across to the big window that looked into the front room and tapped on it a couple of times. Through the fog of the net curtains he could roughly see the outline of someone sitting on the sofa – bolt upright and very still.

He called her name and tapped a little louder.

Myrtle Lewis gave a little jump and looked to her right. She rubbed her nose briskly with the back of her hand. She got up and left the room.

A moment or two later, she opened the door, her face swollen, red and bleak.

'Ah, Mrs Lewis, not a good time, I can tell. You all right?' he asked, deeply concerned.

'Myrtle. Call me Myrtle. I'm afraid you've caught me rather unawares. I was just . . .' she mumbled.

Despite the clear evidence before him, he asked if he might come in. Myrtle stared blankly for a moment, then snapped herself out of it. 'Oh, I'm sorry. Of course. Do come in. I hope you don't mind if I ask you to take your boots off – it's just that the weather is so foul they're bound to leave a trail behind them on the carpet.' She smiled hesitantly. 'On second thoughts, keep them on. You do just that. A bit of dirt won't kill us, will it?' The smile broadened and she squared her shoulders.

Gianni gave a big grin. 'I'll tell you what, Myrtle, how about I'll take my boots off if you promise you won't make me a cup of tea? How's that sound?'

Once inside, he unlaced his boots. 'Hey, I'm sure

you're still feeling a bit dodgy – you've had a hell of a shock, going through a terrible time.'

Myrtle didn't hear him. She had already walked through to the living room and placed herself on the far end of the sofa. 'I'm afraid to say that *my* shock is the very least of it. There are others in greater shock than me right now. I'm afraid I've made a very bad job of things.'

'Ah, don't say that . . . What's up? What's happened now?' he said, moving a step closer to her.

Myrtle's back arched a little. 'Oh, life's unexpected twists and turns never fail to surprise . . .' She stared out into the garden.

'Ah, well, you know, I only popped by because I met your daughter, Beth, the other day. She's a corker. And she said you could do with a bit of help in the garden. And what with being green-fingered and all that, nothing would give me more pleasure than to help you out . . . if you want, that is,' he said, tilting his head to one side as if to try to catch her eye.

'Oh, yes,' she said, 'the garden. I'm afraid it's been rather neglected over the past weeks. Seems I've even made a mess of that. And my darling Beth,' she said, turning to face him, 'always so thoughtful, so loving and caring. Always thinking of others . . . She didn't deserve this.'

'What didn't she deserve, if you don't mind my asking?' he asked, seizing the moment.

Myrtle sighed heavily. 'I'm afraid I've treated her

rather badly. I've neglected her, you see, over the years. I left her to fend for herself and no mother should do that . . .'

'But –'

'No, I'm afraid I don't have the luxury of any excuses – not on this count. She's had some news today and it's all come as a bit of a shock to her, I'm afraid.' Tears filled her eyes and started trickling down her cheeks again.

Gianni came another step closer to her. Myrtle looked down at her lap. 'Don't go upsetting yourself. Perhaps it isn't as bad as you think,' he offered.

Myrtle put her head into her hands. 'I'm afraid it's worse than that,' she whispered. 'For too many years I hid a terrible secret from my daughters because I was made to believe I would get away with it, but I haven't and now I feel a fool because it was never my intention to hurt them.'

'Oh, I see.' He bowed his head. But he didn't. Gianni's mind boggled. He'd come to offer to do some weeding, maybe prune some of the roses, possibly even rake a few leaves, and suddenly he found himself raking up something completely unexpected. What was this? On the face of it she was a mourning widow with starry little eyes, which, from the very start, had drawn him in. There was something behind those eyes – a tenderness, a willingness but most of all a kind of sadness – that had stayed with him since that first day, something that had made him come back and check on her.

'Is there anything I can do?' was all he could say. He was conscious that he should not get too close to her. He didn't want to spook her: there was something vulnerable – fragile even – about her, as she sat huddled on the sofa.

She didn't answer him. 'Can't be undone . . . nothing anyone can do . . . truth is out and it can't be recaptured,' she muttered to herself.

'What truth? What is it you're talking about?' He knelt down at her feet. He didn't care about spooking her any more – this was freaking him out.

Myrtle took her head out of her hands, wiped her tears with her hand and inhaled sharply. 'You might as well be told as no doubt Beth will tell you anyway. Austin – my husband – was not the father of my daughter Gillian . . .'

There was a silence. Myrtle was waiting for a reaction and Gianni was waiting for more.

'Austin wasn't Gillian's father but he was Beth's. They never saw eye to eye. They never . . . got on. And now Beth has told me she's gay and I can't help but feel that somehow it's all my fault.'

'Oh, crikey.' Gianni let out a sigh of relief. 'Crikey! That's not bad news – that's just life. And I don't reckon there's any chance that you turned your daughter gay.' He smiled broadly.

'Don't you see,' Myrtle said, regaining some of her spirit in the face of this man's nonchalance, 'that all her life she's felt at odds with her father and I didn't

314

help her? I didn't defend her and it probably drove her away and made her feel . . . complicated about the whole business.'

Deliberately, Gianni paused. He didn't want her to think he hadn't given her words any consideration. 'Well, relationships with your parents can be a bit tricky, can't they? I mean, I was lucky – my ma and pa were pretty easy-come, easy-go. I let my pa down, though. He wanted me to study more but that wasn't for me. First chance to leave school – boom – I grabbed it like that,' he said, clapping his big hands together. 'Still, you can't choose your parents, can you? You can choose your friends but you can't choose your family.'

Myrtle's eyes went in search of the garden once more.

'What about your other daughter? How did she take it when you told her?'

Myrtle looked down at her hands in her lap. 'I'm afraid I didn't *tell* her. I had forty-one years to tell her but I never did. I'm afraid she found out inadvertently. And that's what makes the whole thing so dreadful . . . I haven't heard from her for weeks. She's refusing to talk to me and I really don't know what to do. I think I've lost her and now it may be that I've lost Beth, too.'

'Oh, you have been in the wars, haven't you?' said Gianni, reaching forward and patting her arm. 'And there I was thinking your husband carking it was your biggest sadness. Now it's the living you have to deal with . . .' He leaned towards her. 'Come here.' He put his arms out and folded them around Myrtle.

Her own arms fell to her sides as he grabbed hold of her. The warmth of his body comforted her. He smelt sweet and his chest was both strong and soft. Her head inclined towards his shoulder and she breathed him in.

'Right.' He pulled himself away. 'I know you Poms like your tea – especially at times like this – but I've got a better idea.' He pulled out a leather-bound hipflask from his back pocket. 'You need a swig of Gianni's remedy,' he said, as he unscrewed the lid and handed it to Myrtle.

She looked at him, at the flask, then back at him again.

She shook her head.

'Go on, I promise it won't kill you! You have my word.'

Against all good judgement, in full knowledge of what Austin would have said and thought, Myrtle reached forward and took the flask reluctantly from his hand. She put it to her lips and took a small sip.

The liquid burned her lips and stung the inside of her mouth. As it travelled down her throat, she was forced to cough.

'There you go,' said Gianni, rubbing her back gently. 'Do you want to, you know, talk about it?' he asked, screwing the top back on the little flask.

She shook her head, feeling her mouth might explode with the intoxicating liquid.

'All-righty. I don't want to trespass. Tell you what, why don't I leave you here, pop into the garden and just give it a bit of a tidy-up, hey? Does that sound OK?'

She looked back at him and they held the stare for a brief moment. She didn't want him to leave. She didn't want to be alone with her thoughts and her wretched emotions. She wanted him to stay by her side so her mind didn't wander again.

But there she sat, while the stranger put on his big, cumbersome boots and his dark mac, then made his way confidently into her back garden as if he'd always known the way and as if he'd always known the land. He raked leaves on the lawn and tended the shrubs.

Myrtle sat and watched as he carried on despite the rain, which fell relentlessly, and she had to wonder at her wisdom in opening up so freely and disclosing the secrets of her life to a near stranger when she'd been incapable of doing so to her own daughters for all these years.

Her head dropped.

She couldn't even make the man in the garden a cup of coffee. Austin would not have coffee in the house and the man did not drink tea. *Perhaps it's time there is coffee in this household.*

Chapter Twenty-five

Christmas was going to be tricky, Geoffrey thought, not just because of the strained atmosphere with Gillian but also the unexpected death of her father and then the fallout from it. It had all been so unexpected – the fallout more than the death – and he couldn't get any sense from Gillian whatsoever on how things might resolve themselves, if at all. But the two of them had agreed, for the sake of Molly, in one of their few mono-syllabic exchanges, to call an amnesty over Christmas – not that there had really been a war of any kind, more a punishing silence.

They resolved to spend a quiet Christmas at home without peripheral distractions or unnecessary interfer-ence. This, in itself, was highly unsettling as Christmases had always formed the same pattern over the years: Christmas Day at Austin and Myrtle's and Boxing Day at Geoffrey's parents'. It was routine that had joyfully become tradition and it felt, for Geoffrey at least, deeply uncomfortable to break with this, even in the circumstances.

The stalemate between himself and Gillian had been broken from time to time by their moderator, Molly, who sensed the stiffness in the air but had no way of evaluating it. Instead, she had managed to make them smile – and her father laugh out loud for the first time in weeks – when she reminded them of how she had one year referred to the turkey in the oven as a 'turtle'. Even Gillian found it hard to suppress a giggle but quickly reminded herself of the punishment she was meting out to Geoffrey and, more importantly, the punishment she herself was still suffering.

Beth had fully expected to want to spend this pivotal, inauspicious Christmas with her mother, but the last bit of news had left her confused, deflated and uncertain. Death was one thing but discovering that her sister was only her half-sister had been another shock.

'I mean, if he was my dad and not Gillian's, then why the hell was it me he couldn't tolerate? It doesn't make sense, Neena.' Beth had started the discussion once again. 'How can you *not* have the blood of one person running through your veins and still be so much like them, huh? That's what I don't get. And why can I be his and not be a *bit* like him?' She was frowning.

Beth frowned a lot nowadays, Neena had noticed – and she couldn't seem to find the right answers for her loved one, regardless of her brilliant legal brain. She felt a bit useless. 'Hon, I don't really know. But I bet you it comes down to that whole "nature versus nurture" thesis – and your situation does appear to come down on the side of nurture, I'm afraid. By nature you're Austin's but by nurture Gillian is – well, seemingly – a bit *more* his . . .' She quickly realized that this was not the positive statement Beth wanted to hear but felt compelled to broaden the discussion. 'I think you're as angry with him as you are with yourself, Beth, for not facing him head on. Don't you think that could be part of it, too?'

No matter how many times they discussed it, Beth remained distracted and confused.

'One thing you *can't* do is punish or ignore your mother – and certainly not at Christmas. I know you want to spend it just the two of us here in the flat but that's not on, Beth.' Neena refused to back down.

'Why not? I've spent enough miserable Christmases without you. This is our first together, properly, and we have a home now,' Beth fought back stubbornly.

'There will be more Christmases, Beth. Just think about how your mother must be feeling. If it's not bad enough that she's lost her husband, that one daughter isn't speaking to her and the other is reluctant, you simply can't punish her by not being there for her. Two wrongs don't make a right and you know it. She needs you. Do the right thing.' Neena was quite forceful: it was as if she felt Beth was so lost in the upheaval, she needed guidance.

'I'll tell you what. Let's not do turkey this year. That's my compromise. Let's take some Indian food over to your mum's. We don't have to have the stress of cooking – we'll just buy it. That way, we'll be bringing a bit of our home to hers. Fair?' She smiled victoriously.

On Christmas Day, Myrtle couldn't help but notice Beth's distraction, in part disguised by an over-enthusiastic Neena, but she had absolutely no clue as to how to approach her, console her or even strike up a conversation with her.

The three of them sat in the living room with plates on their laps, humbled by the silent, sleeping television. The corner of the room that would otherwise have been adorned with the reliable artificial tree Austin had always favoured was bare. Myrtle had not known how to retrieve it from the loft – and even if she had, she wouldn't have felt like decorating it.

She had wrapped a picture from her bedroom dresser of Beth on Austin's lap when she was five years old. It was something money couldn't buy and she hoped it would mean something to her. She also hoped Beth understood the sentiment behind it.

She hadn't known what to get for Neena but the last thing she wanted was awkwardness so she had settled for bath salts, hoping it was not too personal but that the thought counted.

In return Neena had bought Myrtle a set of fragrant body oils she said would lift, energize or relax her, depending on her mood.

'I'm not deliberately making a point, Mum, but I

haven't really got you anything. I'm not being spiteful or trying to hurt you, it's just a really difficult time right now. I couldn't go out and get you something for the sake of it – I don't work like that. It's just that what started as bereavement was kind of stopped dead in its tracks by what you told me. I mean, I would never have believed that something – anything – could possibly eclipse Dad's death,' Beth confessed, in a weary voice.

Christmas had always been rather contained in the Lewis household but this year it was markedly strained, due not least to the underlying silence and a mortally pained Myrtle.

Chapter Twenty-six

It was Gillian at the door on Boxing Day.

Myrtle let out a whimper, uttered her daughter's name and spontaneously held out her arms.

Gillian threw back her head and looked past her through the doorway. 'Are you going to let me in?' Her voice was gentle but firm.

Myrtle hadn't heard this voice before and she immediately dropped her welcoming arms and moved aside to let her daughter past. 'Of course, Gillian, of course.'

She watched her step tentatively into the house and disappear around the corner into the living room. Gillian kept her handbag over her shoulder, standing rigid yet composed, with her arms folded.

'My darling Gillian, you're here! I've missed you so.' The relief in Myrtle's voice was evident as she approached her.

Gillian took a step back. 'I got your parcel,' she said calmly, as she dug the diary out of her handbag.

'You did? Oh, good . . . I'm glad.'

'Is it, Mother? Is it "good" that you took the best part of forty-one years to tell me I'm the illegitimate child of a complete stranger and was brought up to believe that the man who looked after me was my real father?

That's good, is it?' She turned to her mother with more self-control than Myrtle had ever witnessed in her.

'Gillian, dear, no. It's not good. That's not what I meant. I'm not good . . .' she took a deep breath '. . . I may not be a good person . . . I know that,' Myrtle said, bowing her head slightly.

'You see, Mother,' continued Gillian, poker-faced, 'I don't really know where to start. You harboured a secret from all of us. You took ownership of that secret and treasured it in some sad, romantic fashion, cherishing a lie with impunity. A lie with which we have all unwittingly and obliviously lived, like some kind of growth festering away inside, waiting to make itself known and strike us down. I can only hope that the saving grace was that Daddy actually knew.' She forced the words out with contempt in her voice but her face remained deadpan.

'He did!' Myrtle was keen to reassure her on that point.

'Well, that may be, but it's not much to be proud of, is it, Mother? In fact, there isn't much you *can* be proud of, is there?'

'I'm proud of you, Gillian. You must know that,' she pleaded.

'So proud you couldn't help but lie to me all my life? So proud, in fact, that you were willing to allow another man to carry the burden of your big mistake?'

'There was no mistake, Gillian. You weren't a mistake.'

'Funny, that, because according to your *diary* the

man who fathered me sure as hell made it look like I was,' she said, almost lackadaisically.

'Gillian, don't say that. You were wanted. You were very much wanted. I wanted nothing more in the world –'

'Except, perhaps, PC Horton,' Gillian butted in.

'No, Gillian, that's not true. And your father wanted you, too.'

'Which one, Mother? The one who took you in the back of his car or the one who cared for me so diligently for forty-one years?' Frustration had crept into her voice.

'Oh, Gillian, please don't talk like that. You know I mean Austin.' It felt odd to refer to Gillian's father by his Christian name – he had always been Daddy.

'Is that so? Well, Mother, in *Austin*'s untimely absence, I'll just have to take your word for it.'

'Please stop it, Gillian! I wanted to tell you! I was *dying* to tell you all along but it was your father who wanted to keep it a secret. It was one of the conditions of him taking me on . . .' Her raised voice had startled Gillian – it had even shocked Myrtle.

'Won't you sit down, Gillian, please?' She waved in the direction of the sofa without looking at it.

'No. I don't want to sit down. I don't believe there's much to be said between us . . .'

Myrtle's heart was breaking – breaking and sinking. 'How can you say that, my love? You mustn't talk like that.' She knew she mustn't let Gillian go – she had her here and she mustn't let her go. 'My darling Gillian,' she pleaded again. 'We must talk, we must. There has been too much silence in our lives already and for too long – please . . . You must believe me when I tell you that you were very much wanted. I struggled very hard to keep you, against a barrage of disapproval, shame and humiliation. I was living a complete lie, I'm afraid.' She looked up at the ceiling and sighed. 'But I will never forget the first time I held you in my arms – never. Saying that, you hadn't much desire to be born. It seemed you liked it in here,' she patted her stomach lightly, 'but when you arrived, the smell of you made the whole ordeal worthwhile. I remember holding you and touching you – your skin was so smooth it almost disappeared between my fingers – and your little face . . . oh, it was a joy to behold. And your cry! Your cry was a force to be reckoned with.' She smiled tentatively.

'Yes, well, that may be so, but it doesn't excuse the way you cheated Dad into taking you on and forcing him to bear the wretchedness and humiliation of your mistake. Not least bring up a child who wasn't his own.'

'Oh, but you're wrong, Gillian. You're very wrong. Your father wanted me and he wanted you. He was intent on bringing you up as if you were his own. It shames me to say that all the while I was carrying you – waiting interminably, it seemed, for your birth – I used to pray each night that . . . that the man who made you would come and rescue me and take us both away. I was so feverishly in love with him that I hoped he would see the error of his ways – change his mind – and come back for me. But when you were born, Gillian, and I saw the way that Austin, your father, held you and looked at you, I used to dread, with every knock at the door and with every ring of the telephone, that PC Horton would show his face. I believe I loved him once – he was my first love – but your father showed remarkable kindness and generosity in taking me – us – on.'

'That's stating the obvious, isn't it? But you didn't love him, did you?' asked Gillian. 'Your diary says as much. And I don't know why I'm so surprised. I mean, it wasn't as if you and Daddy had any difficulty keeping your hands off each other, was it?'

'It's complicated, Gillian.'

'Don't belittle me!' Her voice rose. 'Please don't treat me like an imbecile. I'm an adult and perfectly capable of understanding emotion – don't you dare pretend I can't understand.' She stared at her mother.

Myrtle breathed in deeply. 'Well, then, you must know that I was passionately in love with PC Horton. I was young, romantic, suggestible – foolish, perhaps. I was very impressionable and I succumbed to his charms. But your father, Austin, offered me the one and only chance of having you and a respectable life of sorts. Things were different back then. A young girl, pregnant and unmarried – it was simply not as acceptable as it is today. Your father had the strength of mind to take me in.' Myrtle looked at her daughter, whose arms remained defiantly folded.

'So you keep saying. But you didn't love him?' she repeated.

'I wasn't in love with him, no, I can't pretend I was. But I believe I grew to love him in some way. I respected him immensely for what he did – how could I not? But we were different, your father and I. We were passionate about different things,' Myrtle replied.

'So, you *didn't* love him?'

'I wasn't *in love* with him.' This was, Myrtle felt, becoming a war of words but she was determined not to be bullied. Not now, not at this most important juncture. 'I think we both compromised, Gillian. He saw that he could offer me a solution, and thought his unwavering love for me would carry him through. I, on the other hand, doubted I could ever love him the way he wanted me to – the way he deserved to be loved – but I promised to remain loyal to him until . . .' She faltered.

'Until the day he died? Is that what you were going to say?'

'Yes, Gillian, it was. I just wasn't expecting it to happen quite so soon. I hoped it would be me who would go first.' She lowered her eyes to the floor.

'Well, you must be relieved, then, that now you're free as a bird and no longer have to *compromise* . . .' swiped Gillian.

'Don't say that! I know you're angry but, please,

please, I implore you, try to understand that I did what I thought was best at the time. And your father was insistent we never told you about PC Horton – I was under the strict instruction that his name was never to be mentioned. I wanted to – I sometimes looked at you and all I could see was him. But I never said a word. I kept it all in here.' She patted her chest. 'I never said a word, out of respect. But it didn't stop me thinking of him from time to time and wondering what might have been. That's the truth, Gillian.'

'So, do I look like him?'

'Oh, Gillian . . .' Myrtle's voice started to dissolve '. . . when you were born, you were the image of him, and your features always pricked my conscience, but there were times when I saw flashes of Austin in you, too. Remarkably, I believe you became so close to one another that it was not only his mind that rubbed off on you. I convinced myself you two looked alike. And . . .'

'And what?'

'Your name. The reason for your name was, well, it reminded me of "Julian" and was as close as your father would let me go . . . That was why I gave you your name. Your father afforded me that luxury, at least.' She cleared her throat.

'Well, thanks for that. Perhaps my scientific mind should have decoded your encryption sooner. Then who knows where we might be?' There was no change in Gillian's tone.

'Gillian, with every day that passed I was terrified you might find out,' Myrtle confessed.

'Well, you've behaved abysmally, is all I can say. Problem is, I don't know what to do with you. Or your diary. I have this rage inside me that I can't extinguish. I have a large hole – blank pages in *my* diary – a part of me that's broken and another part that's void. I don't know what to fill it with.'

After a long pause between them, Gillian asked pointedly, 'Do you know where he is?'

'Who?'

'PC Horton. What happened to him? Is he still alive?'

'Oh, Gillian, I have no idea. As you know, all I was told was that he had moved away. I don't know any more than that.' Myrtle took a step closer to her daughter. 'Are you going to look for him, Gillian?' She could hear the thuds of her own heart.

At first Gillian said nothing, then, 'I don't know . . . I don't know.' She turned and walked towards the window. 'I don't know if I want to see him, know him or . . .' She frowned at a shaft of light coming through the window. She turned her back on her mother and moved towards the door. 'What I can't bear is this idea, this *fact*, that I can't be angry with you because you didn't mean it – you didn't intend to do it. So, tell me, Mother, what do I do with my anger, my hurt and my frustration? The irony isn't lost on me that *I* am the person who has to work it all out and heal my pain – not you. It's me who has to make the repair even though I didn't break anything in the first place.' With that she walked out.

'I hoped she might find it in her heart to at least try to understand,' Myrtle said to Dorothy, when she phoned her a couple of days later. 'I don't know what in this world made me think for all these years that I could get away with it.'

'My dear girl, after the story you've just told me, it's little wonder you hoped you would, but it wasn't your decision to keep the truth from her, was it? Don't let her take advantage of that,' was Dorothy's immediate response.

'It's all such a terrible, terrible mess. The whole thing – all our lives.' Myrtle sighed.

'For a quiet one, you do make quite the actress,' joked Dorothy. 'Who'd have thought the little woman next door had so much colour in her life? Look, this is *not* a disaster. If anything, I believe it will eventually bring you closer together. She just needs time to stew in her own self-pity. You did what you thought was right at the time, and no one can punish you for that. She just needs to get her head around the history of it all . . .'

Myrtle couldn't quite explain why she'd chosen to open up. It might have been a clear case of desperation, if it hadn't been for the fact that Myrtle had chosen to trust her instincts for the first time in ages, and her instincts had told her that there probably wasn't much Dorothy hadn't heard before. There was something about her colourful, gregarious, lively neighbour that invited her confidence. But, most importantly of all, she knew Dorothy was a neutral observer who was likely to have a strong opinion. And Dorothy didn't disappoint.

'I think I've even lost Beth,' Myrtle lamented.

'What on earth makes you say that?' enquired Dorothy, on her mobile, from the comfort of her aunt's house many miles away.

'All those years when she really needed me, I never stood up for her when her relationship with her father collapsed time after time after time. And the irony of the whole thing is that *she* was actually his . . .' Myrtle toyed with the telephone cable.

'Well, why didn't you?' Dorothy ran her fingers through her hair.

Myrtle was taken a little aback by her directness. 'Because I was scared, I suppose. Because I was grateful for what I had and lived in fear of jeopardizing it all . . . foolishly.' She sighed.

'Good Lord, woman, I can see I need to drag you kicking and screaming into the twenty-first century. But I'm afraid that'll have to wait for a bit. I shall be at my aunt's for a few days and when I get back I'll pop over to see you. Remember, a new year is just around the corner – and who knows what that might bring, hey? In the meantime, be sure to put on that top I bought you – if nothing else, it might cheer you up. I must dash – my battery's running terribly low.' She bade Myrtle goodbye and wished her a happy new year.

'Aunty Zita,' said Dorothy, as she turned to the woman sitting on a reclining chair behind her, 'why is it that other people's problems are so much more delicious than our own?'

Chapter Twenty-seven

'Don't you just hate New Year's Eve?' said Gianni, with a big smile, when Myrtle opened the door.

'Oh, goodness! What a surprise!' Myrtle had no time to hide her delight.

'Personally, I reckon it's overrated.' He winked. 'And I thought, I bet I know someone who wants to bin the last year and start afresh ... So, here I am!' he announced, waving a bottle in one hand and a plastic bag in the other.

'Oh, I'm afraid I'm not much company ...' she responded self-deprecatingly.

'Would you give me a chance here?' he butted in. 'I just thought you might want a bit of company ... unless you're already taken up, of course?' he said, raising his eyebrows. He still had his trusty shorts and big boots on but under his jacket he was wearing a shirt.

There was an awkward silence. Myrtle smiled but couldn't find the words. What was it about him turning up at the most inopportune moment and making it feel so opportune? Since she'd last seen him, she hadn't been able to bring his face to mind, but now, as he stood on her doorstep, it was as familiar as his presence was comforting.

'What are you doing here, may I ask?' She smiled. 'You mustn't think me rude but I'm not much fun to be with.' Her hand dropped from the door. 'I don't have anything to offer you, I'm afraid, nothing to give, nothing to contribute. I'm not of much interest to anyone or anything unless, of course, you've come to indulge your curiosity in which case I'm a spectacle to behold . . .' she said, with a hint of irony.

Gianni slipped his big boot over the threshold. He wasn't going anywhere. 'You're no spectacle, love,' he said softly. 'And you didn't have to tell me any of that – I can see it in your eyes.' He stepped through the doorway. 'I can't put my finger on it,' he looked her straight in the eyes, 'but I always had a feeling there was more than *just* sadness behind those eyes. I haven't come to pity you or gloat. I'm here because I like you, Myrtle Lewis, and I think you need a friend. Am I right?'

She blushed. At that moment she felt eroded by the past, drained by the present and intimidated by the future. She felt weak and defenceless. She moved aside and let him in.

She watched as the man who had come so unexpectedly into her life went about her kitchen as if he knew every cupboard and drawer, unpacking groceries and extolling the virtues of Italian food, how good it was, especially for the soul. He offered her a glass of the red Italian wine he had brought and she was embarrassed to admit not only that she didn't drink but that she didn't have a corkscrew.

'No probs,' he said, and plucked a Swiss Army knife out of the pocket of his shorts, unwound the foil across the top of the bottle and dug a corkscrew into it. 'You know, you really should try a bit. Italian wine is the finest in the world – in my humble opinion. We're the ones who kicked off the whole wine-making thing . . .' He poured some into the glasses and held one up to her. 'Go on – won't kill ya,' he said, as he drew his close to his nose and inhaled deeply. 'Now, just breathe in the land in that bottle. You can smell the earth . . .' He took a big sip.

Myrtle was entranced and automatically put her glass to her lips. She let a small amount of wine soak her tongue and anaesthetize it. She felt her shoulders drop.

'How d'you like that, then, Myrtle? Just wait till you have it with the food,' he said, smacking his lips. 'My pa always joked with me about how Aussie women didn't know how to eat pasta, and he said that if I really wanted a good laugh, I should order a bowl of spaghetti on a first date.' He giggled like a schoolboy.

Myrtle liked the way he said 'pesta' and 'spugheddi': it sounded so informal, so familiar, so embracing.

'Now, I don't want you to get any fancy ideas that this is a first date.' He leaned towards her and smiled. 'And don't think I've come here to laugh at you neither.

I just . . . well, I just . . .' he looked as if he was searching for words '. . . I want you to try some real Italian food. I bet you haven't eaten properly since . . .'

She was just about to answer him when he took a step closer to her and asked, 'Have you ever been to Italy?'

'No, I haven't,' Myrtle replied, feeling foolish and interested at once.

'Well, I tell ya, you *have* to go! And you gotta go to Oz, too – it's bonzer. You'll love it.' He smiled broadly.

He talked and talked as he took charge of the kitchen, and all Myrtle could do was touch her tumbler of wine lightly with her fingers, watching him with fascination – and gratitude that she felt so at ease. She put her glass to her lips and took another sip.

Holding a spatula, he turned to her. 'You know, death is a terrible, terrible thing but there are other losses which can also knock you sideways.' His face was sombre.

Myrtle tilted her head.

'I've lost love.' He shook his head, turning back to the stove. And Myrtle was left wanting more. She wanted to know what he meant: how he had lost love and who his loss was.

She couldn't be sure if he was just trying to reassure her and make her feel better – or perhaps he was trying to retrieve some bit of his own past through her. Whatever it was, she preferred the former: she liked the idea of him caring for her.

She looked on silently as his tanned, muscular hands waved the ladle and, from time to time, grabbed the saucepan, moving it backwards and forwards in gentle, rocking movements. She observed how he'd chopped the garlic with speed and accuracy, occasionally looking over his shoulder to smile and check that she was all right.

'I'm making you a *puttanesca* sauce. I think you'll like it – though you might not like the name much.'

'Oh,' was all Myrtle could say, her eyes fixed on his back.

'It kinda means "lady of the night", if you get my drift.' He winked.

She didn't mind what he made. She hadn't had someone cook her a meal like this ever in her life. The scents were warm, earthy and strong. The garlic smelt rather sophisticated. Gianni held his glass of wine with the same strong grip he had held the trowel the day he had offered to help her in the garden.

He served the food and insisted she try it, joking that he wouldn't leave until she'd finished her bowl. Myrtle scrambled for adjectives in her sub-conscious but couldn't come up with any. She just smiled. He winked again and said he was glad she liked it.

'You must miss him an awful lot, your husband . . .' said Gianni, when he'd finished his food. He pushed his bowl away and folded his arms on the table. 'Crikey, you must have been together a good forty years, am I right? At least you were lucky you had all that time together . . . not everyone has that. Bet you were close, you two. Must be hard for you now to be on your own around the place. I feel for ya.' He picked up a stray piece of pasta from the table and put it into his mouth.

'No,' said Myrtle, quietly.

Gianni looked up.

'No.' She exhaled. 'It wasn't really anything like that . . .'

Gianni was taken aback. 'I'm sorry if I've upset you. I didn't mean to.'

'I don't really know what I'm doing . . . Why, Austin would die at the thought of another man in his kitchen, let alone me even so much as touching a glass with wine in it.' She laughed nervously.

'Crikey! Was it some kind of religious thing?'

He looked genuinely put out, thought Myrtle. 'No, no, no . . . Well, yes, it was really Austin's religion – but not mine,' she said, looking straight at him. 'He was a good man, in many ways.' She sighed – a little louder than she had intended.

'I'm sure you loved him very much,' said Gianni, mildly.

'Well, gratitude is no substitute for love. Love should be passionate, vigorous, intense and, above all, instinctive. What is it they say – "If it isn't madness, it isn't love"? No, love should be vibrant and responsive,' she said. 'I didn't give Austin anything resembling that. I was impassive – detached, even. I was not a good wife.'

'I don't believe that for one minute,' smiled Gianni. 'You seem like a good wife to me.'

'Dispassionate and hard-boiled, that was me,' she blurted out. 'Dutiful, perhaps, but indifferent all the same.'

'Nah, don't put yourself down. You mustn't. Puts years on ya . . .' He got up slowly to clear the dishes away.

'I didn't realize I would miss him – and at the same time I feel some peculiar and overwhelming sense of relief.'

'Of course you miss him. He was your hubby – why wouldn't ya?' Gianni said, as he walked to the sink.

'Because I thought I would learn to love him, like he said I would. But I didn't. And now he's had the last laugh – the last word, if you like. He leaves before I do and I sit here choking on my own self-pity, with regret and longing and two daughters who can hardly bear to speak to me.'

'Oh, love,' he said.

Myrtle looked at him with surprise.

He dropped the bowls into the sink and walked towards her. 'Don't talk like that. You know what they say – "You can't choose your family but you can choose your friends."' He knelt before her.

'I don't seem to have huge amounts of either!' She smiled into his kind eyes.

He put his hands over hers. 'Then I'll be your friend, Mrs Lewis. I'll be your friend.' He picked up her hand and kissed it.

Chapter Twenty-eight

A shriek of delight came from Molly's bedroom. 'I can't believe it, Mummy! I just can't believe it! It's snowing! In England!'

Gillian made her way slowly upstairs to her little girl's room, labouring with each step, as if her legs were made of lead. That wasn't all that felt cumbersome. Last night's conversation had left her entire body exhausted and devoid of any will or resolve. By the time she reached Molly's room she was less than thrilled to find Geoffrey had beaten her to it.

Molly was perched on the end of her bed, elbows on the sill, head pressed against the window. Gillian forced a small smile. Her mind was arid and drained of the enthusiasm she needed, as a mother, to muster at a time like this. Self-control and self-restraint were in short supply; tenacity and mettle had left her. Even her teeth had unclenched.

Maintaining an air of martyrdom was harder than she could ever have imagined. Staying silent or screaming had fatigued her, which had, eventually at least, forced her to listen.

'Love,' Geoffrey had said, in dulcet tones, towards the end of their talk the night before, 'I'm laying myself bare here. I'm without barriers, without bias – if I wasn't dressed, I'd be naked in front of you.' His attempt at a joke had been met with a blank face. 'I want you to do the same – lay yourself bare, too. Talk to me, Gill. I just want us to find our way back to being a couple again – not just parents with purpose and duty. I don't know about you but I desperately need to get off this terrible treadmill of obedience, liability, practicality and obligation. Just because we have responsibilities it shouldn't mean we have to be so damn responsible – constantly.

'You know me, Gill, I've never been bothered about who's in control, who wears the trousers. I gladly handed you the baton when Molly was born. But now the balance of things has gone to the extreme and I don't seem to have any power – I'm not even in the race. I'm telling you, something's got to change.' At this point his voice had risen a little for the first time in years.

He had closed his eyes, aware that he had over-stepped his own mark. 'If anything, Gill,' he had continued, more quietly now, 'it should be a relief for you to let go a bit.' He had looked straight at her, his eyebrows seeming to plead for the tiniest hint of agreement.

What is it about him taking control like this that suits his broad, rugby-playing shoulders? was all that ran through Gillian's mind. *Well done, Geoff, I admire you for that. Well done for not letting me walk all over you entirely.*

'And, yes, I have to admit it's been a bloody awful shock and truly terrible timing that you've inadvertently discovered Austin wasn't your real father – but what can I say? There it is – the truth is out now. And your mother can't be enjoying this any more than you are, love. I have to tell you, I haven't met a kinder, meeker woman in my whole life, Gill. Don't be too hard on her, please. Even you've got to see that what really matters is intention. She never meant to keep the cards so close to her chest. And I hope you know that I had no intention of splitting our marriage open by taking a colleague to the cinema.'

He had moved towards her and reached out to put his hands around her waist. In many ways, learning that his wife was the product of someone else had made him hope that maybe some of *that* person's character might at some stage shine through because at times he had felt he was living with a replica of Austin. But he would never dare to say as much.

'Gill, you should think long and hard about investigating the whereabouts of your other father and just consider the consequences. But I want you to know that if you do want to pursue it, I'll be by your side and support you in every way I can, OK?' He had kissed her right temple.

It was this dead end that had left her feeling so defeated. Try as she might, she could no longer find fault with a man whose relentless love and support had accepted – suffered, perhaps – the volatility of someone such as herself. He wanted nothing but the best out of and for her. And she had been determined to squeeze every last drop of badness out of him – and that hadn't amounted to much in the end. She had felt so safe within her marriage that she had given herself permission to push him, accuse him, blame him for all and sundry, because she knew he would never react or even be offended. But now she had to accept that there wasn't much left to complain about. She had gone as far as she could. Not only had she run out of energy but she had exhausted any desire to deaden their relationship.

'Don't let Molly take her gloves off and make sure she's wearing her hat at all times,' Gillian called after him, as he headed out into their garden, which was covered with snow.

'Come on, darling, come out with us!' Geoffrey's breath was on her cheek – she was sure she could hear his heart pounding. He had caught her off-guard, as she stood lost in thought in Molly's room. He had put on that big, chunky knit Gillian had banished to the back of his drawer and a woolly hat Molly had chosen for him last Christmas.

He grabbed hold of her and jigged her gently but provocatively from side to side. 'Come on, let's get you in that sexy all-in-one ski suit you used to wear when we first met . . . the one with the belt and the hood and the awful floral pattern on it. Come outside and have

some fun – relax a bit, take your mind off things ...
What do you say?' He tilted her chin up.

'Oh, I don't –' she started, but Geoff put his fingers
to her lips to hush her.

'Oh, kissing, kissing, kissing!' shrieked Molly, from
the doorway, clapping her hands frantically, high in
the air.

'You wouldn't catch me outside for love nor money,'
Dorothy said, over the phone. 'This is the kind of
weather for explorers and pioneers, not for us beau-
ties.' She laughed. 'So, I'm afraid it doesn't look like I'll
be coming back home to see you any day soon, more's
the pity. I can't tell you how desperate I am to get back
from Aunty Z's.

'Really, Myrtle, visitors are like fish and always go
off after three days and I've well and truly gone off –
I'm way past my sell-by date here. I've done my good
deed for this year and next at this rate. Apart from
anything else, I've run out of stockings and I couldn't
play another game of flipping dominoes if you paid
me. The smell of Vicks is really getting to me. And
some of the involuntary noises coming from Aunty Z
are quite something,' she added chirpily. 'Still, that's
old age for you. She keeps moaning, "Oh, to be seventy
again" – like she was any perkier then! Anyway, I just
called to see if you could keep half an eye on the
house ... and I nearly forgot – how are you?'

'Oh, I'm fine,' Myrtle replied, wondering what it

was like to have guests to stay. She'd always rather longed to do that but Austin had never encouraged it.

Beth, too, had felt it would be treacherous outside. 'Mum, I really think it would be suicidal to try to ride my bike on the roads in this weather. If it's any consolation, I'm going to be housebound, too. But if you really, really need me, I can try to come over with some food later today or tomorrow at worst.'

'Oh, goodness me, no, Beth, there's no need for that. I know I'm not a whiz in the kitchen but I've certainly got enough to keep me going. You look after yourself and don't worry about me – you're very thoughtful,' she said, and put the phone down.

Myrtle had seen snow quite a few times in her life. But this time felt different. It had fallen with such silent fortitude overnight that it had stirred up in her wonder and excitement that would have been curtailed or interrupted by a disapproving Austin: 'This wretched English weather, Myrtle, I ask you – is there no let-up? Just look at it! It's as if it's going out of its way to make work for me. Now I shall have to clear the drive and the car – not to mention the caravan!' He would have shaken his head, drawn in air through narrowed lips and tutted. 'That flaming roof! Do you have *any* idea of the dangers of accumulated snow on house roofs? Do you?' But Myrtle was never given the chance to reply. 'Would you just look at those children out there! I ask you, what kind of parent lets their child play outside in such dangerous – nay, lethal – conditions? It's beyond me. I cannot understand people's ignorance. How can anyone take any pleasure in the stuff?'

Now as Myrtle watched the huge flakes sway elegantly to the ground from a bedroom window, she couldn't help but wonder at the possibility of not having to leave the house for days – if ever again. Seeing each unique snowflake oscillate with such dignity, leisure and freedom through the muted air was extremely calming. Knowing that they would settle and create a sort of insulation around her was reassuring, and with Austin's words still ringing in her ears, her enjoyment made her feel mischievous somehow.

As she made her way downstairs, she heard the sound of loud, intermittent scraping. She peered out of the side window of the front door on to a garden suffocated by snow. She gasped and her hand flew to her mouth. Had she seen Austin in the front garden? She moved closer to the window, squinting. On closer inspection it wasn't Austin. Gianni was shovelling snow in the drive. He looked up through the white-speckled air, waved his spade to the skies, hands held aloft, and threw his head back in a celebratory fashion. Myrtle smiled back coyly and wondered what on earth it would take to make that man wear trousers.

She looked away from the window and into the room where everything stood so still – everything in its rightful place – unmoved, motionless, stagnant.

Mementoes, frames and ornaments stood impassive, hushed and still as death. Life, she was more than aware, appeared to continue, but inside Myrtle and inside the house things had – for far too long – remained distinct only by their obstinate, featureless emptiness. Outside the soft, slow flakes of snow persisted in falling, despite Austin's spiritual disapproval, and Myrtle felt something stir inside her.

Double-quick, she made her way back upstairs where Austin's clothes hung in meticulous order behind paralysed wardrobe doors.

I was powerless with him and now I'm powerless without him, she thought, as she caught her reflection in the mirrored doors. *I was helpless before him and now I'm helpless after him.* Without further hesitation, she threw on yesterday's clothes, stumbled awkwardly into her shoes, put on her coat, went outside and slammed the door hard behind her.

'Hey, Myrtle, isn't the snow wonderful?' called Gianni, as she passed him. 'Where are you going? You shouldn't go out, you know – the roads and pavements are pretty lethal,' he pleaded.

Myrtle stopped, lifted her head and felt flakes of snow melt on her face. 'I've got to go somewhere, I'm afraid. It can't wait. I won't be long.' As the snow fell on her lashes, she looked at him and smiled. 'Thank you, Gianni. Thank you for everything you're doing.' With that, she walked past him.

As she turned right out of her drive, she scrunched

her eyes and ploughed her head into the wind. The snowflakes that had earlier seemed so gentle had gathered momentum and united in their onslaught on every moving thing. The snow had built up on pavements and roads alike. Nothing was distinct – meticulous, regimented gardens, pavements, trees and benches were all draped with a top dressing of snow. Myrtle would have struggled to see her hand in front of her face. Her shoes had already been penetrated by the wet and she couldn't feel her toes for the cold. The firm, steely grip around her handbag refused to loosen. It was as if she was holding on for dear life, every step she took on the unforgiving ground jeopardizing her very being.

Myrtle walked and walked, occasionally skidding and losing her balance. It was hard to see anything but, through the persistent snow against a grey sky, she could just about make out the abandoned cars on the road, their drivers stranded inside them. People stood huddled in hope at bus stops. There was an unusual and unnerving silence, occasionally interrupted by whoops of delight from rushing children armed with makeshift sledges made from plastic bin-lids, laughing as they slipped and fell.

Myrtle could have walked the four-mile journey with her eyes closed – she knew it like the back of her frozen little hand.

Passing the Methodist church on the right, she looked up and, squinting, she could only just read the writing on the snow-capped placard at the front: 'NEED A FAITH LIFT? COME INSIDE, JESUS IS YOUR FRIEND.'

No, thank you, she thought, as she pinched her eyes tighter still and ploughed on. Inside her coat, she was hot and bothered; on the outside, she was frozen, like an ice-lolly. She didn't care. A mile or so further on, past the redundant pick-your-own farm and the cluster of houses on her left, she had reached her destination. And it was Austin's, too.

The persistent snow had already laid claim to paths and was in the process of enveloping little places of vigil, memorials, floral tributes and dedications, which were struggling for recognition under the blanket of white.

There, in the far corner of the cemetery, past the gates that separated the headstones and crosses from the memorial garden, stood a frugal, desolate and undecorated iron cross, bearing Austin's name on a small plaque. The snow in the surrounding area lay smooth and undisturbed. Myrtle bent down, brushed some snow off the cross and felt a small bump on the ground directly below. It was a delicate posy of flowers about to lose their battle against the snow. As she stood back, she looked around. She could see no one in the vicinity.

She cleared her throat.

'I'm sorry, Austin, I've not been here since the funeral. You see, I couldn't find it in me – and what with everything that's been going on, I was beginning to think you were, perhaps, punishing me by going first and leaving me to sort it all out . . .' She paused briefly. 'I've come . . . I've come – not to pay my respects – I was never short of respect for you, Austin Lewis, you know that. Rather, I've come to apologize, to say how sorry I am for not loving you the way I should have done. Maybe you deserved to have someone good loving you – someone who knew how to love you properly. I had hoped I would. I hoped I would grow a love for you somehow, perhaps in the way I grow my plants in the garden – a love that would thrive in its surroundings and be resplendent in its glorious generosity and affection. But I couldn't. You were a difficult man to love. There, I've said it – you were. No matter how hard I tried, for forty-one years, I felt not love but . . . but more an *obligation*. And now you're gone, it seems I miss you for all the wrong reasons. I miss your ability to arrange everything, mend things, sort things.

'I'm afraid I was no good at anything. But you knew that, didn't you, right from the off? They say age brings with it wisdom but sometimes, I think, it comes alone. And I have spent many years trying to work out why you chose me. Why it was me you wanted when you would, I'm quite sure, have had a real chance of happiness with someone else.

'I have felt so grateful for all you did for me, allowing me to have Gillian and never truly forcing romance upon me, but all the same, gratitude was not what you deserved. My gratitude was also my guilt. I felt terrible guilt over Julian Horton, loving the wrong man at such a tender age. Then, as it turned out, I spent the rest of my life feeling guilty about loving the right man wrongly. I wanted so desperately for you to move me – to touch my heart and stir me – but I'm sorry to say you never did. All I felt was some kind of terrible relentless numbness. A numbness that made a grey, lacklustre life for both of us – one that only faded with time. I had to presume there was something fundamentally wrong with me. I cheated you, I know. But you cheated me, too, by being so impossibly tricky and unbending. You made me believe that this was some kind of love. And never – never once – did we speak of these things.

'Fate not only took you away from me but your death told Gillian you weren't her real father – in one fell swoop. I'm afraid she's taken it very badly. And so has Beth – and perhaps that's my fault.

'And now you've gone so I can't ask you what to do. What *am* I supposed to do, Austin?' she said, falling to her knees in the snow, which softened her landing. 'What should I do?'

Chapter Twenty-nine

Every cell and every fibre of Myrtle's entire being ached. From her very core to the outer layers of her skin, the flu had brought with it a pulsating, throbbing head and tenderness throughout her body. Shooting pains attacked her ears, and her throat was thick with infection and inflammation. Her lower back felt rheumatic.

She struggled to move in her bed – weighed down by her own perspiration and the soaked bedclothes. She felt dizzy and disorientated.

Lying on her back in her delirium she was sure she saw Gillian walk into the room, sit down on the bed and administer tablets with a glass of water. She turned over a few times, stirred by her own moaning and groaning, and still Gillian remained at the end of the bed – talking to her softly and slowly, all the while patting her mother's legs.

Day turned into night and the only reminder that she was, indeed, alive was the relentless soreness and the punishing ache deep inside her body. The doctor came. She heard his voice but didn't have the strength to open her eyes.

Beth was there – she could vaguely hear her in the background.

She woke in the night, gasping for water, feeling that if she could just have water she would instantly recover.

Austin was once my remedy and now he has become my illness. The thought passed in waves through her mind.

A few days later the pains began to subside and were replaced by an overwhelming exhaustion, which left her feeling worn, broken and listless. It bore a resemblance to the disarmament, helplessness and defeat she had felt after labour, when hours of sustained, unceasing pain had been compounded by the cries of an unsympathetic midwife who had told her to 'Dig deep!' and 'This is not like riding a bicycle!' The little being in her arms at the end had wiped her memory clean but the pain of the last few days had left her feeling fundamentally empty.

A note on the kitchen table from Beth explained that Gianni had put a thick, traditional Italian soup in the fridge; it only needed heating. Myrtle made it stretch for three days in small, remedial portions.

The snow still covered the ground, the trees and the roofs. Everything felt quiet and subdued as if the stabbing pains in her ears had been replaced by a kind of sound buffer. There was a freshly swept path from her front door to the garden gate. She smiled to herself – Gianni – and her face softened.

Knowing that Austin would have forbidden her to wash her hair on such a cold day, she went straight to the bathroom and did just that. As she stood in the shower, allowing the warm water to pour over her pale, pain-free body, Myrtle knew she must take charge of Austin's clothes and do something with them. Leaving them on their hangers or folded in their drawers would be morbid and desperate – if not unnatural. The girls should share fairly between them any belongings of his that might be of sentimental value. The rest would have to go to the charity shop. She was no Victoria: the keeping of a husband's memory alive with his dead clothes should be reserved for more dedicated wives.

No, she wouldn't cry again – with regret or some sort of shameful gratitude for a man she hadn't loved properly. She was exhausted by the constant feeling that she was balancing precariously on some high-wire of emotions – one wistful breath too many might send her in freefall towards the burning furnace of damnation and guilt. Regret and obligation had had their time. She had served her years in the house of disrepute where her supposed easy virtue had forced her to bow down and abandon all sense of pride. Her parents' way to atone her early transgression had forced her into the arms of a most dignified man – one she hadn't loved – and then left her to get on with it. Now she wanted to move on from a life ruled by an inflicted sense of helplessness and incapacity.

'Myrtle, I think it's quite safe to say that you don't really know your own mind,' Austin had said. No sooner had the words come out of his mouth than Myrtle had instinctively lowered her head to hide her dropped jaw. 'And if you ever did, I think we know it to have badly misguided you and distorted any sense of clarity. No, you have – how shall I say it? – more than blotted your copybook and I think, therefore, it really is best to eliminate alternative and choice altogether. You trust me, don't you, Myrtle?' He hadn't waited for her reply. It was like all his other questions – rhetorical. 'It's best all round if I put forward an opinion on your behalf. I see it as part of my role, as husband and mentor, to shield you from further complications. That is my role as protector, too.' He had smiled proudly.

The years of neutrality, apathy and abstinence had left their mark on Myrtle. She had felt reluctant at the thought of taking the reins and making decisions of her own, but death had brought with it the unexpected and that, in turn, had altered her own sense of where she was going. Ridding herself of everyday reminders of Austin was the direction in which she was veering.

No matter how illicit, underhand and disloyal, no matter how much she knew Austin was incapable of stopping her, she had to do just that: open his wardrobe doors. But instead of feeling wicked inside for disposing of him so capably and so unceremoniously, she was overcome with relief and an unfamiliar energy – she suspected it stemmed from having nothing left to lose.

'Good God, Myrtle Lewis, you look dreadful!' Dorothy had wasted no time on her return from her aunt's house in popping over to see her neighbour. 'What on earth have you been doing? Your face has disappeared! Your skin is translucent and your cheeks, well, they're sallow.' She turned her head from side to side, inspecting Myrtle.

'Oh, I was horribly unwell for a few days,' Myrtle replied.

'Right! Well, I, for one, am in need of some normality after ten days spent with older people who were not afraid to be original, let me tell you.' Dorothy barged past Myrtle into the house.

She made herself at home on the sofa and Myrtle couldn't help feeling how nice it was to have her friend back.

'I want you to know, Myrtle,' she looked up at her earnestly, 'I have every sympathy for what you're going through. It's appalling to lose the love of your life,' she said calmly.

'I'm not sure I could describe Austin in *that* way.' Myrtle smiled awkwardly, conscious that this might bring about a more profound conversation than one about old people or snow.

'No?' was all Dorothy said. 'Well, let me tell you, I know how *that* feels. Many, many moons ago, when I was considerably less wrinkled, I had a true love of my life. It ran very deep – deeply passionate – you know, an eternal kind of love, or perhaps you don't. Anyway, before I knew it, I found myself pregnant. I, of course, felt it was meant to be, but apparently my body had other ideas and within months rejected my aspirations of motherhood. And whatever it was that killed the poor little baby killed our love, too. So, that was that, really. Took me years to get over it, truth be told. I've never allowed myself to get close to a man since. Always kept them at arm's length – not wanted to expose my true self, make myself vulnerable again. Once bitten, and all that ... You see, I've lost love, too. So, you're not alone. Only yours is considerably more tragic, I guess, losing the love of your life so unexpectedly like that –'

'Well, it really wasn't quite like that.' Myrtle felt it only right to set the record straight.

'What do you mean "it wasn't like that"?' Dorothy frowned.

'I once had what I thought was love – but probably only amounted to a passionate schoolgirl crush. I see that now.' Her eyes fell to the floor. 'But I lost him. Pregnancy does take the wind out of the sails of passion, rather. Anyway, he was the father of Gillian. It was Austin who became my protector – my keeper. And what makes it so dreadful is that I didn't love him. I wasn't able to love him – not for want of trying, I can tell you. Little wonder, really. Once you got past Austin's sense of honour in taking me on, you were left with one of life's great moderators – a principled man of overwhelming restraint and self-control. Nothing like me, I'm afraid.' She smiled again, a little nervously. 'And now he's gone and part of me is still carrying a terrible, terrible guilt. It's something I've carried most of my life – old habits die hard.' She tried to lighten the mood with a smile.

'Well, we all carry guilt one way or another. As women we're programmed to do so. God knows, we're made to feel guilty about causing our mothers so much pain at birth and that's just for starters, let me tell you. From that moment on it's a veritable *smörgåsbord* of guilt-trips – one after another. You must understand that guilt is the most painful companion of death – it is the very nerve of sorrow. So, let's hope we can get rid of that somehow. But you, my dear, need to take charge of your life – no more namby-pamby, self-indulgent self-pity. It's about time you grabbed life by the horns. What do you say, hey?' She got up and walked towards Myrtle. 'It's about time we did something about you. I'd never forgive myself if I allowed you to carry on as you are. This is a new year, remember. Life's not over by a long stretch – you must have at least a third left.'

Chapter Thirty

It would have been foolish to attempt to do anything much about the caravan before the snow melted, and much of the country was lying dormant. Besides, Myrtle had needed to be sure she was making the right decision, too, that she wasn't selling the caravan for the sake of it or simply to provoke reaction in others.

She looked out on to the drive where the coldest winter she could remember had left the lawn a depressing yellowy-brown and the border plants shrinking in sheer shock.

The only thing that hadn't changed about the front garden was the greying Sprite caravan, which looked, after only a few months, utterly neglected and even more unwanted than it was.

Myrtle wondered whether she would miss it once it was gone, whether it was a crucial piece in the puzzle of her life or such an integral reminder of Austin that she would regret letting it go. It had felt wrong not to ask the girls' opinion about relieving herself of the unsightly fibreglass monster that blocked the majority of the short driveway. Perhaps she hadn't discussed it with them because she was more than capable of anticipating their responses. That, she consoled herself, was a relief: it was a good sign – even in the current atmosphere – that she knew her daughters very well.

Myrtle agreed with Dorothy that selling the family caravan was a step in a certain direction – which direction she couldn't be sure. According to Dorothy, it was a step into a new world where Myrtle would take control of her life rather than allowing others to make decisions for her.

She had wanted to point out to her friend that she had always been capable of thinking for herself: she just hadn't been granted permission to put her opinions into action.

Dorothy, in return, had been forced to acknowledge that Myrtle was unlikely to move at the same pace as her – Dorothy had had years of experience when it came to doing what *she* wanted. And, as irritated as she was by Myrtle's snail's pace into a life where men did not rule women, she found it incredibly endearing and encouraging that she had made such headway with a woman who had so blatantly been left behind.

When Myrtle had eventually told Gillian and Beth that she intended to sell the caravan, she had been proved right. Gillian had been nigh on incapable of hiding her knee-jerk reaction – even though the therapist she had seen twice had suggested she might be more accommodating of other people's decisions . . .

'Gillian, many people come to me because they need to assert themselves. They need to take control. Could it be that you are here because you want to relinquish some of yours?' she had asked at the end of their first session.

It was at this point that Gillian had burst out crying – disintegrating in the home of the woman who had asked her to call her 'Diane' not 'Mrs Matthews'. It had been the informality that had struck Gillian when they first met, that this woman had not seen it as her role to scold Gillian and tell her how disastrously wrong she had gone but instead to befriend her and not judge.

'I guess I am,' Gillian had mumbled, with her chin tucked into her chest. 'I'm just so exhausted. I find myself irritated to the very core by other people's decisions. It's not that I *want* to be controlling, it's not that I always know best – it's just that I can't seem to help myself. I just find it so much slower to trust others and there never seem to be enough hours in the day . . .' Her eyes burned with tears. 'I can't bear people who dawdle on the pavement – from sightseers and tourists to friends simply chatting as they stroll by the shops. I despise women in high-heels and groomed faces who lack any sense of urgency. I can't stand mothers who don't trim their children's fingernails regularly, and I can't abide couples who relax over glasses of wine while their children run amok in the back garden. I can't stand people without a sense of purpose.' She inhaled deeply.

'I understand, Gillian. You mustn't think you're alone,' said Diane.

'I'm not?' She looked up pleadingly, her face puffy, swollen and red.

At that moment, thought Diane, she had the innocence of a young girl. 'No, of course you're not.' She smiled. 'But I hear you talking a lot about other people and what they do and don't do. I want to talk a bit more about you . . .' and that had been the start of peeling away the layers that made up Gillian Lloyd.

Gillian took a deep breath, closed her eyes and counted to ten in her head. 'I would just like to say, Mother, that that caravan has been like a member of the family to me. I can't even begin to tell you how much it's meant over the years. I mean, it's steeped in happy memories of my childhood and our wonderful holidays.' She turned her face to the heavens to stem the tears that threatened. 'Obviously, I have to respect your decision – I know I do. It's just that the caravan became a second home during the holidays, if you remember . . .'

She had hoped the last sentence would somehow tug at her mother's memories and subsequently perhaps her heartstrings. She had decided against trying to describe the caravan's familiar musty smells and the creaking, thudding, humming sounds it made. It was hard enough trying to control her agitation. She finished simply and sadly: 'I can't imagine life without it. If there was anything in the world that represented Daddy, that caravan was it.'

Myrtle had been very impressed with her daughter's relatively controlled response, but it was for the exact reasons Gillian had given that Beth had been so thrilled at the prospect of the caravan being sold. 'Good riddance!' she'd shouted down the phone. 'All those miserable bloody holidays with Dad controlling our every move and being so entirely anal about where everything went! I won't miss the bloody thing, that's for sure! I can't believe some anorak actually wants to *buy* it . . . The whole idea of getting into it after a four-hour car journey to some lame, uninspiring caravan site fills me with dread to this day. It wasn't even as if we went anywhere the weather was good. While the rest of the country discovered air travel and Europe, we were stuck up in Cumbria freezing our tits off.'

Myrtle hadn't expected quite such a tirade of abuse towards a relatively harmless inanimate object but she was perfectly positioned to understand it: there had never been, for Beth, an object that so completely and unequivocally personified her father as the caravan. So, Myrtle wasn't surprised that it had created such a stir inside her, particularly as Beth was still trying to come to terms with the abrupt end of her unsuccessful relationship with her father.

For the first time in Myrtle's life she resolved to do what was best for *her* and not what others wanted or expected her to do. It had been a boost to have Dorothy nearby to guide, reassure and convince her that she was a capable woman.

Always preceded by a loud, jovial 'Cooee!', she would pop her head around the door. Often she stayed for a chat. By now Myrtle had tea *and* coffee to offer, but Dorothy's face still spelled disappointment.

'My dear girl, there's nothing wrong with a little afternoon tipple once in a while, you know!' She chortled as she squeezed past Myrtle in the doorway. 'Darling, today – like every other day – I'm here to make you feel so much better. I've brought some goodies with me! I hope you're up for a bit of fun and indulgence.'

Myrtle followed her, feeling she had been caught unawares.

'Don't panic, dear,' Dorothy said, as she placed a carrier bag on the kitchen table. 'I come with reinforcements. And I can tell you for starters, I'm not taking no for an answer.'

Myrtle took strength from that – in any case, she was rather looking forward to whatever it was Dorothy had to offer.

'Now, I know you're not exactly known for your courage, so I want you to have at least half a glass – just for relaxation purposes, of course,' she said, as she lifted a bottle of wine from her bag. This was swiftly followed by various tubs and sachets, a bottle of beer, some eggs and a large cucumber.

Dorothy placed Myrtle in one of the kitchen chairs. She talked about the virtues of facials, deep conditioning treatments on tired hair and split ends, how unlikely seaweed and mud were as beauty products but how they really worked, and that Myrtle would love the effect of the beer and egg application on her hair.

Before she knew it, Myrtle's hair was covered with some treatment or other, her face blackened with a mud and seaweed concoction and her feet soaking in a bucket of warm, salty water. She smiled to herself. She couldn't help feeling a little ambushed – but there was very little choice with a person like Dorothy around. For that she was grateful. She couldn't imagine herself complying quite so easily a few months ago. But she rather liked this feeling of the unexpected.

The doorbell rang and Myrtle jumped.

'You expecting someone?' Dorothy wondered.

'I don't believe so,' Myrtle replied. Hurriedly, she took her feet out of the bucket and, skidding on the linoleum floor, ran to the door and opened it.

'Holy Dooley!' exclaimed a shocked Gianni, taking a step back from the porch. He gaped. 'Well, don't you look a picture! Blimey, Myrtle, what's happened to you? You look like you need a bit of a wash.'

'Oh, Lord,' exclaimed Myrtle, putting her hands up to her face and smearing the seaweed and mud mixture. But before she had a chance to say another word, Dorothy emerged behind her and pulled the door wide.

'Well, look who it is! Gianni D'Amico! What on earth are you doing here, you old rascal, you?' She pushed in front of Myrtle and gave him a big hug.

Then she turned back to Myrtle. 'Mrs Lewis, I didn't know you were receiving visitors!' She fanned her face theatrically with her hand. Her arm remained around Gianni.

Myrtle felt a little stab in her heart and was grateful the mess on her face concealed her blushing jealousy.

'Ah, nah, we're just gardening buddies, aren't we, Myrtle?' Gianni winked.

'And first-name terms, too, hey, Myrtle?' Dorothy winked, too.

Myrtle wished all the winking would stop. It was suggestive and not helping her embarrassment.

'Well, I've clearly come at the wrong time so I'll be on my way and pop by another time,' Gianni cut in. 'You two ladies have yourselves a lovely afternoon – and good luck getting that muck off your face.' He gestured in Myrtle's direction.

''Bye, Gianni!' Dorothy waved enthusiastically. 'See you at salsa on Wednesday.'

Myrtle closed the door on the visitor with a feeling of dissatisfaction, which suddenly appeared to have eclipsed her embarrassment. She couldn't work out if it was the fact that Dorothy had acknowledged Gianni in such a familiar way that had irritated her or whether it was the idea that they would see each other again on Wednesday night.

As Dorothy followed Myrtle into the kitchen, she overtook her, pinching her bum. 'You dark horse, Myrtle Lewis! You dark, dark horse!'

'What do you mean?' Myrtle tried to conceal a smile.

'Just you look at me, young lady. What are you hiding from Miss Perkins? Come on, you can't keep anything from me!' She took Myrtle by the arm and swung her around to face her.

'Honestly, I don't know what you're talking about,' Myrtle riposted. 'He's a very charming man and he's been kind to me. He shares a love of gardening and he's helped me out with that, too.'

'Who are you trying to convince, Myrtle Lewis, me or you? Why, if it wasn't for that mask on your face, I'd put good money on the fact that you're blushing right now!'

'Oh, don't be silly,' Myrtle said. But, try as she might, she failed to straighten her face.

'Well, jolly nice for you, my love,' Dorothy said. 'He's a lovely man, I can vouch for that.' She patted Myrtle's shoulder.

When she had gone, Myrtle finished her glass of wine and headed straight for the shower.

As she stepped out, she stood in front of the mirror above the sink and wiping the steam off it, she dared herself to think that the mask had done something to her face, not least put some colour into it.

Chapter Thirty-one

There weren't many people Gillian trusted – not now, not ever. But she had always trusted the weatherman, come rain or shine. It was a huge relief when he announced that, after weeks of the country shuddering under perishing January temperatures and perilous amounts of snow and ice, the thaw was finally on its way.

What people failed to grasp, in Gillian's opinion, was that meteorology was a near exact science – and you could trust science, even when you couldn't trust people.

Alongside the general population, which had been fighting a losing battle with the Arctic weather, Gillian had been fighting her own battles. It seemed pertinent that, as with the weather, another thaw was occurring – one that, slowly but surely, was tenderizing an other-wise rigid Gillian. It was something she had, perhaps, to thank both her therapist and the weatherman for.

She knew the address. She even knew its distance from her home. Over the years she'd sent enough Christmas cards there to keep several charities afloat. Except, that was, for the Christmas which had just passed. It was only a few months ago that she had struck everyone off her card list in an act of fury and defiance because there was no point in *pretending* you wished everyone a merry Christmas when, really, you didn't give a jot.

So, as she stood in the street, it felt odd to see the place for the very first time. She couldn't deny the feeling of awkwardness – but it was not linked to a sense of obligation.

Whatever it was, she was rather impressed by the large stuccoed windows of the ground-floor flat – they must be ideal for letting the light flood in: perfect for an artist.

'Bloody hell, Gill, what are you doing here?' Beth blurted out, as she opened the door to a dark, narrow hallway with a single, failing light-bulb dangling from the ceiling.

'Well, if it's not a good time, I can always –'

'No, hell, no, of course not,' Beth interrupted, for fear of losing this highly unexpected opportunity. 'I just didn't think you knew where . . . well, how to find it.'

She led her sister down the hallway to the first door on the right, which stood ajar.

Once inside the flat, Gillian didn't know where to look first. It was a sensory overload of burning incense, brightly coloured walls and loud jazz-type music playing. It was, in an opinion Gillian would keep to her new restrained self, a shambolic mixture of mismatched materials draped over a large, deep, yielding sofa, an extraordinary collection of exotic ornaments, half-empty boxes pushed against corners and walls, books piled high on two small desks in the corner, hundreds of framed photos, paintings and pictures plastered across the walls and redundant clothes drooping over chairs.

'I'm living the cliché, aren't I? Bet you're horrified, Gill. It's not normally like this but, no matter how I try to make space for Neena's things, I'm gradually realizing that compromise appears to be the key to the future. Yep, compromise is the word of the year so far . . .'

'Isn't it just?' Gillian said quietly. She didn't necessarily want the coffee that was placed before her on the low table but, with the word 'compromise' still rattling around in her head, she wrapped her hands around the mug. 'I wonder why it's always winter and bad weather when horrible things happen . . .' she said, staring out of the large bay window facing out into the street.

'You won't remember,' she continued, 'but I reckon I must have been about ten or eleven when Granddad Hale died. It was dismally cold then, too. You were only tiny but I remember Mummy really crumbled – sort of secretly, anyway. She tried to hide her tears from me but every so often she would disappear into the bathroom or go and rest on her bed in the middle of the day. Granddad Hale was a doctor – did you know that?'

'Er, no, I didn't,' Beth replied, wondering where all this was leading and whether there was a catch. 'I mean I've seen pictures of him and Mum always talks of him fondly, doesn't she? But she never mentioned Grandma . . .'

'No, she died a few years later. Don't think there was much love lost between them. Maybe it's true what they say about mother–daughter relationships being notoriously tricky . . .'

Ah, there it was. Beth nodded to herself. That was why her sister had come.

'Anyway,' said Gillian, aware that her presence was unexpected, 'I just wanted to say sorry . . .'

'Sorry?' Beth probed, keen for a full and frank disclosure.

'. . . for my silence, for not speaking to you after I found out about – you know, Daddy . . .'

'Oh.' Beth listened intently. It was more than three months ago now.

'Truth is, I didn't know where to put myself. When I found out, I wasn't sure how I was supposed to feel. I've always known how you should feel – when you marry you feel happy, when you give birth you feel pain . . .' she was grasping for something else '. . . when you put out the bins and the dustmen even take that extra bag of rubbish – you feel satisfaction . . .'

'Ah, I don't know about those last two. Especially as I'm just thrilled if I even remember to put the bags out on the right day.'

Gillian looked at her with a straight face and Beth inclined her head, as if to pave the way for her sister to carry on.

'It was a bit of a shock, you might understand. And I felt angry. I was furious with Mummy for not telling me sooner – I felt it was my right to know. I was even angry with myself for not working it out . . .' She looked at her sister to gauge her response.

'Well, maybe that's not as daft as it sounds. But in the circumstances I would have put money on it being me . . . you know, who wasn't Dad's . . .' Beth smiled.

'Well, therein lies the irony. My silence must have seemed selfish – indulgent, even.' Gillian paused. 'Your face tells me as much and I don't blame you. But the irony is that I couldn't speak to you because at the time I was so jealous of your biology – I begrudged you your natural history with Daddy . . .'

'Blimey, Gill, you had something considerably more tangible, wouldn't you say? You had a proper relation-ship – you had a connection, regardless of genes. I had something I didn't particularly want – his blood running through my veins but no affinity with him.'

'Oh, but you –' Gillian started.

'No buts, Gill. It's just the way it was – is. And when he died, I missed something I hadn't ever had, which, in itself, is pretty warped, isn't it? I just hated the feeling of being wronged, being denied, being made redundant right from the start.' She smiled at her sister as if to indicate that it was all right – it hadn't actually been – but that was just how things were.

'Geoff says I lionized him. No one quite measured up to Daddy. I put him on a pedestal. Perhaps he was too high up for you to reach . . .'

Both women were silent for a moment. Then Gillian put her mug on the table. 'And there's Mum, of course,' she said, fidgeting in her seat. 'Who would have thought such a mild-mannered, quiet little woman would have such a big past?'

'Yes, sizeable indeed. Weird and pretty shocking, if I'm honest,' Beth admitted.

'She sent me her teenage diary, penned like a Barbara Cartland novel – except with an illegitimate child.' They smiled. 'But it was like I was reading about this woman I'd never met – it was as if there was this whole other woman we never, ever knew . . .' Gillian shook her head in wonderment. 'Strange, isn't it, that you think your childhood is normal and everyone else's is peculiar? I mean, I never questioned the lack of affection between them – the absence of affirmations of love and the odd bit of romance. It didn't really register. I just saw them as old and that that was how people behaved.'

'Sssh!' said Beth, suddenly, with a finger over her mouth. 'Did you hear that?'

'What?' Gillian replied, clearly spooked.

'*That*, just then, dear sister, was the sound of the two of us talking . . . not fighting, not winding each other up, just talking like grown-ups.'

Gillian frowned. 'Oh, for goodness' sake, you had me worried then.'

'Sorry. But it's nice, isn't it? It's just a shame that it's taken a death to bring it about.'

'A death, a meltdown and a little help from a therapist . . .' Gillian smiled coyly.

The floodgates had not opened. Rather, this was the merest perforation of something that had hitherto been a solid partition. The conversation trickled on until Gillian looked at her watch, made her excuses and got up.

At the door, Beth moved towards her, arms open.

Gillian hesitated, her arms only lifting to reach her sister's waist. 'I'm not sure if it's a good idea for you to hug me. I fear I might still crumble,' she whispered into Beth's shoulder. 'It's something I'm still working on.' Her voice faltered.

Beth let her go. 'Well, you work away. But I'm here if you need me,' she said, as she closed the door behind her.

Chapter Thirty-two

The middle of March saw snowdrops with their fragile, pendent white flowers pushing through the thawing ground much later than normal and daffodils pointing large yellow cups towards the spring sun, and Myrtle felt her heart lighten a little. When she had first laid out the garden many years ago she had so wanted to plant 'Queen of the Night' tulips but Austin had strongly objected to their maroon-black flowers as much as to their name. He had insisted Myrtle should stick to the plain 'Bellona' – a single-cupped tulip that would complement the other spring flowers.

Myrtle reflected that she hadn't stood her ground even about something so seemingly trivial but which had been significant to her. This coming autumn she might change the planting and rectify the matter of her age-old compliance. She thought how nice the garden looked and finally recognized that, despite the turmoil of the last few months, with such prolific germination and the increasing daylight blessing it, the garden had always given her a tiny sense of hope – hope that was now starting to blossom.

How could I not look forward to Gianni coming over in the week? She smiled to herself, looking down on the primula he had brought her, which she had longed to plant out. *And that smarting feeling you had in your stomach a couple of weeks ago when he was unable to come – what was that about, Myrtle Lewis? You couldn't settle all day, you know you couldn't. It wasn't indigestion, much as you pretended it was. It was something else, wasn't it? Was it longing? You'd do well to be a bit more honest with yourself, you wistful old fool.*

'Now then, Myrtle, no peeking! I want you to guess what plant I'm holding behind my back,' he'd said, when he'd turned up the following week.

She had beamed. 'Oh, Gianni, there's absolutely no need for you to bring me a plant every time you come! It's quite enough that you –'

'That I what? You nearly said it then! That I just turn up? Is that what you wanted to say, hey? Well, you're not wrong there. But I love your little face when I bring you something for the garden.' He handed her a pot. 'Now, how's about you talk me through some of your planting today? What d'you say? C'mon, Myrtle, get those gardening gloves on those cute little hands of yours and let's get out there in the wilderness.'

She had laughed at his persuasive powers – and had been quietly grateful for his persistence: she had truly missed the sense of calm and reflection in which she could indulge while she was in the garden.

'Now,' he turned to look up at her while he was kneeling by one of the herbaceous borders, 'once spring is in full flow, I reckon we should take a trip out to Hergest Croft Gardens – you know, out Herefordshire way. They've got the best collection of rhododendrons. And you want to see the magnolias – ah, they're to die for. And the cherry trees surrounding the main house! Just you wait till you feast your eyes on them! I've been a thousand times and it just gets better and better!' he'd said with such enthusiasm and gesticulation that he had almost lost his balance.

She had wanted to show some dignity in her response but instinctively she exclaimed, 'Why, I'd love to!' Austin had never shown much interest in visiting gardens and it was such a thrill to have someone so enthusiastic and willing.

'Really? Would you really think of coming?'

'It *is* rather a long way to go . . .' she mused. 'I don't know . . . would it be so wrong?'

'You know what, Myrtle Lewis? There's something of the Catholic about you, something kinda orthodox. Now, I'm not religious or nothing but the way you give yourself such a hard time – it's like you've got huge sins on your conscience, crimes to answer for . . . like you're condemned or something. I should know. I was brought up a Catholic and I left it all behind. But you, you give yourself a good beating, don't you?

'Oh, I'm sorry', Gianni interrupted himself. 'I don't want you to do something if it doesn't feel right. That's the last thing I want. I just thought . . .'

'I know, I know, and you're right. It's been years and years of this unbearable, burning pain in my heart and it's been in my throat every time I've wanted to speak.'

'Sssh.' Gianni stood up. 'You mustn't talk like that. I only wanted to take you to see a garden.'

'And I would love to go! Maybe part of me is scared . . . because it feels like I can't possibly deserve to go with someone quite as kind as you.'

'Oh, no, that's not true at all. You mustn't feel like that. And if it will help you to stop feeling like that, then we *must* go,' he said. Then he had lifted her chin with his hand. 'Who knows? By May we might even get to Chelsea!' He landed a light kiss on her cheek.

Chapter Thirty-three

It had been such a relief, some weeks later, when Beth, out of the blue, had asked if she could pop around because she had something to show her mum.

Myrtle didn't feel fear or anxiety this time, as she had done on a few previous occasions when Beth had simply turned up unannounced, saying she needed 'a talk'. This had invariably turned out to be, by Myrtle's standards, more of a conversation of great profundity – and always about Austin. A few times Beth had brought Neena with her for what Myrtle could only assume was moral support but also, it turned out, to act as mediator for opinions or versions of events that had a tendency to clash or simply differ.

At times, Myrtle had to admit that her daughter's anger, which manifested itself in an agonizingly infectious silence and an almost touchable kind of darkness, had forced the atmosphere to become incredibly strained.

'My darling Beth, it's one of life's great ironies that you, who are your father's own flesh and blood, have turned out to be very little like him and that your sister, who was rather more imposed on him, is so similar. I have to be honest with you, Beth,' Myrtle had taken her hand, 'I was perhaps as surprised as you. You see, for me it seemed almost predictable that your father would reject Gillian in some way. I was fully expecting it, but he never did.' She had smiled and gazed into the distance, past Beth.

'Yeah, some irony . . . But I just can't imagine hating your own child,' was Beth's response, and her mother was immediately brought back into the room.

'Oh, no, Beth, stop this talk of hate. He didn't even dislike you – that much I do know. But I can't help thinking that he felt threatened by you somehow. Does that make any sense at all?' she asked, but didn't wait for an answer. 'You see, he liked to be in charge, your father. He liked to be in control. He liked to know where he stood. He certainly wasn't a man who cared much for unpredictability, and maybe he felt uneasy with your fearlessness and willingness, your brilliance and radiance. Your father wasn't one for colours – he was a . . . How shall I put it? A monochromatic man. And not a tolerant one at that.'

'I just can't help feeling he judged me against his and Gillian's standards and I simply didn't measure up. That's a horrible feeling, Mum. It's just horrible.' Beth shook her head.

'I know. I really do know. If it's any consolation, my mother, your grandma, whom you won't remember, she preferred your aunty Wren. I'm afraid she didn't take to me at all. So I know that feeling, Beth, all too well. No child should ever have to feel like that, never.' Myrtle had leaned over to embrace her beloved daughter.

Myrtle didn't know what came over her during those conversations because never before had she been capable of putting so many words to her emotions, but she had to presume that it was a remedial mixture of Austin's absence and her maternal instinct to protect her daughter, which she felt she had failed so miserably to do up to that point. She wondered if the presence of Gianni in her life had anything to do with it, too . . .

Beth had been intent on taking issue with her mother on many occasions because, as things stood, the situation seemed so intangible: there was nothing for her to cling to, apart from her own hurtful words and her subsequent lonely silence. She craved noise, volume and some physical substance – anything that would amount to her father's presence. It simply wasn't enough that her mother showed such relentless empathy.

When Beth was at her noisiest and most objecting, Neena had stepped in with words of depth, wisdom and understanding, which helped defuse the situation. 'I'm sorry, Beth, but you're just being unreasonable now.' Neena had acted on the urge to raise her voice, although she knew that in court this would not necessarily be acceptable. 'You can't run roughshod over your mother and not listen to her,' she continued, as she moved from her side of the kitchen table to where Myrtle was sitting. She stood behind her and placed an arm around her shoulders. 'Self-pity is fully expected in the circumstances but sometimes you're positively overdosing on it! You have to hear her out. Perhaps it's taken your father's death for her to be able to speak. Maybe she's been terrified all these years to say anything for fear of the consequences. This isn't *just* about you – and you know it. This is about a complicated network of liaisons from the past and the present. Myrtle can't be ignored or bullied into submission, can you, Myrtle?' she said, looking at her and smiling.

Myrtle smiled back hesitantly. She couldn't help but warm to Neena. Lovely Neena, with her flawless skin, shiny hair, bright mind and impeccably clear vision . . . Myrtle smiled every time she thought about her. When Neena leaned forward to kiss Myrtle goodbye and rubbed her arm reassuringly, Myrtle no longer recoiled or failed to reciprocate. It seemed only natural and right to express her gratitude to her.

This time when Beth called she sounded different. Her voice was buoyant and excited. 'Right, well, I just wanted to make sure you're in. And I want to make sure you're in a good mood. Are you?'

Myrtle thought she could almost detect a giggle in her voice. 'Yes, I'll be in, of course I will. Am I not normally in a good mood?' she dared to ask.

'Of course you are, but I just want you to have an open mind.'

Myrtle didn't quite know what she meant but she was encouraged by the conversation because it felt like a sign that they had – against not insignificant odds – made some headway in the state of their relationship.

Myrtle's fearful, pessimistic, glass-half-empty side sometimes forced her to keep positivity at bay in favour of nervousness. Beth was very clear that Neena would not be coming with her this time, and Myrtle couldn't help feeling a small longing in her heart, in the way a child might without its comforter or security blanket. Could it be that together they could now fly without assistance?

When Beth arrived, she made sure her mother was seated in the living room. She went out and returned with a large canvas covered with an old towel. Myrtle thought it must be at least four feet by five, and although it was light, it was clearly a struggle for Beth to get it into the house.

She put a kitchen chair directly opposite Myrtle, across the coffee-table and leaned the canvas against its back. 'Mum, these past few months have been a struggle, haven't they? I mean, it was the biggest curve-ball anyone had ever thrown my way – well, our way. But for me it was complicated. I've gone through the whole gamut of emotions – I've made no attempt to hide it, I know – and I *still* haven't decided which one to settle on . . .

'But part of my insane cathartic process has been to do what I always do when I'm in turmoil and that is to paint. Maybe it's what I do best – I'm not much good at anything else . . . Although I'm not sure Daddy would even give me that. But then this was really kind of inspired by my new friend, Gianni . . .'

Myrtle frowned quizzically.

'I like him, you know. He's got really good energy. He's a great listener and he's made me look at things in a different light, I guess. Anyway, it was his idea originally. It took me some time to get going, I can tell you, and I had a few false starts, but I wanted you to be the first to see it, Mum. I really hope you like it,' she said. With one hand behind the canvas, she grabbed the towel and whipped it away.

And there he was – Austin Lewis: no longer in pain, in conflict, in between daughters or incongruous – just in oil, looking sombre and confident in a suit and tie painted from a photograph taken of him a few years after their wedding. Myrtle couldn't help thinking how very little he had changed over the years. He had been a man who had looked old before his time, she thought.

'Jeepers! He *was* a miserable-looking chap, wasn't he?' said Dorothy, in all seriousness, as she walked into the living room and clapped eyes on Beth's painting. 'I mean, no disrespect to your lovely Beth, she's right on the money with the quality and all that, but by Christ, he exuded seriousness even at that young age, didn't he? I mean, you can say that now, can't you, M, now that he's gone?'

Myrtle smiled. She liked Dorothy calling her 'M'.

For one, it indicated a familiarity between them – something she had not been afforded by friends since she was a young girl. It was also a genuine term of endearment – which Austin would have balked at. Terms of endearment were reserved only for the unctuous. But for Myrtle, Dorothy's passing reference was the acceptance she had longed for.

Myrtle, looking at the painting, tilted her head to one side to work out if she could see something in Austin's defence. She wouldn't give in to the nagging feeling that it wasn't right to talk about Austin in that way. 'You're quite right, Dorothy – he does look flaming miserable.'

Myrtle had been thrilled with Beth's painting – more for Beth's sake than her own. Clearly, the act of committing brush to canvas brought Beth alive, and Austin, too, in the way she needed him to be. There was more colour in his face than there had ever been in the photograph, and that was of Beth's making. The exaggerated facial creases and the two distinct frown lines between his brows had very successfully immortalized him in the way a photograph never could – the texture and thickness of the oil on the canvas had created a 3-D effect.

It was Beth's impression of her father; it was her description of him and her expression of his very being. His tightly shut lips looked thinner on the painting than they had been in life. He was a serious man, and there was no denying he had often been miserable, but that was just what he was – nothing more and nothing less. When Gianni had seen it, he had said there was honesty in the painting.

Beth might not have liked the fact that her relationship with her father would remain unresolved for all time but she had at least accepted that she had done all she could. She could never deny – as she had felt obliged to admit to Neena – that she had probably 'subconsciously' come to cling to Gianni, as if he were some kind of adoptive father-figure. Neena saw no shame in that and actively encouraged their friendship. And Myrtle agreed with whatever Neena had to say because she knew it was highly likely to be right.

'It's clearly what she sees. It's her knowledge of him and it don't get much more honest than that, does it?' Gianni had said. 'Do you like it?' he persisted, after receiving no reply to his first question.

'Well, I'm not sure if it's for me to say whether I *like* it or not. I like Beth's talent and I like the fact that she has created it. But I don't much like the subject,' she said, looking straight at it from the doorway of the living room. 'It's funny . . . All this time I've been thinking I didn't *love* him but now that he's here – right in front of me – I suppose it tells me what I've always felt, that I didn't like him much. Perhaps I had some kind of love for him . . . I don't know.' She walked into the room and immediately turned to look at Gianni.

'What I don't understand is why you suggested she

paint it in the first place?' It sounded confrontational and it was supposed to. She was questioning his thinking, but perhaps more than anything, she was challenging his motive.

'Oh, you know, it was just a thought I had. It was like putting two and two together – it seemed obvious. I thought, having seen some of her work, that she'd not only make a bloody good job of it but that it might do her some good, you know, help her channel her feelings into something . . . productive, artistic . . .'

'Is that it?' said Myrtle.

'And I wanted you to have something of him and of her – something reminiscent of him for you to have. But I didn't want you to think for one second that I was trying to muscle in – take his place or something. And I figured that if you had this, you would keep him a bit more alive – if you know what I mean . . .' His explanation petered out.

'Well, there's nothing new in that – people thinking they know what's best for me . . . Maybe I don't want to keep him alive any longer. Did you ever consider that?' She kept a courageous stare on him.

'Er . . .' he mumbled.

'Gianni, there's something you should know.' She moved closer. 'You could never take his place. Apart from anything else, I wouldn't want you to take Austin's place, as such. You, Gianni, are a warm, funny and considerably more lovable man.' She turned her head to one side and smiled, and he smiled back.

Chapter Thirty-four

Gillian hadn't been terribly keen on the painting but she had made every effort to be civil about it when she realized what tremendous effort Beth had put into creating it.

'I didn't say as much, of course. I've been told by Diane to "assess my levels of tolerance" on a day-to-day basis,' Gillian told Geoffrey, as they drove to pick Molly up from a birthday party one Saturday afternoon nudging Easter.

'Well, we could all do that,' Geoffrey replied encouragingly.

'Hardly. You've been quite tolerant enough. The funny thing is, I think she really hit the nail on the head about tolerance. I've always *wanted* to be tolerant and I've probably always hated myself for not being very good at it . . .' she said, leaning towards the car window. Her breath left a cloud of condensation on it and she brought her finger up and drew a mindless squiggle. 'Diane wondered if I might have been resistant to changing my behaviour all these years – my *intolerance* towards others – because I feared it might be rejecting Daddy in some way. It does sound ludicrous, doesn't it? But I've given it some thought and there might be something in what she says.'

Geoffrey was given no chance to interject.

'I mean, I know I'm so much like Daddy. That's the irony of the situation. I'm impatient. I can't bear the dawdling of other people. It burns me up inside.'

She turned to him. 'Diane suggested that my low levels of tolerance may also have driven the wedge between me and Mother . . .' She waited for a reaction but none was forthcoming because Geoffrey was keen to listen: he had never heard Gillian speak like this.

'It's as if the slower she moves or acts, or the more time and understanding she shows others, the faster I go, and before I know it, I've succumbed to a complete lack of rationale. Does that sound right? Does that sound familiar to you, Geoff? Tell me.'

He was itching to respond but it seemed unethical; it seemed as if he was siding with the therapist and he didn't want to discourage his wife – he didn't want to kick her while she was clearly vulnerable.

'It seems I've failed miserably to preserve even the tiniest crumb of understanding for my mother's patience and tolerance. I know I'm snappy, I know I'm highly strung. It's a ghastly feeling, Geoff – exhausting, too, I might add. And it's not making me very happy. So, the aim is to take responsibility – as long as my mother does too, of course. And then there's the other fifty per cent of me, which I don't know about at all,' she said, putting her arm on the car-window ledge and resting her head on it.

So, while learning patience and tolerance was a big step, she understood that she also needed to learn something about 'truth and reconciliation' in order to achieve closure, if nothing else.

She needed to say things she didn't particularly want to, and when she had explained that to her mother, *she* had pointed out that 'wanting' and 'needing' had been two very different things for her entire life and perhaps always would be.

The two of them had done something they had never done before – not even with Molly: they had met alone over a pizza in the centre of town.

The Easter holidays had started and the restaurant was bustling with people, mostly families but also couples. While some were taking off coats, hanging them on the backs of chairs, others were attempting to pin lively children into high-chairs and stopping menus being deliberately dropped on the floor by irresponsible older siblings.

At the far end there was an authentic-looking pizza oven with a stout round top and small mouth, open to receive the round, flat pieces of dough heavy with toppings.

The smell was welcoming and nurturing, and made Myrtle's stomach churn from hunger, not nerves.

'I've been more or less instructed by Geoff to have a glass of wine. He says it'll relax me. He also recommended you have one, too,' said Gillian, eyeing the menu but not taking any of it in. 'I felt we should meet somewhere . . . er . . . *neutral*. Gosh, that makes it sound like some kind of war-zone or something!'

Myrtle smiled and shook her head. 'No, it's all right, Gillian, I understand.' She paused. 'This is nice, though, isn't it? Just you and me. It's a shame we haven't done something like this before. It just didn't occur to me – and there hasn't really been the need for neutrality between us before. But I'm glad you asked me – regardless of what you have to tell me.' Myrtle maintained her smile.

'Yes, well, let's order and then . . . you know, talk,' Gillian responded.

'There's been more talking these past few months than there ever was over the past forty years,' reflected Myrtle, looking up from the menu. She felt comfortable, she didn't know why. She could have done without the wine but she enjoyed drinking it because she could, and she'd become rather accustomed to having a glass once in a while.

A waitress arrived, asking to take their order.

'I'll have the Quattro Stagioni,' Gillian said, closing the menu firmly on the table. 'But could you leave the artichokes out, please? And I don't want any anchovy, either, if you're putting some on – and please go easy on the cheese.'

'Gosh,' said Myrtle, 'that does sound fancy. I think

393

I'll have one of those but you can keep all the bits on, the way they're supposed to be.'

The waitress repeated their order in her broken English, and as she turned to leave Gillian called, 'And please don't overcook it – not too brown!'

There was a silence between mother and daughter. Gillian was the first to break it. 'Look, Mother, there's nothing dramatic about today, really. I just wanted to see you and talk to you and tell you where I am . . .'

Myrtle smiled but resisted the temptation to say that she was sitting right in front of her – which Gianni, rather cheekily, would have pointed out.

'I guess I no longer have to worry about the possibility of subarachnoid haemorrhage like Daddy's being hereditary . . . But it's weird knowing that somewhere out there, potentially, at least,' she pushed some hair away from her face, 'there's another half of me I just don't know about.'

'Oh, I see,' said Myrtle, trying, unsuccessfully, to disguise her disappointment.

'I keep thinking I can just carry on and not be interested in where he is. And it's not even that you and Geoff and Molly and Beth aren't enough for me. It's just that I can't avoid this feeling of displacement. Sometimes I even wonder if it's why I've been so angry these last few years – that I've felt instinctively that something's been awry but I haven't been able to put my finger on it.' She took a sip of wine.

As she placed the glass back on the table she reached

towards her mother's hand. 'I don't even know if he's still alive. By rights, he shouldn't be – not if Daddy had to go so soon – but I need you to know that I'm going to look for him.'

'Oh,' said Myrtle, inhaling sharply.

'I wanted you to hear it from me and know there is no malice in it. I'm not going to tell him anything about you – unless you want me to.'

'No, no, not at all, Gillian, no, not at all,' Myrtle answered quickly.

'I'm not even after his version of events . . . I have yours and that's all I need.' She squeezed her mother's hand. 'I guess I don't know what I want – perhaps just to see him, even if only from a distance and the safety of my car.' She sighed. 'Listen to me going on and on! I don't even know if he's alive.' She forced a laugh.

'My darling Gillian, you must do what feels right for you. I couldn't love you more if I tried – regardless of what you do. It's a mother's prerogative, as you well know. That man hasn't had a place in my life or my heart for decades. For my part, at least, he's been dead for years. But if you do meet him, be sure to thank him from the very bottom of my heart for giving me you.' She clasped her daughter's hand firmly and Gillian was quite prepared to let the tears roll down her cheeks without feeling the tiniest need for restraint or control.

It must have been an evening in late April when they had taken a stroll up to the cricket ground, which would soon undergo rigorous preparation for the season ahead.

It had been the kind of day April sometimes grants England completely unexpectedly, with no strings attached, which has its residents believe it's summer. It had been warm – balmy, almost – and the smell of expectation in the air was undeniable, one of sweetness, fertility but, above all, the scent was abundantly floral. The birds sang into the early evening as if, after months of neglect, they were reminding everyone of their presence. Myrtle felt as if she hadn't heard them all spring, perhaps not for longer than that, but now, suddenly, their salute to the warmth was doubly joyful and refreshing and was bound to lift even the most darkened soul.

At the top of Warner's Hill they looked out over the fields of new, vulnerable bleating lambs.

'Golly, that hill does take it out of me rather,' puffed Myrtle. 'Phew,' she said, with a hand on her forehead.

They sat down on the well-worn bench they had come to visit regularly. Without turning to Gianni, Myrtle said, 'You've been very patient not asking me what Gillian wanted.'

'I figured you'd tell me if you wanted me to know or if you needed my help.'

Keeping her eyes fixed on the view, she continued, 'Well, I do want you to know. Gillian has decided to look for him.' She hadn't needed to clarify who she was talking about – they both knew. *He* had made his way into many of their conversations over the past few weeks.

'Oh,' was all he said at first. Then he took her hand and faced her. 'Are you OK about it?'

'I'm rather surprised that I am. I think after all these years – after all the anticipation and anxiety he brought to my life – I feel rather calm about the whole idea of him, fearless, even, about the possibility of Gillian finding him.' She turned to Gianni and gave him a big grin. 'Who'd have thought it? The man who shaped my destiny and caused me so much heartache is really just a memory. Is that what time does to you? It makes you a little fearless?'

Gianni squeezed her hand and put it in his lap. He stroked it gently as they looked out over the undulating hills past the village and beyond. 'I guess it does.'

He paused briefly before putting his arm around her. He breathed in the spring air and exhaled loudly. 'I'm proud of you, Myrtle Lewis. Myrtle, my turtle, if I'm not mistaken, you're coming out of your shell.' He turned her face towards him with his forefinger and kissed her on the lips.

Chapter Thirty-five

There had been no grand plan. No manipulation of destiny, no malevolence, just a plain old-fashioned feeling that the time was right.

Austin had always said, in their camping days, that it was crucial not to cut across people's pitches: you mustn't interfere. He would repeat this several times on each and every trip, as well as reminding the children that they must wait in line for the facilities. One of his favourite rules – the one for which he was a real stickler – was that you should always clean up after you. This had been so popular, had worked so efficiently for Austin, that he had seen no reason not to extend it to every other aspect of his life.

It was little surprise to Myrtle, then, that discipline and the idea of clearing up after yourself was the one rule in life that had stayed so vividly and poignantly in her mind. It was the only thing, thanks to Austin, that she had ever managed to do all those years ago when she had fallen pregnant with Gillian.

The idea of doing it all by herself – making this particular arrangement for a random weekend in May – ensuring it was properly organized, had become not only the obvious thing to do but, in so many ways, a necessity.

She wanted it to be a casual affair because that was how she fundamentally felt. In itself, that was really quite a revelation.

Gianni's influence on her life, she was now more convinced than ever, had been an extremely positive and calming one. It was strange, Myrtle kept thinking, that you don't realize you behave in a particular way until you start behaving differently.

Maybe that was what Gillian had meant when they'd met for pizza and she'd talked about the changes she was trying to make in her life. Myrtle hoped she would achieve everything she wanted, just as much as she hoped Gillian wouldn't entirely lose her tense, neurotic and controlling ways, if only to keep Austin alive. The idea that she might confront the remaining 50 per cent – which was the very sum of her – did not threaten Myrtle at all. Myrtle already had some excellent male influences in her life and she felt satiated by them. Geoffrey continued to be a wonderful, mild and understanding son-in-law – more so than she could ever have imagined, and perhaps because she had never had reason to ask anything of him until Gillian had fallen apart.

Gianni had been meant to come into her life, of that she felt sure. There was no way on earth she would ever subscribe to the idea that he had been *sent* by Austin but the way they had first met had been, without doubt, because of him.

As much as she had tried at first, she had not succeeded in keeping him at arm's length. She wasn't sure if subconsciously she hadn't wanted to all this time and therefore hadn't tried hard enough. The fact that Beth had struck up a friendship with Gianni – and, as Beth was keen to point out, not him with her – had made it all the more difficult to keep her distance from the Italian-Australian.

While there had been a time in Myrtle's life when she had thought she could have written the end of her life story and perhaps even that of her immediate family, she now felt delirious at the thought that she had no idea what might happen next. Strangely, she found that more comforting than she had ever found predictability. 'The only constant in life is change,' Dorothy had reminded her, and she had been so grateful that she had a new friend in her – no matter how different they had once been. Myrtle hadn't even found it in her to question how well Dorothy knew Gianni when she had opened the door to him with her mud face-mask that day. She hadn't asked because she hadn't wanted to know the answer, but that day had been significant in making Myrtle realize that something about Gianni plucked at her heartstrings in a way she hadn't experienced since she was seventeen.

There was no family significance to the event – no birthday, anniversary or celebration. The significance was purely Myrtle's and she thrived on that idea alone.

Seeing them all sitting expectantly but at ease in the living room, Myrtle hesitated in the doorway to take it all in. She observed them for a moment, knowing they couldn't see her, and felt a flush of pride and happiness, excitement and fulfilment.

It was a true sign of the room's harmony, she felt, when she walked in and placed a platter of finger-food Gianni had prepared that morning on the coffee-table, and the conversation did not cease. She sighed with contentment and watched them all tuck in without so much as a glance at her.

Molly was sitting next to Gianni on the sofa, where he was teaching her an Italian nursery rhyme. Beth and Geoff were talking across the table to each other and Neena was discussing a legal matter with Gillian.

Myrtle cleared her throat. She felt thrilled that she was forced to do it more than once to get their attention. 'I wonder if I might say a word or two.'

Molly clapped her hands. 'Speech, speech!' she shrieked, and the others laughed.

'Ah, my darling Molly, thank you, but it isn't really a speech. It's just a few words. First, though, I want to say how lovely it is to have you all here. Thank you so very much for coming.

'Austin would have loved to see you together like this . . . although, on reflection, I'm not sure he would have approved of the wine or the crumbs on the floor.' She smiled.

A hint of laughter dissipated through the room.

'It's strange. Your father's absence is felt in so many ways – he was a good father and a loyal husband, but you don't need me to tell you that.' She nodded at her daughters. 'However, I mustn't be scared of saying that I also feel I'm learning to function without him, and there really was a time when I felt I wouldn't – even a time when I felt I didn't want to.

'It has been suggested to me on more than one occasion, these past few months, that I might like to get a cat as a companion. But I can't help thinking that a cat doesn't need me and I don't really need a cat, so what start is that to a friendship?

'Instead I have found a wonderful friend in you, Gianni,' she looked at him seriously, 'and I'm grateful to Austin for having been so fastidious as to insist on a name and address label in his fedora, or you might never have found your way to this house.

'We knew so much about your father, girls, because he was so very black and white. But there was something none of us really, really knew, and that was the true extent of his personal discipline.'

Beth and Gillian were clearly intrigued.

'It turns out that your father was not only a very bright and intelligent man but he was incredibly shrewd, too. Girls, do you remember how he refused to let you send postcards from Scarborough to your friends because he said it was a complete waste of money?'

Both women smiled, bemused.

'I only wish he hadn't been quite so shrewd and had enjoyed life a little bit more,' Myrtle went on.

'Mum, what the hell are you going on about?' Beth said irritably.

'Sorry, I'm not deliberately talking in riddles, it's just that I'm trying to find the right way of telling you – perhaps I'm dressing it up too much . . .' Myrtle turned to Gianni, who winked at her.

'The thing is – it turns out that when your father passed away, he left a lot of money behind . . .'

'What?' Gillian whispered.

'He left the best part of one and a half million pounds and there was no mortgage,' said Myrtle, with a mixture of pride and sheepishness.

'Oh, my God!' exclaimed Beth.

'Strewth, Myrtle!' bellowed Gianni.

'You didn't know about this?' said Beth, turning to him.

'No! You're kidding – why would I?' he answered.

'Fact is, I had no idea until he passed away either. I thought we were still paying a mortgage on this house. But the point is that I don't need that kind of money – I really don't,' Myrtle said. 'I would like you, Beth, to use some of it to buy yourself – and Neena, of course – a flat. Perhaps one with enough room for an art studio.'

'Mum, don't be ridiculous! What are you talking about? I don't want –'

'Don't interrupt me, Beth, I haven't finished. Gillian,' she said, turning to her elder daughter, 'I'd like you to have a sum of money, too. I want you to put it towards whatever you want, as long as you promise me you won't be as prudent as your father. Perhaps it will buy you some time off work or some nice holidays – I don't know. It's entirely up to you.'

'Mummy, I don't understand. Why this and why now? How come you didn't tell us as soon as Daddy died?' was all Gillian could think to say.

'I was desperate to tell you but I just couldn't. I was fearful you might think I was buying your affection at a time when things were so disjointed and you were both so cross with me,' Myrtle said.

'Mummy, I really can't take money from you,' objected Gillian.

'No, really she can't,' came Geoffrey's support.

'Well, you must and you will.'

'But what about you, Myrtle, what are you going to do? You've got to have a good chunk for yourself,' Neena said.

'Oh, yes, there'll be plenty left over, I should imagine.' The sense of anticipation in the room was noticeable. 'I'm thinking of buying myself a tumble-drier – despite your father's claim that clothes dry best on the line. I'm afraid I never agreed.'

Her words were met by silence.

'And I think I might get myself a passport.' She smiled at Gianni. 'I've never actually had one and I don't think I'm past travelling – not at my age.'

Gianni stood up. Smiling broadly he walked over to Myrtle, cupped her face in his hands and planted his lips directly on hers. He held the kiss for some time. 'You're a wonderful, wonderful woman, Myrtle Lewis, and I'm so proud of you,' he said, his hands still around her face. 'Does this mean you might consider a trip abroad with me?'

'I think that sounds like a lovely idea.' She blushed.

'We could start with Italy.' He was beaming. 'D'you fancy Australia, even?'

Acknowledgements

I would like to thank all the lovely Penguins at the Strand for their kindness, enthusiasm and tremendous support.

Jessica Killingley and Clare Pollock for guiding me through the Publicity and Marketing so impressively.

Louise Moore for making my childhood dream come true by believing that the seed of this novel was worth nurturing. Thank you, thank you.

I have been truly blessed to have my editor, Mari Evans, by my side throughout the writing process. Mari, you've not only offered me more support than I could have hoped for but you've been a wonderful mentor. You have shown me patience in times of need and conviction in times of great self-doubt. I am humbled by your faith in me as a writer.

Alice Shepherd, Mari's assistant, who has been so kind, sweet and patient.

I'd like to thank Hazel Orme – the best copy-editor in the business – who also showed patience by the bucketful in the face of my overzealous exclamation marks and commas. Thank you for your kind comments, too.

Wise Gordon Wise – what would I do without you?

I want to thank you for your wicked, wicked sense of humour, but most of all for your never-ending support.

Emma Draude has worked on the PR with such enthusiasm and I've not only loved your approach but think you're a fantastic person. Thank you.

I'd like to thank my children, Cameron, Bo, Martha and Malcolm, for their lack of support; their lack of belief that Mummy was actually writing a book and wasn't just sitting in her study at home engaging in a bit of internet shopping. I hope you can now see that I have actually been working . . .

And my darling husband, Brian – you are truly incredible. Without your continued support, endless patience and sheer selfless and unconditional love, I would never have been able to see this book through the terrible pain I have suffered. I'm so glad I found you. I cannot imagine life without you. Bubble.